Acknowl

I would like to thank my family, friends and Katie for their continued support and guidance throughout the creation and publication of both Seadogs and Criminals books.

I would like to thank Nik from Book Beaver for creating the covers for my books, listening to my ideas and giving the books professional identities.

I would like to thank Grosvenor House Publishing for taking my work on to be published and for guiding me through the process. You have opened doors for me and my writing career.

I would also like to thank you, dear reader, who bought this book. I hope you enjoy reading my work.

Prologue

For hours on end, his hand had been hurting - his fingers were cemented into a contorted stance to grip his fountain pen, and yet despite the discomfort he could not release it nor cease its movement. Charlie Munson could not stop writing; there was too much to record, too many details that couldn't be left out. He'd never been an active man – academia had called him into its studious embrace early on – yet he found himself sweating profusely in a manner he found embarrassing. Not just because of the constant scribbling and pressure to not miss anything, and certainly not because of the limited exercise of retrieving a blank sheet of paper, but because he was intensely gripped by the enveloping story that unfolded from Joseph Winter's lips. He felt, and he was sure his fellow writer and companion Alex Drayson did too, that he was within the adventure as well. Just as the hardy crew of the *Victoria* had been, he was hooked by the mysteries and intrigue, the adventure and desperation, and wanted to join the worthy cause that drove the condemned city souls into a tumultuous voyage to seek out the infamous Lost Loot.

Just as Joseph armed himself with a dagger and pistol after listening indignantly to the whispers of mutiny from the gloom of the hold, there was a high-pitched scream from the deck above and . . . the story suddenly ceased, and a deafening silence filled the drawing room of their house. The crackle of the hearth abruptly took on the ferocious roar of a forest fire. Charlie suddenly remembered he was not aboard a ship at all and was, in fact, on dry land. Both Charlie and Alex looked up at the sudden quiet and saw Joseph breathing deeply, looking beyond them with eyes that were glistening. A tear spilled and rolled down his cheek; he blinked, breaking the self-inflicted trance. Joseph sniveled, wiped his eyes, and gave a cough. 'Sorry about that. I . . . I need a minute.' He got to his feet and walked from the room.

His wife looked to the doorway in concern, then to Charlie and Alex. 'I'm going to see if he's alright.' She then pushed her chair back, minding her pregnant belly, and left the room.

'Of course. Take all the toime you need.' Over the past three days in the company of Joseph and his wife, their tale had paused from time to time for fresh drinks and food, stopping fully only to sleep, but this was the first imposed break where overwhelming emotion had been involved. Honestly, he was surprised Joseph hadn't become overwhelmed sooner; their tale had its fair share of trauma and heartache – just from a listener's perspective. To have lived through it, experienced it firsthand – to put it plainly, Charlie would've been crying much earlier on and they hadn't even reached the crescendo or ending yet. Both writers knew there was much more to come and, in an unsettling yet intriguing way, they were impatiently excited to discover what else occurred upon the voyage; be it beautiful or horrifying.

For now, they were both left alone to wonder. The wonder, however, was short-lived as they painfully broke their hands free from their pens, jokingly suggesting a crowbar to snap their fingers from their cramped crookedness. They looked down to their sprawl of papers - scrawl-filled, ink-spread and messy - and hoped in their bewitched state that they had remembered to number them. Tidying the table, they squared off the used paper and placed the stack into their leather cases before retrieving fresh sheets and new ink cartridges, preparing their workstation for when the couple returned.

They then donned their jackets and hats and, informing Joseph and his wife, exited the house for some fresh air. It was a glorious afternoon with a sea breeze that lazily pushed the warm air around, cancelling any humidity. Walking beneath the tree outside the front of their property, Charlie picked a cigarette from his pack and lit it between his lips. He puffed, thinking on all what had been divulged so far, when Alex sounded his thoughts in his thick Australian accent. 'I wonder how it will end. What more happened to them to

It moved so sleekly, so effortlessly, and matched speed with *Victoria* without struggle. It was larger than he'd imagined dolphins to be, at least three metres long and had a strip of white blended between a light grey underside and a dark grey top. He admired its large fluke that oscillated powerfully, propelling its body forward and its head that narrowed into a stubby beak. It was mesmerising to watch, a beautiful creature of the oceans. He spotted movement beyond it and saw another dolphin fin breaking the water, and another, and another until he realised they were sailing amid a large pod.

Suddenly a dolphin broke the surface entirely, leaping completely from the water before it arced and dived back in. Another leapt out, and dived in, and then another and another; not one of them landing on each other, each knowing the exact distance from its neighbour. Joseph laughed in delight, the crew were ecstatic, forgetting their troubles and hunger for the moment and enjoying the life that swarmed the ship, basking in the glow of life-giving energy the ocean had delivered.

Despite moments like these being a rarity, when they eventually arrived they brought forth a sensual and invigorating buzz that proved this vast desert of water was brimming with existence; that they were only visitors passing by, never to be able to fully inhabit, never to be able to fully conquer for their own.

He took Victoria by the hand and led her to the bow where they observed dolphins leaping from the water in front of the stem. They leapt, arced, dove and swam; playing with the ship and toying with each other in a peaceful grace. He looked at her then, in the light of the afternoon sun, and observed her smile as she peered out to the frolicking waters; a grin of happiness, of purity, where there was enough life surrounding them that it infected her, infected everyone, and had banished the pessimism for but a fleeting moment; and in that moment he revelled and wanted to stay. It was beauty within beauty. Grace and magnificence folded together in a peaceful mix where, in their situation, it never should've been able to exist. He moved beside her, and gently kissed her on the cheek.

Then, just as fleetingly as the appearance of the pod, it vanished. They lessened, and soon only a few remained until they, too, followed the pod away from *Victoria* and swam into the open ocean of the southern Atlantic.

The sea seemed calm now, and empty as it had always looked. The waves rose and lowered, ebbed and flowed, undulating and ever-changing. They stood waiting, sadly hoping for the dolphins to return. After a moment, Joseph picked out some tobacco and pushed it into the bowl of his pipe; the stuff was foreign and cheap, but it kept the shakes away. Suddenly they heard Robertson call, 'Master Rigger! Attach bonnets to the foresail and mainsail; the wind speed has dropped slightly; we could do with the extra canvas.'

The old sailor turned and saluted as he smoked his pipe, 'aye, aye sir.' And hobbled off to complete his business. Hugh went with him to control the halyards, and Rob attended to the belaying pins to loosen the correct lines. Billy left for his own station with a cigarette between his lips.

Robertson called again. 'Now you're all done watching the waves, we have rope that needs coiling, and some caulking wouldn't go amiss on deck afterwards either. The Devil's waiting to be paid. Pine tar should be in the hold; remember how I showed you to do it. That storm last night didn't do the wood any good; just a layer should help until we reach Madagascar. Then swab the decks sparklingly clean; I want to eat my supper off them tonight. Bosun, I'll leave you to supervise that one.' By "supervise", he meant join in.

Victoria sighed; caulking was a hard job to perform. Her fingers were still sore from the last time she'd caulked. Coiling rope she would choose any day. She turned to Joseph, 'see you at the evening bell.' She smiled again, but the purity of it had gone.

He nodded and smiled warmly, 'until then.'

She joined Tess and Poppy, who was looking increasingly frail, at the top of the companionway and they went down together to start on collecting the correct fibres from the rope. Suddenly Joseph found himself alone with Dave, whose face was still partly swollen.

get them here, to make them who they are now. From how he is, Joseph is a completely different man from the one that set out from London.'

'I agree.' He replied, 'I guess after everything they've been through; they wouldn't be the same. They've both changed, and I can't wait to find out not only why, but how. We still don't know the entirety of the story; there's a big chunk missing, and I think our answers will be in that missing chunk.'

Alex nodded as he took a drag and blew it out, leaning against the trunk of the tree. He looked pensive. 'What they've been through, what they've done; it's – it's incredible. It's a fascinating thought, eh? How far would you go, how much could you take, how many limits would you test - for prosperity?'

He smiled, 'Prosperity *and* freedom. Honestly, I don't think I could've done it. I don't have the patience mate. You know I'm no good at waiting. I think I'd have given up and lived in Lisbon.'

'Lisbon? Nah, Charl' – you wouldn't have even made it on the ship. You'd have probably made it out of prison then laid down for a kip right there in the street.' He laughed, then flicked his cigarette away. 'Let's go and see if they're feeling better.' Alex slipped his hands in his pockets and strode back to the house, itching to get going again.

Upon their return, they found Joseph and his wife prepping the evening meal for the four of them, and, not wanting to interrupt, Charlie and Alex stepped back into the drawing room and sat down. Taking off their hats and jackets, they unbuttoned the top buttons of their shirts and rolled a part of their sleeves up, ready to continue scribbling.

The writers could hear them talking and laughing from the kitchen and could tell they were happily married, carrying no burdens nor stress that came with adult life. Being around them gave a sense of ease and warmth – there were no judgements, no bitterness or pride; it seemed they had moved on from it all and lived richly, thoroughly, sweetening any atmosphere into a peaceful one. They acknowledged each other romantically, yet they had not stuck to the formal attitudes of a husband and wife; if anything, they sounded like best friends that happened to be married. They were aspirational, and both men couldn't help but to feel envious of their marriage. *Perhaps I need to work on mine a bit more . . .* was a thought shared by them both.

Eventually, Joseph and his wife entered the room, looking refreshed and ready to continue. 'Sorry for the delay gentlemen,' Joseph started as he sat down, 'dinner should be ready soon.'

'Sounds great.' Alex answered, 'there aren't very many men that cook, yet alone help out with the cooking. Some would consider that quite radical.'

'I suppose some would see it that way, but what's life without a bit of radicality?' he shrugged, 'I endeavor to not be a product of my time and generation; I'd rather live how I choose to with an open mind. We cook together as often as we can if I'm not at work, or we'll take it in turns to cook, but that's not to say I'm any good at it.' He winked and smiled.

'Of course.' He replied, 'I meant no offence.'

'There was none, don't worry.'

'You say you work,' Charlie asked, 'what is it you do?'

He gave a sly expression. 'You'll soon find out. I don't want to give anything away. Jump the gun, as it were. If you want the story, you'll have to hear it properly without any present-day tainting.'

They smiled, 'very well. Do you feel ready to continue?' they asked them both.

Joseph glanced to his wife. 'I'm ready when you are.' She said, her hands on the table.

He nodded and looked back to the writers who had their pens at the ready. 'If you need to stop or pause to take a moment, don't hesitate to tell us.' Charlie added and Joseph nodded again. His lightheartedness and ease were forthwith whisked away as he dredged the memories of their fateful voyage and his eyes, once again, became pools of reflection as he revisited *Victoria* sailing the waters at the base of southern Africa.

'We were at the Cape of Good Hope when I first heard the whispers of mutiny. Looking back, I think of how apt the name was since we were going to need hope, a lot of it, in order to endure the events that were to come. The whispers set me on edge, but it was the scream from the main deck that sent panic down my spine. The mutiny, I thought, it's begun . . .'

Chapter Twenty

Exploding onto the main deck, he held his pistol tightly and his breath even tighter. The light of day was bright; his eyes ached, and the humidity fell densely in his lungs. On edge, he expected a scene of hostages and violence and was ready to take on anyone who challenged him. Puffing his chest, he tried to look as intimidating as possible. The scene he was presented with, however, was not anything of the sort.

Everyone, bar Robertson at the helm, was huddled against the sides, hanging from the shrouds or crowded upon the forecastle. Excitement was in the air, not panic. Confused, he saw Rob leaning over the railing and pointing and Poppy next to him, tired but enthralled with the waves below. Billy stood overlooking the bowsprit and the other men were equally as entertained at the sight overboard as they clung to the shrouds for a better look. He frowned and slowly tucked the pistol into his belt under his shirt and stepped to Victoria at the top of the ladder. 'What's happening? What is it?' he asked urgently as he ascended.

She grinned at him as her tied hair played in the breeze. 'Dolphins! Come look!' She peered over the side and he joined her, standing close. Over the side of the ship close to the hull, he spotted large glittery movements of grey flittering through the shafts of refracted sunlight. A dorsal fin broke the surface and split the water in two; there was a puff of air, then it slid back under the waves. Joseph could understand the exhilaration now, never had his eyes seen marine animals of the sort; in fact, never had he seen any animals apart from horses and the creatures of the market. He found himself grinning, and, like Rob, leaned over the bulwark for a closer look.

He pursed his lips, *oh god, please - anyone but him,* and nodded, 'Alright, Dave?' he sucked on the pipe and puffed out the smoke.

Dave nodded as politely as he could, 'I'd like a word, Quartermaster.' The way in which he gave his address, especially the last word, had animosity. Its delivery was bitter.

Joseph shrugged the bitterness away, 'what's on your mind?'

The breeze played with his black hair and tugged lightly at the patchy black beard he was growing. His cheek bones were showing, and he looked so thin his shirt hung on his shoulders as if it were clipped to a clothesline. Joseph hadn't taken much notice until now; he hadn't wanted to stay close enough. 'I'm coming on the next venture to land.' Dave said bluntly, both knew small talk wasn't wanted. 'I need a break from the ship. The last time I set foot on land was Lisbon and that was on the other side of this wretched world; I need stability, at least for a while. I want to come on the next expedition.'

He shrugged again, 'It's not really up to me. It's Jim's decision who to take.'

Dave's eyes narrowed, 'I thought it was voluntary?'

'It was last time, but I'm not sure this time. Especially what happened after . . .' *Harold . . .* he didn't say his name and let his voice trail off. He took another drag. 'Look, it's going to be a different expedition this time. Madagascar won't be the same as Gabon.'

'You're the map-holder, an't you? The Quartermaster or First Mate or whatever you want to be called now. You have a say in the decision. And I know it's not the same as last time, it's a completely different place; that's why I want to come along. After all, you're the one who gave us all the grand speech about the chance at a new life beyond London. I've had my fair share of ships and seas now; I want to explore, it's my turn. If this is a "new life", I have a say in what happens in it, don't I?' he said firmly. It was clear he didn't want to be talking to Joseph as much as he didn't want to be talking to Dave.

Nonetheless, Dave James had a point. Joseph had offered them this opportunity and he had followed, there was no argument there.

Getting to the real reason behind his hesitancy, Joseph didn't want him to come because he didn't want to spend time with a character such as him; he was stubborn and merciless and took regard of no one else apart from his own skin. He could dish out the insults but could never taste them when served by others. He believed himself to be at an uppity station in life, always seeming to be in a state of podsnappery; not the sort of man he wanted to be around. Joseph sighed, *perhaps I could let him come. Maybe all the ratbag needs is a break from the sea.*

He sucked on his pipe, then took it from his dry lips. 'Alright. I'll warn you now, it won't be an easy journey. I haven't an owl in a barn who will be there, what they'll be like or whether they know of the map at all and, regarding the next clue – I don't know where it'll be, what it's going to be or how to get to it. It could be inland, coastal or hidden away in a mud-hut somewhere. All I've to work with are four lines written over a hundred years ago that happen to rhyme. This an't even including the risk – it's going to be a dangerous journey, more dangerous than you think, so when we get to shore, you *must* listen and follow the Captain's orders. Do I make myself clear?'

Dave nodded, his eyes forever sharp. 'Crystal. I'm ready, and when the longboat is on the water, I will be in it.'

Joseph pursed his bearded lips, hoping he'd made the right decision. 'I'll go and check with Jim and make sure all is well.'

'Aye,' he nodded, 'and make sure you let him know I'm volunteering for this, and I an't a one to back out of things.'

Joseph would've chuckled, *apart from when you're getting a battering mate.* Beneath the hardened surface he wasn't anything more than a shady coward. He slipped his hands in his pockets, 'aye. Right. Now why don't you hop back up in the Nest and keep a lookout.'

Dave gave a mocked salute, 'aye, aye *sir.*' He turned confidently away and strode to the mainmast's shrouds, beginning to climb. Joseph watched him go with contempt.

Hurriedly, he descended the forecastle ladder (Robertson had told them it was time they start calling the stairs "ladders" if they were to be proper sailors) walked the deck and climbed the ladder to the helm to where Robertson steered. His eyes were trained on the horizon ahead and sporadically darted from place to place to check on the crew, the masts, yards, sails, lines and direction of wind. Joseph stood beside him, trying to keep in the shade of the mainsail as the sun continued its afternoon arc. He cleared his dry throat; important matters had to be discussed, but first, 'Dave wants to join the expedition to Madagascar.'

The captain gave him a quick glance then his eyes were back on the ship, 'oh? I'd have thought after what happened to Harold he wouldn't want to come.'

'No.' He shared Dave's opinions. 'I said it would be alright and, to be frank, I don't think he'd have had it any other way. We're just going to have to bite our tongues for the venture, as we know what happened last time when tongues were given freedom.'

'I wouldn't worry about tongues; it was your fists that seemed to have found their freedom last time. Alas, I see no problem with it. All he needs to do is follow my orders.'

He looked at him and his burnt red cheeks. 'That's what I fret, Jim. He's not a man to follow orders. He could ruin the entire trip. What if we have to make friends with the natives but he won't listen and starts scrambling and being aggressive?'

'Here, take the wheel.' Robertson passed him the rungs and Joseph held onto the wheel, feeling the Agulhas current trying to persuade the rudder. Robertson turned to him, 'have you seen him around natives of a different skin?'

'No.'

'Then we can't know for sure how he's going to act. Honestly, I'm not sure how anyone is going to react, which is why we need discipline and attentiveness. If he can follow my orders, he can come.'

'And if he doesn't agree with your orders, yet alone follow them?'

'Then I'll make sure he will.'

Joseph hushed and gripped the rungs, turning it starboard slightly and then to port to keep them on a straight course. There was a knack to it, he'd found. *How do I go about telling him what else I heard?* He gulped and itched his head; his hair growing longer. 'Jim, there's . . . something else.'

Another glance, 'yes?'

'I . . . I,' he paused and scanned the deck. Lowering his voice, he spoke as calmly as he could, 'we have rats on the ship.'

Robertson looked about, uncertain of the importance, 'yes, I know, it's quite common aboard ships. I've seen the bastards scurrying about the hold. We should've bought a cat in Lisbon.'

'No. What I mean is, *we have rats that are starting to act differently.*' He looked to the sea, trying to make their conversation look casual.

Robertson paused whilst processing, then, understanding, his eyes narrowed and he quietened too. 'How deep have they burrowed?'

'It's hard to say, but they're building a nest and filling it with scandalous thoughts.'

'Are there many in the nest?'

'Only two that I know of. I heard them squeaking in the dark.'

'Do these rats have names?'

'I'm not sure. Their squeaks were noticeably quiet, it was hard to tell. They have a leader though.'

Robertson pursed his lips, his brows hunching over his eyes. 'Rats are clever, they know how to survive. I just didn't expect there would be some aboard our fine *Victoria*. But I guess long hardships at sea breed contempt and in turn breed false thoughts of opportunity. Those ideas are like ticks on the rat's back, once they're there their roots dig deeper and it's hard to rid of them. I'm afraid how much this has progressed without our knowledge; if we're not careful, we'll have an infestation on our hands and the ship will be overrun with vermin.'

'What do we do? Can't we stop them before it gets too far; before a mutiny begins?' he asked.

'No.' He shook his head, trying to think, 'no, we can't. For one thing we don't know who the rats are; they could be anyone. Secondly, if we misjudge then it'll break out anyway; provocation without preparation is a nasty business, Joseph. We'd have a mutiny on our hands either way.'

Just then Rob climbed the ladder and stood at the top. 'All finished with the bonnets, Captain, and the foresail is full to starboard. The outer and inner jib's strung and flying.'

Robertson turned to him and replied lightly, 'good lad. Now go down to the hold and tidy. Empty barrels and sacks to one side and those with food still left in them to the other. I'm damned if I go back down there again and spend twenty minutes only to find a stale maggoty biscuit.'

Rob smiled and nodded, 'aye, aye sir.'

The captain turned back to Joseph and spoke low. 'Speak to no one else of this, do you understand? No one. We sleep lightly and be alert at all times. I'm afraid trust is now a thing of the past.'

Joseph looked to the horizon, his face stern, 'it's already gone.'

The rest of the afternoon passed swiftly, and the breeze wavered enough for them to begin trimming the sails but keeping the bonnets attached. They slowed to a steady five knots and rounded the very base of southern Africa, reaching the bottom of the south-eastern side and into the Agulhas current by the time the sun began to set.

Brilliant displays of gold and yellow stretched across a hazy sky and once again colour was drained from the sea to allow for this mesmerising phenomenon slowly sinking below the edge of the world. Beyond, a calm darkness loomed with scuds of grey clouds.

No one enjoyed the dusk this evening though, and after anchorage had been found offshore, a rationed supper had been eaten and a warning of cholera from the captain had been heard they retired to their hammocks racked with fatigue. It was only this far into exhaustion that Benjamin gave a solitary complaint of his joints aching, but for the landlubbers the laborious work on such little sleep was enough for them to flop into their hammocks and want to cry with the pain of their throbbing limbs. There were no tales tonight, nor any tunes from Billy's fiddle, which was why, after the sun had set and the night was in its youth, Robertson was surprised to hear a knock on his door. Through a suspicious crack he peered through, to see Tess standing in the dark. It was her turn on watch and he wondered if all was alright.

'Yes, yes. Fine. I just need to talk to you is all.' He welcomed her in and offered her a drink to which she politely declined. 'I was just wondering how far we have until we reach Madagascar?' She asked, taking a chair to sit on. She looked drained, her eyes were rimmed with dark circles and her hair was dishevelled; she'd managed to tie her humid curls and lay them over her right shoulder, but it had been done half-heartedly and looked knotted and dry. He wasn't a one for noticing emotions, but he was sure she'd been crying. *I'm not surprised; a storm and then half a day caulking would make me want to cry,* he thought, *the Devil's toll is always a toil.*

'Not too far. Two days at the most depending on how the Mozambique current treats us, and with the wind kissing us a southerly goodbye it could make the waters a slippery spot but, with fortune, we'll reach the southern end of the island by then, and then it's the east where we need to make landfall.' He took a seat on the other side of the table, unsure of how to approach her feelings. *Do I ask? Do I wait for her?* He took his pipe out, pushed a pinch of tobacco inside and lit it with a match, the smoke wafting in the lamplight.

She looked at the wooden table, the lamp illuminating her soft young features, her unhappy, drained complexion. 'We're going to run out of food.' She said calmly and morbidly, as if she was mentioning the weather.

Robertson had realised this. Their stock was to last them until morning and then that would be all, the food, even the stalest morsel, devoured. He wasn't sure what Madagascar would offer but he hadn't heard of a grand trading port selling goods to ships, which was what they desperately needed. Vessels didn't venture to this island to sell and buy stock. Slaves perhaps, but not food; in fact, the only interest he'd heard was of missionaries visiting to convert the local people to Christianity, but religion was not going to fill their bellies. They would starve, but at least their souls would be satisfied. *Satisfied for a god watching us starve. How droll.* Still, he hadn't heard if the missionaries returned alive. All in all, he hadn't the slightest clue what to expect, but food was a necessity and took priority over the next clue. 'We'll find food when we reach Madagascar,' he reassured her, 'there will be something there, even if we have to hunt it ourselves.'

The thought made Tess smile, 'fresh meat would be nice. I can't remember the last time I ate it.' She paused, 'I gave my rations to Pop tonight. She needs the strength. She—' her brow furrowed, 'she hasn't been feeling well of late.'

'Oh? We have a bottle of opium and some laudanum and last I checked some absinthe too . . . Our stock of medicines is quite scant I'm afraid and even so I'm not trained in that profession. Victoria's got some experience, but she's not a doctor or surgeon. Here, let me get some.' He got out of his seat and went to the cupboard to find the small stash.

'I'll try but I don't think it'll be of much use. She's . . . very weak,' she looked down to her hands sadly, 'she can hardly do the work you set without needing a lie down; her arms and legs are sore most of the time and have sores on them too. She's lost colour in her face, there's not a glow or blush anymore and her skin is a starched yellowing sheet. When I try to comfort her, her hair snaps off in my hands as if its straw. Is that considered normal? I mean, for sailors?' She looked up worriedly, her eyes welling with tears. Tess started talking quickly, 'I've seen a lot of bad things before; gangrene and tuberculosis, cholera and cancers, the city's awash with diseases and sickness that us poor souls have to live in and I usually know how to handle them, how to help but this one I haven't seen, and I feel powerless against it. Powerless. I can't . . . help her, I can't make her feel better.' Tears fell from her eyes, 'I've been taking on her jobs for her, so she can rest but she just an't recovering; she's worsening no matter how much she rests. Captain . . . Jim . . . is there anything we can do to help her? What is it that plagues her? Is . . . is she . . .?' There was no need to finish the sentence.

Robertson could do nothing but sigh out smoke and lower his head; he gulped, knowing exactly what the plague was but knowing nothing of how to say it. If he was being frank, he wasn't surprised. It was bound to happen; it was bound to strike with their poor diet aboard this ship. He cursed himself for not buying lemon juice when they were in Lisbon; nowadays it was as much as a necessity at sea as having a Bible on board. He had that in a drawer now in case they had any more psalms come up, but the Holy Book wouldn't save Poppy Mills, and from the sounds of it nothing could; she was beyond aid. Thinking of the bluntness of truth at this moment, Jim Robertson hesitated and decided to give it to her straight. He turned from the cupboard and spoke with the calmness of an ebbing tide rolling along sand. 'I know what it is, Tess, and it's a merciless ailment when severe. Scurvy is what weakens her. I'm sorry Tess, but without the proper medicine, the correct diet or the blessing from a priest, she,' he exhaled, '. . . she won't make it.' He looked her in the eye, 'I'm so sorry.'

As the words sank in, he walked to the cabinet and picked out the bottle of Old Pulteney and poured the last of the whiskey into two glasses. He'd vowed this was for emergency use only, and he classified the present moment as one.

Tears ran down her face in wet streaks although her face was surprisingly calm, as if she'd guessed as much but needed to hear the words from somebody else. 'Scurvy . . . What a horrible thing to die from, and so young, oh my heart!' She began crying, 'what do I say to her? Do I tell her? Do I tell the rest of the crew? How am I supposed to tell a child she is going to die soon? Tell me, Jim, tell me.' Her shoulders started to shake as she sobbed. 'What do I . . .'

He placed a hand on her shoulder and passed his handkerchief. 'You don't have to say anything to anyone, if you wish not to. And as for me, not a soul will know, on my honour as a seaman and Captain of this ship. Time will eventually tell the crew of her fate.' Gently, he placed the glass on the table for her.

After a time, she snivelled and breathed and dabbed her face with the handkerchief, 'the world is cruel. She needs to know.'

Really? Does she need to know she's going to die soon? She's twelve years old; a child. Let her run her course in peace. He thought but did not say, he instead squeezed her shoulder and sipped his glass, trying to soften the sombre mood with the warm caress of Old Pulteney.

Tess looked up to him, her eyes glistening and bold. 'She needs to know,' she repeated, 'she . . . she isn't my trueborn sister.'

The sentence hung in the air like a seagull hovering on warm drafts, unable to come down. His eyebrows knitted together, perplexed. 'What?' Robertson asked, taking his hand away, 'she *isn't* your sister?'

She sighed, 'No.'

He walked back to his chair and sat down, pulling straggles of hair back to his head, his mind sifting through other possibilities of how these two people could be connected. All along she had been telling a lie. He rearranged his pipe. 'Is she your daughter then?'

A shake, 'No.' She wiped her nose.

'Niece? Half-sister? Bastard-born?'

With a sigh, Tess managed to get her lips moving. '. . . Poppy and I, we're not related. Her real name is Poppy Kettlewell. I was friends with her mother when I worked in a women's dress shop as a young girl. Well, we weren't exactly friends; we knew of each other and we spoke rarely, if at all. She was three years older than me at the time, and beautiful. She always caught the eye of men that came into the shop from time to time, men that came in with their wives, but it was her their eyes were looking at. She was kind, friendly, worked hard; I aspired to be her, what teenage girl wouldn't? I was only fourteen; she was seventeen, and even though we hardly spoke I felt I knew her,' she nodded, 'even though I never knew her. I didn't know what was going on in her life, but I wanted to be like Katherine.

'As time went by, she grew a bump under her dress. She tried not to draw attention to it, but it was obvious what it was. She was with child. I . . . I was confused, she wasn't married (not that I knew of) she wasn't courting a man and yet there under her skirts a baby was growing. Young as I was, I'd heard of girls that went into other establishments for extra coppers, that sold her purse to fill her purse; maybe this was from that. I didn't know. Of course, once everyone discovered her secret, she . . . lost her job. She had to go, and so she did.' She sniffled, looking down at her glass, 'walked from my life without a goodbye, not ever a hello. It was heartbreaking; I cried for a long time.

'I later discovered her story and felt terrible that I'd thought her to be a prostitute. Katherine wasn't a fancy girl, wasn't a hedge-cropper at all. The fact of it was that her mother was deeply religious and her father not at all, well, not on the inside. You could call it the story of the saint and the sinner, and, oh, what a sinner he was. He drank too much and had too little sense; a recipe for a monster, yet he was dastardly clever in a way that his wife, Katherine's mother, never found out. He did awful things to poor Katherine; godforsaken things and it was a blessing when he died – but left her an eternal reminder of him . . . growing in her belly. The only fruit her womb was to bear was to be from her own father. She wanted to abort it, but her religious mother wouldn't let her, forbade it and rejected the claims of what her husband had done. As she was only seventeen, she had to oblige. It was her body, but not her decision. A woman's body should be her own possession, not anyone else's. It is a cruel world indeed.' She took the glass and swilled the contents and took a gulp and in silence, staring at the table, she reminisced.

'I met her two years later. Her religious mother had rejected her and tossed her to the streets. There she sat against the wall, loitering in the London Mud and city filth, her clothes torn and dirty, her face aged by a lifetime; she was still beautiful, but her face was lean now, her eyes had far more stories to tell. Around her skirts was a two-year-old girl, the girl of incest. I had heard of stories to do with children of incest; that they were stunted with too many fingers and toes, that they were disfigured and hid under beds; but this girl – this girl was normal, with normal brown curls in her hair and a normal interest in the world around her.

'Katherine saw me and beckoned me over, and suddenly began to weep. She told me she knew me and told me I used to work in the dress shop. She . . . she told me she had a disease and wasn't well, knew she didn't have long left, especially as a vagabond on the streets with winter around the corner. Her child would die too, she said, and begged me to take her and keep her safe.' Tess looked at Robertson, her heart in her eyes pumping tears down her face. Emotion was thick in her voice. 'I knew if I took the child people would think it was mine and my mother would never agree; I would be thrown out of my home, abandoned, forgotten, but what was I to do? What option did I have? So, I did what any good person would do. I promised her I would look after her, that I would raise her. And my best friend smiled tiredly, peacefully, and told me the girl's name was Poppy.

'Katherine . . . died within days, nineteen years-old. A young death even in our days; a tragedy. I cried for days when I saw her lying dead on the street with people walking around her, ignoring her, treating her like another bit of litter; the woman I never knew and yet knew everything about. She gave me aspirations and she gave me my sister. I'd never forget her face. Never. Even now I can see her there, standing beside you on this ship rocking with the waves. I see her in her daughter. I saw her mother days away from death, and here I am ten years later watching her daughter die too. Why does God punish those trying to help the world he made? Am I a sinner for taking a daughter away from her mother? Am I . . .' her voice trailed off to the gloom of the cabin, leaving the room in silence with only the whisperings of the wind outside to listen to.

Robertson studied her. He had no answers, and for the moment, no words. He took another sip of whiskey and closed his mouth, but before he could stop himself he asked, 'why haven't you told her this before? She has a right to know.'

He expected anger, a slap, a storm out the room, but he instead received a nod, 'I was planning to. I was going to tell her when she was a woman grown, so she could understand the premise of why I had to take her, of who she is. She needs to understand. How am I supposed to tell her now, a twelve-year-old girl, that she is the product of incest? That her mother was raped by her father and she was going to be aborted, that her mother died a poor vagabond on the dirty streets of Camden and that I, who she's thought as her sister her entire life, am of no relation to her at all and that she has no one in the world who would love her and care for her as I do? If you could give me the words to help me explain this to her on her deathbed, I'd be grateful. Do you have those words, Jim?'

He didn't want to answer, he held his tongue. A light smoke rose from his pipe. Pursing his lips, he said, 'I don't.'

Tess dried her bloodshot eyes and finished off her whiskey. 'Then the world is tormenting as well as cruel. It's a small wonder why people find appeal in suicide; death becomes the relief whereas life becomes the torture.'

'Life can also be the saviour,' he replied, 'it can give you chances where in death there are none.' She didn't reply, but a fresh stream of tears ran down her cheeks. She needed sleep. 'Why not try and get some rest, Tess? We've all had a long day, and, in the morning, you can decide on what to do with a clearer mind.'

Tess nodded slowly, looking exhausted, and rose to her feet. 'Goodnight Jim.' She walked around the table and kissed him on the cheek, 'and thank you.' Tired, she left the room and closed the door behind her, leaving Robertson sitting in silence sifting through the information. He knew she wouldn't get much sleep tonight, and now he guessed he wouldn't either.

Dawn came grey and humid, with an overcast sky not letting any heat out and not letting any sunlight in. There was movement in the air but not enough to fill the sails and push them at the fast pace they all prayed for, yet it was enough to keep them moving. It was better than nothing. The sails were untied and eased, the halyards were tightened and tied to the belaying pins and the bonnets of each mast were unfurled again, aiding them in their efforts to get to the next checkpoint as quickly as possible.

The grey forlorn sky became appropriate when they discovered the last of the food was no longer edible and the water had to be rationed. The mood lowered sharply as everyone aboard knew another hardship was on its way. Starvation and dehydration; gnawing, empty, horrid feelings that brought shaking limbs, short tempers and a loss of focus to all.

Only a few more days to go, a few more days . . . Was a thought that kept them going, yet it set Joseph on edge as he perched on the foreyard stitching a tear in the foresail. A few days of aching hunger could be the trigger the mutineers were waiting for. A time when tensions were running high and when morale was running low; a time when those whispering rats decided now would be a good time to enforce new management. His fingers ached as he sewed, and they constantly fumbled with a lack of precision and focus. *No, it can't be today or tomorrow or the next day. Hunger will be on their minds, not mutiny. If they attempt to take the ship, they'll be too weak to carry it out and what's more, they'll have an empty ship with hungry hostages . . . if they keep the hostages, that is.* With a dry throat, he gulped and pushed the needle through, pulling the line tight and was about to continue when he became aware of the sound of crying from the main deck.

He peered from his perch and saw Tess leaning against the portside railing, her shoulders hunched, sobbing. As quickly as he could, he clambered down the shrouds and noticed she had a bundle of sewn sailcloth at her feet in unmistakable human shape.

Joseph suddenly realised and was taken aback by shock. He'd been wound so tightly recently he hadn't noticed the situation behind the scenes, and as he looked down to the bundle, to Poppy, he noticed this grey day turn a shade darker. He turned Tess and hugged her, 'I'm so sorry Tess.'

Approaching from the forecastle, Victoria put her hands to her mouth, her eyes wide and already beginning to fill, before hugging Tess tightly. 'I'm so sorry, Tess. I'm here for you if you need anything at all. We're all here for you.' She paused, 'it was a pleasure to have been a part of Poppy's life.' She let her go, dabbing her cheeks.

Hugh then gave Tess a hug and stood back solemnly, his hands in his pockets. The rest of the crew appeared and joined her in mourning. Silently, Billy came and stood beside Joseph, his face still. Even Dave looked mournful, something Joseph found surprising since the man was made of stone. Robertson arrived last of all from the helm and seemed to have a look of understanding on his face; sad, but accepting, as if it were the ways of the sea, the rise of a swell. Ashes to ashes, tide to tide. He stood beside her and took his hat from his head. 'I'm sorry, Tess. She was too young. Would you . . . or would you like me to?'

She wiped her red eyes and managed a heaving sigh, a sigh of grief and a hint of relief that Poppy's pains were gone. 'Thank you, but it should be me.' Everyone stood around her in a sorrowful silence, a melancholy of respect that could only be found at a funeral. A floating funeral. As was tradition, Captain Robertson said a passage of peace and love from the Bible and spoke some final words as he had done with Harold. 'Poppy Mills. The finest Cabin Girl in the Empire, the finest sister and the finest friend. Your troubles are gone now, your soul may rest. It is time for you to take your place in the Kingdom of Heaven. You will be dearly missed by all.'

Tess picked up the body at her feet, wrapped in the sailcloth. The body that was so light now, she wasn't even a struggle to lift. She lowered her into the longboat and stood in an absolute silence for a minute, only the sounds of the sea could be heard but even they were tame. 'My sister, my love and my joy. Goodbye Poppy, your suffering is over now, my sweet.' They heard her say quietly to her sister, 'be at peace, your mother will take good care of you.' She got into the longboat and was lowered to the waves and they watched as she gently placed Poppy on the surface where the waves took her like a petal that had landed in a stream, floating gently upon the surface.

They raised Tess back up to deck and a moment of silence pass until, one by one, the crew dispersed to their stations, and after Victoria had given her another hug, Tess and Robertson were left alone together. They stood in silence at the bulwark looking out to the horizon where the faint coastline could be seen through a humid haze, 'did you tell her?' he asked.

Tess stood still, her eyes glazed but the air of peace that surrounded her could not be missed; it was the passing of a loved one who was finally free from suffering, like watching a beautiful bird fly from its cage where it was never meant to be kept. 'No. In the end, I felt I didn't need to.' She said calmly, 'she will always be my sister, no matter where she comes from. I think she'd be happy with that.'

Chapter Twenty-One

The ship felt different, empty almost, for a day, until the changing scenery and current predicament numbed the mourning. Tess hardly spoke a word from then on, except from short conversations with Victoria. Soon, the crew joined her in this, and a harrowing silence descended. They carried out their duties silently, trying to focus on moving forwards yet thinking of nothing but the past. *Victoria* became a ghost ship, where her crew spent their time haunting the decks, getting lost in memories of days long gone. They escaped from the present as often as they could, as that was too harsh to endure. Everyone knew what this episode was. Starvation and dehydration; a pair of haunting spectres suckling the life from them all.

It was strange, Joseph found, the effect that deprivation had on the body. He'd seen people obsess over money before, over possessions and even people, but he never thought he'd find himself obsessing over two such simple things: Food and water. They became all he could think about, his every waking moment. They haunted his thoughts incessantly, tormenting him with their necessity; yet he was ceaselessly reminded of their absence.

They became spirits, only existing in his memories; memories that heightened with each passing day so that details of food became finer to the point of realism. The freshly baked bread was golden with a heavenly crunch as one broke the crust and had such a soft inner of white down, like that of a swan's plumage, you could use it as a pillow. The toffee pudding was perfectly rounded and succulent, sweet, with thick custard glazed over it, glimmering in candlelight like a rich honey drooling from its comb. The steaming porridge was of the perfect consistency, soft and smooth; the perfect temperature, warm but not hot and the perfect sweetness; so perfect it could hold on your tongue for but a moment before it began to melt. The vegetables were vibrant with fantastical colours and zinging flavours. The meat was tender, beautifully seasoned and succulently soft as teeth kneaded it like dough. The water was cool and clean and tasted sweet as it poured down his throat, replenishing his mouth, his senses, pumping life back through his veins. Then there was the . . . flick of breeze and sea spray; he blinked, and the visions disappeared.

His mind had been fed but his stomach yearned for the substance that came with such wonderful sights. Even the tobacco had ran out and he was feeling the withdrawals: the shakes, the sweats, the crawling skin and wriggling teeth. He wanted to groan, to holler in anger and collapse to the deck and weep, but instead forced himself to turn away with his head throbbing and his body aching, desperate for any type of sustenance to absorb.

Days began to pass slowly, and their minds swam in disconnected thoughts whilst their stomachs whined painfully for something to gnaw on. Their joints ached with each movement and their eyes strained to focus. Piss turned a dark brown colour and constipation was the new norm. Madagascar was not too far away – a desperate hope they clung to. Joseph was sure *Victoria* would have arrived sooner if it were not for their two days' delay where the wind, the tide, the entire planet seemed to grind to a halt. Not a breath of a breeze dared to sigh, not a wave cared to push. Everything had fallen still, silent, immobile. There was barely a ripple in the water. The Mozambique current they entered in was a foul one; Robertson had said the seas of this area were usually harsh with gale force winds, or states of utter becalm, yet Joseph already knew what this was. He'd seen it all before and fell to his knees in exasperation.

Yet Captain Robertson was perplexed as the Doldrums could not reach this far south of the equator and guessed it to be from a huge storm out east in the Indian Ocean and this was a weather ripple it had created. It was the only way he could explain the phenomenon as colour drained from his face. It was then that Joseph saw a pure bleak fear behind the man's eyes, a type of fear that was contagious. As he looked out beyond the bulwark, he remembered what a sinister place it was to be stuck in – with the water so still it looked like they had run aground on a giant mirror reflecting the sky, as if they were now sailing through the clouds but had no air to breathe. The water was glass again and they were witnessing two suns rise and fall through the strange horizontal pane, until they touched and disappeared altogether. Then the stars appeared but this time there were double the amount than usual, galaxies upon galaxies emitting so much light that even in the thick of night there were shadows, the only places where darkness could continue to lurk. They were suspended in animation again, travelling not to a landmass but to a lost nebular deep in the universe, sailing on a cosmic tide. Surprising himself, Joseph was growing to love these rare and serene nights where he would stand on the deck for an hour or more watching the night sky streak with the flaming tails of shooting stars.

Spending time in such a vast, empty and unmoving world of parallels was simply terrifying and even though they were out in the wide-open, claustrophobia set in with unmatched might. There was nothing to do as the ship would not be moved, and as the days passed, they heard Billy play forlorn songs on his fiddle and wander the deck singing songs in such a melancholic way they became sinister. Joseph, although frustrated, could sympathise; he was only trying to cling to sense. They understood why Robertson feared this place, indeed, they had grown to fear it too. It was where insanity could slowly burn until you lost your mind altogether in a furnace of madness, to forever smoulder in this taunting mirror.

Yet this "ripple", as Robertson called it, was kind and after two days of unnatural calmness a harsh northerly gale snagged their sails and hauled them forward without the need to tow. No one had the energy to. Another day rolled by with a fierce wind until, in the thick of urgent desperation on their fifth day, Dave cried land from the nest; Madagascar was in their sights at last.

Pushing hard, they sailed the ship from the southern coast to the eastern and dropped the anchors to the shallows as a flock of greater frigate birds soared high overhead in the warm coastal drafts. The longboat was quickly lowered, weapons and small gifts were stowed and those that had volunteered climbed aboard to visit the shore, some for the first time since leaving Europe on the other side of the hemisphere. Only Benjamin had decided to stay to watch the ship, 'me ol' bones need to rest for a while and explorin' is a young man's game anyway.' He'd told them as he jumped down from the shrouds.

Billy and Dave pulled the oars, their struggle evident with grunts and groans and sharp facial expressions. Even minor movement was becoming painful – climbing shrouds to get to the yards seemed an arduous feat; Joseph dared not to imagine what pain they must be enduring to pull this boat to the eastern shore of this long-awaited island. Suddenly he heard Billy mutter a rhyme to himself as he had done these past few days, looking down to his rowing arms as if they weren't his anymore,

> *'Oranges and lemons says t' bells of saint Clements.*
> *You owe me five farthings, says t' bells of saint Martin's . . .'*

As Joseph sat on the sternsheet and looked weakly up from his spinning compass to the incoming land, he realised how little the tide influenced him anymore. Waves didn't feel like waves. When they set out from London, he could feel the slightest roll of the water in their large vessel but now it seemed like this vast undulating liquid was the new solidity. Each rolling swell was just a bump to walk over. All in all, he felt something akin to pride (perhaps the only feeling he could recognise apart from the overwhelming hunger, thirst and craving) that he could no longer call himself a landlubber. He was a man of the seas now, weathered and experienced. A criminal turned sailor. A seadog. *A tired and hungry seadog, that is.*

Peering up, he shielded his eyes to see a clear blue sky behind the streaking white sprawl of stratus clouds. The humidity was increasing but try as it might it could not dry out their parched throats further. His tongue was swollen and had nothing to wallow in or swallow down; his tastebuds felt like a wire brush scraping his palate clean of any leftover moisture. Even perspiring was now a treat for the body. Joseph guessed what was on everyone's mind – food and water and the excitement at receiving both. Essentially, so long as there was something to eat and drink on this godforsaken island, he couldn't have cared less about the poxy clue.

He looked down to the note in his quaking hand:

Sink below the equator but float to the continent's east,
Under crux and canis major is where luck will never cease.
Strange lands and strange predators there are: be warned
of Tangena's bite,
Seek along the eastern coast, pray and do not lose sight.

Help Merina and Merina will help you.
H.S E.S.

Well, I'm praying, and I doubt we'll lose sight, he thought, *and Merina best have a table ready. Dinner for seven please. With extras of everything, and to wash it down, a cool jug of clean fresh water. Yes, yes please! Then to set me off to sleep; a nice long cigarette to smoke until I forget what fresh air is.* With his head slowly turning to the water and waves, he realised how challenging it was to string that thought together.

'*. . . When will y'pay me, says t'bells of Old Bailey.*
When I grow rich, says t'bells of Shoreditch . . .' the Irishman
continued.

Ahead, he saw a crop of trees yet no beach beneath them and instead they seemed to grow straight from the water. *Where are they finding the freshwater? How can they possibly grow in such salinity?* Once again, he found himself envying the plants and their remarkable evolution. Their roots stood above the surface and were a grey green colour after the mud and algae from the last high tide, they were compact with a roof of sickly green leaves not permitting any passage through. The closer they rowed, Joseph saw they were sharp too and a murk lurked in their knitted depths. This was not an entrance, but they were in the shallows. Flies began to buzz and swarm about the boat, sandflies and mosquitoes alike finding interest in these pallid wasted things they mistook for corpses.

'Mangrove.' Robertson cursed, 'we will find no landfall here. Turn to port and we'll sail along the coastline until we reach a beach.' His tone was meant to be strong, but a hoarse crackle only made him sound weaker. Joseph had noticed his beard looked like straw too, black lined with grey ready to snap off at the lightest of touches; his lips had split and had dried blood in ragged lines.

> *'When will that be, says t' bells of Stepney.*
> *I do not know, says t' great bell of Bow . . .'* Billy tugged
> the oar harder.

The boat turned and they bobbed along the coastline, passing long stretches of mangrove forests, tropical labyrinths that harboured their own coastal mysteries. No one offered any suggestion to climb through them to find land, no one had the energy for suggestions.

They continued onward at a slow pace until finally the mangrove lessened and gave way to white sand and tall placid palm trees shrouded by bamboo. Many birds they could not see but hear in a cacophony of chirps and warbles, from the cuckoo-roller to the giant coua and from the air they watched African palm-swifts chirp and sweep into the palms whilst plovers darted from the edge of the tide into the green brush. Greenery was profound and flourishing and the wide range of flowers made the growth sparkle in a wealth of colour.

This was the eastern coastline and it looked visionary; they did not wait to find another spot. Once again, the boat brushed up against the sand and all its passengers clambered out to the beach, hoping beyond hope that there would be some sign of life close by. Some sign, some form, and if they were fortunate, that form's name would be Merina. Unlike Gabon, they could not fully appreciate the beauty, not when they were ready to collapse yet its beauty was astounding nonetheless. Everyone was quiet as they observed, except for Billy Baker, who finished his rhyme and made the others wish he would've stopped at the great bell of Bow.

'Here comes a candle to light you t' bed,
And here comes a chopper to chop off your head!'

Joseph turned around to him, peeved, wanting to glare but Billy wasn't thinking straight and innocently looked on to the trees and beach. Blinking slowly, he doubted anyone heard his sinister ending. He hoped not, the last thing any of them needed was to hear about a beheading when arriving on a strange land with strange predators. *Be warned of Tangena's bite.*

Their muscles ached as they stepped up the sand, their minds adrift and struggling to discern what was reality and what was a cruel conjure of the mind. Walking slowly up to these odd trees, a type of tree they had never seen before, they looked up with curiosity. It grew in a gentle curve from the sand to a splay of bright green fronds at its peak, and had round brown, green balls attached just beneath, sheltering in the shade. Coconuts, but how were they to know. Joseph scanned it, wondering how a plant could be so green and luscious in such rampant humidity. *What are those balls? Are they edible?* But the thought of climbing to get them seemed like a long and tiresome, impossible effort.

Rob helped Billy pull the longboat to the sand and anchored it away from the water. The captain nodded and looked at his dishevelled party. 'My crew. Madagascar now awaits us. For now, we stay together and head south along the beach. If we separate now . . . in our state, I doubt we'll be able to find each other again. Lord knows it's hard enough to keep thoughts straight and sharp, so we must not split until we find someone.' He paused, thinking of his next string of words. 'If all else fails, we'll venture inland to try and find food and water, but we mustn't dawdle and if nothing is found, we return to the boat and try again tomorrow. Any questions?'

No one spoke, everyone looked drained and thin; Tess looked like she was wilting. She had been crying again but dehydrated in such a way, she'd been grieving dryly; her face showed her raw pain.

'Savages. If we find any, what do we do?' Dave quickly mentioned, with Harold on his mind.

The captain licked dry lips with a dry tongue. He replied with his hoarse voice, 'if you find any savages, run away as fast as you can. You have no hope of fighting them in this state. That's not to say that every person we come across on this island is a savage; remember what the clue states, that we've got to find Merina and *help,* and they will help us. Let's say that if they look threatening – run, but if they look friendly enough then wait it out and see how *they* react. Do you all understand?'

Everyone nodded. Hugh swatted at the flies buzzing around his head. 'Right then. Let's walk.' He said and walked as well as he could on the slipping sand. Dave followed close behind and Rob then walked, and Billy, Hugh, Tess, Victoria and Joseph started moving; their legs feeling rubbery on the sand. With solid ground feeling like liquid, they waited for the trees to rise and the sea to fall to find balance.

They walked for twenty minutes, with each minute feeling like an hour and each step a mile. The sun burned brightly in the cloudless sky. The heat was unbearable. Billy fell beside Joseph, his hands in his pockets. He breathed heavily and said, 'y' know, me Ma had a name for a day like this. The Devil's Day she used t' call it.'

Joseph frowned, 'why'd she call it that?'

'Because anywhere y' went, be it outside, inside or in the shade it was uncomfortably hot, and made her feel what Hell would be like. "Y' be a good boy now, Billy, else you'll end up with days like these every day; all heat and no air, with no escape from it and the Devil will sit there with a pointed finger and laugh for eternity." She used t' tell me.'

'Sounds like a fun woman.' Joseph said and managed a smile.

Billy shrugged, 'Devout catholic and liked things to be even and tidy. Not too hot but not too cold, y' know the deal. She was lovely but tough when she needed to be. Ironic though,' he said looking up, 'she died of a heart attack on a Friday, the thirteenth day of t' month walking through a graveyard. Huh, and they say t' Irish has luck. She may have kept faith close, but she was far from luck.'

Joseph smiled again, but his lips were too sore for it to be prolonged. 'I can see what she means though, today is too hot. Us city rats just called it the dog-days.'

Billy forced a laugh. 'Happy Dog-Day to y', Joe.'

'Happy Devil's Day to you too, Billy.'

Suddenly, Robertson stopped, and everyone halted.

Ahead was a boy. A teenage boy, by the looks of it; dressed in next-to-nothing and stepping along the sand. A string of beads and stones and animal teeth hung around his neck and he carried a small spear, probably fishing for the afternoon. Feeling eyes upon him, he slowly turned and stood frozen for a moment. His face had a pygmy look and was rounded, his ears stuck out and his eyes were wide. Wide with fright, with curiosity? Joseph believed it was a blend of the two.

The boy didn't move and made no suggestion that he was going to use the spear on them. Robertson advanced with a gradual movement, a non-threatening step forward. He spoke slowly, although they doubted the boy could understand a word. He motioned to his mouth. 'Food. Water. We need food and water. Can you help us?'

The tanned boy tilted his head and blinked, giving nothing away, and quickly turned and ran up the beach to a grove of trees. Not knowing when they were to find another person and out of sheer desperation the group fell in pursuit, moving as quickly as their weakened legs could manage. Unsurprisingly, the boy was light on his feet and had disappeared into the brush, only leaving a light scuffle of his bare feet to show where he went.

They followed as best as they could. Soon, sand thickened into hardened earth and grasses began to sprout long green blades. The undergrowth became fuller with bushes of ferns sporting great fronds of leaves. Some plants they had never seen before and marvelled at their magnificence; great pulsing explosions of colour and leaf like that of the traveller's palm. Trees were broad and unique; bamboo grew in thick patches and ferns waved them by in broad fields. Passing through the growth, they noticed countless insects of all shapes and sizes, all colours and sounds, and spotted lizards and snakes and small ground-dwelling birds with sleek colourful feathers. Peculiar looking monkeys chattered and jumped from tree to tree, their stripy tails a wonder they'd never seen the likes of. Despite the wonderous scene, Robertson led them on and tried to stay focused. A subtle and narrow path wove its way through the brush, a path that could've been easy to miss but once on it, easy to follow; and so they did, until tall trees towered above and wonderous plants surrounded them.

They became aware of how large everything seemed. The growth of nature was existential – since when were trees, plants, flowers, shrubs and twigs so fruitful, so divine, and so *green*. After a lifetime of living in the drab grey of stone and cement and a long time at sea with nothing but the brown of the deck and the blue of the sky and sea; this place was like walking through the spectrum of colours. None of them noticed, but shreds of the jungle's life seemed to have some effect; their bodies were aching, but their souls began to soothe with tensions gently melting. Walking through the dappled sunlight and the shadows of the trees was a blessing they didn't know they needed. Feeling the soft leaves brush against their weathered skin was comforting – following the winding track no longer felt like a chore, it was a road to redemption, a journey to rid them of this starved and torturous purgatory.

After a time of trekking through the gardens, they arrived at the end of the track . . . and the front door of the jungle's inhabitants. Through the trees, they stopped short and gasped as they looked upon a vast clearing and a large community of thatched-roofed huts.

Only a few trees were left standing around the huts, but these were large, prosperous; respected and kept amongst the village. A small river ran through the edge of the clearing, and a bridge had been built to cross the separation. There, along the banks, the crew saw black women and children of the village. The women wore rectangular lengths of coloured cloth wrapped around their torso, chest and then up over one shoulder. Babies were carried on their mother's backs in the folds of this colourful cloth as the children played and ran bare-chested and barefoot. Some of the women were carrying large jugs full of fresh water to the huts whilst others carried smaller jugs for the plants and flowers that grew up one side of each lodging. Thin grass covered the mud-packed ground and hairy pigs, bleating goats and plucky chickens grazed freely, roaming the land and keeping their settlement trimmed and fertilised.

People walked and worked and stayed in the shade of the trees without any sense of savagery about them. Instead, the crew felt community and well-being, and surprisingly, welcome. They were stunned, no one said anything. It was a sight none of them could forget, mostly because of how *false* all the tales they'd heard were. It was clear these people were not savage. True, their skin was dark but there was not a presence of threat nor incivility about them. Hostility was not on the villagers' minds, and Joseph found himself embarrassed that they'd brought weapons. Although the dagger he was to keep on his being at all times: the jungle may have soothed, but it had not cured the paranoia.

As he looked at the placid scene, he found it strange to see no white people anywhere. None in a drab brick building overlooking the villagers, none walking around or working or beating the black people. The people here were happy, they were free. It was true that slavery had been abolished in the early century but there were still conservatives who kept black people as servants, and almost all those freed were still treated poorly with equality a long way off. Never had he seen an entire community of black people without any white around. Baffled, he blinked and felt his mind stretching to new perspectives. He had nothing against black people, and from how white people treated each other in cities he found it refreshing to see the other side. A land free from separation, degradation and racism; he was sure these people didn't even know what the words meant. They had never had to know, and Joseph wanted to keep it that way. There was peace in this land, a peace he didn't want to ruin by enforcing their nineteenth-century views on civilisation. *I wouldn't want to spread our twisted views anyway. They've got a good thing here.*

And then, just like that, the peace shifted. Suddenly Dave stepped out toward the river, but Robertson quickly grabbed his shirt and yanked him back. The sailor shot daggers at the man, 'it's water. *Fresh water. We haven't had anything to drink in days and it's right there!*' he argued angrily with an outstretched arm.

Captain Robertson glared back, 'this is not our water, sailor.' He said sternly, 'if we go in there without their permission, we'll all be killed for trespassing, do you understand? We must wait to be accepted onto their land, so they know we're not a threat, and we know they aren't either.'

'I thought you hadn't been to this place before?' Victoria queried.

Robertson muttered to her without taking his eyes of the people who were now looking at them, talking about them. 'I haven't, but that's the simplest rule of hospitality. How would you like it if strangers burst into your home and started drinking your water?' he hushed quickly, and then muttered, 'everyone, leave the talking to me. The boy's bringing the leader.'

Out from a large hut nearest to the biggest tree, came the teenage boy they had met on the beach and following him out from the shade was a short man, followed by a shorter man. Like the women, he wore a long rectangular length of cloth that wrapped around his waist and chest with the end reaching up and folding over his shoulder. The cloth was brown with white flecks and tapered to a bold red, it was unlike any others they spotted; these were the colours of the chief. Behind, the other man wore only a small piece of cloth to cover his intimates. The boy led his chief and the other man toward the group of Londoners, who saw for the first time what a real tribesman looked like.

The chief was lean, his muscles refined and toned after a lifetime of labour, but his skin looked vitalised and fresh, apart from his pygmy face where small wrinkles were tugging gently at the corners of his eyes and mouth. Nonetheless, his face was friendly, and he looked almost unsurprised at seeing white people entering his village. *He's not even shocked,* Joseph thought, *are we the first whites he's seen, have there been others?* Atop his rounded head he had a crop of short black hair and had ears that protruded widely, and had large hoops stretching his earlobes into an obscenity that made their empty stomachs quiver. Around his neck was a necklace of teeth, rodent skulls and sparkling diamonds. Walking with a large stride, he was barefoot but moved with such pride and elegant masculinity that it was clear he oversaw this community. In his hand he carried a spear with a rare diamond head, sharpened to a point.

The boy stood in front of them, then moved aside as if to welcome his superior.

At a first reaction, Joseph was surprised. *Blimey, he's short.* The chief stood at five feet tall, but his eyes carried such an intensity that they knew he was a man of serious agenda. There was a moment of silence, neither leaders sure of who to speak first. Everyone eyed each other awkwardly, but the tribesman behind looked on with a diffused gaze. It was Captain Robertson that eventually caved in, smiling and handing him a smoking pipe and a patterned handkerchief as gifts which the chief accepted. 'Greetings. We are sailors. We come from far away. We've had no food or water for days now. I'm not sure if you speak English but we're all desperate and that river is looking better by the second, as well as one of those chickens.' He spoke slowly at first but as he tired, his words came at a normal pace. Joseph doubted the chief could understand a single word. *Oh balls, we really didn't think this through.*

The chief eyed them suspiciously and tilted his head as he mused. 'Food?' he said suddenly in a thick accent. 'Wau-ter?'

'Yes! Yes! Can we please have some? Any you have to spare?'

He turned back to the other man and spoke to him quietly in Malagasy, and the other man with a flattish face and broad shoulders blinked once. Then the chief looked back to them, reached, and softly placed his hand on Jim Robertson's shoulder. A sign of welcome, or was that acceptance? *Or was he just getting a huge spider from his shoulder?* The gesture was short-lived, and he retrieved his hand, but it was the other who spoke. 'Chief Tulyaka welcomes you to this village. He decides you not threat and will help with your needs.' His English was broken, the words short and punctual. 'Follow, friends.'

The chief turned and began walking away with his translator close by. Excited by their chance at sustenance, they hurriedly followed them to the river where they could approach the water's edge. The villagers watched with curiosity.

With shaking legs, weak at the sight of such a delicacy, Joseph fell to his knees on the bank and felt the soft earth. Moist earth. Rich earth. He leaned to the water and his lips made contact, instantly taking in long gulps. The water was the sweetest nectar he'd ever tasted, sweeter than any he had known. Sweeping away the dust as it flowed down his throat. Even the feel of it rushing around his lips and face was a blessing, and to feel it passing over his tongue and into his body felt like the touch of God himself as a reward for his suffering. Joseph had been through hardships before, lord knows a life of abject urban poverty had taught him how to endure certain things, but never had he had to face such a debilitating ordeal that had been so intent of sucking the life from his weary bones. He drank deeply until he felt full and lifted his head from the river, water running down his face and dripping from his beard and breathed heavily, before leaning in again for more.

After a time, and as replenished as he could've been, he pulled himself from the water and wiped his sore lips. The others were along the bank as well, all drinking and splashing the water to their faces. Now thinking about it, he doubted Robertson needed to explain what they needed, surely the chief could see. They were all haggard, thin and pale with blistering sores breaking out and ugly welts appearing around any place they had slightly bumped. Red spots from mosquitoes had pocked what remained of their skin and their hair was a helpless case. Their appearance must've been a shock to this man's village, small wonder the people were talking; they looked like they'd just been pulled from the edge of their graves and told to walk five hundred miles to reach this river. *Lord knows it felt like five hundred miles.* He lowered himself again and drank more before splashing his face with the water and wetting his hair and beard and washing it as best as he could.

When he had finished, Joseph pushed himself to his aching feet and walked back up the bank to join Robertson, the chief and the other bare-chested man, who called himself Yalla. Again, Joseph found himself expecting a white man to walk out and do the talking for them, but he had to shake his head and dismiss the thought. Some accustoming had to be done. The captain looked round to him and made the introduction. 'My First Mate and Quartermaster, Joseph Winter.'

Joseph held out his hand. 'Nice to meet you. Thanks for having us.'

Neither shook his hand. Neither understood the gesture. The chief turned again and muttered in Malagasy and Yalla spoke brokenly, 'Chief Tulyaka welcomes you . . . Jo-seph Wintah. On this night, you all join for feast around fire to greet.'

Joseph nodded, lowering his hand and felt himself trembling at the thought of food. He heard Jim Robertson muttering next to him, 'I've asked for food and water to be brought back to the ship for Benjamin and so we can begin stocking up again. We'll trade things for some nets, or whatever these people can offer us to fish with as I doubt they'll have much in terms of preserving food. It's eaten fresh or not at all.' Joseph nodded again in agreement and addressed the chief and his translator.

'Do you have a person called Merina in your village? Do you know of anyone by that name here or in the area, neighbouring tribes perhaps? We're looking for Merina.' Yalla took a moment, then translated and the chief smiled and gave a laugh, even Yalla found himself smiling.

He looked from one to the other. 'What?'

Yalla answered, 'Jo-seph Wintah has met Merina already. Chief Tulyaka is Merina, I am Merina. We all Merina.'

Joseph frowned and believed he was being mocked. A flicker of anger sparked inside of him; a raw emotion brought on by the insatiable hunger. He was just about to begin pointing fingers and raising voices when Yalla explained further. 'Merina is us. The people of this land.'

Great. Well now things have got a whole lot harder. How are we meant to help everyone? Do I tell them about the clue? He blinked and brought a tired smile to his face. 'Well then, my new friends, we need your help.'

Chapter Twenty-Two

Today had been strange. Usually, or you could even say ritually, events of each passing day within the village ran like clockwork, with each cog in the system playing a vital role in keeping everything balanced and everyone fed, but as soon as seventeen-year-old Honlu saw the newcomers on the beach he knew very well that this day was bizarre. He had run back to the village to warn his people of odd-looking strangers, yet destiny (or desperation) had intervened, and they had followed. Begrudgingly, he blamed himself for leading them here. *I only wanted to catch crabs, not people.*

As Honlu sat amongst his friends in the orange glow of the bonfire eating pieces of chicken and slithers of slow-spit fish, he wondered how these intruders had managed to become their guests. *Guests?* He had thought, taken aback at hearing of their celebratory welcome feast tonight; *they are dressed in strange garments, their skin is white, they look like bones and they followed me back to our village with weapons. How are they now our guests?!* Honlu had spoken as much to his mother in their hut, but she was swept up in the excitement and dismissed his suspicions by reminding him of their role to play in hospitality, and even joked that maybe *Vazimba* had sent them. He held his tongue and kept his opinions to himself for the rest of the afternoon, knowing he'd be disagreed with. Perplexed, he'd watched on as his people gathered and offered them food and water, observed them eating greedily and drinking heartily, never seeming to fill, and saw the bonfire being prepared; he knew the village was officially welcoming them. *Have they forgotten what happened last time we had white people here all those years ago?*

If anyone had placed a plate full of the finest pork, goat, breast and seafood London had to offer, Joseph wouldn't have been able to tell the difference with what he was eating now on a large thick leaf. At first the feeling of food passing his lips was a strange sensation, his tongue had almost forgotten its other role, but as soon as it understood the concept of consumption his body trembled and wolfed down anything that was in front of his face, which was anything these kind people had to offer. Still, his body yearned for more.

All afternoon they had been eating and drinking and now that his body had overcome the raw necessity to intake food, he was able to enjoy the tastes and textures that came with it. The favours, ah the flavours! As he bit into the chicken, the meat was tender and soft, nourishing and fulfilling, flavoured with special herbs he'd never tasted. The pork, oh! He felt the meat melting on his tongue and its juices flow into him; he barely had to chew it before it was swallowed. Even the fish was a gorgeous morsel, tasting of actual fish and not salt, and the rice and fruit that had been offered too gave the most wonderous flavours he'd ever tasted. Some of these strange fruits he'd never seen, never heard of, and he had to ask how best to eat them: mangoes and pineapples, Papayas? Coconuts and bananas? They sounded strange to the ears and odd to pass on the tongue but the way they danced upon it was astonishing; their sweetness, firmness and brilliance were astounding, each having their own identity with taste and appearance. He loved it.

The freshness of everything was awakening; his lids had been open before but now his eyes could see. He could feel life pulsating back into his body, and the painful gnawing cramp that had burned from within was doused by these heavenly pleasures. The pain was retreating, and he felt somewhat human again. Joseph lifted his cup and drank the fresh water until it was empty and sighed, enjoying a full stomach for the first time in days. Looking to the spit, bowls, rocks and folded leaves situated carefully around the glowing embers cooking more food, he guessed it wouldn't be long before he would be hungry again. He wasn't expecting it to be only five minutes before crushing stomach cramps left him wincing, and ten minutes before he had to rush to the trees to void his agitated bowels. One by one, they each had to rush away as food was reintroduced to their digestive system; he wondered what the villagers were thinking.

Around the glow of the bonfire, fireflies dotted the air, and brave, big-eyed monkeys they now knew to be called lemurs, ran through the congregation snatching food from the unwary. For their entertainment and as part of the celebrations, dancers jumped and frolicked around the fire in fluid movements whilst the village watched and talked and laughed. The dancers skipped to the beat of a drum and the playful tune of an artfully crafted flute; strings of colourful beads and petals covered their essentials and rattled and swayed with each alteration, adding a sense of delicate beauty to their ritual. All the dancers were women, and the crew were mesmerised by such a beautiful display of feminine motion. The men of the crew were transfixed by the wonderous caper, as well as the slips of breast on occasion. Joseph found himself watching, and hoping for a slip, but as he looked around, he found the stern face of Victoria eyeballing him and he looked away innocently pretending to be interested in the fireflies. Of all, Hugh was lost in a trance with his eyes not moving from a specific dancer.

A long smoking pipe was passed around the congregation with each taking a drag from it before passing it along. Joseph watched with anticipation, as well as the other smokers of the crew, and when it came to his turn, he put his lips around it and inhaled a lungful of the strange-tasting smoke. It was thick and heavy, herbal yet powerful, sucking sense from his head leaving him feeling dizzy and acutely aware of the distinction of colour in his surroundings. He coughed at the density, his eyes watering. He thought it would've done the trick to calm his cravings, yet it left him longing for the shitty city tobacco even more. On the plus side, the aftertaste was rather sweet.

Beside Joseph, Robertson wiped his mouth and sighed with relief at having a full stomach, then asked a question that had been on all their minds. 'How is it you know English?' He spoke to Chief Tulyaka, but the question was aimed at Yalla.

The thicker-set man, who had now tied the village garb, called a *lamba*, around himself for the meal, answered slowly and as best as he could. 'Many years ago, we were visited often by groups of . . . religion . . . men, to spread word of Christ. I was small boy when King Radama first accepted these religion men to Madagascar. These religion men . . . from England, they come, and when I was in youth, they come often to teach . . . Christ-ianity along coast to Cotier pee-pole. Religion men also teach English to me and to others who learn quickly. Chief Tulyaka understand . . . little words, and I, Yalla, is helping him learn. They also give us sheep and goats and chickens as gifts, and we breed them.'

Joseph gazed into the fire behind the dancers and remembered the influx of pious men volunteering as missionaries in the quest to spread the word of God to lesser-developed countries, but he never would have imagined them travelling this far for it. He'd been fascinated by the concept of travelling, but his belief in God was a fracture that had never healed and so he never put himself forward as an agent of the Lord since his faith was lacking somewhat. He remembered telling Lucy . . . he winced, *Ah, Lucy . . .* "if *He* can't take care of what he created then surely he can't be that responsible. An irresponsible father leads to irresponsible children, and here we are with poverty, disease, death, war, overpopulation and corruption, not to mention the huge gap in social ranks – all because the bloody hornswoggler couldn't keep an eye on us. The only time I'll have faith in him is when I've got a pocket full of pennies and a cupboard full of food. That's when I'll accept the invitation into the Kingdom of Heaven." He reminisced as Lucy rolled her eyes and tucked the Bible into a drawer, but he found himself frowning as he struggled to focus on her face. If anyone had asked the colour of her eyes, her hair, he wouldn't have been able to answer. She was fading, along with the memories of his hometown, and he was confused about how he felt about that. Joseph looked around at the people of the village, *and yet here we are where those missionaries turned up. After all my sins, I've followed the path of righteousness,* he found himself smiling, *fate can deal some swift hands.* 'Why did these missionaries stop visiting?' he asked them.

Yalla chewed his meat and swallowed, then spoke to Chief Tulyaka and he replied, as if confirming, and Yalla spoke. 'Religion men not come back for nearly five-teen years. Merina pee-poles were taught *Kristianisma*,' his brow furrowed in his language confusion, '*Krist* . . . We were taught that Christianity was what made pee-pole whole, yet soon we learn it is not a whole t'ing. It is broken into pieces with some religion men teaching other ways of Christianity – Christian and Catholic and Prot . . .' he struggled and moved on, 'but all lead to same eventual t'ing. I am confused by this. We were taught Christianity to be most peaceful and forgiving religion, yet all its *sampana*–' he paused again, '–all its branches have caused war and conflict. You do not hear of tree's branches warring because one has different shape of leaf; they all part of same tree, and the tree supports all the same way. This is not way of it though. I am sad. I liked idea of Christianity. I hear they not come back because Andriana, the noble pee-poles of this land, were taught another part; prote-protest-pro-'

'-Protestantism?'

A nod. 'Andriana, were taught another part and fell out with religion men; send them home. Some of Merina say they pushed out by slave traders wanting big of plantations, others say their Christ called them home because they finished spreading word of God.' Yalla gave a gesture that was akin to a shrug, 'Religion men not come back.'

'Or maybe it was because they didn't like the blackies.' Dave muttered sourly. Joseph overheard and winced with a flash of anger, but fortunately Yalla did not pick up on it.

Victoria swallowed a mouthful of food and asked, 'there are plantations here? I thought that was only in the Americas.'

Yalla conveyed in Malagasy, Chief Tulyaka confirmed and muttered to Yalla and Yalla muttered back, then replied. 'Plantations set up along coast of Madagascar, yes, close to sea so it is easy for *mpivorota* - for traders to reach. Strange plants they like; sugarcane is what they work on to trade, as well as pee-poles. Plantations are spread along the coast but there are still ancient lands owned by Merina tribes; coastal villages – our village – between. We rarely see plantations; we stay within our boundaries. We know our limits. Often, we see runaway *andevo*, many slaves, pee-pole thin and tired like you, but they not stay long and move on.

'Land here is changing, it is dev-develop-ment. Future is slow coming to Madagascar. It is happening more inland but not reaching all of land, yet. Places are still as they have been for generations.' He smiled, showing his gapped teeth, 'our village is developing; our village knows English and has traded with English before. Fortune comes to you, pee-pole of England, for finding our village. God blesses to you all.' He said with pride. Just then, as the dancing stopped, the musician approached and gifted them the flute he had been playing. It was bamboo and had intricate swirling designs chased in its surface. The most musically orientated of the crew, Billy examined it with delight, excited to learn how to play.

Tess reached and spooned herself more rice and picked up more chicken. In the glow of the fire, she looked worst of them all, completely drained with her cheekbones showing, her reddened eyes sunken and her jawline a knife edge: a walking skeleton. The passing of her sister had taken a part of her too, but thankfully this hospitality had enabled her to have faith and open her mouth to speak more than two words to someone. 'God blesses you too and thank you all for the food. It is very lovely.'

Yalla smiled at her and again muttered to Chief Tulyaka, who turned and grinned at her. He lowered his head and managed to speak, but his accent was so thick he struggled to push the words through the tangle of tongue. 'Woo-man is . . . kind. Tulyaka well-comes all to village.' The Chief looked at her in a calm way, 'Woo-man is welcome to stay again . . . he is 'appy.'

A silence passed through them all, and Joseph almost hitched up his food. *Did he mean . . .?* Tess looked at the chief quizzically and gently shook her head. 'What do you mean "again"? I've never been here before.'

'None of us have been here before.' Added Victoria.

Chief Tulyaka blinked and leaned back, then muttered Malagasy to Yalla. The Merina man placed his leaf on the floor which the lemurs hastily scrambled to and sat up straight, 'Chief Tulyaka sends many 'pologies, he confused you with other woo-man.'

Joseph swallowed and spoke quickly, 'have you had white people like us here in your village before? Other than the missionaries?'

'No.'

'Oh.' Joseph could not help but to feel disappointed, the chief's few words had stirred interest.

'Not for long time.' He continued, 'it was before Yalla's time, before Father's time. Chief Tulyaka and village only knows of it from one story left behind, passed from *ray* to *ray*, father to father. It more of an *angano* – a legend. Most of village do not believe it.'

Without realising it, all of them leaned forward and listened. 'Do *you* believe it?' Joseph asked.

Yalla then muttered something to Chief Tulyaka, a sentence Joseph could imagine being: *why do all English folk believe in such old tales? The old missionaries believed in stories written in a book thousands of years ago.* The translator looked at them in thought. The bonfire crackled and spit. The villagers spoke quietly amongst themselves. The lemurs, tired of their snatching, bounced back to the trees. 'Yes, I believe it.' He replied at last. 'Only because I have seen . . . *porofo* - ev-evi-' he stopped and looked down, sighing.

'Evidence?'

He looked up sharply, almost in relief at finding the word, 'yes. There is legend and there is evidence. Only by whispers through the elders we have been told they link together. Just like Bible and Christ.'

'What is it? The legend and the evidence?' Joseph asked eagerly.

Again, Yalla talked to Tulyaka almost asking permission. The Chief nodded and Yalla pressed on. 'In the times before father's father and mother's mother, the land was a different place. Our world was small, but our village was much bigger, and we knew little of world and its pee-poles; pee-pole were 'appy with that. No plantations, no slaves, no religion men and no hearing of any Sons of Gods on big wooden crosses. Only us and *Vazimba* and our own beliefs. The jungle was where we hunted, the beach was where we fished; the sea was just a place for crabs and canoes; mother's mother and father's father never would have believed that it was the sea that connects world together. That's why, one day, they *tohina* - so shocked to see big ship nearby and pee-poles with white skin come to beach.

'In legend, they say five come to beach, but different pee-pole say different things. Villagers were surp-surprised: they had never seen other pee-poles with other skin before. It strange, and they believed *Vazimba* sent them, how else could such big boat sail and not sink and move these white pee-pole from one land to next? How, when there were other villages on coast, did they find ours? With group was man and woo-man; they made friends with villagers, they friendly but others have problems. One is sick and two others are sick with greed.

'The five stay for four days and in those four days Sick Man dies and Two Others try take value-able tokens and our woo-men at night, but Man and Woo-man manage to fight and bring back tokens but not our woo-men. Two Others take our woo-men back to boat and village never sees them again. Village offers thanks to Man and Woo-man for help and village helps them by taking in and keeping safe somet'ing they leave. They then leave, and village never sees them again. It all happened so fast the village doubts its truth and the story becomes myth.'

The group sat silently, pieces slowly fitting together but they needed more proof. All of them hoped, but still a niggle of doubt was present; it sounded real enough but maybe it was just a legend, or perhaps this man and woman were not the man and woman they were hoping for. Victoria argued, 'don't you have evidence to support the legend, though?'

'Yes.'

'Then surely it can't be myth, it has to be the truth?'

'Bible is ev-evidence of Jesus Christ dying and yet pee-pole still question it.' Yalla stated.

Joseph spared the nit-picking and asked bluntly, 'what was it they left behind? Who were the man and woman?'

Yalla's eyes turned to him and focused intently, his dark eyes probing. 'From both, they left one small t'ing in villagers care. A small box.'

His pulse quickened, 'And their names? Do you know them?'

His dark eyes probed again, and he was just about to reply when the Chief opened his mouth after picking up on certain words. 'Man and Woo-man's names known only to few. Woo-man there looks . . . like woo-man before, how she is told in myth; des-described in myth. Do you . . . know . . . names?' he pointed to Tess.

She sat straight and gulped as she felt everyone's eyes turn to her. Remembering Benjamin's tale, Tess named who she thought they were to be. 'Eve and Henry Scott . . .' She said as a statement, but it sounded like a question.

The Chief and Yalla did not answer at once, they sat quietly, almost deep in thought, or was it surprise? The interpreter then cracked first. He pursed his lips, 'you know them?'

'We know *of* them.' Joseph mentioned, 'and we've been following a trail they left behind on their travels and I think that maybe . . . maybe that small box they left in your village's care is what we need to continue the trail, the next part we need to find.' He paused, thinking how to word the next part properly without sounding desperate, 'we need that box. Where are you keeping it?' *Hmm, maybe that did sound desperate.*

The two Merina men closed their mouths suddenly and appeared taken aback by the abruptness. Robertson snapped around to him, his eyes glaring, knowing that when it came to asking for certain things from strangers in their homeland the brashness of an Englishman was not the way to go about it. Although, surprisingly, Yalla answered with a politeness that avoided Joseph's curt tone. Either that or he didn't know how else to respond. 'Our village treasures not seen by stranger's eyes. It is rare they are seen by villagers' eyes; it only seen by Chief and cared for by Chief.'

'–But you *do* have it, don't you?' he pried further.

Robertson decided to step in to ease the conversation. 'What my Quartermaster is trying to ask is if we'd be able to see it, to verify that it's the same one we're looking for. We've seen the type of box before; it could be similar.'

Suddenly Joseph jumped in again and made Robertson wince and want to land a royal back hand to the man's head. 'Would you be willing to trade for it?' He asked quickly, not wanting the topic to change, overwhelmed by a want - a *need* to get the small box, since so much had been sacrificed for it. Additionally, now his thirst and hunger had been absolved his craving for tobacco heightened, wearing his patience ice thin.

Yalla listened and replied without even confiding with his superior. 'You all have come from boat with nothing: no food, no water and no hope. If you had nets you would have fished; but you do not have any. If you had other clothes you would have worn them, but you do not have any. If you had other fresh water you would have drank it, but you do not have any. No luxuries, you have. Let me ask you, Jo-seph Wintah, what could you have to trade when you not have anyt'ing? What could we want from pee-poles that do not even have simple food to trade?' He sat forward, arms over his *lamba*, his eyes open and flickering in the firelight; there was a tired look in them. For a man who had never set foot in a city or knew of business, stocks and shares; he was firmly aware of the meaning of a healthy transaction.

Pursing his lips, Joseph felt stumped. He looked away to the fire; knowing that they had nothing of worth to offer. He ground his teeth together in frustration and felt the quake in his hands returning.

'Weapons.' Billy spoke up, 'we have guns and knives and pistols. Now I don't know about you foine gentlemen, but I'd prefer some proper arms instead of spears and arrows and the power of a taught string.' For a moment, Joseph wondered if the Irishman had ever had a role in sales before – he pitched it perfectly. A spark of hope.

The two men were silent for a moment, then Yalla translated and Chief Tulyaka spoke Malagasy and they conversed for a minute.

Eventually, a decision was made between them and it was the village's leader who joined the discussion. 'A trade . . . can . . . be met.' His deep yet smooth voice said, 'we want . . . no'ting of . . . material from you. We want . . . y-your help, as trade.'

Victoria sounded confused, 'you want our help? Help with what?'

Tulyaka smiled, 'collecting underground stars.'

Everyone fell silent. Hugh looked to Dave quizzically and Dave only lowered his head to his hand in a hopeless expression. Was the chief being serious? Did he not understand what they were talking about or was he trying to divert the conversation? Jim Robertson studied the two men in earnest, seeking an explanation - *or maybe it's us that don't understand?* He tried to sound calm, 'I don't . . . what do you mean? Does that mean something else in your language?'

There was a moment to process the words. Tulyaka sat back, 'No. Same t'ing. Next day you all . . . understand.' Then he rose to his feet. 'Merina will help you . . . if you help us. You may . . . sl-sl-sl-' he turned to Yalla and muttered.

Yalla translated, 'You may sleep beside fire, or return to boat if you wish. Too-morrow we walk far. Chief Tulyaka goes to rest now, bidding you good nights and God blesses.' Tulyaka then nodded and smiled, turned and headed into the gloom toward his hut with three women following.

Others of the village were now retiring to their huts, slowly filtering away from the light and leaving the fire feeling empty. Soon Yalla left them and returned to his hut until it was only the Londoners left. No one felt like talking, and after eating some more and drinking their fill they lay on thick beds of leaves that had been prepared around the fire and tried to rest. The sounds of the nocturnal rainforest life were cacophonous, making them wonder how much rest they were likely to get.

Joseph bundled his waistcoat to lay his head on and checked for insects before looking up to the night sky with Victoria lying next to him, resting in the crook of his arm. They listened to the crackling flames and watched the fireflies when she asked quietly, 'do you believe them?'

He thought for a moment before looking at her and whispering back, 'I think so. They've no reason to lie.' *My god she looks beautiful in the firelight.*

'Everyone lies, sweetheart. If that's one thing I've learned living as a woman in a world ruled by men is that everyone lies, especially when there's some sort of gain . . . or when they've got secrets to hide.'

His stomach sank then as he remembered what he'd heard back in the hold and knew he was becoming slack in his efforts to prevent the mutiny. He sighed, 'then how do you find the truth?' he asked.

'You learn how to tune your ears into the finer details and to trust your instincts.'

'What are your instincts telling you about this, then? The clue did say "help Merina and Merina will help you", and that's what we'll be doing. We're following the instructions of the last clue.'

She was silent for a moment. 'We're following the instruction, but I can't help but to have doubts. Underground stars . . . I don't know, it just sounds . . . peculiar.' A silence settled. She leaned over, 'goodnight Joseph.' She kissed him, and he kissed back.

'Goodnight.' He said as warmly as he could, yet he felt cold. Distrust and apprehension weighed on him, and the memorial necklace – Harold's carved elephant – brought back dark memories as it lay heavily on his chest. Mutiny was on his mind and made him shiver next to the flames, and the night sky, with all its twinkling wonders, offered no remedy for the insomniac.

Morning arrived quickly and the first few pale colours had barely touched the sky when the visitors were awakened, tired and aching, by the same boy they had met on the beach. One by one they were roused and given water. Gasping in the humid air, they saw the dancing flames of the night were now no more than smouldering grey and black chunks of lightly smoking char. Surveying the village, they saw the pigs beginning to wake and wander with the chickens beginning to crow, and rounded lemur eyes peered out from the dark brush at the edges of the clearing. It was warm now, but they knew as soon as the sun reared its head above the horizon it would be an intense heat at all hours until it sank again. These equatorial countries had vicious humidity, wrapping them in a warm wet lethargic blanket extracting moisture and air from them, day and night, until they craved a breeze. If it were not this, the coastal air was just as vicious in its opposites; the nights would be cold enough to shiver and the days would be hot enough to sweat; shiver and sweat, shiver and sweat, never to cease. As Joseph sat up and rubbed his bleary eyes, feeling a sweat already, he could understand the necessity to leave now and gain as much ground before sunrise when the humidity would become rampant.

Standing just outside the camp, Yalla wrapped himself in his stripy red, white and black *lamba*. 'Morning's to you.' He greeted, 'we leave now. This boy is Honlu; I have been teaching his English. He says you all have meet him before.'

Honlu raised a hand, 'Morning's to you.'

'Morning matey.' Joseph replied. Almost everyone was awake and on their feet after a few minutes, now noticing Hugh and Dave were missing. They were not in the camp, but Joseph fretted nor feared and instead lowered his brows in frustration. *For Christ sake.* 'Hugh! Dave! Time to go!' he called out and waited a few moments before the two men stumbled out from two separate huts, buttoning their shirts and stringing their braces. Yalla looked round to Robertson and Joseph plainly. Not having any words, Joseph shook his head as the two men joined the group looking flustered.

Hugh gave them all a sweet smile, 'Sorry, one o' those dancers led me back to her hut. I wasn't gonna' stop her.'

Robertson was just about to retort when suddenly Billy yawned, 'Why, look, ain't you the wee boy we met on the beach yesterday?' He asked, nodding at Honlu, uprooting the seeds of an argument before they could germinate.

Honlu looked confused for a moment and looked hesitantly to Yalla before replying. 'I was . . . on beach, yes.'

'Nice to meet you, Honlu.' Joseph said, ignoring Hugh Jackson's shenanigans.

Dave had to add in, 'Funny looking lad, he is.'

'I t'ought that was you!' Billy said with a grin, 'cheers for leadin' us back t' the village.'

The lad smiled and nodded, although they all knew he had no idea what Billy had just said. 'Let us leave, now.' Yalla instructed and turned, making a beeline to the trees on the edge of the settlement making no comment on Hugh's or Dave's actions.

Awake and prepared, even if they were feeling under the weather, they followed suit with Hugh taking up the rear and Honlu coming in at the end, making sure no one was left or veered astray. Over a shoulder he carried a wicker basket.

Robertson was behind their guide and was astonished to find a narrow, barely visible pathway that led through the trees. It was overgrown and led straight into the rainforest, winding challengingly – the path had been tracked *with* the vegetation, not *through* it. As they walked, they realised the difficulty in moving through such density, especially when the gloom of the rainforest floor allowed no light in. They tripped and shimmied and waded through tough undergrowth, wondering how on earth these people managed to hunt in this environment. The leaves were thick, the vines were cloying, the plants, especially razor grass, grabbed at their clothes whilst insects inspected their sticky skin; nothing could penetrate through the mass, not even light, not until the sun appeared. Whilst they all struggled, they noticed how swiftly Yalla manoeuvred himself through the tangle, how easy he made it look. He was moving with the motions of the rainforest, just like swimming with the currents of a tide. It was effortless, and not once did his woven *lamba* snag.

The rainforest was a harsh environment with mysterious chirps and chatters, screeches and cries in the trees above; alive and thriving even in the gloom. Here and there a blur of movement caught their eye, yet they failed to see clearly. Yet as they trudged on, light gradually melted its way through the canopy with colour pulsating through the web of wood and leaf. Stark blue petals rested against bright green leaves, white flowers with red stamens bloomed powerfully against murky green vines, bright pink teardrop petals of the Madagascan periwinkle opened and breathed as the orange and white petals of the comet orchids pointed the way. Bark became a spread of light greens and browns, wrapped in vine or cloaked in leaf, or naked they stood proudly in the brightening light. Some trunks were crowned with plates of colourful fungi, fringed by thickets of fern surrounded by creepers and thorny vines entwining with shrouds of bamboo. They walked in wonder; it was as if a painter had tripped and spilled his pots on the canvas, suddenly sending streaks and splashes of extraordinary dye to these once dull, and additionally tormenting, forms of life. The brighter things became, the more their eyes opened to an untouched virtue. The walk became enlightening without them even knowing.

Winding candidly, the path elevated, rising through the dense undergrowth until the trees and thickets thinned on one side and morning light poured through onto the path. Yalla halted and turned back to his sweaty troop, 'careful here. Edge. Down is water.' Then he continued onward, leaving them to try and piece together what he'd said. They walked no more than ten paces until they understood and stepped into the warm light overlooking a steep slope that descended to a beautiful blue pool. Through the remaining trees and tall traveller's palms, a waterfall cascaded into it from a higher point across the gap, sending colourful sprays of mist into the morning sunlight. Flowers of all shapes and colours, red and white periwinkles and blue and white orchids, dotted the greenery of the descent; all open, stamens reared, absorbing the warmth of the early rays. Nearer the bottom, smooth brown rocks cut sharp shapes and drops as the plants found no footholds to root. At the very base was a crystalline blue pond that jittered and jived from the entry of the waterfall with white froth and foam spilling from its centre.

The cascade was loud, but the sounds of the rainforest were louder. It seemed as if the competition was on and everyone wanted to be heard, but the waterfall was winning in the competition of wanting to be seen; it was exquisite beyond comparison.

They walked on, leaving the pool behind. No one said anything; everyone wanting to remember it as it was so when times became hard again, they could return to it and bask in the serenity; a reminder that the world gave light and dark sides to everything. They stepped on through the trees behind their guide with lemurs bouncing from trunk to trunk in pursuit – some were grey, some milk-white, some ink-black yet all observed them with wide, rounded inquisitive eyes and a face that looked like an old man's. Wild hairy grunting boars snorted through the roots as they dug for insects. Colourful birds flitted around the canopy, some were spotted with extraordinary tails fanning out as they danced on the branches and whistled a fantastical song to attract a mate, whilst others darted through the undergrowth, small and heavy, their plumage the colour of polished earth. Paradise flycatchers, cuckoo rollers, pygmy kingfishers, giant couas and sickle-billed vangas; none of the crew knew their names, yet they saw them all and heard each and every voice. From the wet leaves and trunks, vibrant frogs hopped (although they were warned these were not to be touched), chameleons were spotted on branches nearby and spider's webs, huge and obtrusive, were avoided at all costs.

As the sun climbed higher, the chorus grew louder until they could barely hear their own thoughts and wondered what all these sounds were; the cries, the whines, creaks, howls, chirps; what creatures could make such a strange cacophony. Amidst the crew's tiresome panting, an entire community - no - an entire *city* of bustling life was waking up to see tourists passing through. With wide eyes full of awe, Joseph looked up to the trees and saw fantastically coloured birds with long curved beaks, calling out from their branches to try their new loaf of bread; he spotted two ring-tail lemurs swinging through the canopy, howling the news of the day. Creatures large and small whined and chittered like the bustling markets he'd grown up in. The constant high-pitched ringing of the cicada insect was a drone of which he'd never known, as headache worthy as the grinding new-fangled machines the city was now sprawling with. Swerving quickly in fear, he missed a large green striped snake, somehow climbing through the trees without any limbs, just as the old vagabonds would slither the streets even though they were without luck or fortune. From somewhere in the trees, a Madagascan Ibis rang its signature call – the rainforest's Big Ben chiming the hour. *When will y' pay me? Says the bells of Old Bailey* . . . Suddenly London was alive in his mind again, a throbbing memory resuscitated by the bountiful life around him. The two settings had nothing in common, yet everything in common. They thrived, they evolved, they *existed,* continents apart.

The crew stared in bewilderment at this exuberant ecosystem, shocked to see how different the creatures were and how well they were adapted to their environments. Some of these creatures they had never seen before, not in a photograph, nowhere in their imagination. It was exquisite, extraordinary; a natural wonder to behold. They felt like David Livingstone, exploring the wilds of Africa, away from the city, living and breathing in a lavish freedom.

They walked on, trudging higher; the trees gradually thinning until shafts of sunlight were able to break through the thick rainforest rooftop, but these bounties came with consequences. The humidity intensified, and they perspired constantly with every garment soaked through with sweat, which attracted the mosquitoes in swathes. Soon, other flies joined the cloud, and they were assaulted by the pests, feeling their skin being leeched. Leeches themselves soon found a place on their skin, much to their disgust. The tribesmen Yalla and Honlu, however, didn't seem to notice their presence and strolled gaily as if they were out exploring in their garden. Joseph envied them, all envied, especially when Joseph spotted Yalla was walking barefoot through this wilderness. His own boots were damp and hot and continued to slip, not helping his tormenting ache as his plantar stretched tight and corns began to grind; blisters were forming, bursting and healing. A terrible itch had been plaguing him for days now too.

The path led them to the banks of a large pond where overhanging creepers dangled precariously above the water, exposing their great red thorns. Despite the thorns, it looked captivating and utterly blissful. Here, Joseph spotted several large flying creatures that silently swooped down, gently touched the surface and rose in haste. *What in the name of the dear mother*

Mary . . . he counted ten – no, twelve – twenty? *Thirty?* Through the scattered trees he saw up to a hundred flying through the clearing, their wings sweeping and membranous. He could hear their thrumming flutter. 'Yalla?' he called out above the din.

Their guide turned, surprised he'd called.

'What are those creatures?'

He followed Joseph's gaze and smiled, 'we call them *ramanavy.* Bats, I think, in English. They eat fruit. Lots of them, come in mornings like this.'

Victoria studied as she breathed, hair clinging to her face. 'They're not drinking the water; they're just dipping their bellies on it.'

Yalla tried explaining with added hand gestures, 'touch wah-ter . . . wet fur . . . drink on droplets on fur when hang in trees. No time to stop to drink, no. Danger lies beneath.'

'What's in there?' Hugh asked, wiping his dripping forehead.

'*Voay.*' He replied. Ready to ask what one was, Hugh was suddenly cut off by a sudden shrieking and splashing as a fruit bat flapped in the water, before silencing, and in that silence, they knew it had not just simply fallen into the water; it had been snatched. In that silence, they understood what a *voay* was. They didn't need a translation. *Crocodile.* Suddenly the pond no longer looked inviting, they were dissuaded by the sinister scaly secrets lurking beneath. 'Come.' Yalla ushered, 'we move on.' He continued walking with the group following, all happy enough to move on past this pond now knowing what called it home.

After two exhaustive hours of traversing through the thickset rainforest flora, they noticed a shift again, almost as if the soil were providing a different set of nutrients for different species to flourish. The path levelled and snaked its way onward at a slight downgrade. The trees, once rabbled with branches, coated in leaves and pregnant with fruits, nuts and fungi, were now tall, spaced apart with a broad naked trunk growing all its skinny branches and hardy leaves in a cluster at its peak. They reminded Joseph of a tall man wearing a bowler hat. Despite their rather bleak, dull appearance the crew felt awed at such a strange and beautiful spectacle. Such an odd-looking tree, a horticultural ultimatum, not that the urban folk could judge having spent their lives in structures made of stone. They were called *Boabab,* Yalla told them, and were a timeless species that were relics of this land, managing to endure throughout droughts, floods and near enough anything. Yalla walked to one and placed his palm gently on its trunk, just as Tulyaka had done to Robertson: a sign of peace, respect and friendship.

The sailor walked with wonder through the euphoric scenes, no longer caring if his clothes snagged and ripped, forgetting the weight of the carved elephant against his chest. It was all only material, it could be repaired; this was a journey of hardship, yes, but also of exultation – a wander through a dreamland. An inspirational transition that no one could take away from him. Joseph blinked in the sights and felt his soul awaken. There was more to life than what he'd thought.

They stopped to rest, drink and eat, but this break did not last long, and they were back trekking once more through the wilderness of this strange island. They trudged for a further hour downward with the landscape changing evermore so into a rockier crop where plants grew between crags and roots tangled and spilled over smooth black surfaces. Trees surrounded them still and shaded them under their greenery, but the ground was more shingle than earth and it crunched underfoot as if the rainforest had managed to take root over a landslide. It was a different kind of wonder. At points, Joseph had to question himself of the situation they were in, how they got here, what they'd done, and was indignant of his own past. *It feels like a different life now; so bleak, so bland and void of wonder; trapped in a pit of greed and profit. How petty.* People did not do these things, never, especially not the low-class gutter-rats. They lived and died in the city. He smiled tiredly, feeling proud at what they had achieved, but that feeling subsided when he spied their path toward . . .

Yalla slowed to a stop. He looked around, muttered to himself and traced paces, touching trunk after trunk, to a large tree with huge, impressive struts rising from the ground. They were its roots, he guessed. Joseph couldn't tell any more, it was all a mesh of life.

Obediently, they followed to where Yalla stopped again beside a towering strut and stepped aside to show a large crevasse that ran deep underground, under the tree, a blackness darker than ink that allowed no light inside. Spindly entrail-like roots hung over the edge clinging to the rough crag, begging to not be released. It was large enough for them to walk through single file, and it seemed to decline at a steady angle as if it ran straight to the bowels of the earth. They all stopped and looked at the gap, all pleading him to turn another way and lead them to another spot, a less daunting spot. *Please don't say what I think you're going to say, oh dear lord please don't say it . . .*

Yalla smiled, 'we are here.'

Chapter Twenty-Three

Peering into the black craggy fissure, Joseph felt more than simple apprehension; what he felt was a sheer instinctive force to pull away from it immediately. It was not that he feared the dark or what might be lurking in the eternal shadows, it was the thought of not finding a way out again that dried his mouth and made him tremble: being trapped; lost, wandering through the darkness praying for a glint of light, of hope. Surely there was a mistake, and as he glanced at Robertson suddenly looking perplexed too, he knew he was thinking the same. Licking his waxen lips, Joseph looked the tribesman up and down, his eyebrows lowering as his eyes darted questioningly, searching for a sign, a flicker of a ruse, that he was pulling their leg.

There was none. Yalla had the strongest poker face Joseph had ever seen, which meant he was positively serious. *Blimey he'd be a master at cards. The old mush can sit by me any day. This has got to be a bluff...* 'Uh, are - are you sure? This is where you've been leading us – to this big crack?'

The rest of the crew were silent, hoping beyond hope he was not about to say, 'Yes. This is place. This where collection takes place.'

His stomach dropped as the gravity of the situation sank in. Curiously, Rob stepped to the mouth of the yawning cave and peered into the entry of the earth and cursed under his breath. He turned back to them, 'I an't too keen to tell you the truth. That's enough to make a stuffed bird laugh down there.' He said matter-of-factly.

'You can hook it if you think I'm heading down there, I an't doing it. Not for nothin'.' Dave snarled, folding his arms. 'I may be off to meet the Old Scratch one day but it an't going to be today.'

Joseph winced. The last thing they needed was confrontation out here. Yalla and Honlu had taken them all the way out here and they intended for this to go ahead. *There's got to be some other way we can do this, some negotiation we can agree on, come on, think man!* But then Victoria, tucking her damp frizzed hair behind an ear and wiping her forehead, seemed to already know what to ask. A hand rested on her hip, 'are you sure there's no other way we can do this deal? We could help you with the chickens instead. We could help hunting and fishing, with sewing? I'm good at that. I could show you some tricks.'

'So can I.' Tess added.

Yalla's grin faded and with Honlu by his side they looked slightly threatened. Again, Joseph found himself wincing. *No, that's not it, if anything they look offended we're shirking this.* The man shook his head in defiance, 'No. Chief Tulyaka wants you to collect diamonds underground. That – for box. No other way.'

Hugh spoke up and took an interested step forward. 'Diamonds, you say?'

Finally, it clicked what Tulyaka had meant last night when he said he wanted them to collect underground stars. 'Yes. In cave, *diamondra*. Very of value, yes. We call them *kintana fanahy.*' He added.

Suddenly Hugh, Rob and Billy found a new interest to the darkness, now knowing what lie within. 'What does that mean?' Tess asked.

'Soul stars.' He smiled, showing the gaps in his teeth.

'Why do you call them that?'

'We bury *diamondra* with our recently dead. Our village belief is when you pass along the dark road to rest, these stones light the way, help guide you to other side, to Heaven, where those passed will return stones to sky. They shine, like stars, for infinity. We do not have many left. Need more.' he smiled again. He wasn't even breaking a sweat out here in this humidity. Joseph was filled with dread at what it would be like down there, but he looked toward the entrance and nodded slowly, accepting their ordeal.

Tess smiled, her yellowing teeth having no effect on the prettiness of the grin. A tear formed in the corners of her eyes as she thought of her sister. 'That's beautiful.'

Robertson looked at the entrance firmly, then asked, 'are you coming with us?'

Stepping forward, Honlu managed to tell them he was.

Licking his lips again, Joseph wiped his forehead with his sleeve. A pointless act: his sleeve was soaked through anyway. He could've done with another drink, of stronger stuff this time; a tot of the Old Pulteney Jim kept, or any whiskey. Everyone was nervous, tensions were high. They all knew this was not optional.

'Right then.' Captain Robertson started with a steely British optimism, 'let's get to it.' He stepped toward the cave tentatively, the rest following suit. He turned to Yalla, 'You'll be here when we return, yes?'

Smiling again. 'Yes. I stay.'

'I'm stayin' too.' Dave stated and watched them stop and look back. 'I don't care what the negro says, I am *not* going down in some shady cave.'

Anger flared, 'Dave, you are coming down with us whether you like it or not. Remember our agreement.' Joseph snapped, not only because of the rejection but also because of the language he was using in front of their hosts.

'What agreement? Captain said I could come, he allows it, and so I've come, but I an't going down there.' He retorted aggressively, 'you'll all be grinning at the daisy roots.'

Beginning to crack, Joseph made a step for him, but Robertson held out a hand calmly. 'I'll talk to him. He'll listen.'

Joseph backed down flaring his nostrils and breathing harshly, 'make sure he does. We are in this *together*,' he said, sparing an eye for Dave, 'even if some of us are cowards.'

Robertson went to Dave and spoke quickly and quietly, with everyone watching. Yalla, who seemed unphased by the insult, watched with interest. Eventually, they joined the group and Dave kept his head low and mouth shut. Joseph couldn't bear to look at him, *just get me in the dark so I won't have to look at that goddamn face any longer,* he thought, *else I'll smack it again, harder this time. One more strop and I swear that ratbag's face will be bleeding.* He sighed, trying to release some anger, and followed Honlu into the crevasse where the gloom instantly swallowed them. It was darker than it looked. Intimidatingly dark. Willing his legs to move, he walked under the thin slimy creepers and stepped into a world of silence.

One by one they stepped inside and instantly felt the temperature change; the drop as the hot air met the cool air, and the smell of moisture and minerals replaced the pungent aroma of rot and vegetation. It was a completely different atmosphere, reminding some of walking into a cellar or walking through the streets after a heavy rainfall. Wet stones and smooth - *'Ow! Argh ya bastard!'* Billy cried and limped along after them, biting his lip - rocks. The ground was rough to walk on and crunched underfoot but this shingle soon petered out the further they trekked down the clearway and turned to a pocked jagged path; dimpled after years of moisture erosion.

Without any sensation other than touch and smell to iterate their surroundings, claustrophobia set in making quick work of thinning the air and closing the walls either side of them. The path was only wide enough for a single-file passage, but here, where the ground began to slope and the tunnel turned, was like trying to fit through a pipe that led to nowhere.

Drips began to echo through the tunnel, bouncing off the rocks to reach them but from where and from how far deep they had no idea. How many fathoms did this cave descend? How many miles did it stretch? Was there even an end . . . or a way out? Joseph moved with his hands against the cave walls beside him trying to get some relief. They were slick with dry patches and sometimes had cracks and fissures of their own. No relief was found, only a rising sense of panic.

He followed the sound of Robertson's heels clacking against the stone and the light shuffle of Honlu's feet ahead. There was shuffling from the rest of the group, sounds of boots walking, of clothes rustling, of mouths breathing and lips smacking and gasping for more air, and quiet whispers of prayers, and the drips and the drips and the dripping . . . 'Have you been down here many times, Honlu?' he asked, relieved to have broken the silence.

Pausing, he replied from the front, 'Two. We reach . . . soon, yes. Soon.'

Joseph nodded. 'Soon.' He muttered, hoping the boy's idea of "soon" was the same as his.

Onward they walked. At times, the rock wall beside them bulged excessively on one side and the other side disappeared; the rock became smooth and dry at this section. Then, as they continued, the ceiling would lower, forcing them all to duck, wincing and praying for this nightmare to be over. The dripping sound became monotonous and merged into a trickle, swiftly becoming a stream of water that ran through their path down an eroded gully fashioned through years of movement. They followed this stream for some time, cursing at their wet feet and sodden shoes, until a faint light shone ahead.

With a faster pace, they marched and emerged into the bottom of a narrow canyon with a small waterfall rushing at the other end. The light was coming from above, through a gap that ran all the way along this underground river making the water twinkle as it bounced along its stony course. Leaves, vines and roots hung over the edge and connected as the gap narrowed near the middle where the rock wall, smooth and coloured, bulged again, bloated by the weight of millennia resting above.

At last, Honlu turned back to them and pointed ahead, 'near.'

Sighs of relief were shared, and they pressed on, walking through the water. Only when they neared the waterfall, they saw where Honlu was heading; there was no way around it, no entrance beside – a dead end, but not to the experienced. Honlu walked to the edge, turned back and smiled, then stepped straight *through* the torrent, disappearing into the froth and foam.

Pausing, Robertson considered the possibilities; *is it a trap? Where is he taking us?* But there was no choice, they had to move forward. He pursed his lips and took a breath, then walked through the cascade. Joseph followed suit and the rest passed under. The water was cold and refreshing, a powerful rush blasting onto their heads and shoulders. It soaked them, cleansed them, rinsing the sweat and flies from their bodies almost as part of a ritual to what they were about to witness.

Through the waterfall was a short and straight passage, a connection to their destination. Light was at its end and as Joseph stepped out of the dark, he entered another world. An open cavern, brimming with wonders and brilliance, yawned wide, stunning them all into a bewitched tranquil. They were dripping wet and tired, yet shocked beyond comprehension; everyone stood still, their eyes alight, gripped with an overwhelming understanding of Yalla's explanation.

Soul stars indeed.

'Oh Christ . . .' he heard Billy gasp from behind as he entered the cavern. Tess involuntarily crossed herself.

The sailor took a step forward, his mouth agape. *What Mad Vinny wouldn't give to be here now. Too bad we couldn't see eye to eye, eh?* Shafts of light lanced through fissures in the rocky cavernous ceiling; a tremendous feat that something so fragile could manage to penetrate through the depths to reach this subterranean expanse. Despite the light entering only through cracks, the level of illumination was astounding – they could see almost everything by the light reflecting from masses of shining diamonds scattered over the ground, the walls and the ceiling.

Some scattered over the rocks, some were embedded in them; others were mounted together up the walls and protruding from the ceiling in huge glittering clusters of sharp angles and points. Possessing no colour other than hints of the lightest mineral blues and blinding whites, their eyes had to accept that these crystals were transparent. Small pockets of reds and purples twinkled amongst the white and creamy blue minerals whence the diamonds formed, showing some diversity to the collection of rare stones. As they stood transfixed, they struggled to grasp that these were raw minerals and materials; they hadn't been touched by human hands, not by the wealthiest or even royalty.

Essentially virgins, these gems and diamonds had been forged by eons of intense pressure. It was nothing more than nature wielding its blacksmith's arms in such a forceful way that a lump of rock was subdued into change, was sculpted and reimagined until its paradigm altered altogether – reiterating its atoms, its appearance, its name, its value. What was opaque was now transparent, what was grey and dark was now piercingly clear like a crisp morning sky after a stormy night. A mine of miracles was what they now stood in, and Joseph felt overwhelmed as the glitters sparkled in his eyes. It was a phenomenal sight he could not believe existed in this world.

Stepping further into the cavern, he saw it was larger than he'd anticipated. It was an incredible expanse and yet every inch had been decorated in such an exquisite way, in such an untouched manner – everything was rugged and raw and yet pristine; not a speck of dust or dirt tainted this capacity, and everything was where it was meant to be. Architects would have envied, and the wealthy would've had itchy fingers, ready to pull out their bulging wallets only to discover there was no such price for an accommodation such as this. A room expensively furnished by nature's finest items and supported by grand pillars of smooth natural mineral rock that rose, in places, to six feet tall. A décor like no other. He gulped and walked past structures he had never seen before, listening to a gentle and echoing drip.

Protruding from the ceiling and rising from the ground, stalactites and stalagmites reached out to each other, connected only by the single drip of accumulated moisture that fell often enough to spread its minerals. Some of these formations were small, no more than ankle-height but some reached heights he couldn't see the top of. They glistened in the fractured light, their surfaces smooth, never to be touched by the external elements; no erosion, only expansion, and looking up was like looking into a mirror – moulded from the ceiling was another great pinnacle pointing directly at its neighbour below. Small stalactites hung from the ceiling in a mass like bats, but only a few had formed enough to be an identical partner to the stalagmite underneath. He couldn't begin to imagine when these structures had begun to form.

Honlu set the wicker basket down and called out to them, breaking their trance. It was intended to be quiet, but the aweing silence amplified his timid voice, 'to drink . . . if need, pools have fresh . . . wah-ter.' They followed his movement as he walked over to a small pool directly below one of the fissures where a steady stream of drips and a blaze of perfect light fell from above, seeming to brighten the cavern even further. He knelt, splashed his face and drank some water. Then he looked up to them and saw no one had moved, all were stupefied into submission. He could understand that; he had been quite fascinated his first time in the cave. 'We start on *diamondra* now. Much s-s-sacred to village, yes. Pick big and lit-tle *diamondra*. Leave the other colour, red, they . . .' he paused, searching, 'rare; they val-hoo-blue. *Val-yoo-bul.*' He struggled to get the word out, then gave up. 'They stay.'

'What can we pick them with? Are there tools here?' Asked Rob.

Honlu tilted his head, not understanding the words, but he guessed the meaning and walked back to the basket where he picked out a special type of sharp granite. Then, stepping carefully with his bare feet, he reached a crop of diamonds and stooped, aimed carefully, and with a sharp strike he hit the base of the largest diamond and broke it free from its purchase. He stood straight and looked to them, holding an object so rare and valuable people had paid for it in blood and began to toss it from one hand to the next aimlessly, as if it were nothing more than a cricket ball for the upcoming game, unaware the people of the world craved such stones, killed for such things. To Honlu, it was only an item of importance when someone died, and occasionally it was fashioned into a necklace or shaped for the head of the Chief's spear. What other use could these stones have?

They began to fan out into the cave, each exploring their own pocket of diamonds to marvel at. Billy approached Joseph, who wandered over to the pool to drink before he began to mine. 'I t'ink we've hit the jackpot here, Joe. I mean, would ye' look at it.' He took another wide glance at the scene and giggled, 'wouldn't ye' know, the lucky leprechaun did manage to find the pot o' gold.'

Joseph drank the water using his hands, and splashed his face washing the sweat from it, and smoothed down his beard. The water tasted of minerals yet no less revitalising. 'It's beautiful. I've never seen anything like it.' He stood, 'the lads who grew up in poverty, running the benjo streets barefoot, down for a long stretch in prison – and now here we are in the bowels of the earth mining diamonds on a tropical island.' He smiled, 'not bad.'

The sounds of clinking and tapping started, shattering the tranquil of the cave as they attempted the collection. Billy smiled, 'Funny what a bit of desperation can do to ye, eh? It's a bastard to be in, but we wouldn't be 'ere without it.' He tucked his hands into his pockets and in that movement, Joseph glimpsed at a sheathed knife tucked under his shirt and instantly the sentence changed from a friendly quip to something other, a provocation? A warning? *Since when did Billy carry a knife?* Either way, it reminded him to be careful and he found himself nodding and smiling. There was a pause where an ever-so-slight atmosphere settled before Billy asked, 'how many o' these do we need?'

'Don't know, ask the lad.'

'Honlu!' he called.

The boy turned, surprised to hear his name being called.

'How many do we need to take?'

'We fill it.' He said, pointing over to the wicker basket near the entrance. Three diamonds had already been added. 'Need to . . . leave before . . . moon.' He said slowly, carefully, choosing the right words.

Billy nodded, 'I'd best get a move on then. See y', Joe.' He walked off toward a cluster of blue-white diamonds.

'Happy mining.' He said, then headed for a patch of scattered stones but saw not the sharp edges of the diamonds now; instead he saw the sharp edge of a knife.

'An Irishman in a cave full o' jewels, he's bound to be happy!' Billy called back.

Joseph walked back to the basket to collect the granite piece before scouring the ground, stooping and examining a large diamond roughly four inches in length poking from a cluster. He aimed and struck the base of it. There was a crack, but no split. He hit again, and again multiple times and finally broke it free from its purchase, realising how easy Honlu had made it look.

He held it up to the light, seeing the rays refract through the strange transparency. It was like looking through water, through ice, only this was rock. It had weight to it, yet it sat daintily in his palm. It was remarkable; he could see why the lust for them was so great, so sought after. *This is something kings and queens wear, something that hangs on the necklaces I once stole, sits on rings I once took; and here I am now holding it free of charge – the only time in its existence where it holds no value or credit, before people slap a number on it and deem it worthy only for the wealthy.*

In his other palm, he held the granite he used to break it free and compared the two; the stronger one used to break it and the prettier one that deemed the exercise worthwhile. So similar yet so different, but he knew which he was attracted to more, which he had always been attracted to. His hands began to tremble with a sudden want. To slip it into his own pocket was easy, too easy, and he wanted to do it; to claim it and keep it for himself. A lifetime of picking rare and shiny things was not something he could easily forget. A magpie could not easily shed its trademark.

After a moment of hard deliberating and with great difficulty, he walked over and placed it in the basket. Exhaling, he didn't realise he'd been holding his breath. *You've got to start letting it all go, you little skilmalink, enough of the secrets and shadiness. You an't in the city anymore, chuckaboo. Stick to the truth, keep it clean; you'll have a lot less problems to deal with.* Quickly looking away, he continued to forage. It was tiresome work, and after an hour, the novelty had worn thin and they saw why they had been elected this job as their part of the deal. It was an awful, horrid job. Their hands began to cut from the sharpness of the granite and diamonds, their fingers became sore with awkward gripping and it was a struggle to clutch anything. After two hours, their blood was spreading on the diamonds and the basket was filling with red-smeared stones. Groans became the new sound and gasps possessed a new meaning; no longer did it have an awestruck quality; it was now full of pain and discomfort. It became laborious, hard work and was as Billy described it, as "tryin' to do the gardening with glass for weeds."

Soon, the lacerations hurt so intensely they struggled to strike the diamonds any more without yelping in pain. It became clear, *crystal* clear, why Chief Tulyaka chose this job as a trade for the box: because it was a torturous ordeal that no one wanted to do twice. Joseph imagined the thought process: *Might as well get these fools to do it for a silly old box.*

Eventually, Honlu stepped back from the basket and turned to them, 'basket full. Time to go now.'

Everyone looked up, too exhausted to express any form of joy but feeling a rushing sensation of relief. The pain was getting unbearable; every edge and point felt sharper and those places that were not cut were tender and sore to touch. It was strange, Joseph found, that even though the diamonds were as smooth as glass they now felt as rough as the rock from which they'd been hewn. 'Thank fuck for that,' Hugh complained standing and beginning to walk back toward the entrance with the others, wincing at his bleeding palms, 'my hands are so sore!'

Billy smiled and took the opportunity even though he was tired. He hastily retorted, 'funny, that's what yer mother said when she lay beside me after I'd finished.' Rob and Joseph laughed, and Dave even smiled.

Hugh forced a laugh, 'har-har, as if I haven't heard that one before, you Irish git.'

'Yet it still cracks a laugh every time, it's gold!'

Hugh shook his head tiredly, 'it's a good job my hands *are* sore else a smack would be coming your way, Baker.' He winked.

The Irishman laughed and pretended to walk faster. 'Easy now, easy now. Not in front o' the wee boy here.'

A chuckled spread through them, and Robertson shook his head exhaustedly as a mother with two sons would do. They reached the entrance where Honlu stood waiting with the basket strapped to his back by two woven lengths of vine. When they all joined him, he made his way back through the tunnel and through the waterfall, and this time they all appreciated the coolness wash their sweat and clean their stinging palms. Despite its beauty, Joseph found himself eager to get back to the rainforest.

The walk back through the tunnel seemed to take longer, it certainly felt longer and tighter than before. It occurred to them that maybe Honlu had taken another route, but they didn't see another opening, nor did they see him take it. It was the same path, with the same rocks and same dripping; the only difference was the level of exhaustion. The darkness seemed less foreboding this time though; Joseph could see some of the walls and the rocks they walked past but even so, the gloom had little to offer, especially after basking in the cavern full of diamonds and wonderous crystals.

The group quietened, and the jokes ceased; the darkness snuffed out the humour like fingers pinching the flame of a candle, and the claustrophobia reset as they walked along. Timidly and almost nervously, Victoria reached back and took Joseph's hand, holding it tight. He winced at the pain of the soreness, but he kept holding on. Her hand was sweaty but so was his, and they felt comfort in this. He felt the cuts and her worry and wished he could have taken her in his arms just then and kissed her as he had done on the beach that humid day, underneath an arch of flowers in a country they never knew existed. Suddenly he felt something more for her, something internal that warmed his chest, a feeling he hadn't felt in a long time. Love? Was that it? A carnal desire? He couldn't pinpoint it exactly, but something was there for her and he felt scared, scared that he might lose it if he told her. How do you even tell a person you love them? He was never good at it but as he walked, he wondered if she felt the same.

Through the murky tunnel, they pressed on, walking as quickly as they could, single file. Suddenly Joseph bumped into the back of Victoria, and Rob bumped into the back of him. The line had stopped moving. 'Oh God.' He heard Robertson say from up front.

'What? What is it?'

'Honlu. The boy. He's . . . he's gone.'

Joseph frowned in confusion, along with the rest of the crew. 'What do you mean he's gone? He was walking right in front of you.' Hugh called.

'It's a single pathway, he's got a faster pace than us. He's probably ahead.' Suggested Victoria, trying to stay calm.

'How did you not see him go? It's not as if there's a lot of room in 'ere Captain.' Billy pointed out.

'I wasn't looking. I was looking at my boots trying to not trip, then I looked up and he wasn't there. He was gone.' He argued back, sounding more surprised at himself than angry.

'*Walk-er!*' groaned Hugh.

'He was light of foot without any boots on.' Tess reminded them, 'and over the sounds of our boots I couldn't hear him. He probably walked off and is at the entrance waiting for us. Let's keep going and meet him there.'

The rest agreed. 'We keep going and pray we don't hit a fork.' Robertson declared and set off again at a faster pace than before, his heels clacking against the stone.

What started off as a fast walk turned into a jog and before long, they were running through the darkness, managing all the twists and turns and bends. No longer could they hear the dripping, their hearts were beating too loudly in their heads, pumping sheer panic down their throats. 'I knew we shouldn't have trusted them!' Dave cried from the middle as he ran, 'I knew it! Never have I trusted 'em!'

'I got to agree with Dave on that one,' Hugh said, 'They cook good meat but they're a strange folk.'

'Do you really think you should be talking so loudly? These walls echo if you hadn't noticed.' Victoria said in between breaths.

Dave was adamant though, 'I doubt they're even there anymore, Vic. They've gone home, they've left us here in the caves to get lost. They've got their diamonds now; they've got what they wanted.'

A scornful quiet settled between them, unsure of who to listen to.

At long last, light was seen from around the bend and shingle crunched underfoot; the shapes of the rocks were in sight, the crags in the walls had shadows. Breathing heavily but eternally thankful, they burst from the crevasse and back into daylight where green of the trees seemed extra vibrant and the afternoon sunlight seemed blinding compared to the darkness of the tunnel. Blinding though it was, both Yalla and Honlu were nowhere to be found.

As they stood catching their breath and listening to the cries of the rainforest fauna again, they realised Dave was right: the two villagers had tried to abandon them, believing they would get lost either in the cave or rainforest. Awash with betrayal, they stood around the crack and tried to calm their racing thoughts, but the only one who seemed to have a clear run of them was Dave James, who stood in a dominant stance with his chest heaving. 'I told you! I told you all, didn't I?! I said I didn't want to go down into the caves, I told you the niggers an't no good; I knew they were going to try something like this, some treachery! *Ne-gro* is a *no-go* is what I've learned and it's a damn good thing I learned it. I wish I'd have said it earlier and stuck with it! And let's not forget who it was that killed Harold: the fucking blacks!'

Joseph looked to Robertson, who was biting his lip and looking to the ground in thought. *I don't care, Jim. I can't do it anymore. I'm speaking my mind and you can't stop it.* 'Dave,' he looked him in the eye and felt the rest watching, 'on islands like this there was bound to be black people living here, so let me ask you one thing: if you kenned it already, *WHY DID YOU ASK TO COME WITH US!*' he yelled, scaring some birds into flight. 'I told you what it was going to be like, I told you what to expect but *you wanted* to come anyway! You've been nothing but a fucking thorn in my side the entire time, what with your snide little insults you thought no one heard and your constant complaining—'

Dave's nostrils flared as sweat trickled down his brow, 'I didn't expect to be left behind by them, and in case you hadn't noticed we've been abandoned in a fucking jungle, on an island I can't even pronounce! They don't like us, the blackies *do not want us here*. It's a message, and since you're so good at picking up clues I'm surprised you didn't see that. They dragged us out here to labour for them, cutting our hands in the meantime and then they abandon us once they got what they wanted. They *used* us. Maybe it took you to see it through my eyes. Maybe I *shouldn't* have come along. Maybe it was *your fault* you let me come.' He paused, 'I want an apology.' He folded his arms in an act of superiority.

The atmosphere was as thick as the humidity; the rest watched on in anticipation, unsure of whether to step in, or *when* to step in. Joseph's glare fixated feeling the same rage as before, only this time, it had built up to boiling point. It was like a jabbing pain that had gradually turned into a white pinprick, a splinter in the crook of a finger that ached and hurt as time wore on. With great difficulty he restrained himself from swinging a punch, from whipping out his knife and stabbing it deep in his neck. Sinisterly, he hissed. 'You know, when I met you, I thought you were a decent bloke, not great, but decent enough to bring along, but now, now I can see what you really are and I can see I made a mistake,' he growled, 'I shouldn't have trusted you in prison, I shouldn't have broken you out. I should've kicked you off the ship before we even set off. I never should've let you join this expedition. I heard travelling changes people, but I can see that don't always work; no amount of countries or places you go to, work or people you meet will ever change who you are – you'll still be the same stubborn, stupid cunt I met before. Except now I've got to live with it without any escape.' He hacked up and spat in front of him, 'that's your apology, you fucking prick.'

A mist seemed to settle over him. Dave relaxed his arms and looked as if he was about to swing, then in one swift movement, he pulled a gun out from under his shirt and aimed it at the Quartermaster's forehead. It was so close Joseph could smell the powder of where it had been messily primed, but never did he flinch. He stared down the barrel, faced that black hole of oblivion and the callous man behind it and startlingly felt nothing at all. No fear, no chill down his spine; only a rising clarity.

There was a moment's hesitation and Joseph Winter knew he had him; the man was not going to pull the trigger. A moment was all it took to decipher those that meant to pull and those that did not intend to. Hesitation meant he was thinking, and a man thinking is a man not meaning to kill. If he'd have wanted to do it, he would've already done it. Dave had already spent too long holding it and doing nothing, the little sense in him holding his finger back.

A coolness ran through Joseph's veins and he felt suddenly sharper, 'go on.' he hissed as he placed his forehead against the barrel. 'Pull it.'

'No!' Billy cried and shoved his arm away. The gun exploding into animation, flashing and bursting its bullet. The sound of the shot ruptured the rainforest's calls; birds tore away from their perches and flew into the air, lemurs scarpered away; the echo rebounding from tree to tree silencing and frightening the fauna.

Joseph ducked holding his heavily ringing ears. '*Avast! Stop this now!*' he heard a muffled voice exclaim and looked up to see Robertson glowering and snatching the gun from Dave's grasp. '*The hell do you think is going on here!* That's enough collieshangles! All the while you two have been bickering I've been trying to remember the way back and as it turns out I can't even turn my back for a second without some fucking squabble! You two are *men* for God's sake, we all know you don't like each other but you're forced to live together, so buck up and get on with it!' He tucked the pistol away into his own belt, 'Mister Dave James, when we return to the village you are to keep that rabbling squealer shut until we get this blasted, cursed poxy chest and get back on the ship and on our merry way. These people *are* black of skin, but they are also our *hosts* and at the minute, *our only hope.*' He hissed, 'you'd do well to not offend them and to keep those opinions to yourself. Do I make myself clear?'

Dave looked to the ground like a sour child and nodded.

'*I said*, do I–'

'Yes sir!' he shouted, standing upright, glaring coolly ahead.

'Good. Now for the love of the Christ and his dear mother Mary can we please make a start on getting back to the village before dusk, else we all might as well be worm fodder.' He turned and looked at the man who had, only a moment before, been staring into the barrel, 'And Joseph, you try a stunt like that again and you'll be going to heaven without a head. You're not a fool, so don't act like one. Do you have your compass?'

Joseph stood, his ears throbbing, his palms stinging with blood and sweat, indignant of what he'd just done. His voice sounded muffled, as did everything else, but he got the gist. Reaching into his pocket, he picked out his compass and noticed it was spinning where it should've been still. He frowned and shook it. The needle wobbled, balanced, then swung this way and that. 'It's broken,' he heard his voice say hazily.

Captain Robertson pursed his lips and exhaled sharply, then addressed them all. 'Right. It turns out this day was to test us after all. Now, I think I can remember certain parts to get us back on the path. It's going to be a long journey and we've got a lot of ground to cover and I want to get back to the village before nightfall. God knows what prowls around these trees when the sun goes down. The pace will be fast, so do keep up. Now,' he took his hat off, wiped his forehead and pulled his hair back, tying the back of it with a length of string, 'let's move.'

He turned and strode off with large steps and they all followed behind him, trying to keep up and stay cool in the humidity. Nonetheless, the tension between the two men had set everyone on edge, now knowing each carried a weapon of some manner. Now unsure of what to be more afraid of; the nocturnal creatures of this rainforest or these creatures their shipmates had turned into.

They walked on through the craggy forest, leaving the crevasse and rocky crop behind. Rob kept the pace behind the captain, almost springing as he jogged, and Tess managed to keep up, followed by Joseph, Billy, Victoria, Hugh and Dave, whose pale face was sour in the shadows.

The baobab trees were passed without anyone looking up, the rainforest encroached by; no one took any notice of how the trees thickened. Lemurs followed in the trees and called to each other, yet they soon melted back into the canopy. Large cat-like mammals were spotted quickly darting back into the brush; from the defiant looks on their faces, even the *fossa* knew to keep clear, yet the crew barely noticed; everyone was too focused on keeping up with the pace of the group. No one looked as they passed the pond, now still and silent. They swatted flies when they needed to but not surprisingly, they were no longer such a nuisance.

The path wound on uphill, and Robertson, only stopping twice to get his bearings (and to remember to breathe) managed to stay with the path or close enough to it to know where he was going. It was as if a compass was in his head, a lighthouse was guiding him back to shore, and he marched on like a soldier with his troops behind.

By the time they reached the view of the waterfall and pool, evening was in full swing and in the gap of clearing where the path teetered on the edge, they saw the sunlight was a mellow orange, soon to redden. Dusk was not far away with the shadows of the traveller's palms stretching long. The orchids were closing. As they caught their breath, they noticed their clothes were ripped and torn and blood seeped from numerous cuts they didn't know they had. 'We've got to keep moving. We an't far from the village now.' Robertson instructed and moved with a larger stride.

Shadows crept up the bark of the trees and the underside of leaves darkened, flowers began to close their petals as the day drew to a close. The beauty of the rainforest was now lost to them and the vegetation became an obstacle, a hinderance. The path became a clock and as they marched down the second-hand, time slipped quickly away; daylight slackened, gloom rose; they hoped darkness would not push them from the clock's face.

Again, they felt hunger begin to tighten their organs and their throats craved liquid to swallow, their legs burned and eventually numbed. When looking down, they saw only two attachments swinging and flapping beneath them somehow moving them forward, belonging to no one.

At last, they heard cracklings of a fire and voices talking through the trees. 'We're close.' Their captain heaved as he pressed on through the fading light until they saw orange through the trees ahead; orange light, flickering flames. They pushed harder with branches whipping at them and leaves smacking as they ran by. No longer caring for the path, they headed for the firelight with their heads swimming and bodies flailing. At long last they burst through the trees and into the clearing of the village, much to the surprise of the community who looked on in wonder with some running to Tuyaka's hut.

Jim Robertson walked a few steps before falling to his knees, heaving in breaths with mighty force, lactic acid burning up his throat making him want to vomit. The rest clambered through and stopped, collapsing to the ground, but Joseph kept going, knowing that if he stopped to catch his breath he wouldn't want to get back up.

He walked past Robertson and into the village, eyes searching greedily for their guide and the boy who took the diamonds. There was footfall behind him and when he glanced, he saw Billy and Victoria, with, was that Dave? He couldn't make him out, his eyes were shot and bleary.

The villagers looked to each other in surprise. Worry was on their faces, whereas some turned away and headed to the fire in ignorance, acting as if they hadn't seen them, wishing they hadn't returned. *Things have changed, I can feel it. What's happened since we've been gone?* Joseph marched on with sweat running down his face and his throat dry, spitting feathers. He strode under the tree toward the chief's hut where Tulyaka stood at the entrance waiting for them. Before he could stop his mouth from moving words were coming out, 'Oi! Tulyaka, where's Yalla and Honlu? They left us behind! What's all that about? We damn near killed ourselves trying to find our–' he stopped short, seeing Honlu walk out the hut; his face swelled, bleeding and blotched, his cheek red and risen with one eye closing to a slit.

'What the – someone's copped the boy a mouse! What in God's name happened to 'im?' Billy spoke his thoughts aloud and slowed to a stop. The rest halted.

Honlu looked over to them and pointed angrily with tears streaming over his ballooning cheek. Yalla emerged from the hut next, his face red, his features drawn together in rage. He spoke in Malagasy and Honlu answered, but in his anger some explanation was given in short words of broken English. He continued to point, 'they!' he exclaimed, 'they, hurt! That one,' pointing to Dave, 'steal red *diamondra,* I saw! Tells to stop . . . he says no and hurt me!

Beat me! They, they do not stop, try to take *kintana fanahy,* then all hurt Honlu more!' he cried, angry tears streaming down his face.

All of them stopped, absolutely perplexed. Hearts racing frantically, their minds searched for lost words and memories that never happened.

Chapter Twenty-Four

Valla examined Honlu, crying and drawing a crowd, and turned to the four English people and felt emotions he hadn't felt in a long time. '*You! You all did this.*' He snarled, approaching them threateningly, 'you beat him, poor innocent boy! You hurt us! Why? Why do that after you eaten our food, shared our fi-yah and saw our sacred *kinata fanahy* cave?'

'We never - *what? We didn't do that!*' Joseph exclaimed, still partly shocked at the accusations. A thin red line of blood trickled from his brow. 'None of us stole from the cave and *none* of us laid a finger on him. Why would we?! We all picked the diamonds like he told us to do, we did exactly what he said!'

Victoria stepped forward, fuming, 'why don't we address betrayal and abandonment instead? You *know* what that word means, don't you? *Abandonment.* We were following Honlu through the tunnels when he disappeared, then when we came out of the cave, you'd both gone; came running back here expecting us to get lost out in the jungle and not return. As soon as–'

'We left as soon as the Honlu came from the cave with blood on his–'

She held a finger up, 'No, I wasn't finished, and don't interrupt me when I'm angry. As soon as you had your diamonds that we'd collected for you, that we sliced our hands to get, he abandons us in those tunnels to get lost. He used us, *you* used us.

'We held up our part of the deal; we got the bloody diamonds for you so hold up your end and give us the fucking box and we can get out of here and leave you all behind. We know you don't want us here, and we no longer want to be here, so give us what you owe, and we'll be gone.'

'You t'ink we *used* you pee-poles? Like tools?' Yalla looked hurt, he stood in front of her with a red face. Fury was aflame in his eyes. 'We fed you, watered you, gave you a place by fi-yah and gave opportunity to help in return for box. No, it is lies we used you. We *help* you.'

'Lies?! You want to talk about that? Fine. It's a lie we hurt him, it's a lie we stole any diamonds, it's a fucking whopper of a lie we did anything wrong.' She snapped, spitting flames. 'I really don't think you understand the place where we came from. We've dealt with lies all our lives – we know what they smell like, we've dealt with far worse people than you or that skilmalink Honlu and we *all* know that none of us hurt that boy there or stole anything!' With her voice raised, the rest of the villagers looked over and Robertson, Hugh, Rob and Tess quickly hurried over to see what was happening.

Yalla's eyes narrowed, his voice lowered and in the rising gloom he appeared even more hostile. 'Religion men taught us to respect other pee-poles, to love thy neighbour and to help weary travellers as Jesus wanted us to do. They do not tell us pee-poles from ships would be so selfish, so hurtful, beat our children and lie to our faces. The way you talk to us, I do not like. I am offended. The way you evade truths is not good, not when it is to your host. It is worst. Bad pee-poles you all are.'

'Look mate, ye got your diamonds, just give us the box you owe, and we'll be gone.' Billy said exasperatedly, 'it's the only reason we're still here.'

'We don't have all *diamondra* from today. You took the red; Honlu told you not to take, to leave them. Since you no listen, we take them back now.' He held out his hand.

'*We didn't take them!*' cried Joseph, agitated, 'none of us took any of the red ones.'

Yalla looked over his shoulder to two other men and called out to them in Malagasy. The two then approached and began to search, patting their pockets and ripped clothes. They let them search, knowing they'd find no rogue stones. When the others arrived, they were patted as well. Robertson looked to Joseph questioningly, wondering what was going on. He let them search too, not wanting to cause any more friction than there already was.

'What's this for? What's happening?' Hugh asked, watching them search Robertson.

Suddenly one of the men gripped something in Dave's pocket, but before he was able to draw away and pull it out, Dave's face narrowed and he grabbed the hand before it left his trousers and he hissed harshly in the man's ear, whether he understood English or not. *'You pull that diamond out and you're dead, nigger. I've killed before and I'll do it again if you cross me. I know how to do it; I know how to make blackies die slow. Let go of that and move on.'* He let go of his hand and the man cocked a stern look at him, considered the conditions, then tore his hand from his pocket crying out, *'Diamondra! Diamondra mena! Mangalatra aminay izy ireo!'* Diamond! Red diamond! They steal from us! He held the red diamond in the air for all to see and handed the stone to Yalla, who took it knowingly.

Dave stood chillingly still, his teeth grinding, wishing he still had his pistol. If he did, he knew exactly what to do, who to aim it at. And this time he would pull the trigger hard.

'They steal! They did it! *Nokapohin'izy ireo i Honlu, mandainga izy ireo!'* They beat Honlu, they are lying! 'They beat Honlu, steal soul stars and lie! They did it!' Yalla exclaimed, 'Honlu tells truth!' Suddenly the crowd of villagers erupted in shouts and yells and cries at the atrocities these people had brought upon them.

The crew's eyes fell on Dave with indignation and hopelessness. How could anyone believe their defence now? To the villagers, they had committed everything Yalla was accusing them of and deserved punishment. At that moment, Joseph had never felt as much hatred as he did just then. It was like a bout of hellfire had infected his heart and was now pumping raw contemptuous flames through his veins. Before, he'd have never considered killing; it was a messy and dangerous business, but now the thought of it was becoming increasingly appealing, and he found himself wanting this man dead. No, he wanted more than that; *he* wanted to do it himself – to pull the trigger, to slide the knife in, to pull the lever releasing the trap door and watch his body drop into the noose. He wanted to see him jitter and struggle, twitching as life left that man's eyes and feel the joy that would come with such malevolence. The thought became more desirable than the thought of getting the chest or even the Lost Loot itself. He hated him, but not only because of what he'd done, the grief he'd caused; he hated him because he had awakened the worst inside himself and made him want to commit atrocities he otherwise would've never considered. He would've never wished death upon anyone, until now.

In fact, everyone looked at Dave with a newfound emotion, a new set of eyes. A perspective that would take a lot to shake off. They saw a man who had committed crimes against the law and should've stayed in prison. He *should've* been kept there, but they broke him out. They gave him another chance. *Joseph* had given him a second chance.

Joseph clenched his fists, not only feeing fury but feeling guilt too; shame that he had allowed this beast to join them, that he'd given him a new life he didn't deserve. And now he was going to take that away. Reaching under his shirt for the dagger he kept, he grasped its hilt as Yalla continued to yell. Even though he'd never stabbed anyone, he knew exactly where to stick the blade.

Sensing this, Victoria turned and faced him and looked into his eyes whilst holding his hand around the knife. '*Please, no,*' she whispered, 'it'll only make things worse. Listen to me. *Please.*'

With great force he managed to tear away from Dave and looked into Victoria's eyes, her calm eyes, and considered; his fingers slightly loosening.

'*Enough!*' Chief Tulyaka roared, and everyone silenced. Fireflies began to light above them and around the tree, the sounds of the rainforest suddenly amplified. He walked forward from the entrance of his hut and moved toward them, 'I have heard. Ears are open, and I now judge what to do.' He then gestured to Yalla to continue in English for him whilst he spoke his native tongue for the gathering crowd to understand. '*Ny anglisy dia nangalatra ny diamondra masintsika masina ary nikapoka an'i Honlu rehefa hitany ny nataon'izy ireo . . .*'

Yalla had his eyes and ears on Tulyaka but his mouth was speaking another language, and kept up as each word passed, 'English have stolen our sacred red diamonds and have beaten Honlu when he saw what they had done. The evidence is now clear. But . . . English *did* collect diamonds and hold up their part of the trade. The box . . . is here, in my home, but events . . . unfold, make t'ings difficult.'

'*Tsy maintsy miatrika ny rariny ny anglisy amin'ny asan-dry zareo ao amin'ny tanànako . . .*' Tulyaka held up a finger when he had finished speaking.

Yalla interpreted, 'English must face justice for their crimes in my village. As Chief, I say if English pass the trial, they may take box and leave my village, not to come back until end of days.'

The crew looked at each other, puzzled, except for Dave who looked over to Hugh, and then faced forward with a glint of pride in his eye, almost as if he'd forgotten the feeling of being caught out in a crime. He was relishing it.

'Trial? What trial?' Robertson asked.

Tulyaka smiled, as if he had been waiting for that question and wanted the pleasure of answering it. By now, most of the village surrounded them, engaged spectators awaiting the final judgement. Tulyaka raised his arms, 'Trial by Tangena!' he yelled, and the village cried with him.

The word rang a bell. Joseph recognised it, as well as Tess, Victoria and Billy; those who had been present at the revealing of the prior clue.

Strange lands and strange predators there are:
be warned of Tangena's bite;
Seek along the eastern coast, pray and do not lose sight.
Help Merina and Merina will help you.

Tangena.

Joseph felt his stomach drop and his mouth dry up, he closed his eyes and sighed. Tangena was the exact thing the clue had warned them about. *Help Merina and Merina will help you. Oh, the irony.*

Suddenly he found himself wanting to laugh, what else was there to do when things had turned so horribly wrong?

Tess appealed, 'You have the red diamonds now; you have all the diamonds, let us take the box and leave? Surely, you'd want us out of your hair sooner rather than later?' She hoped a different tack would change his mind and prevent them all from facing a trial, and, for some, the second and third trial in their lives.

The finger returned and pointed at her; all eyes then turned to her as they listened to their chief's decision. '*Tsia! Lehiben'ity tanàna ity aho ary manapa-kevitra. Ianareo jiolahin-tsambo anglisy tsy maintsy mandoa . . .*'

Yalla continued, 'No! I am Chief of this village and I decide. You English must pay, yes. Trial take place at rising of sun, on new day. Tonight, you all . . . spend in the pits.'

He had barely finished speaking when the warriors of the village grabbed them and hauled them away from the scene, from the excited village, and hassled them toward the edge of the clearing. They knew they had no choice; they did not struggle. Suddenly Victoria and Tess were taken apart from the group and guided on different route. 'We'll get out of this! Don't worry!' Joseph called to Victoria when he saw they were to be separated. He was surprised, even out here they still preferred men and women to be apart, but then a crafty slap around the head cut his thought short.

'*Tsy miresaka amin'ny voafonja!*' *Do not talk to the prisoners!* the man declared in a deep voice. The six men were taken into the trees and were surprised to see a deep pit in the ground with a template of bamboo bars tied to many rocks sitting over its edges acting as a door: a cell door. One of the men lifted the bamboo bars and the other urged them inside the dark pit. It was darker on the inside, or so it seemed in the gloom of the new night, and the earth was cold against their hands as they clambered down. Joseph hoped Victoria and Tess had a better treatment, something above ground at least.

The bamboo door was lowered; he could almost hear a metallic clang as they shut, and the two men stood by in silence, leaving them to their thoughts. No one spoke. The sounds of the rainforest cried and cawed as creatures began the night shift, but that meant even worse things were now awakening too; things that chose not to make a sound as they took over the trees and prowled their territories in the darkness.

Joseph looked around the pit, noticing its length and width, its surprising depth and saw shadows of objects on the ground; skeletons of animals that had fallen in no doubt. He looked at the shadows glumly, used to having poor conditions in a cell. *A cell of earth; that's a first.* This sentence was only to be for a night though, and his cell mates were numbered at five. He found himself shrugging, *at least there's room here for six prisoners, in the London gaols there wouldn't be this much room.* The tension between them was thick and Joseph feared that if anyone spoke, especially Dave, there would be a confrontation. For once, Joseph was glad it was night in a cell, as, if it were day, he would still have to look upon that man's face and see its proud sneer.

The evening's gloom layered darker shades, pulling it into a deep black that none of them could see through. Even the firelight could not reach them; sight was unavailable, but their hearing sharpened, and they listened to the crackle of the flames and the chatter of the people around it in the village. There were howls and chatters from the trees and the creaking of insects, but none offered any comfort, and they knew sleep would elude them this night. After a time, they heard footsteps and the same two men opened the bars to lower food for them in guano bowls, and then they handed a seventh bowl down. Joseph was confused; there were only six incarcerated. 'You've brought one too many, there's only six of us down–'

'Hang on. That one's mine.' A voice called out, and hands reached up and took the guano bowl.

Joseph jumped, startled, and the rest turned in surprise. The voice was unfamiliar; it was not a part of their crew. Someone else was down here with them.

The bamboo bars lowered, and the two men stood guard by the pit, leaving the prisoners to discover their inmate. 'Who - who are you?' Joseph asked, eyes probing the darkness; his ears waiting for evidence of the existing. He nervously began picking out the food and eating, his stomach gnawing.

'I–' the man chewed and swallowed from a back corner; none could see him, but all could hear, '–am your new friend.' More chewing, 'Thomas Sharp was what I used to go by, or Tom, Tommy, Thomas – call me whichever you prefer, I don't have a care anymore. It's only a name.' There was a weak chuckle, 'I'm just relieved to have some company down here. I tell you, I can't remember the last time I heard that London accent! Music to the old lugs, so it is! Who are you all? I think there's six of you. I can't see you, so I won't have a clue what voice to put to what face in the morning but tell me anyway. It's great to hear someone speak.'

'Joseph Winter.' He answered, and the rest gave their names out and as soon as they did, he had to ask, 'Tom, how come you didn't make a noise when we came down here hours ago? Where were you?'

'Oh, I was just sleeping over there in that corner. That corner, there's my corner, I sleep there, and it gets dark, in my corner. And might I just say how bloody lovely it is to talk without anyone stopping to ask what this word and that word means. You've no idea how infuriating it is to speak with constant interruptions.' He replied, taking another bite.

'You. You're the one that's been teaching them English?' Robertson asked from what sounded like the other side of the pit.

'I'd say it's the only damn thing keepin' me alive right now. It's my only use to them – teaching them English. That translator, or he might as well be "vice Chief" Yalla from how much influence he has around here; he's the one most interested, visits me most to have lessons so he can teach old sourpuss Tulyaka.' Now it became clear how Yalla's wide range of vocabulary came to be.

'How long have you been here?' Rob cut in with interest.

'Oh, years.' Thomas said, 'I've seen babes grow into children, that've grown into youths about to take part in their ritual to make them an adult. Some visit from time to time, learn a few words, then the novelty wears off and I don't see em' anymore.'

Hugh interjected, 'how come you an't tried to escape?'

'Well, strangely enough,' another bite, 'there's a few reasons for that. One: I'm on an island, how am I meant to get away? Two: I don't have a ship, boat, canoe, or raft supple enough to take me to Africa where even then I wouldn't know what to do or where to go. Three: I'm being kept prisoner with full-time guards to teach the village English and Christianity as penance. They take me out for walks occasionally, to give the legs a bit of stretch but most of my time is spent in this glorious hole. Believe me, I've tried escaping, more times than I care to count, but I never got far; these people know how to track better than anyone I've ever known.'

'How did you get here?' asked Joseph, 'it's not exactly a common country to visit.'

A nod in the dark. 'It was popular for the missionaries about fifteen years ago.'

'You're a missionary?'

Chewing, 'tried to be. I was in training.' Swallowing, 'Wanted to be a priest. Nothing made me happier than making God happy. Mother told me *"nothing can help God more than spreading God's love to other people, especially those where they don't have a church to go to on a Sunday or a Bible to pray with."* So, I left England on my twentieth birthday, ready to spread the Holy Word, to teach the ways of the divine as best as I could. Went to a few countries, shared some passages and the love of God and then I joined the expedition here. And here's where I found out some "missionaries" weren't so interested in God as I thought. They seemed interested in women just as much, with one even getting a woman from the village pregnant.' The voice trailed off and they heard a strain as the man sat down.

'Well, as you can expect, the village was in uproar. A missionary getting a village woman pregnant out of wedlock – *the scandal!* Naturally, villagers pointed to me as I was the youngest. The other missionaries pointed to me because I was the youngest *and* newest to the job. The expendable one, I suppose. The others left after the village got tense; they left me here to uphold my responsibility of wedding the woman as religiously and Christianly as I could out here and to father my bastard village-child. The village kept me here to not only teach them English but also to father this child that wasn't even mine. It was John's; he was the one who always wanted to preach and pray to the women, and as it turns out he was praying in a physical as well a spiritual sense. There goes your future, Tommy-boy, there goes your freedom, tarah! Shake hands and wave that one away! I got the blame, the sack, these bars and a muddy pit in the ground, all for trying to help spread God's word, and what did He do for me? Nothing at all, completely, what-so-ever.

'I tried to keep my faith. For years, I prayed for my freedom and my justice, telling myself about His intricate plans for everyone and that one day I would find salvation and be redeemed and rewarded for keeping my faith.' His voice faded '. . . yet after years of repetition, the words begin to lose their potency. I wasn't going to be saved. I wasn't anyone special. No one was looking for me. Here I've been for years, sitting in what's basically been my grave, waiting . . . and waiting . . . waiting for what? I didn't know. But now I do; because you're here.' He smiled in the darkness.

Suddenly Joseph heard Billy whisper from behind him, '*is it just me or is he two sandwiches short o' a picnic?*'

'What happened to the baby?' Robertson asked.

'The baby?' He repeated, as if he'd forgotten the reason for his imprisonment. 'The baby that was born, that I had apparently fathered, died when she was two from malaria. Poor thing. Yet the hopes at being released from my imprisonment were dashed when the Chief declared that I was to remain their prisoner as punishment for allowing this to happen. As a man of the cloth, God's actions channelled through me and had let this child die. So, from then on, I was an oath-breaker, sinner and murderer, all in the name of the Lord.

'But don't get me wrong, I still held onto hope. I always did. I may have lost faith in God, but somewhere along the line I found it in myself which became even more potent. You could say I found my salvation. Your options, opportunities and optimism become limitless when you have self-belief in the present moment to keep you going. You can be the strongest person, able to withstand anything when you find presence, yet this doesn't mean you are all powerful; it's merely finding power from within. A power that enables you to surrender to the flow of events rather than swimming against the current, yet this surrender doesn't mean you are weak. This means acceptance for your situation rather than resistance.

'Within this pit in the cold earth, I came to discover that resistance to presence is the source of suffering in the world. By becoming present, you can allow things to be as they are, and that is the freedom we all seek. It allowed me to keep hoping when I'd lost everything and to remain open and accepting to anything that came up . . . or came down, I should say, into this pit. And here you are, the chance I've been waiting for.'

Joseph listened in wonder, intrigued and fascinated by this strange, enlightened man. He had never heard anything like it and wanted him to keep talking, but Billy spoke up, finishing his last mouthful, 'I'd still hold onto that hope if I were you matey, we're all up for trial in the morning. Tangena's what we're against.'

There was a pause as the words sunk in, then Thomas's voice uttered, 'Tangena? You've got trial by Tangena? Christ, what did you do?'

'Stole some diamonds and apparently beat up our best friend Honlu,' Joseph said bitterly, but had accepted it now. 'What is Tangena?'

'Ah, Honlu. Yes, he's certainly a character. Spread around I'd been teaching him to swear, even though I hadn't. They're good at framing things, these people.'

'What is Tangena? An animal?'

He took another bite, shaking his head. 'Tangena's a plant. A tree with highly toxic nuts; they crush the nuts, mix them with water and make you drink it. That's the trial; it's not very fair. If you throw it up, you're innocent; if you die, you're guilty. No jury, no judge except the lining of your stomach. Surprisingly, not many people *are* innocent; quite hard to defend yourself when you're being poisoned outright. It's mostly banned around the country now, a medieval tactic, but this village is one o' the last traditional ones and mainly keeps to itself. Tangena still happens here, you lucky lot.'

'Sounds about as fair as the trials back in London. Strange how no justice system seems to work properly no matter where you go in the world.' Joseph said, sitting down. 'All we needed was that poxy chest and we'd be back on the ship.'

There was another moment of silence. 'Unless you didn't have to go through with it . . .' Thomas added.

Their ears pricked up. Heads turned to the direction of his voice. Suddenly no one was tired. 'We're listening . . .' Joseph urged, hoping this man, this poor strange, marooned man, could help.

Chapter Twenty-Five

The morning was humid and unwanted. The hard-packed earth around them offered no warmth, no comfort. Sleep eluded them throughout the night; an hour's worth was all they were able to snatch, not only from the frigidity of the pit but also due to the numerous thoughts racing around their heads. Things had to be remembered, ideas had to be kept fresh, yet nothing could stop their imaginations running free; the darkness a black canvas for them to paint their worries upon.

Joseph peered up at the faint light eking its way over the top of the pit and knew it wouldn't be long now. Reaching down his back with unwelcoming clammy fingers, anxiety reaffirmed its grip once more; the following hours were a dread. Now that dawn had broken, the guards would soon be lifting the weighted bamboo and march them into the village where . . . he gulped and felt it catch in his throat. That was the thing, he wasn't entirely sure what was to be there. With the other trials in his experience, there was a wooden pedestal, benches and a high seat for the Welch Wigs to sit upon and judge. *That sounds like beer and skittles compared to this.* Thomas had given them a rough idea, but even so, he'd confirmed he wasn't one hundred percent sure; nonetheless, Joseph and the rest had taken his word for it, as they had nothing else to base a plan on. One thing was for sure, however; 'if I help with this, all I ask for is to not be left behind. Frankly, I couldn't care less where you're off to, what your plan is or who you people are. I swear I'll swab, calk, thread, reef and rub your achin' bunions at the end of the day without one complaint. The only thing I ask is for a place on deck, you understand?'

Help Merina and Merina will help you, yeah, right. More like help Thomas and Thomas will help you. Joseph crossed his arms and waited for the guards, wishing for nothing but a pinch of tobacco to smoke. The layer of frosty sweat on his back was not just from the cold and neither were his shakes. Once more, *and I'll get on my hands and knees and pray this'll be the last,* he stood, awaiting trial.

They were all awake and waiting by the time the guards approached. There were more of them now; Joseph counted eight. They were in their warrior's garb, wearing nothing apart from a slither of material to cover their manhood, holding tribal spears and small painted shields. White paint lined their cheeks and spread in three lines from their chest around their shoulders to their forearms. Their muscles looked toned in the morning light and their piercings looked inhumane. '*Manantena aho fa noana ianao, ho feno ny sakafo maraina.*' *I hope you are hungry. Your breakfast will be filling.* One of them said and the other snickered as he lifted the heavy bamboo bars and slid a ladder down. The guards knew none of them could understand Malagasy, and as far as Joseph could understand, they didn't care; they were enjoying the power and excitement for the morning's events. The crew had stirred a gripping drama last night and had aroused the attention of the village; he wouldn't be surprised if some of the villagers had taken bets on who would go down first. Then again, he couldn't blame them, he'd do the same if he were in their position. Oh yes, he'd make a bet, and he'd put all his money down on the black stallion Wicked Dave, hoping that dark horse would be the first to drop.

One by one they began climbing out of the pit, groaning and huffing with their cramped, aching muscles. In his spare moment, Joseph turned and finally, in the pale light, was able to see what Thomas looked like.

A pale, skeletal man sat with his back against the mud and had his thin hands resting on his bony knees that were drawn up to his chest. He had a head of thick dark hair, long and matted that blended into his bushy unkempt beard, yet his cheekbones were so pronounced they made his face look thin and drawn, as if his hair and beard were oversized wigs. Wearing - no, he wasn't wearing them anymore - his loosely fitted and ragged long-sleeve top draped over his coat-hanger shoulders and a pair of ripped-to-the-knee moth-eaten trousers were tightly bound to coat-hook hips by a length of twine. They would've looked small on him, years too small, if his body were not so feeble.

Bushy eyebrows raised at the look of Joseph: his thin appearance, bearded face, long hair, weather-beaten clothes. Thomas realised these were not navy sailors passing by as he envisioned in the dark, these were men who looked almost like himself. Poor and rugged, but otherwise friendly. A look was in the man's eyes, a look that he had seen a lot of things, some goodness and some bad – his eyes were bright and clear and clever, sharp and attentive but amiable all the same. He had a grand tale to share; but now was not the time to ask. Thomas's thin lips smiled and lightly nodded, and Joseph nodded back before turning and climbing out the pit last of all.

His legs ached terribly from their venture yesterday, and he slipped on his way up falling to the undergrowth and kicking one of the rocks out of its divot in the ground. One of the guards laughed and kicked him. With trembling legs and painful, weeping hands, he pushed himself back up and took a helping hand from Billy to get him on his feet.

'Cheers.' He nodded and followed the rest of the crew out of the trees and into the clearing of the village where the morning light glowed in the east over the tops of the trees. The air was stifling already.

The huts stood quietly in the growing light; the trees appeared to be hushing. Only the sound of water came from the village, the river; he'd heard somewhere that the sound of running water was supposed to calm the senses, but today this did nothing to ease the knot in his stomach. The thud of footfall from the men walking to their judgement could be heard, and it was deafeningly loud. With hopeful eyes, he looked over to where he last saw Victoria and Tess being taken but saw no one walking toward them. *Maybe they're getting them once we're in the village?* He slipped his hands in his pockets feeling the broken compass, Harold's carven elephant hanging heavily from his neck. His mouth shut, he breathed through his nose, trying to deny his body the right to panic. *Your fists are clenched mate; relax. You are in control.*

His insides grumbled yet he didn't feel hungry at all. It was nerves churning the contents of his stomach. He was thirsty, but after hearing what he would have to drink this morning, thirst was the better option.

They walked closer to the village, still not hearing or seeing anyone around. *You know why that is, Joseph?* His thoughts asked, *because they're all waiting for this trial, for you all to stand up and drink the toxic mix; waiting to watch as each of you foams at the mouth, crumbles to the ground, writhing in pain until you eventually and mercifully die a terrible death.* As forcefully as he could he pushed the thought from his head, not wanting to think of images like that.

Nevertheless, the truth was there; entertainment couldn't be more popular and thoroughly enjoyed throughout history than watching other people die a gruesome death. The worse the ending, the faster the word spread. Funnily enough, hanging a person until near dead, drawing that person's innards out whilst they were still alive, burning them in front of their seeing eyes and quartering that person's body into four to spread to different locations never failed to draw a large crowd. People loved it; people made a day of it; the gallows were the hotspots to draw the community together. Public executions were good for socialising and entertainment, as well as business – he'd been to many hangings as he grew up, they were good opportunities to draw a fine profit with so many people in one area and so many pockets to pick. They were fond memories for a poor London lad. As they passed the first hut, however, and saw the entire village congregated near the burning bonfire, peering to the crew as he once looked at the criminals about to face the noose, they realised the gallows were not what they were facing. Not today.

Eight large stakes had been driven into the ground near the flames, not close enough to burn but close enough to sweat. Eight large stakes, like those used to burn so-called witches upon. Joseph suddenly felt scared, could feel fear beginning to grasp, and could relate to how those poor women must've felt, how those criminals he watched must've been feeling; this was not going to be a trial, oh no, this was going to be public torture and execution. Death by consumption of high toxicity; Tangena was waiting for them to take a bite.

The villagers began to turn as the group approached, led by a high-ranking guard. The Londoners walked solemnly, acting as if they were guilty of the most heinous crimes. The congregation parted for them to pass through with all eyes focused on them; they could feel their gaze, could feel their judgement. Mothers held their children, families watched on. Hushed mutters passed through the crowd and Joseph felt on edge, he wanted to shout at them but what good would that do? He dug his hands in his pockets and forced his eyes to the ground. This wasn't a trial where you were given a date of execution and had the laborious task of waiting for it – this was swifter.

As they reached the stakes, he looked up and his stomach dropped. Victoria and Tess were already there, tied to their stakes. Their hair was tangled, their clothes were ripped and muddy and had handprints on them. Their necks were red; cuts and bruises were on their face and arms. Victoria's cheek was black and swelling. The men of the crew didn't need to assume, it was quite clear what had happened and how light a treatment they had received. Joseph felt his cheeks blush, not with shame but with rage. His gaze moved to the other end of the stakes where Chief Tulyaka, Yalla and the red-faced liar Honlu stood, wearing their wrapped *lambas* with their faces and bodies painted in the white stripes too. Tulyaka was wearing a thread necklace today, its decorations hidden beneath his woven garment.

'Oh, Christ.' Robertson uttered and turned to the chief. 'What have you done to them? *What have you done?!*' Suddenly losing his temper, he made for the Chief and Yalla, punching a guard to the ground in the process. In surprise, the guards hastened to grab Robertson who struggled and kicked. Venting his rage, Joseph then joined him, utilising his rusty skills as the famed bare-knuckle boxer of the Back House. Dave, Hugh and Billy were caught in the fray, beginning to brawl with the warriors to get them out of this predicament. Rob looked on, speechless and pale.

More of the warriors joined, overpowering the brawling few and managing to restrain them and separate them to their own stake, working quickly to get them tied. Billy tried to help. 'Victoria, Tess – don't you worry sweethearts. We're getting outta' this, alright? We'll be foine, absolutely foine.' He called out as they tied twine around his chest.

Tess looked up and gave a weak smile, her eyes ringed in dark emotional circles but Victoria looked blank, pale and blank.

'Victoria.' Joseph cried as they pulled him to his stake, forcing his back to the wood and wrapping a long length of twine around his chest, arms and legs. 'You were right. You were completely right. I'm so sorry. Trust me, we'll get out of this. We have a plan.'

Victoria looked in his direction, 'I trust you.' She managed. The villagers watched on in anticipation, shouting and urging the trial to commence.

Thomas didn't say we'd be tied, he didn't say there'd be stakes - please say that doesn't change things. Concern gripped him along with the anger, anger directed at the villagers and their chief – and himself; it was his responsibility after all; *I should've said something, I should've been stronger. Oh god, what did they do to Tess and Victoria . . .*

Chief Tulyaka walked out in front of everyone. Standing firm, he raised his arms and a deathly silence settled. The fire crackled loudly. He began the proceedings in his native language for the audience to hear, with Yalla translating for the accused. '*Ry oloko, tongasoa eto amin'ny fitsarana an'i Tangena . . .*'

'My people. Welcome to the trial of Tangena . . . You stand here this morning for yesterday's crimes of which you have pleaded innocent. Stealing the sacred red diamonds when you were all instructed against it and for the unjust beating of Honlu, my son . . .'

'*Na izany aza, ianao nanangona ny diamondra rehetra araka ny nandidiako . . .*'

'–However, you all collected the diamonds as I instructed . . . and held up your side of the deal we made to trade your services, your help, for the box you requested . . .'

'*Noho ireo antony ireo dia tsy afaka mandray fanapahan-kevitra mety . . .*'

'–For these reasons, a proper decision cannot be made . . . not by my judgement as Chief of this village. I leave the decision to God to determine your innocence and fate. Live or die, you shall now face trial by Tangena!'

Two warriors then hauled a large bubbling pot from the fire and placed it in front of them for all to see. It looked like a witch's cauldron in the tales Joseph heard as a boy, and the concoction inside was bubbling and frothy like a potion of many possibilities: a liquid lucky dip. One ladle held the power to allow them life and freedom from this trial (of which Thomas had told them that chances were astronomically slim) and another spoonful held the toxic contents from the Tangena tree and would burn their organs and quickly strip, melt away and deplete all that was left of their existence. An ugly choice to place in one simple ladle.

Joseph's heart raced frantically in his chest. Gulping was hard; fear had taken all his saliva and chained his tongue. He wasn't sure what he'd rather have - the gallows and noose, to hang until dead or drink this vile liquid and be burned from the inside out. Either way, both were to kill him in an abhorrent manner. Looking to the thick white water being ladled into a guano bowl; he realised this time he really *had* done nothing wrong. The times before when he'd stood in front of the law, he was guilty of something; of petty theft or stock manipulation, but this time he really was innocent. This time there was no wrongdoing involved. He considered trying to tell them, to yell and struggle to prove their innocence but then held his tongue and thought against it. *They won't listen to you; they won't believe you. You can scream all you want, the only way you're getting out of this is if everything falls into place, which it will, of course it will. Why wouldn't it? Why would Thomas lie? He wants to get out of here as much as we do.*

Why do I feel so nervous if I know he'll come?

. . . Will he?

The bowl was brought to Hugh Jackson first, who was tied to the stake closest to the fire, then there was Rob Epping, Dave James, then himself. He thought their plan was simple enough, as good as they could get with their limited information and finite options. Thomas knew what to do; *so why is he taking so fucking long? Come on, hurry up!*

The bowl was brought to Hugh's thin, quavering lips. In a glimpse, Joseph looked at Yalla watching the proceedings and saw a grin on his face and he knew in that instant he was the one who'd dealt the abuse to Honlu. Perhaps it had occurred as the two villagers journeyed back, perhaps it happened in private; either way, no one saw it. No one knew. A perfect frame.

Hugh tried turning away from it and keeping his mouth closed. 'No,' he resisted, 'no. No, no. Fuck off! Fuck you! Get away, you fucking liars!' he shook his head viciously from side to side, his long straw-like ginger hair tangling, desperately trying to wrestle free but one of the men grabbed his head and forced his mouth open . . . and the white water, the milk of Tangena, was poured down his throat, cutting his screams short.

Joseph watched intently as his throat began to gulp, then opened, filled and backed up. Once the bowl was empty, they took it away and stood back. All eyes were on Hugh Jackson, then. He was the centre. The epicentre. The focal point of the universe. The nucleus of their fates. If he lived, they had a chance, but if he died; they were watching to see what would happen, what *was* to happen to them.

Tangena spewed then slowed to a dribble from the corners of his mouth, dripped from his curly ginger whiskers to his torn dirty clothes. He burped and hiccupped. Hugh looked up, eyes bulging, darting worriedly from one place to the next, breathing harshly as he understood there was no going back. 'Oh god what's to happen? What - what does it do? What will happen to me?' he asked but no one answered. Red flushed his pale cheeks. *'Fuck! Tell me, tell me! How long until I'm clear?!'* he yelled. *'I'm innocent! Tell me how long! Get it out of me, help me! Anyone! Fucking help me!'* he screamed, veins ballooning on his forehead, chords rising in his neck like the strings of Billy's fiddle. No one wanted to play Hugh's music though. No one was listening to what he had to play. He hollered for a solid minute, screaming for help, for guidance and explanations but still no one spoke. Everyone was in a trance. The sounds of the rainforest were miles away. Eventually he quietened and stood in silence, his face gradually reddening. He frowned in anguish, in sadness, in rage, so many emotions trying to tug at his pallid face, until one found the spotlight.

He frowned and began to sob. 'Please. Listen. I'm from a big family, a son of a blacksmith, from a long line of blacksmiths. I was lazy; I didn't take up the practice. I stole from my family, stole from people; I joined gangs; I drank too much; I enjoyed violence. I'm a thief, a constant liar and a serial rapist; I raped women, so many women, I hurt them and I'm sorry.' He sobbed, tears streaming, 'I'm sorry for what I've done, for what I am. I'm sorry, please, listen to me, forgive me . . . remember me,' he pleaded, confessing. He calmed and looked at them all, everyone, with clear eyes, 'I don't want to die, not like this. Not now, not–'

He cut short and hiccupped, blinking in confusion, then vomited violently. Upon a pause, his breathing became ragged, then the screaming really began. These were not the screams of a scared man. These were the screams of a dying man. His face crumpled in agony and reddened to a bright crimson; his lips pulled back exposing his black stumps and yellowing teeth; he howled as his innards crackled and popped and burned and melted inside, spilling their contents, bursting and spilling. His arms snatched up and down, fingers snapping in and out; he howled like nothing Joseph had ever heard before. This was not like the gallows. This was full torture from within; as if someone had opened his belly and was munging, mingling and giving his organs a good old squeeze, rummaging and ripping his vitals. Foam began to fizzle at his mouth, bloody froth whipping at his lips. He ripped open his eyes, bulging and bloodshot as he struggled for breath but could not find lungs to inhale. Hugh tilted his head back and half screamed, half cried and smacked it against the stake again and again.

Until he stopped altogether; and dropped fully into the ties. Deadweight. Void. A husk without the corn. Everyone was silenced, stunned by the execution. Joseph became aware of the sound of crying. Tess was sobbing, as was Rob, who was next in line. Joseph licked his lips with a dry, fat tongue and found tears on his face he didn't realise had fallen.

He'd never heard a man being tortured before. Death he'd seen, but that, that was something worse. Something else. That was a prolonged death, a violent torture; a body shutting down bit by bit; ripping itself apart. Imploding. He realised how merciful a noose was in comparison. Joseph thought of Rob and could have wept for him. The lad had witnessed it all being the closest to Hugh, not just witnessing but being able to smell the reek of burning flesh, vomit and exploding bowels – knowing he was to be next. He'd witnessed it all at the age of fifteen. *Christ, he's still only a boy. Just a lad.*

One of them had been bitten by Tangena, seven more were to go.

One of the men came up to Hugh and undone the ties on his legs, stomach and chest. The body dropped heavily, first to its knees then flopped to the ground with a thump, spilling the contents of his mouth and stomach . . . and pockets.

Dozens of red diamonds scattered from his trouser pockets to the dirt. Their beauty tainted, they appeared melancholy compared to those they'd seen in the cave, glittering sadly on the earth in the golden morning sun. There were small and large ones, a solid collection Hugh Jackson had dared not to speak of.

All eyes fell to the ground and a gasp spread throughout. Majority of the village had not even seen the red diamonds before – they were so sacred. Another moment of stunned silence; an ugly twist at the end of the performance. *Oh, Hugh. What have you done?* Yalla looked pale. Tulyaka was horrified, pointing to the ground he uttered, '*diamondra mena . . . diamondra mena!*' his voice rose in volume, in depth; he yelled for the heavens to hear. '*Meloka! Meloka! Mangalatra amintsika izy ireo! Jereo ny habetsaky ny nangalariny! Avy aminay! Ilay fitenenan-dratsy! Ny kisoa Anglisy! Ireo piraty! Vonoy ireo! Aza miandry azy ireo ho faty, vonoy izy ireo! Izy rehetra dia meloka!'* Guilty! Guilty! They steal from us! See how much he stole! From us! The blasphemy! The English pigs! The pirates! Kill them! Do not wait for them to die, kill them! They're all guilty!

Joseph didn't need to understand Malagasy to know what the chief was saying. The meaning was there, they all understood. 'No!' he exclaimed along with Robertson, Victoria and Rob, all trying to explain the situation. He looked up sharply from the scattering of the island's treasured rubies. *'No! I didn't know about that!* None of us have stolen anything else! Check us! *Please, no!* Stop! Don't touch him! Don't you fucking touch him!' Joseph writhed against his bonds.

The men were filling up the next bowl quickly. The first time was delicate with everyone watching, now they were filling it as quickly as they could with the crowd chanting behind them, *'meloka! Meloka! Meloka!'* Guilty! Guilty! Guilty! They were riled now and hurried to pour this mixture down all their throats. They wanted death; chanted for death and torture to these vile creatures who'd stolen their sacred soul stars.

In spite, the bowl was brought to Rob who wriggled intensely, writhing and snapping his head from side to side, scared witless. The crowd was a storm, a thrum, a thunder whilst the prisoners hurled insults and defence. Rob's head was held, his mouth opened, he screamed . . . and Tangena was poured inside.

The Young Hare's mouth had barely closed before the men were back at the pot, spooning out the next bowlful for Dave.

Rob stood still with the milk dribbling from his mouth, not fighting it as Hugh had done. He stood and wept, frightened of what was to come.

'Vonoy ireo! Meloka! Vonoy ireo!' Kill them! Guilty! Kill them! Tulyaka howled, his face sneering with contempt as the villagers threw their arms in the air and screamed in disgust.

The bowl was brought over to Dave who tried to kick them, tried to pull himself free. *'Don't you niggers dare pour that down my throat! I'll kill ya'! I'll kill the whole lot o' ya'!'* He snarled above the din, but it was a fruitless defence. He pulled harder against his stake, heaving against the twine, barely feeling it cut into him, but before he managed to wrench anything free his head was held firm and his mouth was yanked opened. The bowl was tipped.

Tangena milk spilled from the bowl messily, splashing on his face and in his eyes, pouring down his throat until it backed up and came spilling from his lips to the ground. His clothes were spattered with the milk and bile. As soon as he cleared his airways, he coughed and spluttered, eyes red and stinging, face dripping, '*You bastards! Black bastards!*' he continued raging as they filled the bowl for the next person.

Joseph watched his bowl being filled and felt his heartbeat as it had never beat before. Everything looked blurry now; the crowd, Tulyaka, Honlu, the trees in the distance; everything was a blend, out of sequence, surreal. Terror gripped hold of him, he wasn't sure what to do.

Colour drained from his face, he felt his bladder loosening and his piss running down his leg in a warm stream. He looked sternly at the bowl of the vile concoction and now knew what it felt like to walk up to the gallows, to the swinging noose as a hated criminal and stand in front of the hollering crowd, to look down upon so many people that spewed hatred, and to place his head in that knot, the rough rope rubbing against his bare neck. He knew what it felt like now. He knew what it felt like to look at death and feel it closing in, touching a shoulder, running its cold twisted hands up the small of his back like a lover, feel it kiss his neck, feel its lust to take him wholly.

The men brought the bowl over. Joseph Winter didn't move. There was nothing to do, nothing to say, that would change their minds and prevent this from happening. In those final moments, he did not fight. The bowl was raised. He let them hold his head . . .

. . . open his mouth . . .

The bowl tipped.

Tangena flowed out copiously. It splashed messily on his face. Squeezing his eyes shut, he felt it run down his throat without him swallowing; a warm liquid, tasteless yet its flavour was incomparable; offensively, it even hinted at being sweet. Almost like milk, the sourest and awfullest milk he had ever had to drink. The bowl emptied. The crowd howled. His friends screamed.

There was too much inside him and it backed up, spilling from his mouth like vomit; he spat it out, letting it drool from his lips and run into his beard. Toxic spittle. Now he could understand the disgust. The aftertaste was abominable. It almost tasted unnatural and pumped full of chemicals; it burned the back of his tongue and his uvula was aflame. Still the people screamed.

He opened his weeping bloodshot eyes and saw a different blurry scene now, although in his disorientated stupor he wasn't sure what to believe. The screaming of the crowd was not at the victory of conquering enemies – it was the screaming of confusion and panic and the shouting of instructions. People were going mad. The village was mayhem. Something was on fire in the village. He could see hazy flames and smoke rising in the air. Joseph blinked more, his eyes stinging. It was the tree. The tree near Tulyaka's hut was burning as well as several of the other huts. The crowd was no longer watching the trial – no, it could not be called a trial: executions was a better term – they were spread, running and yelling and crying, collecting water from the river in a frenzied panic. If Joseph thought the scene before looked surreal, this looked completely extraordinary.

Suddenly he felt something rubbing against him. He tried pulling away from it lazily, docile, and managed a yelp, a hiccup and burp. His stomach was flipping, his head felt as if it had been raped. Then, shockingly, the tension holding him tight disappeared and he collapsed to his knees and dropped to the ground with the cut twine flopping over him uselessly. Looking at it incomprehensively, he felt lost and confused, perplexed but feeling like he should be happy about this. *What . . . is happening . . .* The burning tree and huts, the cut twine: was all this a hallucination conjured by Tangena's bite? Someone had cut him free. Holding the twine in his weak hand, he concluded its reality and gently closed his scabby palm. A swell of nausea rose and fell. An arresting sense suddenly gripped him; his mind snapped back into place and one person took priority over everything else. Robert Epping. *Get to him. Save him. There might still be time.*

He sat up quickly, his head swimming, his stomach churning. Something was happening internally, as if his body was deciding whether to accept, reject, dissolve, or implode. Surveying the ground, he saw the stakes, the twine, people running and screaming and Rob laying unresponsive on the ground. Finding his feet, he stumbled over. 'No. No, oh no. Rob, Rob!' Joseph knelt and grabbed him, holding his head in his lap; he was ghostly pale, but breathing. 'I'm sorry Rob, so sorry my lad. My friend.' Words were tumbling from his mouth although it sounded like they were coming from afar, 'but I've got to do this now.' He opened his jaw and stuck two fingers in his mouth until he reached the boy's throat.

Immediately he felt the reflex kick in, and his throat widened and tensed. Pulling his fingers out quickly, Rob retched and turned on his side; his mouth exploding, spewing up white and red again and again until his stomach emptied completely. Blood was on his lips and swirled in his vomit.

Joseph felt relief, but then he remembered his own issue. His stomach gurgled aggressively; a striking pain struck through him at all angles: his body had made its decision. It felt like a stomach cramp, when something eaten does not agree, but this pain was intense and was not to get better. His muscles spasmed and jerked; clutching his belly he cried out in pain. The time was now.

Going against everything he hated doing, he stuck his own two fingers down his throat and felt a retch. Suddenly, his body responded in an abrupt expulsion as his stomach ejected; his head flung forward and propelled its contents harshly. He vomited heavily again, almost seeming to pulse the Tangena from his body, ridding of that dense, toxic mix. He retched and heaved, heaved and retched, barely allowing himself a chance to breathe. It reminded him of his first night dancing with too many apple ladies. When he finished, he saw blood in his vomit too, and, wiping his mouth, saw it smeared on his lips.

Groaning, his stomach ached, and his body felt empty; cleansed almost. He wanted to collapse in exhaustion; his body feeling hollow. There was a sudden heavy hand on his shoulder. Drowsily, he looked up to Robertson's relieved but panic-stricken face. He was pale, but no sign of Tangena was upon him. The fires had worked as a distraction. 'Oh, thank God you're alive! I thought you'd gone; you were silent for a long time! There's no time. We must go now. On your feet, Winter, and you too, Epping. We're leaving this place. Sharp's slaughtered some pigs and goats and some chickens and we're taking them. Now hurry!'

With his head still spinning, Joseph managed to get up and spotted Thomas Sharp's handiwork burning and smoking heavily. The villagers had managed to put some flames out, but it was raging; it would take a while to get that under control. For now, they had a distraction but how long it would take for the villagers to realise their prisoners had escaped he wasn't sure, and he didn't want to hang around to find out.

Turning, he saw the crew running away from the scene and into the morning sunlight; all had been freed from the stakes, from the grisly fate they were to endure. Thomas had done well – even if he had been delayed. Their new friend had a large pig over a shoulder and was heading for the trees with Billy nearby holding onto the other pig. Joseph saw Billy was gesturing a hasty "come on" wave as he looked back to him, then he turned and headed for the trees where they had entered the village only two days ago. Robertson was heaving a goat onto his shoulder and following the rest.

Rob got to his feet next to him and wiped his mouth. 'Let's go.' He said weakly and began to run toward the trees.

Joseph began to run too when he suddenly stopped, remembering something important. 'You go. I'll catch up, I need to get something first.'

The cabin boy turned back in surprise, 'what?!'

Joseph was already running . . . back toward the hysterical village. He turned and yelled, 'the fucking chest! It's the only reason we came here in the first place!' His legs were rubber, trembling beneath him, feeling as if they were carrying the weight of the world above. Pushing hard, he kept them moving and weaved his way through the swarm of people trying to put the fires out.

Everyone was hurrying so frantically no one noticed the one white man slithering through the fray. He couldn't care less if they did; he had no respect for them anymore; if anything, they were just a hinderance. Not that he hated them, he still didn't – he would not and never could stoop to Dave's level of racism; the entire charade here had just soured from bad to worse. What he did pity was the tree, it really was quite spectacular.

Running past the crowd of people near the fires, he spotted the chief's hut and raced for it. Dodging between more people, he reached the entrance and burst inside; his eyes intent on searching, looking, seeking . . . finding. There it was. At the very back of the spacious room tucked near the large bed. At last, the small, ornately designed wooden chest they were after. He recognised it instantly. *Oh, yes. You beauty.* Moving quickly, he snatched the box, tucked it under an arm and turned to the doorway.

Figures stood in the exit. Silhouettes of the Chief and Yalla against the fire and glowing sunrise. 'I knew you come to it. I see what happened. Thom-as, it was him who help you.' The Chief said.

Joseph sighed tiredly and wiped the sweat from his face, still tasting the foulness of Tangena on his tongue. 'Look, I am in no mood for games; there was enough of that yesterday. We all know it was Yalla who beat Honlu and you framed us perfectly and that was a shitty thing to do. I don't know why you wanted us all dead and I don't care anymore. Just step out the way.'

Tulyaka took a step forward, his *lamba* torn and dirty, he looked exhausted himself. 'You have brought death here, Jo-seph Win-tah. You and all other English pigs. In name of *Vazimba* I curse you–' Suddenly Yalla was behind him, yanking him down as Tulyaka reached out and, with great speed, grabbed his neck, making him drop the chest to grab his wrists. Joseph struggled to breathe but managed to pull the man's hands away from his neck. In fury, Tulyaka dove into him and they tumbled to the ground. Little did Tulyaka know who he was dealing with.

Straddling Tulyaka, Joseph punched him hard in a spot he knew would hurt. Tulyaka softened but fought back with tribal ferocity, scratching and hitting him hard, before yanking his necklace off and swinging a hidden diamond blade for his throat but Joseph caught his wrist, halting the killer blow with the blade inches away from his neck. It was a test of strength as the two men clashed, until Joseph elbowed him in the chest making him wheeze and release his grip and necklace. Quickly, Joseph grabbed it from the ground and got to his feet, turning to the doorway where he found Yalla holding the chest and smiling devilishly.

'Give it to me, Yalla. Please.' He said, a fresh trail of blood seeping down his cheek.

He didn't respond, and instead turned and ran toward the flaming huts to dispose of the precious box. Joseph pocketed the necklace and bolted after him, pushing people out of the way, knowing that their futures rested on that chest. He had to get it. There was no other choice.

The man was fast, a lifetime of hunting had honed his feet into springs, but Joseph caught up to him as he reached the fire. In haste, he grabbed his *lamba* from his shoulder and yanked him from the edge just as Yalla launched the box into the flames and lost his balance, falling backwards. Denying instinct, Joseph quickly reached into the fire and picked it out before the flames had caught hold and jumped free, pouncing away with the chest under his arm.

'I curse you, Jo-seph Win-tah! I curse your voyage and your dreams! May you suffer!' Joseph heard him call, but he could worry about curses later. For now, he needed to get back to the ship.

It was awkward to run with the chest at first. It wasn't large enough to be cumbersome, but it wasn't small enough to run easily with, yet he managed as best as he could and darted toward the trees.

Bursting into the foliage, he ran as swiftly as he could, not checking to see if anyone were behind him. It was hard work, obstacles were everywhere, and he stumbled and fell numerous times. Soon, isolation took hold and all he could hear was his breathing, his footfall and his thumping heartbeat; it sounded odd, after he was so close to losing it. His stomach ached painfully, his every joint whined and creaked. *Get to the boat. Get to the boat.*

For now, that longboat was the only place he could feel safe. The only way he knew for sure they had escaped, yet paranoia kept tricking him into seeing eyes through the leaves, hearing ragged breaths down his neck from the canopy above.

Gradually, the trees thinned, and the humidity rose until there was no air to breathe. Sweat lashed out of him, his clothes clung desperately and snagged on thorns and branches. Flies followed his path now, a constant drone in his ear. He didn't swat them. That used too much energy and he needed it all at the minute. Everything he had. Any he could spare.

Soon, the trees shrunk, the vines disappeared, and the bamboo left him to clumps of fern and dry shrubs amongst rocks, allowing him a more comfortable pace. The ground dried considerably; hard fertile earth became softer, grittier, sandier. It had never felt better. He wanted to stoop down, feel it run between his fingers like water, feel it crumble and shift relaxingly. But not yet. *Get to the boat, get . . . to . . . the . . . boat.*

The shrubs thinned to dry grasses that grew in clumps and another type of tree became frequent. Palms. Palms with those round spheres he now knew were called coconuts. Just like he'd seen before on their arrival. He wanted to weep. Just then, another sound entered his small aura: the sound of water. Not rushing like a river, not the tinkling of a stream. The gentle roll of an ebb and a flow. A tide. The sea. The beach. He was here.

Joseph ran onto the sand and slowed to a stop. The sea was glistening in the light of a new day. It was calm, there were no people around. He was alone and, in that moment, he relished it. Spying the waves, he looked out to the deeper waters and saw a ship anchored a mile away. *Victoria* resting where she'd been tucked into her seabed what felt like a lifetime ago. A rush of relief and happiness touched him, and he never felt so overjoyed at seeing the water and his ship again. It meant they could move on, they could leave this place behind, leave this island and its memories and discover where to head next. *Just away from here, anywhere.* Suddenly he heard calling. Someone calling his name. Tuning his ears, he listened intently, eyes searching.

He moved along the beach, speeding to a jog with the sand shifting underfoot and saw there, bobbing on the water, the longboat with everyone in it, waiting for him.

Smiling tiredly, he walked forward into the golden water toward them. The water rushed around his feet, his legs, his waist and up to his stomach. The salt stung his cuts, yet it had never felt better. It was cool, refreshing; he felt cleansed. Lifting the chest above his head, he passed it into the boat and ducked down beneath the surface, feeling the cool water accept him and wash him. He lifted himself back up again, pulling his wet hair to the back of his head and washing the vomit from his beard. It was an intense feeling, as if he'd just been baptised. Never had washing felt so good. 'Let's go.' He said, jumping in the boat.

Chapter Twenty-Six

Thomas Sharp was beaming. With one hand resting over the side of the craft, dipping it into the soft roll of water, a look of fascination and relief found its way to his pallid complexion. Joseph knew that look. The look of escaping a long sentence – true, he'd never stuck around for a stretch as long as Thomas's, but he knew what it felt like and, as they began their journey back to *Victoria*, that feeling was clear on Thomas. It was freedom. The sense of a moral opening as the world suddenly became much larger and much more colourful than a dark pit in the ground. Again, Joseph could relate; they all could. The city had been their dark pit, and now the memories seemed so dull, so drab and lifeless. As the quartermaster sat dripping on the sternsheet, he looked at their worn faces after the last few days. Some shared this look of relief whilst others were vacant, exhausted. Once he stopped and crawled into his hammock, he knew the past few days would catch up with him too.

For now, though, he was elated but somewhat groggy after the trial. His stomach felt stretched, his body scraped from within, leaving nothing but bones and a sad little muscle that bounced to a constant thump. Despite the grogginess and the expedition that had led them to the verge of execution, he'd never felt cleaner. Maybe it was true what people said: innocence was a virtue. Looking to the water, he mused about his own truths. *I suppose it's all about finding a balance.*

The carpenter and rigger were at the oars again, trying to stifle their groans as their lacerated palms bled and the friction of the wood gave a striking pain. It was of great disappointment to Joseph that he saw Dave James still alive and aboard the longboat; it was a shame the man had been cut free and had been able to purge of the Tangena whilst there was still time. *I should've mentioned to Thomas to leave him till last, only releasing him if he had a spare minute,* but there was a positive spin; *if the prick's on here he can be the one to do the rowing.* There was a surprising pleasure in watching the man in pain.

'*Argh, ya' bastard. Christ, 'tis painful.*' Billy muttered to himself, grimacing at his weeping palms. Despite the Irishman's mutters, no one spoke – everyone was processing memories of the past few days, trying to push Hugh's screams out of their heads. It was not an easy feat. Once witnessing the agonising death of a man, hearing his wails of intense agony and guilt, it was hard to think of much else. They'd seen executions before, but not like that; a public hanging wasn't akin. The body dropped, the noose went taught, there was a wiggle and a jiggle, and the corpse was let down; sweet and simple, but what they'd seen and heard was an abomination.

Despite the bloke being a nuisance sometimes, he was still pleasant enough to work with; Joseph would even go so far as to call this silence mourning, and he hated to admit it, they were missing him. It was strange to not see him on the boat, sweating through his receding ginger hair, his freckles reddening with the oncoming sun, itching his ginger beard as he looked out to the horizon. *He wasn't buried or given to the waves; we left his corpse lying there.* A certain guilt was plucked, and Joseph got a case of the morbs. True, Hugh had stolen the diamonds and had hid them well, but he had also paid the price for them; a price only his life could pay for, and in death, the son of the long line of smithies left a personal reminder for them all, an instruction to not be forgotten in haste.

Alas, no one was going to weep for him. His crimes, especially against women, were dreadful and his screams were too intense. Those awful, bawling, inhuman screams, echoing in Joseph's head like the chimes of a bloody big bell, ringing constantly. He squeezed his eyes shut, attempting to block. *That's in the past now. It's time to move on. Time to look at something else. Time to move forward.*

The chest. Sitting by his feet was the fabled casket this endeavour had been about, the purpose of this venture to land. It was a perfect twin to the last box they'd recovered; with dark wood panelling and an ornate metal framework caging it. Age had rusted some areas, some patches of wood were warped and twisted, and moss and lichen had spawned over majority of the lid, but these added a certain authenticity to it, like the beard of a wizened old man. It was a relic after all, a box that had been left over one hundred years previous. A veteran from a different world. The small lock stared at him with its one dark eye. Suddenly it occurred to him. *Oh no . . . Please say the key Elanor gave us works the same for this box. I'll be damned if I'm going back to that village again. I doubt they'll be as welcoming.* It was the same metal, same design, same lock? He fucking hoped so. If not, surely there were some tools aboard the ship that he could find a second use to. One way or another, the chest was going to be opened.

As the longboat rose over the waves, he pursed his lips and frowned at his own stupidity, before looking up to Victoria and her ripped blouse and trousers. The redness of her neck had faded but it left rash-like marks. Her eye was squinting over her ballooning blue cheek. Again, guilt began to grasp, and he felt short of breath. Acting more out of instinct, he reached over and touched her shoulder caringly. 'Are you alright?' It was a stupid question, of course she wasn't alright, but he didn't know what else to ask or how to break this silence and stop the screaming.

She looked to him with bloodshot eyes underlined with black rings, her face was pale in the morning sun. 'I'd like a smoke,' she said bluntly, 'and a bloody strong drink.' It was obvious she didn't want to talk about it, so he didn't pry.

'Christ, make that two.' Billy chipped in between rowing.

'Three.'

'Four.'

'Five.'

'After what we've been through, I'm cracking open the last reserves of any rum we have left, if we do have any, once we get back to our old girl.' Robertson declared and they all agreed as if it was an offer, even though it was not.

Tess kept her legs tightly shut, her thighs and groin were sore. Everywhere was sore. Although she hadn't had any Tangena, her body felt as scraped as if she had. She wasn't a virgin, but it had been a long time since and last night was far from pleasurable. Closing her fists, she realised her fingers were sticky; her hands still had dried blood on them, so she washed them in the water over the side, wanting to rid of any evidence. It had been a long night and she was glad Victoria had been with her, so she wasn't alone. Anger welled up, pumping through her veins but she felt too exhausted to release it; for now, it would just have to settle. She looked to Victoria and noticed that she was looking at her too. Tess gave a flicker of a wane smile and wiped away tears that had fallen from her eyes. She thought of Poppy; the memories of her helped to supress the night, and now helped to supress the screams of the dying man. As she looked around, she noticed their newest member, the man who'd freed them and saved them all. 'Who is that?' she asked.

'Oh, that's Thomas Sharp. He was a prisoner of the village. Met him in our pit, we've a lot to thank him for.'

Thomas nodded, his hand still in the water. 'How d' you do?'

Suddenly the Irishman cut in, nodding to the beach. 'Er, sorry t' cut the introductions short matey but we've company on the horizon.'

They turned and peered at the shrinking strip of white sand where people were gathering, forcefully sliding canoes into the water and jumping in them, rowing furiously. The crew were a decent distance from the beach, far away enough to see smoke visibly rising above the belt of trees, but they were still halfway to the ship – enough distance for pursuit, and capture, to be possible.

There was a moment's pause as everyone took in the scene of the chase. Thomas's grin disappeared, and he paled, along with Rob. Then instructions were yelled from every one of them. '*Row!! Row, goddamn it! Hard as you can! Move it!*'

Billy and Dave kicked into overdrive, pulling the oars with a mighty force. Billy screeched in pain, '*Argh! Me fuckin' mitts! The pain!*'

'Baker! James! Row as hard as you fucking can, lads! Double-time! Triple-time! And if you slow there'll be no time!' Robertson ordered, 'We can make it to the ship!'

'How long 'fore we can get her going, Jim?' Joseph fired the question.

He peered to the bow of the ship to judge her status. A lot needed doing, but instead of telling his crew as such he worded it differently, 'as soon as we're aboard we can get her going. Anchor, sails, lines and the wheel; that's all it is.' Of course, that meant a great deal more work than originally stated.

The distance to the ship closed quickly, and unfortunately so did the distance of their pursuers. There were four canoes, and each had two to a canoe and had less baggage; additionally, their canoes were lighter and possessed a more streamlined quality, much to the disapproval of the crew whose heavy boat was laden with people and stock.

Blood ran down the oars in heavy streams. The groans of pain had become mere whimpers with silent weeping as they heaved the wood with their shredded palms. They began to lose grip on the oars; their hands were slick with blood, and they continually lowered down the oar to keep the pace, to keep their grip but their speed dropped considerably since they were no longer in synch. The boat snapped this way and that as one pulled whilst the other was a moment late; if they continued, the boat would eventually swing in a full rotation. Joseph licked his lips and quickly whipped off his shirt and told Rob to do the same, 'we'll take over. Move. Now.' No one argued. As rapidly as they could they swapped seats and wrapped their shirts around the bloodied oars and pulled as hard as they could. A tightness enflamed around their chests and arms as they were thrown into a sudden workout. Speed increased again and they approached their ship.

'Benjamin! Sailor, ahoy! Benjamin, ahoy!' Robertson hollered as soon as they were in earshot. The old sailor appeared at the bulwark, but before he could utter any greetings Captain Robertson spilled orders as quickly as his tongue could pronounce, like a drunkard who couldn't keep his mouth shut. *'Unfurl the sails,*

pronto! Fore, main and mizzen; I want to see those white wings, make 'em fly! Rig the jibboom! Rig the forestaysail! Winch the anchors! Toss Jacob's ladder! We need to move! Hand over fist, sailor, pronto!'

A salute was seen from the silhouette and he hurried off.

They reached the hull and bumped alongside it, scraping along latched barnacles. Releasing their tingling hands, they saw their shirts were covered in blood, their palms grated and weeping once more.

Quickly grabbing the ropes, Dave and Thomas pulled them close to the side and lined themselves up with the hanging longboat lines and ladder. 'Go!' Robertson ordered, 'Climb!'

One by one they footed the ladder and clambered up to deck and instantly went about helping Benjamin with the heavy workload. Joseph and Rob unwrapped their shirts, dunked them over the side and rinsed them, wringing the blood out. Numb, their hands had lost all feeling – they didn't want to look. A keen shredding had taken place and felt as if someone had peeled a layer of skin from their palms and was rinsing their raw flesh in ice cold saltwater.

Rob climbed the ladder with a goat over his shoulder, following Billy's and Dave's bloody handprints and leaving his own as he got to the deck. Robertson and Joseph tied the lines to the boat's rings at the bow and stern, ready for it to be hauled.

At last, Joseph climbed the ladder with the chest over his shoulder, supressing the sharp pain shooting through each finger as he gripped. It was shocking, he thought, at how large this ship was. He'd never taken much notice before but now he could appreciate its grandeur. Never had he seen a ship so beautiful, and as he clambered on deck with a film of blood and sweat slick on his body; never had he wanted to see her sail so badly.

'Man the yards!' the captain cried from the side, although majority of the crew were already aloft. The deck was a flurry of morning madness with deckhands running hither and thither along the lines to get the ship moving. Suddenly he saw the mainsail drop free - lines tightened, halyards squeaked as the deckhands controlled the canvas before belaying the lines tight to the pin-rail and working on the sheets to adjust the sail's position; it gradually filled with air and he felt the ship tug forward slightly. Spying the foresail, he saw it was already open, taught and tied; only the foretopsail needed flying and looking higher, he saw Billy and Rob working on unfurling it, the Irishman's hands flicking and twisting the reef-points into new shapes as he loosened the sail free from the yard.

Joseph placed the chest down near the pigs and goats and pile of dead chickens and waited near the line for the captain. No more than a minute later, Robertson climbed over the railing and dumped the last pig with the others before grabbing the line and pulling, heaving the longboat from the water. 'She only needs pulling halfway, Quart', we haven't the time to heave her home. As long as she's out of the water.'

They pulled the longboat up and away from the surface, then tied it tight through the ring with an anchor bend knot and pulled Jacob's ladder from the hull. The four canoes were nearing, the warriors of the village rowing hard. Thankfully, now standing on deck, they could feel a steady breeze shifting through the morning haze, enough to get them sailing. Robertson frowned; all the sails were flying but *Victoria* was struggling to walk yet alone run. *We aren't moving, why aren't we moving?* He spied the taught halyards and sheets, the stays and the sails. *She should be moving . . .* Captain Robertson hurried way from the side and threw himself afore the ship, up the ladder to the forecastle and peered over the side to see the anchor ball on the surface; indicating the anchor was still resting on the seabed. *This was always Hugh's job . . .*

He peered up and saw four crew aloft on the yards beginning to climb down the shrouds, and three hurrying around the belaying pins knotting new ropes. '*Mates! Any A.B.S afore here now! The anchors are still abed! Any hand to the stern to winch the other!*' Robertson threw himself on the winch and began hauling the anchor up; immediately feeling the tension. *Please don't snag, there should only be sand on the seabed!* He heaved, but this was a two-man job. At last, the others arrived and jumped on the crank, winching the great metal hulk from the seabed and freeing the ship for movement.

Suddenly the vessel began to move as the wind caught her, but she wandered aimlessly, sailing portside . . . into the shallows and toward the canoes. Robertson spun and saw the wheel was unmanned; but Joseph had spotted it.

The quartermaster flung himself up the ladder to the helm and grabbed the spinning wheel, immediately halting further veering but she was already sailing to port; a situation that was not helped by the sails which needed to be adjusted. He heaved with a red face and peered out to deck, 'Mainsheets hard to starboard, rig an extra jib! Someone unfurl the spanker!'

Sailors ran to pull the sheets starboard. Victoria heeded his cry and unfurled the spanker, tying it tight, then, seeing he was struggling with his hurt hands, quickly hurried to his silent plea and grabbed extra rungs, ceasing the veering and holding the ship straight.

At last *Victoria* began to swing starboard and away from the shallows, heading for deeper waters. She was on the move and sailed away from the coast, away from Madagascar. As they looked back, they spotted the canoes unable to catch them, rising and falling on the tail waves of their escape. Eventually, they steered her away from the coastline and out of reach from any of those brave enough to ride the swell of the sea.

Joseph allowed himself a smile. He wasn't sure where their next port of call was, his skills with geography and cartography were not his strongest but north-east was a good bet, up the east side of Africa and heading toward the Arabian Sea and India, but he wouldn't know for sure until they cracked open the chest to find the next rhyming riddle. *If this next one says anything about making friends and nanty-narking with the natives I swear I'm ripping it up.*

The sun rose through a smudging bank of grey clouds into a blue sky, sending warm rays of light asunder to the clear blue waters of eastern Africa. Warm southerly draughts of air swept through the ship yet from their experience they set the mainsail and foresail slightly to starboard, with the mizzensail and jib pushing her along at an easy five knots. The tide was favourable, and they sailed with it, which meant they were not crashing through. Joseph kept her stable though, not eager to rush off when they didn't know their next heading; instead, he sailed her into deeper waters with the eastern coastline of Madagascar still visible on the horizon before ordering the sails to be reefed in order to slow their speed. Exhausted, the crew went over their jobs half-heartedly, checking the lines and sails, careful not to injure their hands further, patiently awaiting the order for them to break their fast and change their ragged clothes, even though majority of their spare clothes were now ragged.

Whilst they were alone at the helm, Joseph decided to act. He turned with one hand on the wheel. 'Victoria, sweetheart, I just . . . I just want to apologise for what happened to you and Tess. I didn't think that would happen, but I should've known; I put too much trust in them. You even told me to play it carefully and I should've listened. It's all my fault. I'm sorry. I know you had it rough with your husband before, the last thing I'd want to do is to put you through something like that again.'

Victoria eyed him warmly and tried to calm her hair that played in the breeze, 'Thank you, Joseph. I know. And the fault an't yours, how was you to know they were to be like that? Truth be told, I managed to escape the rape. They tried,' she sighed, looking away, biting her lip as she struggled to put the memory into a verbal form. 'They tried to get me, grabbed me and tore at my clothes, clung to my neck, but I managed to kick them and push them away. Eventually they got me, but instead of rape they beat me and laughed about it.' Silent tears rolled down her cheeks, she kept her eyes on the horizon. Despite the emotion, these were not tears of self-pity or sadness; they were full of anger and contempt at how things were toward the opposing sex. A raw conviction of powerlessness against a twisted social imbalance. Why men were the apparent better gender she had no idea; they were sloppy, unruly and greedy, constantly warring, treating everyone as an enemy and keeping their wives in the shadows unable to speak out or stand out. She hoped, she prayed that the future held better days for women. 'They turned their attention to Tess . . . who couldn't – she didn't fight back as well as I did. A petite girl, she . . . hadn't the strength to match them. I . . . tried to stop but they pushed me away and punched, laughing; I blacked out. By the time I came around, they were gone, and Tess sat crying and bloody. She didn't know what she'd done. Oh, Joseph, why, wherever you go, do men still treat women so wrongly? Why are all men such *beasts?*' Her fists were clenched, she turned away.

Joseph wasn't sure if the question was rhetorical, but he gave a pause, in which he hooked the wheel on the bowline rope and hugged her. 'Not all men are like that. I can't deny that most are godawful horrid beasts, but some are alright.' *I love you, Victoria Penning,* he wanted to say but declined. Now was not the time. Instead, he wiped away her tears and hugged her again. 'If Dave or any bloke has the tallywacks to treat you like that again, you come to me, alright? That's if you need the support anyway. I know you're a strong woman.' *Christ, where did that come from? You'd have never said all that to Lucy.*

'Don't worry, I know how to defend myself, but I appreciate it.' She smiled, wiping her tired eyes.

Robertson thumped up the ladder and stopped suddenly, seeing their embrace. He looked away. 'Sorry. Didn't see a thing.'

They detached, and Joseph quickly returned to the wheel. 'Aye, Captain?'

'I'll take the wheel. You and Victoria see what you can do with that chest so we can begin to decipher our next heading.'

He nodded, 'aye, aye.' With a quick look back to the boatswain, he left the wheel and thumped down the ladder with Victoria following. Robertson took the wheel and unlashed it, looking over the deck, surveying its needs.

Descending the shrouds, Benjamin felt the breeze on his weathered face and was glad to be on the move again, and, listening to the banter of the crew, was glad to have them back. He heard the captain call from the helm, 'Baker, you Irish scallywag, get James and strike the bonnets from the sails! We've no need for 'em anymore with this wind,' he cried, 'then, when you're done, find Mills and you two give our saviour Mister Sharp a rundown of *Victoria* and how to treat her. Show him the ropes.'

He watched Billy throw his arms up, 'aye, aye! And alt'ough I appreciate the lovely banter, a please would go swell at t' end of a sentence!' Benjamin smiled and chuckled.

Robertson gave a laugh, 'There's not a please at the end of an instruction. You wanted to be a seadog, get used to the barking!'

He landed on deck and hobbled over to Billy, Tess and the new addition at the belaying pins of the foremast under the shrouds. 'The expedition was a success, I see.' He nodded to the captain's cabin where the door hung open and the chest could be seen in the gloom with quartermaster and boatswain around it.

'Oh aye, we got t' chest alright, and they gave us a lovely flute, but plans went a bit astray, so they did. Things . . . got a bit mucky.' The Irishman said, looking solemn as he glanced to the deck, then changed the topic quickly, 'this here's a Mister Thomas Sharp. Helped us out of a sticky situation shall we say – he's joinin' us, and he's even generously offered to rub our achin' bunions at the end of the day to be on our foine ship, an offer which I have already accepted.' Billy winked as he undid knots and put an arm around the man, 'ye'll have a cracker time on this old tub, my dear chuckaboo.' Then he left for the shrouds to begin working on taking the bonnets down with Dave.

Thomas smiled, looking as if he couldn't believe his luck. He looked ecstatic to be on the ship even though he knew nothing of it; another landlubber to test his sea-legs. As his face drained of colour, all could see he was not accustomed to *Victoria*'s oscillating dance upon the waves. Nonetheless, he pleasantly stepped forward and held out a hand, 'Mister Benjamin. Tess has told me what a fine sailor you are, sir. How goes you?'

The old sailor grinned and scoffed, taking the man's hand, 'well bless me for a gigglemug, I an't been called sir in nigh o' twenty year. Nice to meet ye, Tom.' He turned to Tess, 'where's the Jackson lad? Haven't seen him as o' yet.'

Tess's face fell, but she stood contrite. A posture that expressed numerous emotions of sadness, betrayal and disappointment. 'He's . . . he's no longer with us.'

Benjamin slipped his hands in his pockets, wondering what that meant. Whether he'd ran off or been killed, it sounded like a sore subject to address and now was not the time to pry. 'Oh. I see. Shame. I quite liked the lad, always up for a laugh, he was. Always easy to get along with.'

'He didn't exactly help the situation.' She replied, as Hugh's screams tormented places in her head she never knew were there; replaying his torture, his drop and the spill of the stolen diamonds that sparked everything off.

He shrugged, 'easy to get along with *on the ship*, then, I'll amend.' Just then Captain Robertson hailed him from the helm. 'Aye sir!' he called back, 'I'll sees you's later.' And he hobbled the length of the deck, clambering up the ladder to the quarterdeck where Robertson looked at him with a face that had seemed to have aged tenfold over the past few days. Everyone had seemed to have aged, much to the approval of Benjamin whose wrinkles never smoothed.

'Mister Smith,' the captain addressed, 'your report whilst we were absent?'

He stood to attention, knowing the question had been coming. He took off his scally cap. 'O' course, sir. A couple of fellas and ladies came rowing up on the evenin' ye left off, handing over baskets of fruits, nuts, meats, fish, rice, bit o' bread, a big ol' basket full o' coconuts, few beakers o' water and a couple o' skins full o' milk. Said something akin to you'd asked for food to be sent to the ship, or that's what I came to guess since they spoke scarce English and they mainly used hand gestures, but I was very thankful so thank'ee for that Cap'n.

'Next day, I prepped the meats and fish, saltin' 'em and preservin' 'em as best as I could. I split hemp from the ropes and caulked the deck, sewed some rips and careened for the a'ternoon – getting a few barnacles off the hull, general maintenance an' the like. Then, as the sun set, I made up a make-do net for fishing before cooking me meal and cleaning up the stove.

'An' this mornin' I prepared food for ye all an' that's when I heard ye all comin' back.' He reported.

Captain Robertson nodded slowly, 'good. Very well then. We also managed to bring back some goats, pigs and some chickens with us from the village, so they'll need preparing, their meats salted. Their horns and bones could have many uses too, I'm sure. Preserve as much as you can. Get Tess and Rob to help you with that after everyone's eaten something and rested for a while.' He paused, 'Benjamin?'

'Aye, Cap'?'

The man looked deep in thought into the horizon, seeing the memories play out against the sky, trying to push the echoes from his mind, trying to stop the screaming of Hugh Jackson, the son of the long line of smithies. *I was lazy; didn't take up the practice. I stole from people; I joined gangs; I drank too much; I enjoyed violence. I'm a thief, a constant liar, a serial rapist; I raped women, so many women, I hurt them and I'm sorry . . .* 'Remind me never to go to that island again, or if I do, urge me to visit the west coast.'

He nodded, again knowing it was better not to ask. 'Aye, aye Skipper.'

He nodded, his stomach gurgling. 'Good man. Now ring the bell for breakfast.' *I'm sorry for what I've done, for what I am. Please, listen to me, forgive me, remember me . . .*

Benjamin rung the bell, the sails were trimmed, and anchors were lowered a fathom. Everyone rushed down to the hold and was delighted to see food in it; some stored and, better, prepared to eat with moderate portions. They picked what they fancied with some choosing the exotic fruits on offer, savouring the exquisite citrus flavours now that they knew how to peel them and climbed up to the berth deck to eat, (or mess deck as Robertson had also called it when they ate in the berth). Berries, nuts and salted fish were washed down with goat's milk.

Trouble found its way to the three unfortunate Tangena victims however, as it had left an unpleasant residue in their bodies and made the food taste sour. Their stomachs cramped and tried several attempts at voiding the deposits; it was an effort to keep the little they had eaten down. 'It's just like a bad one after a night up the pole.' Joseph tried explaining, hoping it was what he was guessing, straining to keep a bite of bread below his throat. 'You've got to eat something the next day, no matter how much your stomach doesn't want it; you got to get something else in the system other than the alcohol.' He gulped and felt his guts writhing and his tongue squirming, 'can't deny it though, I'm bloody orf chump.'

Rob nodded in agreement having completely lost his appetite too, but Dave kept his mouth shut, not in spite as before but because he was trying to keep the food within his body. Nevertheless, Tangena had hooked its teeth in and made it a challenge to taste anything, as if the mixture had scorched their tongues of tastebuds. He could've been eating the bark of a tree for all he tasted.

As they were eating, Thomas picked the conversation as he leaned against the mainmast. 'So where is it we're headin' to?' he asked as he effortlessly peeled a banana; they watched with fascination as the curved fruit opened. He noted their wide eyes and almost chuckled, remembering his complete vexation when he was shown the art of peeling a banana all those years ago.

'To be completely frank, we don't know ourselves yet.' Jim Robertson, the Captain, answered.

Thomas looked at them all with bemusement, unsure if he was joking. Ships always had a destination. His brown eyes searched, 'so . . . we're out to sail the seven seas?'

'No.' Joseph swallowed with difficulty, then thought about the reply, 'well yes, in a way.' *How can I word it without it sounding moronic?* 'We're following a trail left by two explorers over a hundred years ago leading to, what we hope will be, the Lost Loot, or you might know it as Scott's Trove. Sounds preposterous, I know, but we've followed it all the way from London and the clues we've been finding have taken us half-way round the world and, if we piece it together right; there's a clue waiting for us, telling us where to head off to next.'

A stern look crossed his face, but then a grin spread making him look somewhat handsome. 'I always loved a treasure hunt! But a one across the world, damn me for a fool, that's just extraordinary. Takes guts, I admire that. I've heard of the Scott's Trove before, but

I didn't know it was the same as the Lost Loot. This'll be like killin' two birds with one stone. I like it. I'm in. Is that why you ended up in Madagascar?'

A nod all round. A regretful nod. 'The clue from Gabon led us there, and as it so happened Mister I-am-a-prick-Tulyaka was keeping the next clue and played the hard card with letting it go.'

'Even then, he didn't let it go. You stole it.' Victoria added.

Joseph nodded and smiled, 'well I had to let them know I was from the backstreets of London now, didn't I?' he winked, 'it was my profession after all. What's life without a little pumpin'-blood?'

Thomas didn't ask why his profession was thieving; before he'd left England, he'd been taught to not steal anything and that there was good in all people through god's eyes. But now his perspective had altered; he cared not where they came from or what things these people had done, only who they chose to be in this moment and where they were heading. 'Where's this one led to, the clue, where's it leadin' us? Where're we sailing?' Hearing himself rabble as such was a habit, not just because of the solitude but because whenever he was forced to teach English, he always offered up alternatives to a question or statement to help the villagers understand the meaning.

'As soon as we crack open this chest, we'll find out.' Joseph forced down another bite then, groaning, handed his food to another, unable to supress the unpleasantness any longer. 'I'm heading up to open it.' He said, unable to tolerate even the smell of food around him. He headed to the companionway and ascended to the main deck before realising everyone had followed in anticipation.

Joseph opened the cabin doors, took the chest from the table and walked it out to the sunlight, placing it on top of a barrel for all to see. It was small, exceedingly small in fact, to what Thomas had in mind. Its size was surprising due to the importance of what was enclosed inside. It could've been the Holy Grail locked within, or the Ark of the Covenant in its level of value, and the crew circling it its disciples having conquered the righteous tests to claim it.

Despite this being Thomas's first encounter with a chest of such, he felt the atmosphere ripen and understood why this was so critical; a quick glance at them all cemented it. All eyes were trained on the chest and a tense silence settled. This wasn't just a chest with a few pieces of paper inside – this was their future, guiding them to their next destination. A prophecy. Their lives were entwined with this journey now, they had nothing else to go back to. Only onward. Toward their future, locked inside this casket. He felt himself drawn to it too and was suddenly eager to find out its contents.

'Joe, have y' got the key?' Billy asked calmly.

He held it up. 'It's the key from the last chest, it might work for this one too.'

'Then stick the fuckin' thing in there! I can't deal with this suspense.'

Lowering the key, he inserted it into the lock and turned it slightly . . .

But the lock did not yield. This was not the correct key.

A surge of panic gripped him, knotting his insides. It was as if someone had landed a fist to his diaphragm and left him gasping for air. He exhaled, closing his eyes in pain. *No . . .*

'It's not the right key!' Dave James cried, echoing everyone's thoughts.

Joseph stood up straight, exhaling sharply, and turned away before he could look at the man's face. At anyone's face. Stunned glances passed from the key to the quartermaster, then to Dave, then to each other as the gravity of the situation sunk. The worst-case scenario was it was back in the village. The best-case scenario . . . there wasn't one. The key was not here. And the thought of rowing back to the village, to the crazed chief and his lying assistant, to the burning village and Hugh's corpse surrounded by stolen diamonds, to ask for the location of the key to the chest they'd stolen was an image no one favoured. All the effort, labour and cost of visiting the "helpful" village to get this chest had been rendered completely moot. It had been a fruitless endeavour, a pointless act that lost them a shipmate and nearly killed them all.

'Where is the key then?' Dave growled, 'Where is it, *Quartermaster?*'

'Oh, don't you start this again, Dave. We don't want another bloody standoff.' Victoria snapped back.

''Tis not Joe's fault.'

'Where's the key, Winter?! Didn't think about that, did you? All this shit about being friendly to the black people to get the chest and you didn't think to get the key to open the fucking thing!'

'Calm down mate, enough now, this is not helping anything.'

'Stay out of this, Tom. This hasn't got anything to do with you.'

'It's got everything to do with him! He's a part of this company now, and he saved our lives don't forget.' Tess flared.

'Yes, he freed us all but now we're a man down on the crew and a chest without a key. And the one chance Mister Map-Finder gets to grab the chest he forgets the key to go with it. In case you hadn't noticed, we lost Hugh back there, coughing up his life's blood as his insides dissolved *whilst* he was still alive; he died for you, bastard. Harold died for you; Poppy died for *you*. You couldn't protect us; you didn't do anything. All this "new life" shite you fed us in the gaol we happily lapped up but instead all you've given us is an early death. What a jape! You should've been a jester instead of a thief, that's where your colours lie.'

Suddenly snapping, he turned to face him and shoved him hard, forcing him against the mast. Remembering what he had in his pocket, he brandished the diamond blade and held it to Dave's unshaven neck. 'If it wasn't for your greed, we never would've been imprisoned and forced into the trial. If it weren't for your stupidity, we never would've faced Tangena and Hugh would be with us now. If it weren't for your actions and attitude, Hugh wouldn't have been poisoned and burned from the inside out, wouldn't be screaming in agony in my head right now! It was the diamonds you stole that turned the villagers against us, so don't you dare blame me for all the misfortunes of this damned voyage!' He pressed the blade into the skin of his throat, seeing a thin red line appear, 'I could do it. I could end this eternal feud right now.'

He knew how easy it would be to slide it across and spill his lifeblood to the deck, yet something held him back.

Please, no. Victoria had whispered, her clear eyes looking into his. *It'll only make things worse. Listen to me. Please.* Joseph paused, grinding his teeth in frustration. Perhaps there was a reason Dave had joined, perhaps there was more to this man than he knew. How could he know what destinies awaited; who was he to intervene? The hesitation was enough to pass the intensity of the moment and, with great effort, he pulled the blade away and threw it to the deck. He released him from the mast and marched away, leaving everyone in a stunned silence.

After a moment, the frustrated crew parted for their stations, leaving the chest atop its barrel with its mystery caged inside.

Chapter Twenty-Seven

Benjamin stood in shock, understanding why no one wanted to talk about what happened to Hugh or the events in the village. It was too raw. He'd seen and done some awful things in his time; a man of the merchant navy had to do his duty and he knew those demons never left no matter how many years passed. He never would have guessed those demons would be lurking in the rainforests of Madagascar, waiting for these poor wretches to walk willingly in. Now the crew had demons of their own and no matter how many years would pass, the torment caused by a painful, laboured death would always linger.

The old sailor looked at the chest and its signs of age, then stepped over to the diamond blade and picked it up, realising it was attached to a woven thread necklace. Decorations accompanied the diamond on either side, small rodent skulls and large sharp teeth from the *fossa*. Fascinated, he examined the tribal neckwear and thought back to his own experience when he was captured by a cannibalistic tribe all those years ago; the similarities between the accessories were astounding. All skulls, bones, teeth and shrunken heads; anything to strike fear into the hearts of the enemy. They, like any powerful country, used fear as a tool, the most important tool anyone could wield into gaining submission; used universally by nations and governments, and tribes. *Perhaps we're all just tribes,* he thought, *wearing different clothes and building different homes, but using the same tactics and living the same lifestyles.* As he pondered over this, looking over the bones, he spotted something encased within one of the skulls next to the diamond blade – something with its end protruding from the snout like teeth. *Metal teeth? That's odd.*

Hobbling to the hold, he picked out a small hammer and shattered the skull against the floor. Nodding, he smiled at his discovery. How Joseph came by this peculiar necklace was beyond him, but from its value this would've been worn only by the chief. Perhaps fate had been looking after him all along. Hobbling back to the deck, he saw the captain observing the chest as he stroked his beard in thought. 'Don't mind me, Capt'n.' he said.

'Oh, of course, go right ahead.' He replied with little attention, his thoughts were somewhere else.

Benjamin nodded and knelt in front of the chest. Narrowing his vision, he squinted hard, wondering if he should've enquired about glasses before he got arrested for loitering on someone's doorstep. His old eyes strained with much nowadays, but back out on the water he could nourish his firm beliefs in the cures of sea-air and deny his age withholding him. He knew he could still play a part. Slowly, he inserted the small key and turned it.

Suddenly he felt the eyes of Robertson gleaming behind him. *Say nothin' yet, Captain. Just watch for now. Let an old boy enjoy this moment.* He got to his feet and took off his cap.

The morning sun beat down on him, sweat trickled down his spotted forehead. Benjamin lifted the lid and looked inside the chest they'd all worked so hard to claim and saw a scroll, tied up with string, and a pocket watch that had ceased to tick for many a year. Time had frozen. Time had stopped.

'It's open! Ben's done it!' He heard someone call but he didn't know who, he was too engrossed. Soon, everyone was crowing around him and the open chest, hearts thumping excitedly.

He reached inside and picked out the scroll.

Even though he struggled to read the written word, this was an opportunity he was not going to miss. A thought passed: *I should pass this onto the Quart'master or Capt'n . . .* but another crossed it out. *No, it's my turn to discover.*

The paper felt soft against his callous fingers, even though its age exceeded his own. With a careful approach, he pulled the string and the scroll rolled open. He held its ends and tried his best to read it, now more than ever wishing for a pair of glasses.

ALEX FISHER

The day was slow after the revealing of the next clue, as all agreed to decipher it after the evening bell, yet this only made them ponder as they worked as it appeared to be no ordinary riddle. At last, though, as the hours waned, the bell was chimed early. They stowed the sails, ate and steadily clambered into the captain's cabin where, in the light of the oil lamps, a slight cosiness settled. The doors were shut, and the curtains were drawn to fend off the evening's encroaching gloom. The space inside was enough to accommodate everyone without feeling cramped, which was a relief, as everyone was present, sitting on a chair or box awaiting the clue to be retold.

Hearing the clue again was the only thing keeping them alert. The day had been long, they were all exhausted, yet no one could purge of the curiosity of the newest scroll. If anything, the passing hours of the day only exacerbated the wonder as each tried to think of an answer to this twisting riddle. Their limits were reached, however, with their little, if any, level of geographical education.

Nearly all knew the winding streets of the city, the locations of the hidden back alleys, the popular shops, the sprawling markets, the best stables, the areas of wealth and the black spots of utter squalor. If asked, any of them could tell you exactly where a particular bakery was if they stood on the other side of the city blindfolded and tell you precisely what streets to take. But the countries of the world? None of them had needed to know, until they'd begun to travel it and experience it for themselves. Now, all wanted to be like Marco Polo, Walter Raleigh and James Cook; constantly driven by the one gnawing question: where to next? The journey had not only become their lives, but it had also become their addiction.

'Quartermaster.' Captain Robertson called clearly as he stood over the map of the world holding his magnifying piece and his compass. 'Let's hear it again. Where to next?'

Slouching in his seat, Joseph Winter got to his feet and removed his scally cap, pulling his lengthy hair back to his head. He craved a cigarette to suck, tobacco to smoke, he craved a haircut and the flavours of food, to feel normal again. *What is normal anymore?* All eyes were on him. He could feel it. Everyone hushed as he picked up the parchment and unravelled. This time he needed not any special glasses or the heat of a burning candle. This one was written in plain ink and quill. The problem was the timing of its creation; it had been written in haste and some words had been smudged, had faded with age or were missing, written with a quill short of ink. Whatever happened on that day, Eve and Henry were more concerned with getting the words down on paper than trying to conceal them in a crafty fashion. However, what they'd done as they hurried was create a clue blatant to the eye but hard to read and even harder to decipher. An almost unintentional way of making it difficult.

But the evening was theirs now and although they may not have had the education, they certainly had the time; the time to spend piecing together this troubling web of confusion.

He took a breath and read aloud for all to hear:

'Hail, ye weary travellers for here the next ... awaits.
Set sail aboard and aloft, keeping true ... ... locate,
As the crow flies is . . .
... you have crossed and ... you ... sail.
But none as the Ind...
Where the land must be lost.
Guided by the setting of Polaris, ... what cost?

Rumours we have heard, to explore is to discover.
Keep the piece ticking.
Heading so . . .t . . .'

Lowering the scroll, he felt even more lost than before. Upon hearing Benjamin first read it, he believed the old dog was losing his senses, or his wit, but now he felt like the witless one. He thought back to the clue he found in the attic of that house, at how nonsensical it sounded until he learned how to see flatly on the piano. *There was an answer there. There's got to be an answer here.*

There were blank faces in the cabin, blank clueless faces. A coastal breeze rattled outside, seemingly amplified by the silence of the room. 'Are you sure there ain't another bit of paper in that chest?' Billy hoped.

Joseph shook his head, 'this was all that was in there, as well as this pocket watch.' He held aloft the piece, just an ordinary timepiece with its face and hands paralysed and wondered what part this had to play.

'Well, I guess we know the answer to the "keep the piece ticking" part. We'll have to wind it.' Added Victoria positively.

'Aye, that we know, just not where to go next.' Said Benjamin, deflated.

'Bloody hell, if this is what all the clues have been like I'm shocked you've got this far.' Thomas chipped in, sitting on a barrel, 'that's not a clue, that's a riddle!'

'Y' know, I'm startin' to t'ink they don't like us very much.' Billy said, half-jokingly but mostly serious.

'Most of them have basically been riddles but not so much as this. Usually we can crack it; they leave *something* in there at least – but this one's just a shamble. We're three sheets to the wind. If it weren't so bloody smudged and broken, we'd have a better idea at what they're getting at.' He corrected himself, '*where* they're getting at.'

'It's almost as if they don't know themselves.' Rob suggested.

Joseph was about to say something, but he stopped himself and looked at the lad in the corner. It made sense. They couldn't add in any details of where to head as they did not know themselves. It was a possibility, the closest notion to lean upon right now. 'I doubt you're far off there, you know. There's no mention of a certain event, of a certain population or what to do exactly. Most of this one doesn't rhyme either,' he looked over the words again, to the aging smudges and missing links. 'It was written in haste, that much is clear.' – *About the only clear thing on this frousy scrap of paper.* 'And how it mentions they've heard rumours and they're discovering as they explore. It's almost as if they're out to find a new place they haven't been to before.'

Surprisingly, Dave contributed something helpful. 'We know what direction to go in, though, don't we? It said, "as the crow flies" which means to go in a straight line, and it says, "keep true" and that means straight line too. A friend of mine who was a docker taught me that.'

Tess nodded, 'He's got a point. Maybe that's just what they did, and they want us to repeat it; to travel in a straight line, to keep going; it said, "heading so".'

To be fair to them, it made sense. *But where to, Tess, travel in a straight line to where?* Joseph nodded, 'That's something to think on, yes.'

Victoria got up from her chair and stood beside Joseph, looking over the scroll. Tucking her hair behind her ear, she read aloud, '*Guided by the setting of Polaris.* What's that? What's Polaris?'

'Polaris was in the first scroll I found, too. It's got to be important.'

Jim Robertson, who had been quiet for most of the discussion, sat forward with his empty pipe in his hands. It was a habit of his to smoke whilst thinking and the exhausted tobacco situation had set his wits short, yet it comforted him to have it between his lips. 'I'll show you. Follow me.' He got to his feet and took hold of a lamp, exiting the cabin with everyone following.

The evening had turned to dusk, and stars were beginning to wink into existence again for another night. With luck, it was to be a cloudless night. It was a strange thought that the stars were always there, that the earth just turned away from them every morning to face the sun again and then they were forgotten until the oncoming nightfall forced a remembrance. They would still be there long after this year, after this lifetime, Joseph mused as he tilted his head; people would grow, work, live and die, technologies would advance, spread and decline, businesses would bud, flourish and wilt; the world would change and develop and evolve, and they would continue to exist. An ancient phenomenon outliving everyone and everything. He spied the shining beacons, observing a relic of the past and simultaneously glimpsing a piece of the future.

Captain Robertson walked out on the deck, pulled out his spyglass and peered up to the sky. Gazing. Hunting. 'There!' he pointed, 'See? There it is.' The ship rolled gently over a wave.

Joseph hunted around at the other stars but did not see. They were small and white, each and every one, how did any appear different? Then he saw one brighter than the rest; it was not central as he imagined, but then he remembered they were not in the north. Only in the arctic would the star be directly overhead. 'That's Polaris.' Robertson explained, 'It's the main star. The North Star, the brightest; no matter where you go it's the one star that stays north and does not move; all the other stars rotate around it. It's the benchmark, so if you're ever lost, you need only to look up and you'll know where to set your compass to find your way again.'

'Aye, 'tis. 'Tis.' Benjamin nodded.

'On the note it says it's *setting*, though. If this North Star can't move, how can it set? I'm guessing it means setting as the sun does, like its touching the horizon and about to go under.'

The captain looked back down to Victoria; her features were slowly melting into the dark, but even in the little light he could see why men would find her attractive. Victoria was an attractive woman, and her wits were sharp, it could not be denied. He involuntarily twiddled his beard in thought. 'I don't know, that's what I've been getting stuck with.'

'If it's the North star, this Polaris one, then could you see it in the south?' Tess asked, looking up to the stars. She couldn't find it. They all looked the same.

'No. Well, yes, but only very slightly, if at all. It disappears the further south you go, so at the equator it . . .' his voice trailed off as he realised the meaning. Polaris *could* set, *would* set, and *was* setting right now. *Guided by the setting of Polaris . . .* Hurrying, Robertson ran past them all, erupted back into the cabin and turned up the lamp, stooping over the scroll.

Everyone joined him back in the cabin a moment later, wondering what he'd realised but he hardly noticed anyone there. Absorbed, Robertson spooled over the clue, muttering under his breath as he did so. 'What is it, Jim? What've you found?' Joseph queried eagerly. They were all gathered around the table.

The captain looked up, 'I think I have our heading.'

'Where?!'

'South. At the bottom here, it doesn't say "heading so…", it was meant to say "heading *south*" but it looks as if the quill ran dry. Polaris *does* set. The lower you travel below the equator, the more it disappears so those in the southern colonies can't even see the star.'

'If we keep heading south, we'll end up there, in Antarctica.' Observed Victoria standing over the map. Most of them hadn't even heard of the place before, to spell it would be a riddle itself.

Robertson was ready for a reply, 'not that far south. I think they're trying to tell us to head south-east.'

'Not having a gas, Capt'n, but how on eart' could you know that? Half o' the words are smudged, faded or missin' and the ones we *can* read don't make sense at all.' The Irishman sat back down; dark rings troubled his eyes. Fatigue was creeping on them all and the tobacco cravings were drawing patience short.

'Here.' He pointed to the line: *But none as the Ind…* 'Indian. I think that's what it means to say.'

'–We're sailing to India?' Thomas sounded hopeful. He'd always wanted to visit. It was a fascinating place; he'd heard in his days around the docks from the ships trading spices as he awaited his maiden missionary voyage.

'No. *Indian. The Ocean.*' He corrected, 'I'm just stabbing in the dark here but I'm guessing it means to say the Indian Ocean. It goes on to say "*… you have crossed… and… you sail…*" so they want us to sail as the crow flies and cross . . . "*but none as the Ind…*". I'm thinking it's saying we've got to cross the Indian . . . then it says, "*where land must be lost*". Well, where do you lose land? Water – a big expanse, a *great* expanse of water . . .'

'. . . An ocean.' Joseph uttered, things becoming clearer.

Robertson's eyes gleamed. 'Precisely! Then you have "*guided by the setting of Polaris*" which makes sense now as the Indian Ocean is *below* the equator, the southern hemisphere where the North Star is hardly seen. And at the very bottom you've got "*heading so…*" –south. Or south-east. That's our heading. That's where they went next. They crossed the Indian Ocean, so that's what we must do.'

Tess sat down, exhaustion weighing heavy, but she still felt sharp enough to contribute. 'Alright, so we cross the Indian Ocean, but where do we go once we've crossed it? The clue doesn't say where to go from there. It's just given us a few directions, not what to do nor where to look next.'

Joseph shrugged; she was right.

'They didn't know where they were going, remember.' Victoria pointed out, 'they've given us the exact same directions as they took, we know as much as they did at this point.'

Joseph agreed, she was right as well.

'So, is this a dead end?' Tess crossed her legs on her chair, her groin aching but she tried not to show her pain.

It was, and it wasn't, he wanted to say. They had a direction to go in, but just not a one that led them to the next clue. The question was whether to gamble it and cross the ocean and see what they found on the other side. It was a risk though; none of them had crossed an ocean, none really understood the vastness of it, the sheer grandeur of open space. Miles upon miles of blue, without any sight of land. The wavy dynamics were gigantic. Although there was doubt, deep down he knew his answer: *We've travelled this far, I'm willing to go further.*

'When did these people lay out this trail?' Thomas asked anyone, breaking the silence.

Rob answered with a speculation as he scratched his head. 'Over a hundred years ago we think. We an't too sure, but it was around the middle of the 1700's, or a bit later. 1750's or '60's, sometime then. When did they meet again, Ben?'

'Oh, er,' he thought back, 'there was the battle; they met there, *Royal Fortune* . . . 1722.'

'Ah! Must've been mid 1700's they laid this then, or around that time.'

'Well, we know where we're going then. This is a different century we're in now, the blank spaces have been filled. They didn't know where they were headin' to, but we do.' All eyes turned to him in astonishment. 'There's a bit of paper right there on the table that says so. Unless new countries have been found in my years of pit-life, I'm sure most of the known lands are there, on that world map.' Thomas walked around the table, his slim frame slipping through the chairs, and stood beside Victoria. He took the magnifying piece and moved it south-east across the labelled Indian Ocean. 'There. That's where we're heading.'

Everyone bustled in closer around the table, eyes franticly looking at what lay magnified under the piece.

It was resting over land.

A grand chunk of land.

Land that had only been discovered less than a hundred years ago.

A continent.

Their destination for the next clue lay halfway around the world from where they started out. Joseph stared at the magnified word on the map, wondering how on earth he didn't see it before:

AUSTRALIA
(*Terra Australis*)

Chapter Twenty-Eight

With a light and silent step, Joseph's feet were whispers passing through the dark alley. The cobbles felt hard against his soles, they were cold and uncomfortable to walk on. He looked down and noticed his naked feet. *No boots?* Small wonder why his toes were numb. Being barefoot reminded him of his childhood when he outgrew his shoes and would run through the streets; the days before it all began, when he waited for money instead of taking it. In those days, his feet could run through the cobbles and would turn thick and leathery by the time his mother had enough money to buy a new pair for him. Now though, they felt less like leather and more like stone, and had crossed many a mile since then. Another pair of boots was needed; another pair to keep going. The corner ahead needed to be reached, the chest was what he sought. Oh, it had to be found.

No one was down the alley. No one was on the roads. A strange, subdued quiet had befallen the once busy thrum. Keeping an eye about him, he pulled his scally cap lower and heard dripping.

He smelled rain in the air. It had recently stopped, and the freshness was a relief to breathe; it would not be long before the next waft of stink would pass through the narrow streets, so he enjoyed the fresh air while it lasted. As he walked, he began to hear squelching. The cobbles were slick with freshly uprooted grime and excrement from horse and human alike; sometimes, after a heavy rain, the waste would run in rivers, bubbling over the stones as if it were a babbling brook in the countryside. *The water in the country's much cleaner than this, I'll wager.* He dared to not look at his bare feet as he walked, any fool on these streets knew how abhorrent they were after rainfall; numb feet were one thing, brown feet were another. Any fool knew as well that it was not wise to run in such conditions, so he was forced to walk briskly, forever chasing the corner, the next bend, the chest; what was in it?

The buildings looming overhead were huge and unfamiliar, a forest of man-made structures to contain society and make it feel as if it were worth something. He sighed; the buildings felt sickening. Constrictive. Unnatural. A prison. Where were the open spaces?

Bile was at the back of his throat when he felt eyes on him, watching his every squelching step. Suddenly his feet were not the ones whispering; the alley was full of hushed secrets and beady eyes. *Don't run in case you slip,* he tried to tell himself, *you don't want to fall in the river.* The apprehension became too much, and his pace quickened. Paranoia and Anxiety were then set loose, chasing him, gnashing their teeth and frothing at the mouth with unruly rabidity. Joseph caved in and ran for the corner, splashing through the ankle-deep grime heading down a slope, which meant more of the river was due to come. The city was full of people and horses, so full of sewage that no one knew what to do with it. Might as well let it flow.

He breathed hard, trying to keep the bile from pressing onto his tongue but the ordeal was hard. The bile was there, it couldn't be ignored. Tickling his tonsils, it threatened ejection. *Get to the corner. The chest will be there, get to the corner.* Yet the corner always felt miles away, oceans away, halfway around the world.

Pressure jumped on his back and rode him up to the corner, its weight heavy on his shoulders, almost impossible to bear and its reign on him was too tight; the bit was tugging so hard in his mouth he thought he was to gag and release this bile. Still the dogs pursued, Anxiety and Paranoia, their claws clicking and clacking on the stone as they scrambled along walls to get to him, craving his bones to gnaw on. Stress then mounted him too – a heavy passenger – forcing him to stumble and run doubled-over. Stress was harsher than Pressure, it dug it spurs in his side and lashed a whip at his back one crack after another; willing him faster to the corner, to the chest but his legs were tiring with the weight of his baggage and the pain became blunted by the searing heat of his legs.

Feet? He no longer had any, the coldness had seized them and turned them to stone; an ugly blue with blots of black, gradually turning grey. The stubbing of them as he ran over the wet, brown cobbles was agonising; he felt his toes crack and snap off. He was tantalisingly close to the corner, to the chest, to the loot itself; he pushed on despite the bile fingering his tongue, pulling it back and pressing it to his palate like a maid washing a bed sheet against a grill.

He rounded the corner so hard he slipped and fell into the grime, his passengers gripping him tight, still cracking the whip. He rolled in the dirty river, felt it stinging in his eyes, the taste of it in his mouth, between his lips. Crying out, his head breached the surface and he sucked in foul smelling air to his burning lungs. Through bleary vision, he spotted the shovel against the wall and the river of waste was pouring into the hole beside. Standing watch over it, an old, wrinkled crone peered down the depth, his fingers clawing, licking his lips. Joseph knew the man, could feel the swamp of negativity he wallowed in. *Frederick.* 'No,' he uttered, '*no!*' He got to his stubby, frostbitten feet and clambered to the hole where the city's sewage was pouring down into, where the chest was, *the* chest it had all been about; the one he'd sought after for so long it had consumed him and became his past, present and future.

Kneeling at its edge in the foul streams, he peered down the hole and saw the Lost Loot below, deep within the earth. Surrounding it were three figures. They were opening the chest. *His* chest. '*Get off! That's mine! Hear me, mine! Get your filthy fingers off it!*' he exclaimed as the river ran over his hands; he could feel it slowly dragging him in. His grip was giving way.

The three figures almost didn't hear him. They looked up, almost in surprise at hearing another voice, and to his great shock he *knew* the figures stealing the contents of the chest, looting his future from him.

Harold Arms looked up with a pale face and wide eyes, his throat was cut, and slashes covered his naked body. Poppy Mills stared at him with a skeletal frame, her skin so drawn and stretched, her hair so thin he could see her dry cracked scalp. Hugh Jackson peered up at him with red bloodshot eyes, his stomach grossly bloated, fit to burst, and his lips quivered with blood beginning to spill from the corners.

Suddenly a new rider jumped on Joseph's saddle, a fat rider with a three-tongued whip, and grabbed the reigns harder than the rest had. Its name was Guilt and it weighed so heavily down on him he felt tears streaming down his face before he knew he was crying. The rider then brought its whip down on his bare back and he shrieked as the splicing pain tore through his flesh. Guilt laughed. Again, it brought the whip down until his grip failed him and he slipped. Hugh suddenly opened his mouth upon seeing him fall and screamed and howled and bawled and shrieked and he spasmed in such pain and fear that Joseph felt the bile in his throat loosen . . .

. . . and he vomited heavily down the side of his hammock to the wooden slats with a splat. With a quick roll he flopped from his bunk, collapsed to the floor and ran for the ladder, holding his mouth tightly. Bursting out on deck, he flew to the bulwark and heaved up everything his body had to offer in a violent and projectile manner, watching it fall to the waves below. A few breaths of air were allowed before a powerful retch kicked up another bout until his stomach was wrung of its juices and his legs felt rubbery. His throat bubbled as it whipped up bodily froth; he winced as his stomach seized. Most of his support came from the railing now, but still he had to check and was relieved to see his feet beneath him, even if they were barefoot.

From what he could tell in between his voiding session, darkness lingered but shades of light were spreading upward from the east, stroking away the black like a painter's brush, line by line. It would be dawn soon.

A hand slapped him on the shoulder, 'Aye, that's it, boyo, get it up, a'right. That's it now, get the lot up. Oh Christ, yer soaked through!' the hand retreated.

Groggily, Joseph looked to the hand's owner and saw Billy Baker in the haze, if but for a second before he retched again and spewed overboard. The Irishman took a step back, 'you've cost me my orange this morning.' The thought of food made him retch again, but he managed to ask what he was talking about.

'We made a bet on who'd be last up 'ere, who had the strongest stomach, and I placed my orange on Dave, but you went an' blew it, ya' tough-bellied bastard.'

He frowned, confused. 'Who's up here?' he asked, wiping his mouth and beard.

'Everyone but Tommy-boy; slept through the lot he did. The rest o' us got woken up by the–' *screams,* he wanted to say, but pushed the thought away, 'by the vomiting. Rob woke me first since I sleep under him, messy codger t'rew up right over me, he did, but I can't be mad, 'specially after what he drank. I helped him to the deck then everyone else woke too. I doubt if anyone slept properly. Then Dave caved in and came up 'ere to the rails, and then you. That Tangena shite really messed you lot up, eh?'

He held back another retch, 'oh really? You reckon? Still, I'd rather have this than end up like Hugh.' The truth was undeniable, everyone would've agreed.

'Aye. Aye.' Billy nodded, 'I got some water for y' anyway, you look like you've been on the lash; pale as milk, you are.'

Groaning, Joseph took the skin and drank a gulp. 'Thanks.'

'Oh, an' Captain's been up giving orders; sails are ready to fly at first light and navigation's been sorted. T'ought I'd let you know, so you can get changed to somet'ing dry; yer soaked to the bone, matey.' Truth be told, all looked dishevelled this morning and Billy had dark rings around his bloodshot eyes, his face had small cuts from their run through the jungle.

Holding his head, a pounding pain began to burn through the back of his eyes. 'Right. I'll get to it. Bill?'

'Aye?'

'You can have my orange this morning. You'd be surprised, but I'm orf chump a bit. I've completely lost my appetite.'

'Eyy!' he smiled and slapped Joseph's shoulder again making him shudder and want to retch, 'lost the bet but still got me orange, how's about that for the luck o' the Irish.'

As soon as he felt stable enough, Joseph left the bulwark and made for the companionway. A sharp pain dug in his calf that made him wince before it vanished, leaving him questioning its presence and reality. In truth, his body hurt all over; aches and pains, cuts and bruises, welts and sores, it was probably just one of the above. As he descended to the berth, his head swam and smelling the deck did nothing to help him feel any better. The air was thick with the stench of spew; it was splattered on the floorboards as well as down his shirt. *Maybe it's myself I'm smelling?* He pictured a great luxury marble bath with alabaster rails and a plug of silver, shining golden taps running warm water, a homely steam rising from the base inviting him in, but in his current station he'd take anything. A barrel full of stone-cold water sounded blissful, he craved a bath so much. A haircut and a shave wouldn't be amiss either; just to feel clean again. Mites and flies were finding homes in their clothes and lice were ever a problem. The beard he could live with once this was all over, but he didn't favour the squatters that took up lodgings inside.

He plucked a loosely fitted shirt from their barrel of spare clothes stolen from Lisbon; it was stained and grey, wearing thin in places and torn in others, but it was vomit-free. He slipped off his shirt and suddenly hesitated upon seeing the carved wooden elephant hanging around his neck, feeling heavy; another burden to carry, *Harold* . . . Thinking back to his nightmare, he saw the butchered man looking up at him from the hole, as well as Poppy Mills and now Hugh Jackson, *who else will die because of this venture, because of me?* Gulping, he tried to push the thought away. Adorning the shirt, he buttoned over it and slipped a waistcoat on, covering the dagger he kept tucked in his belt.

Gazing at the hooks to the left of the clothes barrel, he spotted his navy jacket he'd stolen from the market on his way to the docks. The last thing he'd stolen. It brought a smile to his face, the thought of being chased and the thrill of getting away – he missed it, and before he knew it the jacket was donned; not so much for the sentimental value but because a bitter chill was running through his body, tapping his bones as it ran its skeletal course. *It's just the*

Tangena. It's still in the system. He hoped it was only the Tangena, else he wasn't sure what it could be. God forbid a jungle parasite, he already had enough stowaways on his body, there wasn't room for more.

Avoiding sight of food, he decided to skip breakfast and clean his mess and the mess around the other hammocks and quickly sanded and scrubbed the vomit. One thing sailing had taught him was to always clean up spills quickly, vomit especially, else the roll of the waves only spread it into a wider patch.

The bell rang on deck and Robertson's voice was heard by them all, 'All hands to deck! Rig the topgallant mast, sail and royal sails whilst we're still stationary, let's catch as much wind as we can today. Also, I'd say our old anchors have had enough resting for the time being. Winch the chains, able seamen, haul them and cry anchors aweigh and let's sail! Our *Victoria*'s legs could do with a stretch before she runs. Any who fancy one last sight of land before the crossing take a glance now, for in the hour we'll have naught to look at but Indian waves and Indian water for the foreseeable future.' A pause, 'Quartermaster! Where are you?'

He coughed, 'in the berth, be up in a minute!' He finished scrubbing and brought the pail with him to deck, tipping it over the railing. Dawn had broken, and in the soft early light the coast was a dark line of silhouettes, risen here and there by the hills of the eastern shore; a small smudge of smoke rising to the sky. Guilt lingered for what they had done to their village, from the looks of it, the tree and huts were still smouldering. Pursing his lips at the shambolic visit, Joseph took in the last sighting and knew the next time land would cross his vision would be the coastline of Australia, the fabled continent.

Australia, my god, they travelled that far without a map. They really had been explorers, pioneers in their field. At a guess, Eve and Henry discovered Australia before Captain Cook even conjured a thought of his First Voyage but had never returned home to prove their discoveries like the rest. *But they weren't out to fill in the blank spaces, they were exploring because that's what they loved to do. It was their life.* They may not have planted flags, named a country or built a colony, yet still people knew of Eve and Henry's adventures, whether they believed the stories or not. Whether they believed they left a trail to follow. If anything, it only added to their infamy for not only were tales shared of the pair, but questions were always asked after; *do you believe any of it? I wonder, are they still out there, roaming the seas leaving a trail in their wake?* People could guess since the ending was never concluded. The Scott's never returned home . . . if they even intended to. Some shared a view the couple were pirates never letting their chest out of sight, the last pirates of the Golden Age. Joseph looked afore the ship, to the forecastle and horizon beyond, to Australia and knew their trove was out there somewhere, maybe with the explorers too. *The pirates still clinging to their hoard locked away in the wooden chest, just like the tales of old.*

Watching the coastline slowly melt away, he craved some tobacco to roll and smoke. He couldn't remember the last time he'd had one, and the roaring flame of clawing need had dulled to a glowing ember, gnawing at him for another hit. Thankfully, his skin no longer felt like it was rippling up his bones and his teeth were settled in his gums, but still he struggled to not put a cigarette between his lips. In frustration, he dug his hands in his pockets and felt the compass against his fingers. He picked it out and watched the dial spin, stop, judder, twist and bounce along the other way, unquestionably broken. Grinding his teeth, he wished he'd have been more careful. It was the only thing his grandfather had left him after all, the only memento from his failed voyages. 'Quartermaster, is that two empty hands loitering I see?' Captain Robertson called from the helm, 'or are they awaiting orders?'

The morning passed quickly and with a coastal south-easterly wind *Victoria* tore through the waves, crashing through the white crests at nine knots, leaving the warm Mozambique current behind to enter the treacherous Indian Ocean waters. No currents ran through it, all currents ran around it almost netting the ocean in a whirlpool of becalmed tide. It was to be a struggle, no longer could they ride the water's trade routes; they had to rely on winds, and if they dropped . . . they did not want to think of it, but there would be many a knife stuck in the mainmast and many prayers whispered into pillows. The threat of sudden weather changes was also on the cards, as the sky was temperamental with the wind's moods forever flicking from a smooth breeze to a storm force gale.

For now, though, all sails were open with the spanker, topgallant sails and royal sails reefed slightly to not catch too much of the southerly gale, but the topsail and mainsail of the fore, main and mizzen were all rounded, taught with tension of the pounding gusts. Halyards were tied, sheets were taught, and the tension of the turnbuckles was checked and tight; the stays were in perfect condition. An equatorial warmth was in the air and kept the heat at a moderate temperature, but still it was enough for the crew to break a sweat whilst working. The air wasn't stifling though, and the breeze was kind on their skin as well as the sea spray that kissed their faces; the faint rainbows fading in a delicate mist.

As the sun rose over the yardarm and they ate lunch, the wind dropped its strength but continued moderately and the ship rolled over the waves, riding them with swift ease as a rider would upon a gallant steed. They were sailing with the wind and it was kind, for the time being. Last night, after everyone had departed for bed – apart from the deckhand on dogwatch duty – Robertson had stayed up planning, charting a course and navigating the route and had calculated, if all conditions were well and nothing proved a hinderance, they could cross the Indian Ocean in three weeks. This was only a speculation though, in his experience as a captain he knew not of any routes where the weather responded accordingly. Three weeks – rounded up to six.

Spirits were high in the crew, Thomas especially elated despite having to learn the workings of a ship from scratch as they entered the great vastness of an ocean. His eagerness to learn was refreshing though, like a child at the first day of school, which came as no surprise since he'd had nothing new to learn for years, but Robertson foretold it would wear and either a hardy sailor or loathsome brute would become of Thomas's enthusiasm. Of the crew, they were pleased to be on the move again; that much was evident, even if their work was hindered by their bandaged hands. Those cuts would leave scars, a permanent reminder of that island as if they didn't already have one. That mental scar would never truly heal, that would continue to scream itself open again and again, zapping spirits of their richness every time they looked for Hugh above board.

How well the crew would fare dealing with Hugh's violent departure and an extensive time in the open ocean was hard to guess; Jim Robertson would have to find out the hard way. Open oceans were a test to anyone. He'd heard from other sailors that open oceans were the nutcrackers and the crew aboard a ship were its walnuts. The weakest chipped first, that much had always been true. *I need to keep a close eye on them,* he noted, holding on to the wheel heading south-east, unaware his grip was tightening on the rungs. He was afraid, and any sailor who said they wasn't, was foolish: fear was an enemy to avoid, yes, but it had to be faced. It was the drive to push onward, evermore the reason to get out. As he looked at his crew at work on the deck and upon the spars of the masts, he hoped they were afraid: fear was to get them through this.

Scanning the belaying pins, the quartermaster saw a line was loose and retied the figure-of-eight without thinking. He brushed over the others, checking their security and continued his round of the deck, hitching some lines and reefing others, adding where needed and pulling that which needed to be pulled. Keeping himself busy was helping, but when he stopped his body felt like it was about to implode, not to mention the increasing pain in his calf that was sharpening to a point of agony, but he couldn't bring himself to check it. Pursing his lips to force back a retch, he found the cabin boy splitting hemp fibres from the ropes for caulking, sitting against the mainmast with the sun in his eyes. His hands were red and blistered, but his cuts were healing. Splitting that hemp must've been bloody agony though. 'Alright Rob, my lad?' Joseph asked.

Rob looked up, squinting, his face colourless and bleak. 'Fine. I'm . . . doing alright.' The look of him said anything but. 'How goes you?'

He forced a smile, 'never better. Shipshape.'

There was a forced chuckle, but not at Joseph. Rob looked down to the rope in his hands. 'My mother used to say she was fine all the time. Nothing got to her or made her ill, even though you could see in her face she wasn't up to dick. I remember seeing her two days 'fore she died, on her deathbed, pale and ghostly she was with a bad case of the morbs, and I asked her how she felt. "I'm fine, little Hare, doing fine. Don't you worry."' He glanced back up to Joseph, 'she was lying. All along she'd been lying. She'd felt that bad that she had to lie to me about how she was feeling, even on her deathbed, and I never understood. For once I wanted her to say how she was really feeling. To tell me the truth. It would've made me feel better knowing she could be honest with me. And now here I am doing the exact same thing.'

'She was just trying to protect you, mate.'

'Protect me from what? I could see what was happening, I knew she was nearly passing, who wouldn't? She was thin and pale, dark rings around her eyes and grey wafers for lips. When I think about it, it makes me angry as well as sad. I . . .' he didn't finish his sentence, not knowing what would come out next.

Sensing the confusion, he changed tack, 'what did she die from?'

'A type of cancer, they say. Fought it well, she did, a long and hard battle, held out longer than we all expected, but it caught her. It catches everyone in the end. Rich, poor, nasty, nice, innocent, criminal – we all end up in the same hole one day. There an't no escaping it.' He split more fibres, plucking them and putting them in a sack.

'You don't seem scared of it.'

'Scared of what? Death?' he paused, thought, then replied, 'it's something we've all got to face one day. You can spend your life running from it, hiding from it, fighting it, but it makes no matter; it'll be waiting for the right moment to take you on. I've seen enough of it to know what it is, and that sometimes it's an escape from the torments of life so you can rest at last. I don't know, parts of it frighten me but I'd rather welcome it as a patient guardian to take me onward than be scared to join it on my next journey. It's only my body that will die anyway, my soul will live on to seek new adventures. Mother feared it at first, then toward the end, she . . . she just wanted to be free from the chains cancer had locked her in. She accepted her situation and welcomed her fate.'

Joseph looked at the lad in awe. He'd never thought about it like that; if anything, the boy made death sound like an enlightening experience, that there was nothing to fear. *He's only fifteen! Then again, I suppose he's seen enough to become philosophical.* Squatting in front of him, he said, 'Rob, if you want the truth, I'll give it to you straight.' The boy's eyes were curious, 'I feel absolute shite, godawful horse-piss. I'm constantly exhausted and have a pounding headache from the lack of sleep and dehydration. I've lice that itch and hands that hurt and I'm constipated daily. That Tangena has messed me up and I don't think it'll be a quick affair.'

Rob smiled an honest smile. 'Thanks Joseph, I needed that.'

He nodded and shook his shoulder, getting to his feet, 'have you spoke to Dave, seen how he's feeling? Much the same as us?'

'Last I checked he said he felt like death was teasing him into an early grave.'

Joseph nodded, 'finally, something we can agree on.' There was something pleasurable in knowing Dave felt unwell. He left Rob to his picking and with a quick step made his way over to the railing to retch hard, spilling bile to the waves. Wiping his mouth, he groaned and wondered how long this torture was to last. His coat fluttered in the breeze and the salt in the sea air tasted acrid to his scorched taste buds. Another gag and another heaving retch, but it failed to produce anything.

'How are you feeling, Joseph?' He heard Thomas ask from beside him.

Joseph glanced up, surprised to see that Thomas had sheared his hair and cut his beard off. Stubble and scabs were a patchwork over his head, which looked remarkably smaller than before; his ears stuck out and his jawline was pronounced, but it was an improvement from the yeti they had recruited. 'Awful. How long is this to last, Thomas?' he groaned.

He held a coiled rope over his thin shoulder and moved with the rocking of the deck. 'Not sure. Not many people live to tell the tale if truth be told. It will pass though, as everything does. Everything is only temporary: with situations as well as emotions. Once it's out of your system, I'm sure you'll start to feel better.'

Joseph frowned at his uplifting attitude; unsure he could've had this type of mindset after so long in imprisonment. 'How are you so positive after so long in that pit? How are you not more angry and bitter?'

Thomas chuckled, giving a friendly smile, 'I was, for a long time, until I realised it wasn't getting me anywhere. Eventually the anger runs short of energy and this identity you'd kept alive, this false angry self you thought was you, crumbles and deflates. You're left with nothing but questions about who you really are – you lose yourself, yet find acceptance for it and in that, you recognise your true self. I accepted my present situation for what it was: merely a transition period. I embraced presence in my life and by doing so, found the wonder and faith in everyday things, simple things. I found joy in the mundane and liberated myself without escaping.'

Blinking, Joseph tried to comprehend. He'd never heard anyone speak this way. 'What is this presence you keep talking about?

'It's just being. Being here. Now. Listening to your senses without thought interrupting. You have no idea how much thoughts get in the way and distract you from the world. What do you hear?'

Joseph frowned again, not understanding but he listened anyway. 'I hear the waves and the hull breaking through them. I hear the wind in the sails, the creaking of the lines.'

'What do you feel?'

'The deck beneath me. The hard wood under my palms. Sea spray. My stomach churning and my body hurting.'

He laughed, 'nothing can root you better than sickness. You don't need my help to be present. You're already there.' He placed a hand on Joseph's shoulder. 'Try not to overthink things too much. Learn to let things go. Let them be. It's a long road, but it's the most rewarding road you will ever walk. Trust me.' Thomas left him by the railing, just as he retched again and draped himself over the wood in exhaustion, trying to grasp everything Thomas had just said.

Suddenly Victoria slipped in beside him, 'Joseph? I brought you some bread and fish if you fancied it? Brought you some water too.'

He had to look away, the sight made his empty stomach roil. 'Thanks Vic, but I'll pass. Not hungry.'

'You've got to eat something; you look as pale as a morning mist.' She said with concern. 'Have you eaten anything today?'

A shake of the head and another retch, again with no produce. 'Christ, Joseph! Here, take the bread.' She offered and was faced with another refusal.

She opened his palm and stuffed the chunk of bread inside. 'Eat it. Nibble at it at least. It'll do no good for us to reach Australia without you. It'll do no good to not have you here with me. I'm strong and able, but I don't know what I'd do. I . . .' she paused and blushed, 'I like having you around.'

The thought of Victoria being alone with Dave, being alone with Billy, Thomas or even Jim caused something inside him to stir, and this time it didn't feel like another upheaval. He didn't want it, the thought was not approached with fondness, so he lifted the bread and took a small bite much to his body's rejection. She smiled warmly, so he took a bigger bite. It could've been a lump of lard in his hand for all he could taste, but to keep her happy he'd keep sticking it in and chewing for all he was worth.

She leaned against the bulwark, peering down to the rolling waves. The way the wind ruffled through her hair with an almost soothing caress gave Joseph's eyes a break from looking at hardship. She moved her hair over her shoulder, exposing her face and neck, leaving him wanting to do nothing else than kiss it. The breeze was irritating her, it seemed, her hair kept throwing locks out of place, so she pulled off the piece of string tied to her wrist and used it to tie her hair up, but still loose strands danced and waved freely. The sun glowed upon her face, enhancing her cheekbones and catching the scar on her cheek. *Just kiss her, you fool.* He leaned in, and she leaned away. 'You've got vomit in your beard, Joseph. Maybe later.'

He drew back, ashamed and wiped his beard, only imagining what he looked like. No wonder she drew away. Looking to the horizon, Victoria was lost in thought. 'What will happen once we reach Australia?' she asked after a time.

Taking a small bite of bread, he mulled it around in his dry mouth and swallowed, surprised his body accepted it. 'I'm not sure. Keep looking, see if the locals know anything. In the meantime, there's got to be something we've missed in the clues, another hidden riddle or poem saying what to do. I haven't checked the papers that were in the chest from Gabon yet, perhaps something's in there we missed.'

'Jim's already checked them. There wasn't much on offer.'

'Oh. I'll have a look anyway; a second opinion never hurts. Maybe he missed something, some detail that needs a different perspective. I'm sure there'll be something.'

'I suppose so,' she paused. 'They didn't know where they were going to end up, that's what I don't get. They've laid this trail behind them – complex enough to rid of any wasters but clear enough for the determined to follow once the clues have been found, only to head to a place they don't know and leave nought but a scrap of paper with smudges, scratches and missing links to tell us what direction to head in. There's nothing there to tell us what to look for when we get there. Why do that? Why lead us this far into it but give us only a heading to sail to? Is the clue a fake?' she said with a hint of annoyance.

He blinked, unable to answer any of her questions and he guessed she wasn't expecting him to. Replying as best as he could, he said, 'I never told you how I came about the scroll, did I? It was a job Mad Vinny (not sure if you've heard of him; probably not in which case lucky you) passed on to me. Told me it was in this house and I should check it out, so I took the job. When I entered–'

'–Broke in, you mean?'

He smiled playfully. 'When I was inside, a hunt like this one was set up throughout the house, small hints telling me to try this spot next, leaving me to figure each one out. They got harder as it went on until I got stuck and couldn't rack my brains hard enough to find the answer,' *until I saw flatly,* 'but after some sense came knocking, the answer was in front of me all along, leading me to the attic where the scroll lay hidden and waiting.

'My point is, there's always an answer so there's got to be one here too. They couldn't have left a dead end; they wouldn't have left a trail of this scale unfinished, so I'll have a check over what we've got. The scroll, the clues, try the glasses with different papers and have a hunt for anything that gives any hint of what to look for.' *And pray that it's not a fake.*

'And if you find nothing? What then?' She stared at him, hoping he had a plan. Thoughts were behind her clear intelligent eyes. *If this leads to a dead end, I don't know what will become of us. The clues, this trail, the trove; they're the only things holding us together.* Joseph wasn't the only one to notice that everyone carried their own concealed weapon. It was a sign of fracture; trust was splitting between them and she wondered if Joseph realised the stakes.

Pursing his lips, he leaned on the railing and listened to the squeaking lines, flapping sails and movement of the water as they ploughed onward. He chewed on the bread, beginning to feel less disorientated. Truth be told, he hadn't had much time to consider the possibilities since discovering their destination; his fragile stomach had seen to that. Now though, he pondered. *What then indeed?*

Imagining the scenario, it seemed a dead end: Upon arrival of the Australian coast, they know the treasure is somewhere within the continent. The gravity that they have about three million square miles of landmass where within it could be buried hits home, and they number only nine. They scour the scrolls and papers for anything else and find nothing. They question the local colonies in desperation, all of which know nothing of any forgotten chest. Confrontation arises, and violence ensues. The crew splits and the treasure remains buried until the end of days, the loot lost to the earth, unclaimed, rendering the entire venture fruitless. Lost in a strange land, they have no money to spend on lodgings or food; no skills to trade; no shelter to sleep in; no knowledge of the wildlife and insects that swarm the country; no friends to rely on, and no hope for a worthwhile future since they are escaped convicts in a foreign land colonised by the one country they'd tried evading: Britain. *And we all get caught, slapped in chains and thrown behind bars to serve the rest of our sentences in an Australian prison instead of a British one.* He had to smile it sounded that awful, *well, at least the weather will be better.*

There was no way he was going to suggest that to Victoria. That scenario he classed as the worst. They'd just entered the Indian Ocean, time was still on their side; plenty of time to muse and ponder, presume and predict, and hope. 'What then?' she asked again.

He looked to her. 'We do what we can. We keep looking forward, moving onward and we deal with the problems when they arise. It's all we can do, elsewise we'll spend our time speculating about possibilities that mightn't ever happen and worry the confidence from our veins until we arrive in a spool of negativity – never able to figure out where the chest is buried because our time was spent worrying what to do rather than thinking on where to look. These are our lives, we've only the one and we're in control of them. And, at the minute, we're sailing to Australia with the sun on our backs and the spray on our faces, breathing in the air of the Indian Ocean on the other side of the hemisphere, where we could've been still locked away in prison, rotting with withered dreams. We'll find it Victoria. Trust me, when the time comes, we'll know where to look.' He wasn't sure whether that was the answer she was looking for, but it was the one he gave.

Her eyes looked at him thoughtfully, and she smiled, then she glanced back to the horizon. 'You know, I've known people who'd do anything for money. When I was growing up, men asked me how much I was and was prepared to pay me even though I wasn't a prostitute, and one of my friends told me I was being ridiculous for refusing because I'd turned down offered coin. I was thirteen at the time.

'When I was in a workhouse for a time, I met a woman who worked endlessly, tirelessly, whose fingers bled continuously through bursting blisters, but when I told her to stop, to rest, she said, "I can't, I need to earn, I need the money." She later got gangrene because of those open wounds and had to lose those bleeding fingers.

'I was twenty-one and courting a man who owned his own accommodation, had a stable job, earning well and was charming; a rarity hard to come by. Soon, he squandered his wealth on gambling and ale. He lost the house, the job and then me, and when I asked him why he thought everything had fallen as such he told me it was the money, he didn't have enough - he never had enough. I myself couldn't really comprehend how he didn't have enough when to me a home, a job, income and charm was all that mattered.

'But you, Joseph, you're the only person I've met who has travelled to the other side of the world, who's left everything behind; faced starvation, dehydration, cuts and bruises; learned to sail a ship and survived a bloody Tangena trial, and yet you don't seem one bit interested in the money that's locked away in the chest. Many people would be in this only *for* the money, I should think half the crew are. I'm interested in it, I shan't lie. Many would only push themselves this far for the wealth at the end and the status that would come with it, but I haven't heard you talk about the gold once, if at all. The way you talk about everything is very refreshing, don't get me wrong, but I can't help but wonder. The question I ask is, why? Why do all this if you aren't in it for the gold at the end? Why did you set out on this trail in the first place, bringing us with you?' She asked, as honest as the sky was blue.

It was a good question. He leaned on the bulwark, feeling the waves rumble through the wood and the sea air run cold fingers through his hair. Truthfully, he'd been kept so busy picking up the pieces of the trail he hadn't thought about the contents of the chest. Now the image was upon him, gold painted a pretty picture; rubies and gems and pearls, jewellery and trinkets of priceless value; his fingers began to twitch as the old desire arose to take them, steal them, all proceeds to the trusty bank of the Winter Funds. *Yer only as good as the things you steal,* Vinny's deep voice echoed, *keep yer feet light and yer fingers lighter, Mister Winter… And you stay out of trouble, Mister Jenkins.* He pictured the glittering splendour running through his fingers, shimmering; the loot of a lost history, and he knew what to do with it.

'A new life. Not just for me, but for us all.' He replied after a time, 'a fresh start. The contents of the chest haven't left my mind, I still think of it, but *finding* it has kept me busy enough for the time being. I need the money as much as the next person; I was jailed for pilfering let's not forget, I had a reputation to uphold; I was Trace and the want of more coffers kept me in the business. I earned well from it, and because of it I lost my life in London. I lost everything because I wanted more. If I hadn't left to do that last job, if I hadn't of been so greedy and selfish, I would've been home, around the hearth with a full belly and a warm bed. Instead, I'm here with a fresh perspective; it's not a case of want any more. It's need.' He took a bite of bread.

'I didn't realise it, but the London life was poisoning me. Society and its whims; moving from one scandal and trend to the next to distract itself from its own aggravating problems. The papers, those petty evening wheezes, selling any story that grabbed the eye even though the truth was exaggerated and only half told. The upper classes forever shitting on the lower and the lower classes forever grudging the upper. People always judging, people crying, people dying and still more flocked to the capital with that childhood dream of creating a business and getting rich to gain status. Poppycock and bollocks to it. Codswallop: that's what it is. That life led me to believe I wanted to be like one of those rich sod's swaggering about without a care in the world except keeping in that high class, but out here I saw what really mattered.

'This journey, it's stripped back everything now, so I'm over the moon when there's a bit o' breeze in the air to fill the sails, or the sun's up so I an't going to be wet all day. When the hold is full, so I know we won't all starve, or the sound of seabirds so I know we're approaching land. I don't know, I guess it's just a taste of freedom, an't it? Hard to come by but it makes you care more about the smaller things.' He looked to her, 'I've learned there's more to life than money. Happiness in yourself is worth more; it certainly lasts longer and feels richer.'

Suddenly he felt the rush again, not of love but of sickness. Holding onto the railing he felt his mouth dry up, but he swallowed hard and took a gulp of water, feeing it recede after a moment. He felt her arm around his shoulder, 'Joseph, are you alright?'

He sighed deeply, feeling his body relax, 'I'm fine.' He replied with Rob's tale on his mind, and the possibilities of the future offering hope to the hardy seadog. 'I'm feeling better.'

Chapter Twenty-Nine

Sweat ran down his brow and his throat felt as crispy as the land around him. The relentless heat of the sun delivered its blazing reminder of thirst and all the deadly qualities that came with it; already he could feel moisture being sucked from his body. Before long his wits would be drained too. Madness threatened . . . *I mustn't let my mind wander; it may not have legs but it wanders further than my body.* Running his thick tongue across his cracked lips felt like he was sanding down wood, every step was crossing a mile of hot coals; he cursed every moment that he forgot to bring some container of water. *I won't last much longer*, Joseph realised as he pushed on through shifting sand. Although, one thing he was pleased with was the boots laced to his feet.

Aimlessly, he wandered further into the desert; morally, he couldn't have felt lower. In his hand was a scrap of parchment, in the other a broken compass. The scroll was blank, he'd seen. Nothing was on it to guide him and the compass pointed to every direction it could offer but bore no heading; still, his feet continued to step forward, his boots sinking in the rushing sand. *There's nothing to guide me anyway, there's nought here but dunes.* Landmarks were nowhere to be found; directions were useless; why, then, he persisted to walk through such harsh conditions in search of a lost chest was baffling.

The metal of the compass casing began to burn in his hand, began to sear his already burnt palm; he could feel it but did not let it go in fear of getting lost. Joseph winced; *I need it. I need it to guide me. I need to find the chest.* He groaned and held on, smelling his dusty surroundings and his cooking flesh, which only enhanced his disgust since it smelled wonderful; his stomach groaned with want.

In his lonesome, he wandered the dry plain, never questioning which way but forever wondering where. Never questioning why he was so alone, but forever wondering what had happened. *They were here, right beside me, where did they go? Why did they leave?* They'd been with him for most of the journey, he knew that for certain, but now they'd vanished, disappeared from his life like the endless grains sweeping across the dunes in the warm gusts that appeared every now and then. He knew he should've cared for their absence, but the power of the sun was blinding, and he found himself concerned only with his own mortality. *I need a drink. Anything. Any drink. Piss, stale and stagnant, give it to me strong and neat and pour another. I need it.*

Joseph looked about himself, to the curling tips of the dunes, to the wisps of coloured breeze brushing down the sides, his scorched road to infinity. Looking was painful to his eyes, the yellow of the sand had turned white in the sun, so squinting through his lashes was as best as he was to get. *I need to see . . . I need to see the chest, to find it, open it. Make it all worthwhile.* Every step was hot, the heat was melting away his soles and beginning to cook his feet inside; slow roasting them like a hog, the burst blisters sizzling like fat from the flank. Saliva watered his bulbous tongue at the thought of his roasted feet, yet it hindered the preservation of his throat which seemed to parch even more.

He felt he was close. How, he didn't know, but the feeling was strong, and it tugged at him and forced him to run. *No, don't run! You need the strength. You need to keep the strength for the dance with Victoria.* His feet, those silly old flapping things, wouldn't listen and pushed harder through, never caring if he slipped and burnt his hands on the hot sand.

A gust of wind pushed his back. Not a low breeze that tore at his ankles, a full body gust. Turning, he saw it. A tremendous billowing thunderous cloud of sand rolling across the dunes toward him. *That's not sand,* he thought, *it's the dust from the people who've died out here trying to reach this chest. None of them got it. But I will.* He pushed harder, his blistering feet caked with bloody sand, his slit eyes blinded by the bleakness, each gasp of breath a pain as he sucked in grains, rinsing and exfoliating his lungs with the desert. Even now, as he pushed, he could feel himself beginning to crumble, joining the dust of the hopeless, slain by the honed sword of the beating sun; unbreakable.

The shovel was there! Waiting for him, it was. Standing sentry beside its pride and joy. He knew the hole would be there. The hole it had dug was dark, dark as a grave and cold, cold as a frost on the soul. Yet its contents were far more important; what lay in its base, its bottom, its heart. A value of unknown price. It was his future down there; he'd come to claim it.

Joseph ran with all his strength, pushing through the pain of the burning and melting and crumbling, smelling only the cooking of his own flesh. The sandstorm was behind and the shovel ahead, but he still checked the broken compass and saw it was being held in charred blackened bone. Even the crows couldn't pick that as clean. Despite everything, he smiled.

Reaching the hole, he dove to his knees at the edge and heard an Irish voice in the sky, a voice he knew was familiar. '*Happy Devil's Day to ye', Joe!*' Joseph peered over the edge to the dark cool depths and saw three figures crowding around the chest, *his* chest. Scott's Trove itself. With rotted hands, they picked at the edges and pulled it open. 'No!' he screamed, '*leave it! Leave it shut! It's cursed, I tell you! It's brought nothing but death and suffering! Leave it closed!*'

The figures looked up. Harold Arms was there, grinning with black teeth and flesh that slid from his bones.

Poppy Mills met his glare with a vacant hopeless eye, her skin pallid and papyrus, her body feeble and gaunt.

Hugh Jackson reached inside the chest and brought forth handfuls of gold, so much it was slipping between his fingers, sliding over his bloated belly. He peered up to the edge, to Joseph. 'I don't want to die. Please. Forgive me. Remember me.' He said in a frightened childlike voice, then howled. Howled and screamed and hollered as his insides dissolved. Piercing Joseph's ear, ringing in his head, echoing to every part he knew of – stamping itself there, branding itself in his memory – haunting him, tormenting him, torturing him with the hideous shrieks of a dying son from a long line of blacksmiths.

Joseph awoke with a start, sweating heavily into his hammock. The loose shirt he wore clung to him and his hair felt thick and hot. Even the air in the berth was stuffy. 'Oh, Christ.' He groaned, holding his pounding head. Vomit was at the back of his throat again, but he could just about control it. He slipped from his hammock and into his boots and changed his shirt before making his way over to the scuttlebutt for water.

His head reeled as he climbed the ladder and lifted the hatch. The deck was empty in the light colours prior to sunrise, apart from one who stood afore the ship, tying and retying a length of rope upon the forecastle, looking out to the watery dawn beyond the bowsprit. Last night during the evening meal, the captain had reminded them of the importance of the dogwatch now they could not anchor properly, with strictly no dozing. True, they'd all shared their duties of the watch before but not out here; to watch over the ship during the witching hours. An agreement was shared, but a volunteer for the first ocean dogwatch was harder to find. In the end, Dave James was chosen to take the first night shift and Joseph was now regretting coming up to deck, knowing he was alone with him.

Some good might come of it, he tried to persuade himself, *maybe if you just try talking to him, getting to know him he won't be such a bastard?* Victoria had been badgering him of late to make amends with the man, to avoid another future confrontation; perhaps now was the time to give it a go? *We might even laugh about all this one day, perhaps?*

He didn't want to return to the stuffy berth or his damp hammock, to his recurring nightmares and the screams of the dying man. He wouldn't be able to get back to sleep and, judging by the light, dawn was not far off; the bell would soon be rung to wake everyone. Slowly, begrudgingly, he wandered up to the forecastle with the heavy footfall of an adolescent after having been told what to do. Dave looked over, glared, and looked away. 'Morning.' The quartermaster tried.

Dave nodded, looking down at his rope.

'Get any shuteye?' Joseph asked, leaning against the railing feeling the fresh breeze up his shirt. Goosebumps ran along his skin.

'A bit. Not much.'

'Hugh keeping you up?'

He looked to him, knowing exactly what he meant. Dave had been having similar nightmares. They all had. 'That whole island's been keeping me up.'

And it would've helped the situation if you hadn't of stolen their bloody red rubies in the first place. Biting his tongue was a tiring business, but he managed it once more. A nod was used instead, 'it was a place I'd like to forget. Doubt I will though.' *Not with Hugh screaming away in my head.*

'Aye.'

There you go Joseph, an agreement. You can agree on something. Progress. An awkward silence settled. Joseph looked out to the brightening sky and the faint mist settling over the waves, then over to the seaman. His black hair was thick and dry, dandruff peppering through it like snow. His face was lean, a large forehead with deep-set creases and a scar that cut through the dark stubble of his cheek to his jaw. Long bushy sideburns cloaked his rounded ears. Once, a handsome man he would've been if not for his gnawing personality. Joseph decided to make amends. 'I . . . I'm sorry for putting that knife to your throat and for what I said to you before.'

Dave looked at him and his brows furrowed, he blinked, confused. Eventually, he nodded in acceptance and kept the silence.

Joseph tried again. 'Bit chilly this morning, an't it?'

'It's cold every morning. There's no cloud overhead, nothing to keep the heat in.'

He feigned interest, 'Oh, I didn't know you had interest in the weather.'

Dave scowled at how sarcastic it sounded. 'I don't. It's observation, not interest.'

Despite his name possessing the season, Joseph Winter had never felt colder standing next to such a bitter character. *Why? Why so bitter, what made you into the man you are now?* Half of him wanted to know, the other half was scared to know. One question burned though, and it blurted out before he could halt his tongue. 'Can I ask, and I know there's nought I can do to change anything and what's done is done, but why *did* you steal that ruby when that lad Honlu told us not to?'

He heard a sigh and a mutter. *Cheeky bastard.* 'Why did *you* steal all the things you did when the law ordered you not to? Why did *you* keep going when you knew it was wrong? I'd have thought you of all people would've understood why I did it. I wanted it, so I took it, so I can add it to my share once we find the treasure. A big pile of gold and jewellery with a nice red ruby, rare as rare can be sitting on top of it all. Wouldn't that be a pretty sight? That's if those blackies hadn't have taken it off me.'

'Honlu told us not to, though. They were sacred to that village as part of their culture; they bury those diamonds with their dead for Christ sake. If you hadn't of stolen it, we wouldn't have faced that trial and Hugh would be on–'

'Oh, so it's all my fault now, is it? How fucking typical. Funny how it's never your fault, no matter what you do. You're always in the clear, the mighty Trace of London. Nothing could ever catch you, until it did. You ended up in the same rank old prison I ended up in.'

'No. I'm just saying if you'd have listened to the boy and not taken the red one then we'd all have survived and would be on the ship now.' It sounded blunt and harsh. It *was* blunt and harsh, but Joseph didn't care anymore. *Sorry Vic, I tried to be nice.*

'Oh right, and you always listened to the rules and abided by them, did you? Always listened to the law, always played by the rules and never did anything wrong? You talk so much shit I can smell it on your tongue.' Dave taunted, 'remember who you are and what you did, *Trace.* You were well known about the streets for your numerous crimes and you wanted people to know and remember, so don't think for a minute I'm going to forget all that now you're talking like a vicar and walking like a saint. Take that fucking halo off your head and come back to the real world. We're convicts that escaped and got ourselves on a boat, but that don't change who we are.

'I'm a criminal. We all were and still are. You want to know me? My story? I know you've been dying to ask. I'm a fuckin' low life street rat who grew up with a missing mother, a drunk, abusive, manipulative father; holes in my stolen shoes and a bed on the floor along with the other twenty people we lived with. And the rats too, they loved to scurry around the room, especially with all that rotten food and the privy that was never emptied. At least the hearth was always hot, hot enough for pokers to glow red, hot enough to burn a boy's skin in the name of discipline and the Lord.' Button by button he opened his shirt to reveal horrid splodges of healed skin in between his hairy chest, skin that had healed but hadn't forgotten. 'He starved me until I got rickets, hit me black and blue and then abandoned me to fend for myself when I was seven. Left me, he did, without ever showing any affection or love. But I found my own way to survive. I'm a criminal, that much is true, but not for what you'd think. I thieved and sheltered with vagabonds, scavenged for clothes and food, sold my shoes for half a loaf of bread. I ran with gangs for the protection they offered and to keep out of the workhouse; I did almost anything to keep in their ranks, learning of the limits of society and the people it tried so hard to discard. In my youth, one of the gangsters took me whoring and I didn't stop for years, finally understanding the purpose of women as none had ever shown me love until then, until I met the lovely Dolly and found a type of love that was different.

'She was a prostitute, my favourite one, but she retired as soon as she found out she was pregnant with my child. We married, and we had ourselves a boy, Dolly and me – we made little John. Lovely boy he was, always laughing, until his first birthday when polio took hold o' his leg, shrivelling and twisting it up. John didn't laugh no more. He was in agony and was in even more agony when it spread to his arm. A cripple, that's what he was to be, for the rest o' his life. He'd never work and have a job, he'd never ride a horse; I'd never be able to play games with him, I'd never see him grow and meet girls and have a family; he'd always be named and laughed at, and that's if he lived. Have you ever had that Joseph, have you ever woken in the night to the screams of your child in pain, knowing there's nothing you can do to help him, knowing his future is as bleak as the city he lived in? No. I can't imagine you would. Why would you, you're too wrapped up in your own petty problems.

'Dolly fell pregnant again and that's when I went out, started stealing again, food for the family and medicine for John, started meeting a few friends from the old days, started drinking again. Started spending less time at home, less time with little John. I wanted a break from the crying, and from Dolly's weeping. And don't you look at me like that, you ignorant prick, I'd like to see you sit at home with nothing else to listen to except pain and misery. I'd steal the food, what little I could, and pilfer medicines and potions and herbs for John, anything to help. To shut him up. After a time, the crying got to me. It was driving me up the wall. It was all I ever heard in the end, the constant drone of John's whines and cries, driving into my head, never to stop, never to settle.

'Dolly kept crying, and I kept drinking. I became abusive toward her, becoming more like my father. To numb the pain and earn the pennies she started back in business again, the only thing she knew how to do; small at first but it rolled on. I'd sometimes come home drunk to hear my wife hard at work in the bedroom, groaning and moaning like a virgin, and the sounds of John wailing from behind the curtain, drilling into my head. Afterwards, we'd fight; she's arguing we need the money and I'm arguing 'cause she's fucking men whilst I'm home, and John is still droning on like a fly buzzing around my ear.

'One day I got too drunk: the world-spinning type. Heard my wife fucking another man again and my son bleating away. I blacked out, then, and don't remember a thing. When I came to, I had blood on my hands, spew round my mouth and a head that was knocking the twelve chimes of Big Ben. Bloody footsteps trailed to the other room where my pregnant wife lay naked with her throat slit, her client dead too, and my crippled son next to her with his head turned the other way around. I thought maybe someone else came in and did it, but I knew it was me. Their blood was on my hands.

'The pain was excruciating; the guilt was unbearable. I wanted to top myself for what I'd done. The man who I became was not who I wanted to be. I did things I'd never wanted to and turned into the one person I despised: my father. The root of it all. If he'd have shown me love, maybe my life wouldn't have been so full of pain. The peelers caught me, and I went willingly without any question or grievance and hoped for the noose. I was still waiting for my session in court a year later, but by that time I realised I didn't even have hope. I missed Dolly, John and my unborn child every day and it hurt like a gaping maw. I'd have done anything to escape the pain, the guilt and the memories. I'd have escaped, sailed a ship, starved myself, abused myself, poisoned myself, to escape the agony of my past. Then one day, as I'm with my old friend Harold, I hear a strange, funny tale about a leprechaun and a magic mask by some Irishman. It made me laugh for the first time in years, so I found him the next day to find out the ending and there he was standing with the mighty Trace of London, the ghost that could never be caught – apprehended and incarcerated, imprisoned like the rest of us.

He tied his rope into a tight bowline, a noose, then looked to him, his voice tired and flat. 'So, don't bother with your new talk of innocence, Joseph Winter. No amount of sea air or riddles will ever change what you or any of us did. We've all got our pasts on this ship; we're all sinners behind the masks. I just don't bother wearing mine; I'm a monster, I know I am, and I'm not going to try and be anything different. I deserve punishment, and this voyage has been appropriate penance for everything I've done. Yes, I stole some of their special gems, but at least I'm not pretending to be some false hero. You an't anything special Joseph, no one is.'

Joseph stood, stunned. Small wonder why he was always so bitter and feisty, with a past like that anyone would be aggressive. It was clear he was not over it, buried it perhaps, but he was far from free. One thing was for sure, he never wanted to become like Dave; a fat caterpillar too engorged on its own flaws that it didn't realise one cocoon could give it wings to fly. He'd done things in his life he regretted, who hadn't? but those regrets didn't define his being or days to come. He wouldn't let them. *I was Trace, I still am, but I need to be someone else, someone different now.* He looked him in the eye and sympathised, from one impoverished street rat to another. 'The past is the past, Dave. We've got to move on to find a better future. There's always hope.'

Dave James seemed to find that amusing. 'Right. A future. Roping a group of hopeless fools on a wild goose-chase to find some treasure we an't sure even exists, leaving corpses in your wake.'

'I didn't kill anyone.' He admitted.

The man looked at him coldly, 'tell that to Harold, Poppy and Hugh, who I can still hear screaming, along with my dead son.' He shoved by him and thumped down to the deck to ring the morning bell, leaving Joseph on the forecastle. Dave then turned back suddenly, 'oh, and let's not forget our dutiful Mister Johnson, our first boatswain who's now abed on the sea floor. The master criminal has upgraded to a multiple murderer, it seems to me. Looks like I'm not the only monster that found its way to sea. In a way, we're now the same. Killers running away from our pasts.'

Dawn was clear and bright, burning away the morning mist, and the wind that had pushed them stayed on course, allowing them another day of passage through this watery desert. Despite the beautiful morning colours, the decent portions of food, (the ability to keep the food down) and the day's duties, Joseph felt lost, coasting through the hours with Dave's life of misery on his mind. He sympathised with him, a tragic tale of abuse and pain and death, an almost classic reoccurring generational chain. Surely it had to be on his mind every day, memories replaying, making sure he was to never forget – turning him into a callous goat who'd gotten so used to using his horns he'd forgotten how to bleat. Their chat hadn't made the progress he'd thought of; if anything, he planned to avoid him even more. *The man's bad meat: bow wow mutton if ever I saw one.* No one wanted a dark cloud over their head on a bright day, and Dave was a certain patch of grey that promised rain.

The day passed smoothly with wind in the sails and, as Robertson had told them, every hour their sails were full and not fighting was a blessing they needed to count. Travelling at a steady eight knots with a good tailwind, they made good progress and the crew were in a better mood after a decent night's rest. Thomas was working away at the laborious jobs in high spirits and learning well, much to the approval of Robertson and the deckhands, and Joseph was relieved to be feeling better, if not for the pain that was spreading in his leg. It didn't retreat now; the pain remained as a constant dull throb. Ignorance was something he had grown up with and had to face from day to day on the streets, so ignoring it came easily. The seed of doubt was there though, it had already been planted and was beginning to sprout. Sooner or later, he'd have to check on it, he knew. *Later. I'll have a check on it later, I'm sure it's nothing.*

That night, dreams plagued him once again; displaying a vivid projection of the ship this time, except he was the only mate aboard. Searching, he found no one, but knew he had to find the chest. It was always the chest. The loot. The trove. The motive, the purpose, the fate he was tangled up in, slowly tugging him by his neck closer but ever farther away. What Joseph failed to discern was whether the tugging came from a line or noose, drawing him closer to the gallows for a swing. Waves crashed about him and the ship veered and swayed, banking, heeling and listing; he stumbled and fell and tried to hold on, but the wood was burning with every touch and the masts and sails were alight with Saint Elmo's Fire. Eventually, he made his way into the captain's cabin and found the corpses of the crew strewn, some with their necks sliced, others with their heads twisted the other way, and in a dark corner Dave stood and said coldly, *'we're all sinners behind the masks. I just don't bother wearing mine . . . Looks like I'm not the only monster who found its way to sea.'* Joseph looked to his hands and saw they were coated in blood. The crew's blood. *He* had killed them. When he looked up, he saw Harold, Poppy and Hugh standing in a dark corner huddled around the chest overlooking the massacre with Dave James. Hugh then opened his mouth once more, that big, big mouth with that loud, loud scream.

When he woke, startled and weary, he was sweating and had a headache that was shooting sparkles behind his eyes. Looking made them hurt, and his leg throbbed heavily, the pain felt as if someone has placed a smouldering ember into his calf. Breathing deeply, he wondered if he was the only victim of these nightly terrors, and then realised he'd made it to the deck, had *woken* on deck. The nightmares were turning into night terrors and he was beginning to see strange visions whilst awake. He hoped that was as far as it went. The notion scared him, and he was frightened to look to the captain's cabin. *It might be a side effect of the Tangena.* Suddenly Yalla's last words to him and with wide eyes he worried whether this was the curse the man had placed upon him.

Once they'd eaten, he caught Rob on the weather deck about to climb the mizzen shrouds. The sun was already bright and hot, and the boy had tied a bandana around his head to keep the sweat from running into his eyes though his dark hair still sprouted over it. 'A minute please, sailor, if you've one to spare.'

Rob nodded, 'aye. I was just about to help Ben unfurl the sails, but I can spare one.'

'Ah, Ben'll be fine for a tick. Listen, have you been sleeping well lately? I've been struggling to get a decent kip for a while now.' He could feel his eyes were sore and tired and he hadn't even been the one on the dogwatch. *I think I'd be better off doing that shift since I'm not resting anyway.*

He shook his head, 'not really. I keep dreaming . . . weird things. Nightmares.'

Nodding, he could feel himself sway. The nights and days were beginning to blur through his mind's exhaustion, everything seemed an out-of-body experience. 'You an't the only one, my boy. I reckon it's the Tangena that's the cause. It must be a side effect or something.'

'I think so. Yesterday I asked Tom if there were any side effects to do with it and he said he wasn't sure since not many people lived to discover any side effects.' He shrugged, 'I suppose we didn't ingest it properly, we didn't drink enough to kill us, but maybe it was enough to mess with our bodies. Why it would cause nightmares I don't know.' Rob shrugged, 'are you alright, Joseph? You don't look so good.'

He felt awful. 'To be frank with you lad, I feel a clock short of a cog, a dog without a tail, and these lucid night terrors an't helping. I think I'm beginning to hallucinate too.'

'What's that mean?' Just then Benjamin called down from the mizzenyard for the cabin boy, so Rob had to scurry, 'I'll see you later, Quart'.' He watched him go and decided it was time to raise concern about his injury; his leg was pulsing and painful and wasn't even bearing weight. Victoria was who he needed, and he found her in the hold with Tess, lidding the tops of the wicker baskets and counting the supplies to report. 'Victoria – a word.' Sweat trickled down his brow.

She smiled warmly, and Tess nodded, understanding. She smiled to both before ascending. 'What is it, my sweet?' Victoria asked him.

'You're the bosun, an't you? Does that mean you've got to deal with injuries and the like as well?' he spoke quickly, feeling weak.

Her face fell, concerned with what he was going to say. 'What's happened? Did someone fall?'

He forced a smile, 'well if I keep it quiet any longer, I think I might. Have a look if you would.' He pulled up his trouser leg to beyond the knee. His calf was the origin of the pain.

She walked closer, holding an oil lamp in her hand. The ship rocked with the waves, rats scurried hither and thither becoming a regularity. 'Joseph, how long have you been keeping this quiet?' she asked plainly.

'Few days, I think. I must've got it running back to the village in Madagascar.'

'Oh, you idiot! Why didn't you say anything sooner? Dash my wig!' she exclaimed as she examined a deep red gash, open, enflamed and spreading up his leg; the wound itself was darkening around the edge and was weeping a foul thick pus. The infection was clear to see as well as smell. She wrinkled her nose. 'Right, follow me. I'm washing it and dressing it as best as I can. Then you're taking some of the opium the Captain's got. Or laudanum.

Or a passage from the bloody Bible. Christ, Joseph, why is it always one thing to the next with you?' she said playfully and irritably as she mounted the ladder to the berth deck, leading him to the sick bay.

He followed dutifully and slipped into the spare hammock they'd strung as she left to fetch the bottle of opium. Upon her return, Thomas followed behind. 'What's the problem?' he asked.

She rolled Joseph's trouser leg up to the knee. 'This.' She gestured, 'I need you to have a look at it, to check it is just a normal infection.'

Joseph frowned, 'why wouldn't it be normal?'

Thomas leaned closer and examined, 'ah! I've seen this one before. Smelled it too. You may need to drain it and cauterise it before you dress it.'

'What?! What is it? Why does it need to be cauterised?' exclaimed Joseph.

Thomas turned away to fetch the knife and a match, replying as he went. 'Why, to kill the flesh-eating parasite you have, of course!'

If Joseph was starting to feel well again, this worked well in making him want to retch. Working quickly, Victoria fetched a pail and sat upon a stool beside him. 'Hopefully, the next time we're in this position it'll be on a bed instead of a hammock.' He said with a tired grin and a feverish sweat frosting on his forehead.

She smiled back and had to have a laugh, 'yes, and maybe we won't have rats running around us . . . First, we need to get that clean though.'

His smile disappeared. *Maybe we won't have rats running around us . . .* was that a subtle message? *Does she know something of the mutiny too?* Realisation hit as he'd done nothing to prevent it, but then again how could you prevent for something as such when you lived and worked in close quarters with the people who were involved in the plot? His thoughts were suddenly cut short as Victoria began to drain his wound of pus and cut off the sections of rotting flesh, making him grit his teeth with the stiff upper lip of a typical Victorian Englishman. Thomas returned and, with haste, gave him a strip of leather to bite on and, before he'd had a second to think, pressed the hot knife into the wound. Only now did Joseph scream. Sweat poured from his forehead and his gums were aflame with the amount of biting pressure. Eventually the pain lessened, and Thomas left the sick bay with the bloody knife and its stench of burning meat. Quickly, Victoria washed the wound as best as she could and Joseph spat out the leather, crying out, '*Fuck!* Christ almighty! Why is it stinging so awfully? I thought this was meant to help.'

'Well, we need to conserve all the freshwater we have, so this is seawater, and it might have a bit of salt in it. It'll sting a touch.' She carefully pressed the rag of salt into his wound, bringing the phrase to life. She then dressed it with some scraps of cloth they'd stripped from their winter clothes for occasions such as this, before making him take some of the opium. 'I'll change the dressing tomorrow. You're lucky it didn't turn gangrenous! Just take it easy for now, don't go doing anything dangerous, alright?'

He smiled dozily from the opium hit. She helped him to his feet. 'On a ship in the open ocean, what could be safer?' Another bead of clammy sweat ran down his face.

Suddenly calls for the quartermaster and boatswain hollered from above board. They looked up, not wanting to answer, not wanting to leave the shade of below deck and sacrifice each other's company. It was not often they got to be alone, but duty was a funny thing; everyone knew they had to pull their weight if they wanted to get through this. 'Down here! Sick bay.' Victoria called back.

Thomas met them in the berth and smiled. 'How are you feeling now, Joseph?'

'Well, I've still got my leg so I'm shipshape matey.' He replied, before observing Thomas's bare chest and the cloth about his head acting as a bandana. 'Tommy-boy, if you knew the heat of that sun you would get that shirt back on, else you'll crisp, pop and be as red as bacon by sunset.'

The man smiled and held up his hands, 'I'll get it back on, don't fret. I was only cooling myself down is all, the spray's nice to feel.' His chest was skinny with proud ribs. Although they ate regularly, the food was slowly dwindling, and they were not eating enough to hide their bones. 'Anyway, Captain's calling for both o' you's.'

They walked to the companionway with Joseph hobbling. 'Victoria,' Thomas asked nervously as they ascended, 'I don't suppose you'd know if Tess is married or anything? Any men she's left behind?'

She smiled as they reached the top, 'she's available I think, Tom, as far as I know. Be careful though, she's a feisty cat when she wants to be.' With a wink, they left Thomas on deck standing bemused, and climbed the ladder aft to the helm where Captain Robertson held the wheel, his hat low to keep the shade on his eyes. The spanker creaked gently behind him.

'Ah! There you two are. Bosun, what's the report on our fodder situation?'

She reported swiftly. 'We've enough to keep us going for a week and a half from this point I reckon. The salted meat is keeping well, but I fear for the fruits and milk. These are things that need to be consumed fresh. They'll begin to rot and sour soon enough if we don't eat them first. Plus, we're running dangerously low on fuel for the stove. It'll be all gone within the next day or two.'

'I see. What of the water?'

'Akin to the food. We've enough in the scuttlebutts and skins to get us through another week, but it's hot weather and we're all sweating; we're drinking nicely but not sustainably.' She moved a lock of hair that fell on her face. 'There's some good news though. We haven't started on the coconuts and we still have the full stock of thirty. I spoke to the translator, Yalla, on our arrival to the village and he was telling me the benefits of them – how they can keep anyone fed and watered for days, that they've got all the essential nutrients to keep you alive, so I'm not particularly worried about the water situation.'

Robertson shook his head lightly, his eye on the compass in his hand. He checked the jibboom pointing outward below the forestaysail, keeping it pointing south-easterly even though there was a slight north-easterly rushing up from the Southern Ocean to test the cut of their sails. 'Aye, nothing to worry about there. Not if we have plenty of coconuts. Men have been marooned throughout time and survived on coconuts for months on end. I once met a man in a pub who claimed he survived for five years on nothing but coconuts.' He shook his head, 'I would've been awed if he wasn't drunk, and it's hard to tell boasts from lies and lies from truths when a man has whisky on his tongue.'

He looked to them, 'in the morning we'll have to get the fruit and milk cleared up, pronto. We already have enough rats on this ship as it is, we don't need maggots and flies adding to the problem. After that, I'm afraid we'll have to start rationing again. We needed a full stock when we reached Madagascar and they gave us what they could, but it wasn't enough to get us through to Australia with full stomachs, which brings me to you, Quartermaster.' He shifted his gaze. 'Over the next few days whilst the winds are kind and not battering, we need nets making. Get Baker and Smith to help you; the Irishman has a knack for knots and the old seadog has experienced fingers. I think we still have some material left to us in the hold to work with.'

Victoria nodded, 'it's being used to catch rats but it's there.'

'Ah, lovely. There you are then. I'm afraid rat-catching is another job that needs to be seen to.' His gaze met Joseph's for a second, then flicked back to the horizon. A double meaning was there no doubt. 'Once you've knotted the net, tie it onto a spare spar; that way when we cast it it'll remain open and you've got more of an area to work with. Wrangle some lines and hooks together and we'll bait the fish toward the nets.'

Joseph understood how but didn't understand when. 'How can we fish when *Victoria*'s on the move?'

'When we stop for the evenings, we'll try our luck with it. I'll ring the bell earlier, so we'll have some daylight to work with. Oceans are teeming with life, they always have been – our ships move along the top of them, barely skimming what lie underneath. I'm sure we can catch something.' He shrugged, 'when the winds drop and change their hands, which they will at some point, we'll have our time to fish properly. As for now, I want to cover as much distance with this wind as possible; it's favourable and not gale force, prime time for sailing. The closer and quicker we reach land, the better.' His hands were white on the rungs of the wheel and he looked as stiff as a plank of wood. Joseph could smell the fear on him.

'Jim,' he spoke carefully, 'we'll get there. We can cross it.'

He looked to him and forced a smile to his pale face, 'aye. We will.' It was surprising for Joseph, seeing an experienced sailor so afraid of the open water. They could spend their entire lives at sea and still fear too much water. *No, it's not the water that scares him; it's losing all sense of direction.* He nodded, 'will that be all, Captain?'

'Aye. That'll be all.' Another falsely confident smile.

'Right, we'll get back to work then.' He said and made his way down the ladder, wincing at his bandaged leg with Victoria following. As he descended, he looked out beyond the bulwark. It was blue. As far as the eye could see was blue water. Nothing more. The horizon was the only feature, the *only* feature, and he suddenly understood the fear.

There were no landmarks, no coastlines or indications of movement; there was nothing to tell them they were sailing forward or making any progress at all. *We could veer off course and we wouldn't even know until the stars came out. Veer off course and end up missing Australia entirely. Christ . . .* The thought was terrifying. No wonder the world took so long to be mapped, the notion of sailing into the unknown, *into* the blank space was frightening, unsettling. It was sailing into a void with nothing but water. He felt his face draining of colour and his stomach rising to his neck.

Explorers had managed it through the ages though, had set their course not even knowing if there was land at the other end. Some had done it for fame and legacy, others for money and sheer patriotism, and then those that had done it because of the thrill it brought. Adventure, that's what it was. A drug. Small wonder why Captain Cook had three voyages and Walter Raleigh forever requested more funds for expeditions; not only to plant the Union Jack on foreign soil but because they were hooked on the high of

ALEX FISHER

unanswered questions; forever craving the next hit in the blank spaces of the map. *Eve and Henry did it too, we shouldn't be scared. We should be enjoying it.* Yet still the caution of their latest clue rang in his ears like the chimes of a mourning bell.

To make sense of its confusion, the previous evening he'd copied it on parchment and filled in the blank spaces left behind, guessing the missing links.

Hail, ye weary travellers, for here the next clue awaits,
Set sail aboard and aloft, keeping true for you to locate.
As the crow flies is your direction.
Continents you have crossed and seas you have sailed,
But none as the Indian,
Where land must be lost.
Guided by the setting of Polaris, to what cost?
Rumours we have heard, to explore is to discover.
Keep the piece ticking.
Heading south-east.

Now, as he peered out to the endless mass of water and knew the weary days to come, he could fully comprehend the riddle not only as a clue, but as a warning.

Continents you have crossed and seas you have sailed.
But none as the Indian.
Where land must be lost.

To what cost?

Chapter Thirty

Dreams visited him again that night, forever haunting him with their exhausting theme: the pursuit of the chest. It was the centre, the focal point, the genesis. It needed to be found. As always, his surroundings hindered him and led him, as always, to the three lingering spirits in the hole. Harold looked up in a bloody mangle, Poppy stared at him with wide eyes of innocence; Hugh screamed his nightly chorus with a belly bloated and about to pop . . . and he woke in a clammy sweat upon the deck in the chill of the morning, about to retch.

The morning, however, brought merriment and nursed his wavering wits. Commanded by the captain, the fruit and milk had to be cleared and eaten to save it from being wasted so the crew filled their bellies with the splendour of leftover foods. Some were at the point of turning whilst some had already turned, yet all was consumed in the damp of the hold. Spirits were high, so high the order of rationing from then on did not make a dent. Although, Captain Robertson was wary sharing the cheer as he knew of the hardship that was to come and the open ocean was forever a torment to the sailor's strained eye. Stress wrapped around him in a fearful cocoon.

The day passed and they manned the vessel; a harsh north-westerly whipped up the waves and strained the sails but they knew how to overcome it, experience keeping them on track. Each of them was healing from their wounds both physically and mentally – their hands, now scabless, bore scars from their time mining. Joseph, however, struggled to deal with the vivid visions continuing to appear before him. They ate a small supper before heading to their hammocks with Benjamin on the dogwatch.

Dreams displayed their vivid nightly showing and Joseph awoke sweating and exhausted on deck, noticing worryingly that each morning he was nearing the bulwark. Sadly, breakfast was a bland occasion with salted fish, a slice of stale bread and a few gulps of water. Spirits lowered as everyone understood the begrudging rule that had to be set in place again; rationing and starvation, a ruthless torment that was behind every full belly, ready to return. The ship was manned by caulking the deck, splitting ropes, climbing shrouds and catching rats with the sails constantly needing attention; their tough north-westerly still badgered them to stray off course, and it was gaining momentum. The pulling of the sheets to control the sails was never-ending.

Joseph noticed his leg was feeling slightly better, or was it? He'd accustomed to the heated throb. It continued to pain him, though, and Victoria worried her efforts were being rendered fruitless. The parasite was dastardly, she fretted opium was not enough. Thankfully, the gash itself was closed and healing, yet his mind plagued him with more visions appearing on the deck.

Dinner was salted pork and rice mixed with a splash of water. Billy took the dogwatch as the moon shone bright upon the rising waves.

Dreams plagued him; he woke sweating. Breakfast was the same meal. Spirits began to drag. Joseph's leg ached, he limped from stem to stern. At least the gash was still closed. The jobs began to show a touch of dullness in their repetition. The wind altered course to a southerly gale. Dinner was salted goat with watered rice and Thomas took the dogwatch.

Dreams plaguing. Sweat running. Morning bell chimes. Bland breakfast forced down. Spirit lacking further. Motivation was what they needed now. His leg was beginning to swell. Might need draining again. Caulking, scrubbing, tying, splitting; nets, keep making the nets. Wind forever a nuisance. Dinner was salt with meat and rice and a gulp of water. Rob. Dogwatch.

The chest. The chest made him sweat. Hugh's screaming woke him, he was nearing the railing. Loud morning bell. Breakfast was sad. Work was irritating. Dinner was depressing. His leg swelled larger. Visions beginning to lessen. Victoria volunteered for the dogwatch.

Dreams. Sweat. Tears. Large waves rocking today. Spirit? What spirit? Have we moved? Working. Tired. Leg drained and looks better, does it? Wind changing again. Just eat the bloody food, will you? Dave is watching dog.

Sweating. Bell. Bland. Annoying. Hungry. Pain. Stress. Eat. Dogwatch.

And repeat.

Before they realised, over a week had passed but not a sign of it showed. They ate the same food, worked the same jobs, talked to the same people, fought the same winds and looked out to see the same damn blue water and the same damn blue sky. Once clouds spread over, but they couldn't say on what day or when. Who cared? For all they knew, they could be set on rollers never to move, never to make progress onward but still labouring the ship until they were spent. If there was one thing Joseph managed to note apart from the pain, it was Billy talking as he was tying. 'Tis like the bloody Treadmill, I'm telling ye. Always moving, always busy but never going anywhere. Always moving, but never forward. *Are* we moving forward anymore?' It was a tough question to answer, Joseph shook his head.

'I don't know.'

Sounds nullified; the crashing of the waves was white noise, the clunking and groaning of the ship was mute to their ears but if someone talked it sounded like a shout. Billy's fiddle, now rarely practised, sounded alien and ungodly, screeching strange tunes. He now practised the flute, hour after hour, a horrid and harsh whistle that revived bitter memories. A craving besotted them; a craze to hear the caw of a sea bird, to hear another form of life squalling to make its existence known. Nothing came.

Sight became a sickening, tormenting sense, doing more harm than good. To look right from the bulwark was to look at miles upon miles of blue water cresting white, ending only with the horizon where a different shade of blue, a still, calm, light blue, started. To look left from the bulwark were waves, rising and falling, cresting then flattening, rolling and rolling onward to a broad line where the sky met the sea. To look up was dangerous, the sun was bright all day every day and the blue that housed it was a permanent abuser, a treacherous player that teased feature every morning but changed its hand as soon as the sun showed its poker face. The sky's blue was a light one that had the strength to hold nothing, not a cloud nor bird; a bleak, frozen wasteland, looking more of a glacier with the sun trapped inside. Featureless, everywhere, and the setting never changed. There was nought to look at, for nought ever came nor went, except for the ship below their feet.

The ship. This ship. *Victoria.* Oh, this glorious vessel of transport, able to cross continents and master the world. How they all grew to hate it. It became their torturer; always giving them pointless work without sign of any progress. Always giving little enough food to keep them alive but never enough to satisfy. Enough to keep them working their menial labours to finish the day, only to start again the next. Always keeping them moving with never any hope there was anything at the other end. The bowsprit and jibboom taunted them day in day out with a pointing wooden finger, yet it never gave any idea how far there was left. As Billy said, it became their new Treadmill: a bigger version with worse consequences. With this new floating version, they were not to walk a never-ending staircase until they collapsed, no, they were to work pointlessly with a false hope of destination until they cracked and slipped from the perches of their minds . . . or from the perches of the railing.

Walking through the decks, it was already beginning. The crew wandered, pulling lines half-heartedly, knotting loosely, losing strength and will, slacking in their endeavours. Orders were carried out with a mere murmur as a reply; reports were given smaller every day as there was nothing new to report on. Talking was seldom and scarce as everyone slowly crawled back inside their own heads, trying to find a seed of focus to plant into the soil of their labour but finding nought but dust. Attentions wavered thin. Despondency followed with more standing by the bulwark looking out to the blue void they were sailing through, wishing for a fin, a fluke, a bird, or another ship; anything to observe to ease this mental torture.

Attitudes began to change as the days passed, each taking their own tack to endure this debilitating mockery of a journey. Characters altered under the stressful situation – Billy's light-hearted humour soured to a sarcastic droll landing on anyone who walked past, some would say he was provoking a response only to ease the mind and root it back to reality. Meanwhile Rob barely uttered a word to anyone, drawing into his shell like a frightened turtle. Tess thinned and looked fragile, even her speech diminished to a whisper; a minimal gust would blow her from her feet.

Thomas muttered most of the time keeping himself to himself, working hard and forever bandaging burst blisters but regret was on his sunburnt face, that was clear enough to see; questioning himself whether this was any better than the pit in the ground. Dave James became a ghost; a silent sinister presence with an air of gloom about him that everyone tried to avoid.

Benjamin had tried to lighten the mood with sea shanties like a Drop of Nelson's Blood and Sloop John B when things toughened but even these fell short of an impact after a time. He spent most of his days aloft amongst the shrouds, rigging and yards, checking and tying and repairing, away from the negative cloud that was consuming the deck.

Victoria stayed strong, but Joseph could see she was faltering and weakening, becoming tetchy and irritable as she lost grip and stumbled over noticeable things. He, himself, was a shell; a worker with no passion, a husk of a human, only waking every morning to escape from the horrors he fell victim to every night, endlessly fatigued and accustoming to his painful limp.

Only Robertson remained alert, focusing on the necessity of the ship and keeping her sailing as the crow flies. As stiff as a board he'd become but Joseph was thankful for the rigidity, for a board was what they needed to keep afloat. Foreknowledge had been a useful tool; experience had taught him what was needed of a wandering crew; discipline and a firm Victorian handle on the situation. *Victoria* needed to be manned, even if her crew were faltering. Only if he shoved orders down their throats would they listen, and his fists were ready; it was the only way to push through the isolation, the only way through this difficult time of their arduous odyssey. There was a reason you sailed within the sight of land.

'Excellent! Good job, men,' the captain cried as he knelt to study the finished net. He picked it up and felt it, 'tight as tight can be, aye. We'll be filling our bellies with the finest fish tonight. Dorado's and sharks and the creatures of the deep.' It had been the fifth day working on it, or the sixth? Seventh? Joseph couldn't remember; a blur was what it had become but the net was finished which meant they had a chance at catching some fresh food. Even the salted meats were turning, and they'd started on the stash of coconuts, sad to see their reserves being taken lower. Still, the milk and flesh made a tasty treat.

'Great! Maybe we'll catch a whale and have it pull us to shore, wherever that is.' Billy said, trying to be funny but sounding sarcastic.

'We begin tonight, and every night from now on if the weather permits.' Robertson ordered, and the replies were met with silent nods and blunt grunts. As the evenings rolled by and the winds calmed, fishing became the regular sport at dusk as well as a therapeutic relief, giving their minds something different to focus on. Their nets held well and were sturdy, if but slightly cumbersome, yet their work was not rewarded as well as they would've liked.

Over the course of the next four sunsets, they caught a total of five fish, three small and two large, colourful dorado's that had been drawn to the bait. These were not the only punters though, as shoals of beautiful and magnificent fish swam under their longboat, teasing their hooks and swimming away. They were of all colours of the spectrum, some huge and glittering whilst the smaller swam in shoals. Sharks teased them too, hammerheads scared the fish away whilst threshers liked to advance to their boat and rub alongside the hull, much to their excitement and fascination. Soon, fishing became the sole enjoyment and Joseph, Billy, Benjamin and

Rob were eager to test the waters and fly the nets. It was escapism, everyone could see, but all were happy to watch something else and put their shredded faith into something other than an illusional horizon.

The next day a shift was brought upon them; it was easy to spot and became their full attention for an hour. The winds had altered again, although this time they brought passengers. 'Blimey, would you look at that!' Billy cried, pointing from the shrouds as he beheld the view, sounding like an excited child, 'Christ, I'd forgotten what they looked like.' Clouds. A thick bank of them were sweeping in like a sandstorm, their bases small and flat yet they towered up in great shapes and turrets like a gothic church to a high daunting roof.

'Looks dark over Will's Mother's.' The captain said, 'foulies at the ready, sailors!' The bank moved slow at first but before they knew it a dark blanket had covered the sunset, hindering their attempts at fishing for the evening. The cold evenings they were used to suddenly became warm and a gift was sent from the heavens. Rainfall. It began as a light drizzle, which brought a relief to them all; cheers spread through the deck as the spray touched their cheeks and wetted their hair, but soon it thickened and doused the ship with fat droplets and the wind carried them into lashing sheets.

'Buckets!' Robertson yelled above the wind. 'Make haste now sailors! Grab them, any of them, any container, collect the water!' Hurriedly, they scrambled down and brought forth any container they could find and planted them along the deck until it was crowded; bailing buckets, small buckets, scuttlebutts and empty barrels and bottles; all catching as much rain as they could. They lashed them tight to the masts to keep the waves from taking them. Fresh water, *fresh!* The excitement to drink it was overwhelming; no more stagnant dregs from an algae-slick barrel.

'I tell you,' Joseph said to everyone as he stood with the warm rain running down his face, raising his cup from the container and watching the water spill over the lip for the first time in days. 'This will be the finest of beers, the top draught of the brewery; a brilliance better than any of the rest in the city we named home. For all the good it's done us: to London!' he cried raising his cup and drinking it dry. It was sweet and fresh and invigorating, oiling his joints and easing his soul.

'To London!' the cry echoed, 'London and Ireland! Me two 'omes!' extended Billy, and the crew drank heartily, feeling it fill them as if they'd finished a pint.

Smiles spread from face to face as everyone found themselves hydrated for the first time in weeks and the workload seemed fresh as everything was in a new setting. Everything seemed well again for the time being, until two days passed and there was no sign of any shift.

It did not take long for the novelty to wear thin and the continuous patter to fail to ring anyone's bell. The smiles were quickly doused as they realised it was as bad as working in the heat; now they were to be soaked through every hour of the day, working with slipping fingers, clinging clothes, and wet bodies. Water ran in their eyes and made it hard to see and shivers with slow aching fingers made it hard to grip to anything. At times, the rain froze and became hail, pounding them incessantly for hours upon end and coating the ship in a thick layer, until the rain came again and washed everything away. The days were windy, a murky grey, and nights were wet and black without a moon nor stars to look upon. They constructed a small spar deck – essentially spare spars lashed together and to the mast with sheeting to cover the poor soul on the dogwatch, the shift which became even more depressing since there was no tobacco to smoke to pass the long rainy nights.

Blisters plumped their hands from the damp ropes and their feet ached from wet boots and constantly slipping on the slick deck. An ugly fungus started to nestle between their toes and the bailing buckets were now an eyesore. Conditions were abysmal to work in and their prayers turned; now for the sun to show its bright face again, any heat to dry them, to warm them and let them work in peace.

'Merciful Heaven and for the love of God and sonny Jesus *would this rain let up!* We might as well've stayed in England!'

Rob cried in anguish as his fingers slipped and shook as he tried to reef a snapped line together; the rain adding extra difficulty to perform the slightest of tasks. Taking the role of the classic Englanders, their complaints were forever about the weather – if the sun came out, it was too hot and they burned, if it rained there was a deluge of which no one could dry properly. If the waters were calm, they prayed to keep moving to escape from the ocean and if it was windy the rain spattered in their eyes. Out here in the open ocean it was an exposed world of eternal conflict, a brutal dichotomy, a setting of raw opposites of which no one could escape.

The wind was being unruly too, pushing them hither and thither, forcing the rain to sway and spatter in their faces in grand floating rushes. Indeed, it carried them forward, but the cost was a sodden one; each day felt like two and daresay they missed the sight of the horizon – this dismal sheet of dank grey shortened their sight only to what they held in their white wrinkled hands. Where they were no one knew, no measurements could be made with sextant or backstaff since their twinkling guides were smothered. All they could do was pray.

Six days were spent in this waterlogged world where clothes never dried, and fingers wrinkled so much they ached at the end of the day where the skin stretched back to its usual print. Six days and nights, that's all it was, but it felt like six weeks. At the lighter shade of grey smiles were called upon again, and, shielding their eyes from the rain, they pulled their ragged curtains of hair from their faces at the first break of cloud. Spirits then soared to a height not seen in days, since their escape from Madagascar. 'Sun's a' coming! Look at her! Look how gorgeous she is! Here she comes!' Benjamin hollered with a beaming smile upon his face and his scally cap dripping.

The sun broke free and cleared the air, making the ship and its crew steam. Within a matter of hours free from the relentlessness of the rain, the sun had dried everything making their skin crack and redden quicker. Heat, the familiar warming touch, returned to them with an incredible vigour; its density blasting their energy as a magnifying piece would to an ant. It was penetrating and left them gasping for air and shade like nothing they'd known. 'My god I'm sweating!' Thomas gasped, wrapping a bandana around his head. 'There's no air out here! I always thought the sea air was meant to be good for you.' He licked his dry lips and gasped more. His hair was growing longer now, covering the scabs and the sun highlighted his auburn colour. His stubble had grown out too, darker than his head; he would've been a handsome fellow if it wasn't for the cracking red skin, sores and bruises.

Everyone was burning and complaining, but the vessel had to be manned and they endured the demoralising heat. Captain Robertson calculated they had been blown off course (quite drastically, he didn't care to mention) and with a good wind they could jump back to it in a day or two. Or three. Yet this was the Indian Ocean, it toyed with their misfortune. Nevertheless, the crew heaved sheets and lines, unfurled and adjusted sails and worked intensely throughout. The quicker they sailed, the quicker they reached this coastline and returned to reality.

We're days away now, surely, Joseph prayed as he fiddled with the pocket watch in his pocket and looked out to the jibboom and its taught stays and jibs, and the hazy heat beyond. It had been on his mind, as it had with them all: Australia. It felt so close, but it was hard to tell when even the horizon bubbled and melted to his bloodshot eyes. Despite the hopeful outlook on reaching land, he couldn't help the doubt that had built with each day. The questions still lay unanswered, Victoria's questions, from all those days ago; *What will happen once we reach Australia? What then?* He sighed, remembering his answer; *what then indeed.*

Focus was what he needed, and a keen eye to pick apart the clues to find anything hinting at what to do once they got there. Presently, keen eyes were not something he could claim, as his fatigue from the journey and little rest at nights left him feeling hollow. Hollow and drawn out, like a knife that had run short of the butter it was spreading. A wrong cut of a jib. The only thing he'd managed to adopt over the past weeks was fiddling with the pocket watch, twiddling the broken timepiece for comfort through the tough time.

How he found the grit to keep his jobs completed was beyond him, yet now they seldom needed focus; knots were being tied without thought, nautical terms were understood as well as any city slang and reading signs of direction and required maintenance were second nature. They did not take energy, what did though was figuring out where this poxy clue was taking them. *Tonight, after fishing, I shall make a start, put something together. There must be something hidden amongst the words.*

The day dragged, just as it had done before the rains; a tedious slog to get to dusk whereupon they could finally fish once more. As the sails were being furled and stowed for the night and the anchors were lowered a fathom, the longboat was lowered to the water with a soft slap. The winds were gentle, the waves a soothing rock. This time Jim Robertson joined the fishing mission, along with Benjamin, Rob, Thomas and Tess. Despite its usual failure, the activity relieved the mind for a while allowing hope for something else other than land, and, after the days missed, fishing was as exciting and exhilarating as any horse race. Although, after deliberation and slight regret, Joseph decided to stay aboard to get started on his studies early before exhaustion gripped its firm hold, of which Victoria was pleased to see and offered to help.

They entered the cabin and lit the lamps, collected the papers and parchments and sat at the table. Beginning to sift, they started with the first scroll, reading it through again but only becoming lost. '*Perhaps you'll get a chance to see her aglow?* What do you suppose of that?' she asked.

Joseph shrugged, 'I always thought it meant a lamp, or a candle. What else would you know of to glow?'

She gave it some thought. 'A fire?'

He pursed his lips, wishing for a cigarette, or even his pipe, to smoke even though his cravings had abated, leaving him feeling morose. *I can't even recall its taste,* he realised sadly. 'I doubt they'd try and lead us to a fire. They wrote this, what, over a hundred or so years ago; that fire's been gone for a while.'

She huffed, not appreciating the tone. 'Fine. It's not a fire.' She rolled her eyes with pursed lips and picked up the clue from Gabon but found nothing else or indeed, including, Australia. Neither did Joseph when he perused the second clue written for Lisbon. He tried the glasses and flicked through the different clues and papers, studying the clue leading to Madagascar and their most recent find, trying with and without the second lens, but they revealed nothing. They only linked with the papers that led them to the island on the other side of Africa. Spare papers they picked up, notes they investigated, and objects left behind to aid them in their search were scoured but no hint was revealed. Whatever Eve and Henry had left, if anything, telling them of what to do, it had been very well concealed.

The next evening was spent this way, as well as the next.

Soon his wits began to flounder upon the fourth try and he slammed his fists down on the table with a bang, making Victoria jump. '*There's nothing here!* Every scrap of paper we've scoured and picked apart, every word analysed and there's fuck all here! *How could they leave nothing?!*' He got to his feet and stepped to the window where he looked out to the darkening horizon and the glittering of the waves as they captured the last light of day. 'What if they really did leave nothing for us, Victoria? What if that *was* the last clue and we spend the rest of our days wandering through that blasted country hunting for the Lost Loot until we eventually keel over and heave our last breath to the dust?' he sighed and folded his arms, 'we'll end up as my grandfather did; old, odious, crooked Frederick Winter with leathery skin and a hardened soul void of spirit, rocking in a chair, smoking a pipe, looking out of a dirty window with no one by his side to share love or happiness with. Woe is him, old man. Perhaps a mystery bigger than this one is how on earth he managed to make my granny fall in love with him long enough to have my mother.'

She looked to him; her hair relaxed down her back in waves. She shared his frustration having exhausted her focus, but her hope remained firm, for now. 'We won't end up like him. You won't end up like him.'

'How do you know that? Look at me. My skin's thickening like an oxen's hide, my hands are callous and scarred; I'm weathering like a rock on the shore and I'm losing my mind over a mystery I can't hope to solve. I'm already looking out of a dirty window; all I need is a rocking chair and a clay pipe.'

Victoria laughed. 'You're not alone though. I'm here by your side. So's Billy and Jim and Rob and Tess and the rest. And I refuse to believe that you, Joseph Winter, will ever end up as a woeful old man.'

'No. Just a foolish old man. A foolish old man like him. He who never gave up until he ran short of funds and was bound to live out the rest of his haggard life with regret and failure weighing down his heart as well as his head.'

'What was it he failed in? What was it he was searching for?'

Joseph sighed and looked to her in the shadow of the cabin. 'A hunt for a chest, lost to history. And if the rumours are right from what I've heard all my years, it was the very same chest we're after. Scott's Trove.'

Chapter Thirty-One

Victoria Penning was silent for a moment; she wasn't stunned but surprise was clear on her fair complexion. 'Are you saying your grandfather travelled the exact same journey we're on? Joseph, why didn't you mention this before! The name of Winter I'd heard of, but it never occurred to me it was connected to this.' She gestured to the sprawl of papers and objects strewn across the table.

He shrugged, 'I'm not sure. I don't talk of him often; we never saw eye to eye and he never shared anything about who he was. What I do know of him and his adventures are rumours of what others have told me, or what has been passed as whispers through the vine. I never knew which or what to believe and since I didn't really know the man, I could never judge for myself. Rumours were common though, lord knows I've heard them all my life; some say how he became a pirate, sailing the seven seas in search for gold. Some say he was a hero, saved people whilst enemy ships sank; others said he stashed gold away on some unknown desert island and some day he was going to return to claim it. I even heard one say he became the chief of a tribe that worshipped him, and he left because they didn't know the words to God Save the Queen. Now *that* I find a little far-fetched. Three things are for certain – he *was* a cabin boy aboard the *Endeavor*, he spent most of his life at sea and he came back a man lost, no spirit nor soul to give him anymore passion in life.

'When I was just a boy, I used to think the world of him until I realised what all of it had turned him into. The most common rumour passed along was the most believable and I took it as gospel; he was hunting for Scott's Trove, the lost chest but never found it and, in doing so, lost everything he held dear. Sacrificed his family, friends, savings and life for vanity, wealth and power. Not really the type of man to boast about, yet alone take inspiration from.'

'Even so,' she mused, 'this would mean he picked up the trail at some point and attempted it, maybe he found some of the clues we've discovered. When did he die?'

Joseph left the window and sat back down at the table again and thought, 'what was I? Eleven or twelve?'

'And you only saw him three times?'

Nodding, 'As I say, we weren't close. He wasn't keen on visitors toward the end. Even my mother stopped seeing him as regularly because of how cold he became. I never knew my father, he died when I was two, but I hear he didn't like him either. He was a hard man to please, but as with any plague, his callousness worsened beyond the point of repair and it took its toll on his very spirit and soul. Constantly groaning, moaning, grumbling; sucking any happiness or joy people had in order to turn it into something foul. Nothing was ever good enough, he always had something negative to say. You know that type of dark cloud. "The young'uns nowadays don't appreciate anything, even though they've got plenty o' opportunities that I never had." Was a one I always used to roll my eyes at. I wonder if he was ever nice to be around. Surely at some point he *was* happy, I just can't imagine it.'

'It's a shame, I'm sure he would've had many stories to tell. Did he leave you anything when he passed?'

'A shilling and a compass. Why?'

Her eyes lit up. 'What became of them? Do you still have them?'

'Course not. The shilling I spent within the first day and the compass I pawned for a few bob to get me and my dear mother some food to eat. Damn thing was pointless anyway, I didn't know how to use it; what good was it to be? What could I use it for? I knew my way around the streets as well as anyone; I never expected to get out. Then it turned up again with the scroll. I knew it was mine, it had a *J* etched into its base . . . but its broken now. An't nothing that can be done.' He could see her disappointment.

'Sorry Victoria, that's all he left and when it came down to it, we needed the food more. Times were hard. *Are* hard still.'

She sighed, 'I thought if he found the clues as we have, he might've left you something to help with them.'

'I don't think he found as many as we have.'

'How do you know?'

He scratched his beard and shrugged, 'we would've known. The chain would've been interrupted; a chest would've been missing; a clue would've been misplaced having already been intercepted by him. Every chest we've come across so far has been untainted since it was hidden away. I reckon he had the first scroll and immediately set out without thinking on it, too absorbed, too excited to stop and ponder where it was leading him. He ran around in circles hitting dead ends until he ran short of funds, food and friends and returned to London to live the rest of his life in woe and regret; sour because of the consumption of utter failure in an obsession he'd sacrificed everything for. I feel angry at his treatment of my mother n' me; there wasn't any need for it, but I pity him as a fool for letting it consume him so.

'Fame was what he wanted, to get his name in the history books. I can't deny that he did explore, he did it all his life but had nothing to show for it by the end. Nothing to plant a flag into, nothing to claim for England and the Empire and upon his arrival back to Britain, he didn't open his mouth to anyone about what he'd done or where he'd been, too embarrassed to let slip he had nothing to offer. He wasn't like Eve and Henry, exploring because of the passion; he wanted a return for it, a dividend. I guess he thought people saw his adventures as a waste of time and effort and fell into that perspective too, almost forgetting everything he did; forgetting who he was.' He sighed, his gaze falling to the table, 'what a pity.'

Victoria sat in silence again, leaning back in the chair with the soft glow of the oil lamps casting her shadow against the desk and wall behind. The evening was falling short, nightfall was just around the corner. Soon the longboat would return with or without scaly flapping fortunes. 'Did he mention anything to you about his travels?' she asked abruptly, sounding curious.

In honesty, he hadn't thought about it for a long time. Only snippets remained to him of the old fellow and what he was like, and those snippets showed Frederick in that chair with that window smoking from that clay pipe. His face wrinkled and weathered, hair lank and grey, lips hooked in an eternal frown, so much so it was clear the misery he was in. Not from an illness, but from self-loathing. A depressed state, but how was he to see that as an eleven-year-old, or understand it as a boy who hadn't set foot from the boundaries of the city? There was only one conversation he remembered, a conversation he wasn't in the mood to share. *Joseph,* he could almost hear old Winter's gravelly voice behind him, *this life. This life you've got now, do what you will with it, but it'll always press you down. Press you down and squeeze and wring you dry until there an't nothing left, and you're done for. You'll end up a washed-up bit o' driftwood, flotsam and waste, never good for nothing unless you stay here. Here, you've got a chance.*

Grandfather, what happened on your travels? Mother tries to tell me stories and I hear things, but I never know what to believe . . . "'Travels" he said with a dry chuckle and spat on the floor, "is that what you want to hear, boy? About my explorin' days? There an't no point to it I tell you! No point, says I. There an't nothing out there worth seeing, an't nothing out there good for you; only misery n' woe n' death and a lot o' water. Lot o' water you can't even drink. Why is it you want to hear of my travels anyways, so you can laugh too? Judge me? Remind me of what I could've had? What's a skinny runt like you thinking of things like that for? Balderdash! You an't ever doing it. You'd not last a day with that thin bit o' gristle on yer bones. That life is hard, crush the living daylights from your measly meat in no time, boy. No. Better to stay in London, boy. Wish I had. Wish I had."' Joseph went silent, looking at the table deep in thought. He didn't tell her about the switch the old man carried with him and how he liked to sharply whip it upon him when Joseph stepped too close. Pursing his lips, he added, '*that* was one of the better times I saw him.'

Victoria exhaled in disappointment. It was clear the old man's bitterness stemmed from his own failure and the judgements of others and attempted to stop Joseph from making the same mistakes. She folded her arms, 'looks like he failed again, even from beyond the grave. You managed to get out no matter what he said. How did your poor granny put up with him?'

Joseph shrugged, 'she was a strong woman. A hard but loving woman. Didn't let anything get to her, especially not him. She was like a ray of sunlight that breaks through the clouds. Then, when she died, his bitterness went on free reign. I can only guess he was a nice man once, but the one I met wasn't much of a man at all. Very fearful he was, fearful that the world would try and crush and humiliate him again, so in the end his achievements amounted to nothing except rumours and whispers. A life reduced to a hushed tone and a shattered spirit. He did well in one thing though; he succeeded in emphasising the family name; Winter always brings cold and bitterness every year to every soul in every home.' He sighed in exasperation, as if even the thought of old Frederick Winter was bringing a chill to the room. From beyond the grave his memory was uncomfortable to think of.

Looking at him caringly, Victoria could see in his face how unpleasant it was to revisit such a character. Understanding it was one thing, remembering it was another. Clearly there was nought the old codger could offer to help them on their quest. A shame, but she was positive. She had to be. After what they'd been through, it was a necessity now. 'Come on.' She said at length, getting to her feet, 'we an't going to find much else tonight. Let's see if the fishermen had any luck.' Holding out her hand, he looked up to her with thankfulness in his eyes and took it. Her hand was hard with callus, he could feel the labours of the ship engrained in her fingers, the pains scarred into her palm yet none of it mattered, he loved to feel it; his hands were very much the same.

She led him from the cabin and into the dusk outside to find six large and colourful dorado fish flapping in the net on deck and the crew in high spirits. It was their biggest haul and could last them a few more days without opening any more coconuts. That night, they dined with cheer and retired to their hammocks with light hearts, eager for the morrow where they could press onward.

We mustn't have much longer left, Joseph thought as he lay in his hammock looking up to the gloomy wood, twiddling the crown of the pocket watch lying on his chest. Australia had never felt so close; he could almost hear the wash of the ebb up the sand, see the haze of heat resting on the horizon of land. He yawned; *I'll ask Jim in the morning. Days, he'll say, I wager; only a few days until land will be nigh and seabirds will be calling out congratulations for us.* Seabirds. The thought of them seemed odd, a fantastical creature of the air. He hadn't seen one in so long he'd forgotten the look of them, misplaced the memory of their caw. Falling asleep, he craved to hear their shrill whining cry announcing their odyssey was almost at its end.

Dreams visited him again as they did every night, reminding him of the debilitating themes that lay just under the surface of his subconscious. The chest needed to be found. The journey was a hinderance. The isolation was brutal. The cold glares of the innocent burned; the incessant bawling of a dying friend disturbed. The guilt was penetrating, cracking open wider the crevasses of his bending mind. Instead of waking though, he found himself walking into a room with a dirty window and a wizened spiritless crone watching him, smoking a clay pipe, clutching a cane ready to raise it. The crone opened its mouth and its words echoed in his head, taking the strength from him: *That life is hard, crush the living daylights from your measly meat in no time, boy. No. Better to stay in London, boy. Wish I had. Wish . . . I . . . had.*

Waking in a sweat, he fell to his knees and heaved in the cold morning air. The deck felt hard beneath him; it was a rarity to wake in his own hammock. Tears were streaming down his face and into his beard. After numerous restless nights, his fear strayed away from his own mortality and instead what made him tremble was tripping on his own sanity, stumbling and never being able to get up. He could feel himself slipping day by day, losing grip of details and dainty features, forgetting origins and sense. It was a terrible anxiety. Quickly, he wiped his eyes; it would not do for the crew to see their quartermaster crumbling. Men were not supposed to cry, especially men that had their reputations to consider. *What reputation? What is there to uphold? Who am I anymore?*

Light footsteps came up from behind him. 'Joseph? What are you doing up here? Are you alright? The morning bell hasn't chimed yet; dawn hasn't broken.' Tess said with concern. It was true, the stars were still out.

'Walk-er! Tess, blimey, you frightened me.' He got to his feet and wiped his nose, making sure he'd pressed away the last of the tears. 'What're you doing up?' he yawned and shivered in the morning coolness.

She shrugged and pulled her oversized coat up to her neck. Her dark hair, tangled and dry, tumbled over her back. 'My turn on the dogwatch. I got a bit of sleep earlier, but I wanted to watch the sunrise. What I'm more concerned with is you. What're you doing awake? Are you alright?'

'Nothing, nothing. Just a . . . just a bad dream is all. I've had one every night since Madagascar. I can't seem to rest.'

Through the gloom, her drawn albeit petite face saddened. 'Bad things happened there. I'm not sure any of us have recovered properly – if we ever will. I dread to think what they did with the - *Hugh's* corpse. I feel bad that we left him behind. Billy's been saying they probably ate him like the others did with Harold. He was trying to be funny, but it wasn't.'

'Ah don't mind Billy; he comes out with some dippy tripe sometimes. I'm sure they buried him.' *Perhaps without any diamonds to guide him through death though, I doubt they'd let him keep the ones he pocketed.* 'They didn't seem the cannibal type from what Benjamin tells me.'

Wandering to the bulwark, she leaned on the wood and listened to the lapping waves against the hull. A morning mist shrouded the water, the air was still. 'I don't know what to think anymore. I didn't think they were that bad until we became their prisoners.' She paused, looking to her hands, 'I didn't expect rape of them, but men love power and to play with it when they can. I can still feel the pain from it, Joseph. I ache from the ship, of course I do, but the pain they inflicted is still within me. It's strange, I've always thought I was a good judge of character but now, I'm not so sure.' Tess sighed, 'people have so many depths, so many levels it's hard to judge the good from the bad. I think of Hugh. He *did* do bad things and he *was* a bad man and, toward the end, an honest man, and justice, or fate, caught up with him for what he did. But I liked him. He was nice to me and a good friend. I know it doesn't excuse his crimes in the city, but . . . I don't know . . . When it's quiet, I can still hear his last words, his . . . screaming; I know I won't ever be able to forget. We couldn't take his body with us, but I still wonder if we should've done. Was it right of us to leave him there? Ah, it's all confusing and painful to think of.'

He wasn't sure what to say. If anything, it shamed him that he'd become so ignorant to what others had been through. Dave's voice echoed; *looks like I'm not the only monster who found its way to sea.* Biting his lip through his self-loathing, he put his arm around her and said, 'I'm sorry for what happened to you Tess, truly. I should've been there; I should've done something. Been stronger. Men of this world, of this time, are bastards and I dread to think what the world will be like in the future if they continue to run it as they do. I wouldn't be surprised if there was a war of great proportions; fought with guns and fuelled by egos. As for Hugh, I'm not sure there was much we could've done; we'd have had no place for him if we had taken him; we'd have only given him to the waves.'

She nodded slightly and scratched her head, 'I know, I know. It's hard to know what the right thing is to do; half the time I don't know how to feel. I'm guilty and confused, happy to be away from London but sad friends are dying on this voyage, I'm moving forward but . . . I'm lost at the same time. I – oh I don't know . . .' she said, showing her years as a twenty-something wanting to find identity. She then continued, 'Poppy is with me though. I miss her dearly; I'm doing this for her.'

He peered out to the mist. 'It's hard to know what the correct way to feel is. You can be lost, but I hope you find relief in knowing that we're all lost too, and, in that way, we can be lost together so you could never be alone in this. I'm sorry for Poppy, she was such a sweet, innocent girl.' A voice in the back of his head cried suddenly, *Christ, Joseph, when did you become so caring?*

She smiled. 'Thank you, Joseph. I appreciate it.'

A silence passed between them. He changed tack, knowing her thoughts were now on the rape and the loss of her sister. 'So, you and Thomas then, you're getting on well?'

Tess gave him a quizzical look, but the blush was undeniable, 'yes, we're getting on well I suppose. I like his hair now it's growing back, and he has a friendly face. He's nice to me, although sometimes I don't think he knows when to stop talking.'

'I see, I see.' He smiled coyly, and she reflected it.

'Stop!' she laughed, 'we're friends.'

'Oh. I see, I see.' He repeated with a nod.

'What about you and Victoria? You two seem to get along well too, spend a lot of time together.' she retorted.

A nod, 'she's a fine woman indeed, and that's all I'll add to that for now.'

Tess returned the coy smile, 'I see, I see. For now.'

Just then the morning bell rang loudly and startled them, its chime harsh in the tranquil. 'Up, up, up! Time to move, I want an early start this morning to cover as much distance as we can before the heat kicks in! 'Fore we know it; the sun'll be over the yardarm.' Robertson declared, half-dressed. He slipped a waistcoat on over his loose shirt, undid his top few buttons revealing a chain around his neck and tied the top of his long black hair into a pigtail around the back of his head. Without his hat on, Joseph noticed lines of grey weeding through his black locks and his beard, although bushy, was now losing its colour to a white grey too. Weathering was not the sole reasoning behind this; stress played a big part too, eroding him externally as well as internally. The faded hat was placed atop his head and he spied the pair at the railing. 'Excellent! That's what I like to see, actions even before the instructions have been given. Fair play.' He tipped his hat in a gentlemanly fashion and strode up the ladder to prepare *Victoria* for another day's run.

Tess headed to the halyards and belaying pins of the foremast. 'Happy sailing,' he called out, and she turned and waved in the rising light of dawn.

After the bell was rung a second time, the crew plodded up the companionway one by one. Grumbling and despondent, they were, but they knew better than to moan too loudly. A quick hour passed where they ate their rationed breakfast and the stars winked out; the horizon lightening into a white and pale blue. They then hoisted the sails and winched the anchors and began their duties. Eventually their creaking vessel found her feet, caught the light south-easterly wind and began to cut through the waves.

The morning passed at a gradual pace and it was not long before they were hungry again. Hungry for substance, but hungrier for flavour. Their breakfast consisted of salted fish and a pouch of spare rice they had found amongst the coconuts. Despite having stock on board, the desire couldn't be helped for the basic foods they'd once had. Sweet and savoury; flavours aplenty.

Freshly baked bread was talked of as a happy memory from the old days; meat of all kinds was discussed at regular intervals, nearly always ending with someone calling off the talk as the craving was too intense. Vegetables were missed, as well as honey in porridge, which almost always led to the topic of sweets, oh! The sweets! Nothing could render them more aggravated than the endless talk of the sugared delicacies they'd once relished; the Turkish delights, and mint humbugs, the marshmallows and pastries, toffees and bakes, oh! The bakes! The endless array of pastries and cakes and bakes laced and coated with sugar and syrups, all with a supreme cherry on top; the smell of them all wafting down the streets as the bakers completed another batch. Oh! It was always too much and brought on vigorous emotion, becoming a distraction to the work ethic. Little could stop the flows of memories of personal favourites, yet that late morning's fantasy was interrupted when Jim Robertson hollered from the helm: '*Quiet!* The lot of you!' With beady eyes, he surveyed the deck and puzzled crew from the shadow of his hat. Everyone quietened and looked to him awaiting an explanation, but he only scoured the deck seeming to look for something.

Something was amiss. Something was not here. Not right. Missing. Sweat trickled down Robertson's face, the air became noticeably thicker and heavier. Stress clacked up his spine, plucking nerves and knocking bones. 'What jape is this?' he muttered under his breath as he observed slack sails and loose lines. 'What taunt, what punishment? Haven't we suffered enough?' The ship creaked as she idled forward aimlessly, moving only from the last breath of wind. 'Oh, merciful heavens, we've found it again.' He shook his head, 'no. *It's* found *us.*'

Before anyone could ask what was going on, they became aware of a sudden rise in heat and an expanding quiet, unheard of in the ocean where waves could always be heard. *Always.* Of course, the sound was accustomed to and the crew tended to not notice any longer, however, now they were amiss it seemed deathly silent. Gravely silent. As well as that, the next bitter blatancy was the feeling. The feeling of the ship moving. Of the ship *slowing,* of the ship *no longer* moving. There was always movement as it rode the waves but now, as Joseph, gulping in fear, peered out beyond the bulwark, he was struck by one feature and one feature only.

Stillness. An absolute solemn sheen.

'Merciful heavens.' Joseph whispered in dread as he looked out to a scene so calm it was calamitous. Becalmed waters, a playground for the insane.

The crew looked out to the vast wasteland and muttered their own quiet prayer. The waves, the tide, the wind and spray had vanished, leaving them with this unnatural, unnerving pane of pitiless glass.

'Capt'n, orders?' Benjamin urgently called, shattering the sinister silence. Everyone turned their gaze on him, wishing for him to rouse a solution and give them hope.

With a controlled tone, Robertson replied. It was clear he was trying to keep his wits about him, alas the sinking of spirit was far more evident. He licked his dry lips and smoothed his moustache down into his beard as he mused. 'Orders, yes. Right.' He pointed, 'ease all sails to their fullest; I want to see white canvas on mizzen, main and fore; rig the topgallant mast, topgallant sail and royal sail, attach the bonnets, secure all lines and tighten them taught. We need to catch any, *any* of the slightest of breezes there are: that's all we need to push us through. A gust, a breath, the quietest and gentlest of lover's whispers; they're out there somewhere and our mighty British sails will find them.' His attempts at strength, although brave, fell short when the orders carried out failed to catch any of the suggestions he offered. The only whispers found were those of doubt from the trepid crew.

Eyes peered to him attentively, awaiting another order, hoping for their captain to suggest anything else. A tick of fear had already embedded itself into their mood; a stifling sense of helplessness settled on the deck. If they didn't move, they couldn't travel. If they couldn't travel, they couldn't find fresh food. They couldn't reach land. They couldn't move on. What gave them the most fright though was a grave realisation, a dawning of the seriousness of the situation; a daunting prospect that if they didn't get out of this stagnant state they'd eventually run out of supplies, of hope. Of life. *We could die here,* the quartermaster thought, *we'll have got this far for nothing, stumbling at the final hurdle, not from starvation or disease but from a doss wind. Curse you Mother Nature and your cruel sense of humour.*

Robertson could feel their wanting, desperate glare. The sun was hot on his face. His shirt clung to his sticky back. It was an effort to suck in this thick viscous oxygen. Loosely, the sails drooped, as sad as a wet sheet hanging on a washing line. *There's nothing we can do. We can't row ourselves through this as we did before. We've no energy, no wind; we're stuck. For how long . . . how long until we starve, until we madden?* If he could've resigned, he would of; slammed down the sheet of paper confirming his resignation to let someone else deal with this. Alas, he couldn't. If their captain couldn't handle this, then no one could. Sometimes the truth, he found, was better delivered, and accepted, than a lie. Might as well come clean.

With their eyes upon him, he let out an exhausted sigh and let go of the wheel, the rudder idling as it tried to find the current. 'My crew.' He announced, laying his hands upon the quarterdeck railing, 'I have guided us through the Indian Ocean and for the better part it's passed smoothly, only now its smoothed so rapidly everything has stopped altogether. The doldrums are where we are now, becalmed in a patch of vicious tranquil dreaded by all sailors; as you can see why.' He gestured to the dead water, 'here we are in the middle of an ocean with nothing but water and yet that particular water refuses to co-operate – a traitorous tide, indeed. Judas's swimming pool if you will. A small patch of hell I'm afraid we'll have to endure. There's nothing we can do, except pray the current finds us and takes us away.

'I can't tell you how long we'll be stuck here, so as of now the field has been levelled. Henceforth, until the doldrums have chewed us up and spat us out, I can no longer navigate this ship; I can be your Captain, but all of our jobs to sail this craft have been rendered futile.'

There was silence. 'What're we supposed to do then?' Dave called out.

'We do what we can to keep occupied; swabbing, caulking, careening, fishing, maintenance and the like; anything to keep busy.'

'And when those jobs are done, what then?' Billy folded his arms, frustrated at their predicament, and scared.

'We pray.' He nodded slowly, 'a word of warning must be taken into account at times like these, so hear me and take heed: try to not focus on the conditions of the doldrums; no one has ever come away feeling better after staring at a motionless pool for hours, for days. The mind can play queer tricks on the vulnerable and the doldrums will test your limits, no matter your strength, race or sex. Stay busy, stay rooted and stay sane. Aye, we will get through this.' He took his hat from his head and wiped the sweat from his brow. 'I don't know what your religious beliefs are and to be frank I don't care. Believe what you want to believe, anything to help you, but as for now, I offer a sailor's prayer to those in need of one:

'They that go down to the sea in ships, that do
business in great waters,
'These see the works of the Lord, and his wonders in the deep.
'For he commandeth, and raiseth the stormy wind,
which lifteth the waves thereof.

'They mount up to the heaven, they go down again to the depths:
their soul is melted because of the trouble.
'They reel to and fro, and stagger like a drunken man,
and are at their wits end.
'Then they cry unto the Lord in their trouble,
and he bringeth them out of their distresses.
'He made the storm be still, and the waves of
the sea were thereof hushed.
'Then they are glad because the waters were quiet; and he
brought them unto their desired haven.'

He paused and pursed his lips. 'God have mercy on us all.' Then he turned and strode down the ladder to the deck, whereupon he drove his knife in the mainmast, partaking in the superstition, before retiring to his cabin.

All stayed frozen for a moment, until the Irishman whistled, 'not his most cheery of speeches, aye, but tis' better than the switch.'

The old seadog smiled sadly, 'between this conundrum and a flick of the switch, my boy, I'd choose the cane any day.' Benjamin touched his shoulder and hobbled down to the berth to take refuge in the shade.

One by one the crew filtered out; their footsteps upon the wood were gunshots in the silence. Some went aft to the quarterdeck, whilst others climbed the shrouds to the maintop and foretop platforms to seek whatever sanctuary they could find. Tess and Thomas followed Benjamin down to the berth, leaving Joseph and Victoria standing alone. His hands were in his pockets, twiddling the crown of the pocket watch, trying to grasp the gravity of the situation. A thousand thoughts raced through his head but only one outshone the rest: the thought of that poxy ill-fated chest they sought after and the trouble it had caused. The cursed Lost Loot. It was the reason behind every grumbling stomach, the reason for their constant deprivation and desperation: the bane of his life. As he looked out to the terrifying view beyond the bulwark, his grandfather's advice echoed in his mind and he wondered if he should've taken heed. *That life is hard, crush the living daylights from your measly meat in no time, boy. No. Better to stay in London, boy. Wish I had. Wish I had . . .* 'Joseph,' Victoria said, breaking his anxiety, 'I hate to admit it, but I'm scared.'

Choosing his bravest smile, he displayed it, 'we'll be fine, try not to overthink it. This'll soon be over.'

Despite his efforts, she saw through his façade. 'I appreciate the strength, but I'd rather the truth. Are you scared?'

He pursed his lips and gulped, 'yes.'

She smiled in relief, 'Good. You're not a fool then.' A pause stopped her, then she embraced him, and he wrapped his arms around her. To Joseph, she smelled of sweat and salt and a womanly scent, an aroma he liked. She smelled on him sweat and fear and a musk she found comfort in. Victoria held him tightly, where he whispered in her ear, 'in the darkest time, I'll ask you to dance with me, so that there can be a light to shine through it.' She squeezed him in acknowledgement, then let go and stepped to the wheel to tie it and keep it heading south-east.

The day passed aggravatingly slowly and barely a sound was heard during its remainder; during the evening sup, it was hard to talk over the loud noises of chewing and swallowing. Teeth mashing food together sounded like buildings being demolished; every crunch a blast of exploding mortar. Everyone spoke in their quietest tone as to not disturb the heavy silence that had befallen – a hush was their best bet at being heard. Night passed with Benjamin on the dogwatch. Now, the role had become ever more important, for the lookout was less for any alterations to sway them off course and simultaneously *for any* alternations to steer them. Billy's new sarcastic name for it stuck; wind-watch it was henceforth rechristened, for that was all everyone hoped for.

In the following two days, the crew went about Paying the Devil. Whilst half split fibres from the ropes as quickly as their fingers could manage, the other half caulked the decks, (making them grasp why the garboard seam was named the devil's seam; it was so long and so damn hard to reach) until near all the hemp fibres were used, the pine tar was near gone and all holes were filled, in the berth, orlop and hold as well as the bilge. At least their leak had been filled; about the only thing Robertson had managed to crack a smile at.

The next day was spent in shifts, with half fishing and the other half swabbing; then swapping as the sun climbed over the yardarm. A stunning spectacle occurred an hour past noon, causing the fishing team to withdraw their nets. A wild swarm of jellyfish bloomed as far as the eye could see. They were white and glob-like, like phlegm in the water, pulsing as they drifted through, multiplying in astounding numbers until the patch of ocean they floated on writhed with the ancient creatures. The crew were mesmerised, yet the bloom left them after an hour, drifting back into the depths as spontaneously as they had arrived. By the end of the day, despite the sparklingly clean decks, every hand was red raw, blistering and cracking, and the holystones were as smooth as the water out yonder. As the laborious day drew to a close, all sailors sought for the one missing element, but wind was nowhere to be felt, not even a sigh, and the water was a dreadful and abysmal feature, simply because of its lack in any. It was a feature without a feature; tiresome and aggravating to look upon. Wind-watch was taken by the captain, who was attempting to stay strong but appearing evermore bleak in doing so.

Careening and maintenance was the focus of the next day. Barnacles: with half the crew set on plucking them from the hull above the surface stem to stern. Prying the rock-hard lesions from the salt-encrusted wood was no easy task but it kept the mind busy and it was satisfying to hear the plop as they dropped back into the water. Some would even admit they slowed this job to draw it out, lest they face the deck again. They only had so many bosun's chairs for this task though, so the rest of the crew were set upon maintenance until they swapped duties; tying ropes and testing them, sewing torn fabrics and repairing tears upon the sails and tidying the main deck, berth, orlop and hold as much as they could.

The following day, whilst constantly lending an ear to a whisper of wind, the non-fishing crew set about dressing down the sails. A laborious and dull job this was, supposed to be a punishment for any sailor out of order yet this glacial day they were all being punished. Slabs of wax were melted, and oil was taken from the hold and brushed upon the canvases, each and every one, to renew their effectiveness and seal any rogue holes along the sewed seams. Some saw this as a moot exercise seeing as there was no blasted wind to snag the sails anyway, yet it kept everyone occupied under the treacherous sun, fluorescent and euphoric.

General talk had been active at first, but it shied early, with barely anyone speaking apart from the occasional murmur and even these happenings seemed loud. Billy played his fiddle and flute quietly, escaping in the strings and the melodies they produced, although his tunes were forlorn and wistful, and everyone wished for them to stop. Hours slid away with everyone becoming more frightened now that the list of jobs was growing thin. The focus on chores was holding things together; what came after was something they were afraid of. Lethargy and insanity loomed in dark forbidding clouds.

The seventh day in the doldrums saw the crew at a loss; wandering from one end of the ship to the other; sitting for hours or standing in a daze, looking out to the endless, torturous void. Already they had begun shrinking back into their own beings, wrapping themselves in a cocoon of thoughts and memories, worries and predictions, opportunities missed, and opportunities taken. Regretting those they had taken that led them to his ship. Regretting agreeing to help Joseph Winter on this ponderous, unforgiving quest.

Eight days in and Robertson offered suggestions to keep everyone busy: more fishing which everyone agreed upon, and another which caused frowns and sighs, but they had no choice: rats. Those that could not fit on the fishing boat thundered around the hold, orlop and berth trying to catch the multiplying vermin that scurried constantly, squeaking loudly, as if someone continued to pull a rusty-hinged door. It was a tiresome and frustrating job, but it passed the time whilst the others sat in the boat bobbing away the long hours on the flat surface of the ocean.

It was refreshing, the fishing team saw, to see ripples in the water coming from their craft; an endless row of lines marching away from them, all identical in movement and shape until they, too, calmed. They forgot how much they missed the sight of movement, and it brought forth a longing wrath to see more and to ride the ripples out of this abhorrent pit of stagnancy.

No fish were caught that day, or the day after. In fact, nothing seemed to be moving under the surface at all. This entire ocean, teeming with marine life, magnificent and microscopic, and not a spec was seen from anyone. A craving besotted at them, not only to hear the waves again but to *see* movement of any kind. A fish swimming under the surface would be a tremendous show, a cloud sailing in its own blue sea would be a grand miracle, a bird soaring over heights escaping this heat-trap would be a brilliant sight to behold, worthy of an applause. Anything to witness. Anything. *Please.*

That evening, their prayers were answered in the form of clouds. Not a dull grey bank of cumulus nor the huge gothic spires of an incoming storm, but great whirls and shapeless cotton forms, all separated by spacings and their own individualism. All riding, all *moving* on the fast jet of pressure above, sliding over as if they were on a glass dome. What appeared even more fascinating was the reflection they gave. Just to see clouds in the sky was enough, to receive that moment's respite from the harsh beat of the sun, but to look out from the bulwark and observe the brilliance of their reflection was astounding.

Each person stared in awe at the passing of the tremendous forms, at the gap of soft yet jagged seams of light, painting them the purest of whites at their peaks, melting down to a lemony cream to dazzling oranges and ambers in their breaks; yet knitting them all together in a grand blanket of warm splendour. Then there! Bouncing the image upside down was to reveal another pure, ever-lasting perspective that could not be replaced. Every wrinkle, crumple and fold of the undersides could be seen in clarity; every detail was captured magnificently by the golden fire of evening light.

It was a masterpiece that stunned them all. A rare scene of an unbridled charm that could only be akin to the purity of a first love and the joy of soul-seeking wanderlust, with sparkling, smoothing sublime colours of immensity that opened the eye to awareness of two sides, the good and the bad. A beauty so raw and so powerful it was a gateway to the heavens, immortal and infinite, that every soul sought to reach.

They ate their rations under the passing clouds, watching them slide over the mastheads and enjoying the patches of shade unknown this far out to sea. Even though the setting was unparalleled, envy could not be helped once the clouds moved on past the horizon, leaving them still stranded, marooned on this floating wooden island. The past few hours couldn't be replaced; the crew knew it was something they could never hope to see again in a setting such as this, yet it set a sombre mood. Billy Baker stared wistfully out to the melting amber of dusk and said sadly as the chill of the air sent steam from their mouths, 'if only we could've wrangled those clouds somehow. Wrangled them with our hopes and desperation – they could've towed us from this sickenin' place instead of leaving us behind to rot in this tragic hole.'

Joseph nodded as he slipped his hands in his jacket pockets and pulled his cap down. 'If only, Bill. I'll take the wind-watch tonight. I've had trouble sleeping of late anyway.' He said as he leaned against the railing, watching the stars peep out of the gloom one by one.

'Aye. Alright, Quart'.' Robertson slapped his shoulder, 'make sure you try and get some shuteye though.'

A nod, 'will do, Jim. I'll ring the bell if I feel a breeze.'

'Aye. Goodnight to you.' He took off his hat and departed to his cabin. The rest of the crew departed, and soon after, Victoria left his side to retire to her hammock after giving him a kiss.

Joseph wandered up to the forecastle and stood silent as the night thickened. A brisk chill was in the air; he buttoned his jacket and saw his breath steaming from his mouth. It was novel to see it again; it seemed a lifetime ago he'd been in cold like this, only this time he was surrounded by an ocean of water instead of a maze of buildings.

As the hours lengthened, the night sky suddenly displayed its own masterpiece, revealing it openly to those awake enough to observe. Upon noticing the fantastic scene, he realised he had to get higher. Hurriedly, Joseph clambered through the deck and climbed the shrouds all the way to the crow's nest, seeing everything perfectly clear from the pale light of the distant moon. He stood at the very top of the ship and beheld two Milky Way's stretched and sprawled, perpendicular to each other; one rising into the night sky and the other spreading deeper into the black sea, emitting such a ghostly light that even the rigging and masts had their own shadow against the virgin glow.

The galaxies were bright and vivid, identical in detail and sharing a clarity that Joseph never knew existed in the world. His pulse slowed as he observed the shimmering spread of thick orbital dust sprawling across the night sky, scattering and branching like a blown dandelion, growing and splitting to his naked eye. A great rift tore the galaxy of the sky in two, splitting the white, blue dust as if the almighty had drawn a finger through it. Thicker patches of mass clouded at one end, though when his eye followed, it cut off and began anew within the water, spreading like an astronomical alga, manifesting in the ocean with an incredible sublimity and wonder that made him want to kneel to the silent phenomenon they were sailing through.

Millions of stars, some with grand white tails as they soared, crowded the sky around the galaxy leaving not a patch of black left for the night to claim for its own, as if all had turned out twinkling to pay homage to their elder kindred. Joseph gazed down and saw its twin reflected in the mirror and felt as if he was travelling through the vast vacuum aboard this lost ship, that they no longer sailed upon water but through the stars to the next galaxy, to the next nebula, to infinity. No other thoughts entered his head, he was too overwhelmed; only now could he grasp Thomas's meaning of presence.

Tears involuntarily streamed down his face as an overwhelming sense of insignificancy beseeched his soul. Oh! how miniscule they all were, how the earth was, in comparison to such stratospheric blooms of stars, galaxies, masses and forces of creation, hurtling through the universe on a never-ending odyssey of existence.

After an hour passed, he climbed down the shrouds and walked afore the ship to the forecastle, bathed in nocturnal light. Suddenly his eye was brought to the surface again, as it was now writhing with colour and pulsating bright greens and blues, overtaking the night's reflecting glory to give way to a wondrous spectre space itself had birthed all those years ago. The ocean, as far as the horizon, was alight with this strange pulsing glow, and for a second he believed he'd fallen asleep and this was but a dream, except the reality of it was too phenomenal to ignore, no matter how hallucinogenic it appeared to be. Bioluminescent plankton was its source, but after falling victim to such harrowing conditions the view looked beyond acceptance. Never had he seen the likes of it before, and never would he see it again.

Suddenly his eye picked out movement within the depths. There! Swimming below the surface close to the hull, shrouded in a splendid glow of sparkling green, a humpback whale and her calf gorged themselves on the rush of glowing midnight bacterium that lit up around them, guiding their path through the water. They were huge, streamlined and comely as they swam, moving and twisting, dancing as they fed, through the pulsing glow until they disappeared back into the depths of this bewildering ocean, leaving Joseph awestruck and speechless. It was a moment he was never to forget. Despite his knowledge, his fingers twiddled the crown of the pocket watch; the only thing rooting him to this psychedelic phenomenon.

His breath billowed out straight, before fading in the cold air and he knew what he had to do and who to spend this moment with. Quickly and quietly, he hurried to Victoria's hammock and woke her, putting a finger to his lips to keep hushed. In curiosity, she followed him to the deck where she was shocked to see how bright everything was, as if daylight had come early. Yet the light emitted from the ocean and pulsed, unlike anything she had ever seen, and she gasped at the sight, holding a hand to her mouth.

Joseph smiled and nodded, understanding. Without a word, he led her from the railing to the middle of the deck. 'I hope you don't mind me waking you, but I had to share this with someone.' He said quietly, 'This, all of it over these past few hours, has reminded me of how beauty can be anywhere, thriving even in the darkest of times, if we're only aware of where to look and when to appreciate.' He reminisced Robertson's words, realising how truthful they had been. 'I know how bad things have become, which is why I thought now was the best time. If I remember rightly, I owe you a dance.' Joseph smiled, taking her hand.

Victoria smiled warmly, tiredly, with tears in her eyes as she stepped closer into him. He took her waist and held her. As she rested her head upon his shoulder, they danced, slowly and peacefully, upon the deck. Enjoying each other, enjoying the moment, as the colours of the ocean glowed, and the stars above shined and soared through the darkness of the passing night.

Chapter Thirty-Two

Morning arrived quicker than he expected, and the stars sadly winked from the darkness, leaving the sky a shell of the magnificence it had borne. A dense fog settled over the smoothness of the water as dawn approached, smudging all hopes of a reflecting sunrise. The fog rose to the bulwark and shrouded the deck and masts in a viscous pea-soup. Mist he'd seen before out here, but fog was another matter and since there were no waves to hear and the fog was a sponge to any sound, a heartbeat was amplified, and breaths were as loud as gale force winds. It looked peculiar and ominous, making him feel nervous; yet the light of dawn brightened the murky tone and raised it to a whitewashed grey letting him know sunrise was not far away. Surprisingly, despite the little sleep he'd managed to get, he felt better rested than many previous nights swaddled and sweating in his hammock. *I'll have to volunteer for wind-watch more often,* he thought as he rang the bell to signal dawn. The sound seemed muffled, as if cotton wool were wrapped around the clapper.

The crew woke and began the day, extinguishing the bewilderment of the prodigious night; the glorious spectre he'd witnessed was set back and again he found himself tense and short of breath. Immediately, Joseph felt the surmounting stress weighing heavily, especially when they noticed the cloying fog, then doubling when they saw how low their stash of coconuts was. Another day was beginning and still no sign of change was present. A looming sense of doom hung over their heads.

As they began their day of aimless fruitless restlessness, no one brought up the subject, but it began to play on their minds; the rats. Scurrying hither and thither, it was hard not to hear them – their squeaks and patters seemed to rumble through the wood from all decks. Their numbers were increasing, which brought forth a depressing notion. Food . . . there *were* a lot aboard . . . and it *was* fresh meat after all. Sheer desperation would have to be present, but for now they were glad to have a few coconuts left, as well as scraps of meat and dried fish as salty as the sailors the crew had become. Yet the thought was on everyone's mind and became not an *if* but a *when*. On that concerning morning however, the wizened sailor brought them each a special treat to stave off the vermin-eating.

As the fog cleared, Benjamin, ever resourceful, had sawed the horns and bones of the goats and pigs into bitesize chunks for everyone to suck the marrow from. Barely anything could be tasted, but as hunger began to test suddenly the marrow became better than any boiled sweet in any confectionary shop. There were plenty more, he told them: a rare term aboard this scant old boat.

Deprivation began to show its hard face again; everyone had accustomed to seeing bones, but in trying times they seemed pronounced and sharper, always knocking into things. When looking over the side of the longboat whilst out fishing, Joseph had caught a glimpse of himself in the water and almost didn't recognise the face looking back to him. The cheek bones were pointed, and the beard was dry and scraggly, the eye sockets were sunken and dark, and the green eyes were beady. *Bugger me, who is that? That's not . . . me. Is it?* Reality had to be faced however, and judgements had to be adjusted; their looks were changing, as well as their bodies. Their skin greyed and dried like ash with some crew members yellowing; often breaking out in ugly welts and red sores from the malnutrition - cracking and flaking from the exposure to the sun. Bruises were taking longer to heal, and small cuts had to be bandaged as the congealing process was far too slow, all of which were pleasant compared to the aching joints firing flares of pain through their bodies with every movement, becoming ever a nuisance. Often, they had to walk barefoot as their feet had swollen and the dry fungus and deep-rooted corns that were intent on ripping their toes apart worked forever hard.

The day was spent with the crew laying in whatever shade they could find and pacing up and down the ladders to keep moving, deeply saddened by the sails that hung so limply by their slack ropes. In the end, Robertson ordered the mizzen and foresails to be hauled and stowed as the sight became too depressing. In a vague half-hearted attempt, they tried fishing again but after hours had passed, they caught nothing and gave up; disappointment showing its face once again.

Yesterday's cloudy spectacle was all but forgotten by the time evening came around; the hardship was too great to focus on anything; the memories would have to be rekindled once happier times were found. For now, though, it would have to wait; focus was short-lived on a ship run by ghosts stuck in their memories, unable to look forward and live.

A stressful, strangled quiet settled over the deck the following day. Like the fog, it squatted immobile and no one dared to heave it away. Sounds were too loud now, which meant the mutterings Joseph heard between the crew had become audible, and the eyes he felt on him were unforgiving. *They blame me for this, I know they do. They're blaming me for all of it because I dragged them into this.* Joseph gave cold glares back until everyone shrank further into their shells. The deck was an anxious place to be, but in one's head was even more paranoid.

He noticed Rob spent much of his time aloft in the rigging or the crow's nest now, muttering with Dave. As he paced the deck from stem to stern, Joseph saw Benjamin, Tess and Billy muttering to each other by the slack lines and belaying pins, '*This ship is the damned Flying Dutchman, I'm sure of it, and we're sailing into Davy Jones's Locker.*' He heard as he passed them and tried to supress a mixed emotion. In surprise, he found Thomas sitting cross-legged on the forecastle, his hands on his knees and back ironing-board straight, facing the bowsprit. Joseph frowned, 'what are you doing?'

There was a moment's delay, as if he didn't hear him. Eventually Thomas replied, 'meditating.'

'What's that?'

Thomas exhaled through his nose without turning around, 'sitting in silence to adjust my way of thinking. Your thoughts are more powerful than you think, enabling you to literally create the reality around you – manifesting what you want and controlling your reactions to situations that can either make everything peaceful . . . or paranoid, depending on which thoughts you pay more attention to.'

Struggling to comprehend what he was saying in his state of delirium, Joseph took a moment to process what he'd said. 'What thoughts are you paying more attention to now?'

'Manifestation.'

'What are you trying to manifest?'

Thomas replied with a snivel, and Joseph spotted him wiping away a tear. 'An escape from this suffering.'

Joseph took a step back and quickly turned, feeling his heart thump faster and his blood rush to his head. *You wanted to come aboard Thomas!* He wanted to scream, *you begged to get on this ship, to come with us!* He increased his pace, making another round on the deck, feeling their pretentious beady eyes scouring him like a wire brush on a rusty iron pot. *Bloody ungrateful pricks, the lot of 'em. I break them out of prison and give them another chance and this is what I get for it. I wish I'd have never bothered; I should've done it by myself.* He walked past Victoria sitting meekly against the mizzenmast, her hands on her stomach and she smiled weakly at him through thin lips and a pale face. Only now did he stop pacing, 'Victoria, are you alright?'

'Yes. Just needed a sit down is all. I can't . . . seem to find my strength recently.' She uttered, shading her eyes from the sun.

He sighed, 'me n' all. I don't know . . . where it's gone.' His words seemed to echo from his mouth; for a moment he wasn't sure whether those were spoken words or a run of thought. Either way he felt out of breath with them. Slowly, he blinked. Was Victoria even sitting there or was she a thought too? A conjured image? A hallucination? Was he even aboard this ship?

'How're you getting on with the clues? Have you . . . looked . . . anymore?' she asked, her voice thin.

Suddenly he was in the shade of the cabin flitting through the papers, his skin feeling like it was about to shrink to his bones and flake like autumn leaves. *How did I get here?* He frowned in desperate confusion, *I . . . can't remember . . .* Joseph looked at the various papers over the table and struggled to recollect sitting down. With tired bloodshot eyes, he read through the same clues, the same notes, the same poems and riddles but nothing presented itself at all. He knew he should've felt angry and exasperated again, but he struggled to feel anything. *Ludicrous, that's what this is. Ludi . . . crous . . .* Getting to his feet, he walked to the desk and began opening drawers – he wasn't sure why, maybe he did know why; he just didn't know any more. What did he know? *I know I'm glad to be away from that pack o' dogs out there, whining to each other, away from those . . . prying eyes, that's for sure.* Hunting for clues, he came across a different piece of information.

SHIP'S LOG

Picking out the leather-bound book, he placed it on the strewn pieces on the table and opened it. Dates and entries filled every page from the start of the year. Joseph flicked through, unsure of what month it was yet alone the date or day of the week. In a past life, he used them, he knew exactly what time it was on a Tuesday and he *actually* cared as he had places to be, as everyone did, but out here in this vast waste, days of the week were positively useless. Scanning, he found the final entry from yesterday; the mention of marrow was there and that had been yesterday. *Or was that the day before?* Blinking hard, he couldn't remember, but he could read. He flicked back numerous pages and perused.

- *Ship Victoria has stowaways on board I believe to be treasure hunters and they have convinced me to be their Captain. I believe they escaped from a prison in the city. They are convicts which is a concern; I do not trust them, but they seem willing enough to learn and work. I fear them, I cannot deny. The leader of the group is Joseph Winter, who found the scroll leading to the supposed Lost Loot, and (at a guess) formed the group and persuaded me to be their Captain to lead them on this quest. My crew was dropped off a few miles from French coast, I pray they found land well. Have given each member a role and named Joseph Winter as my new First Mate and Quartermaster since he found the scroll. Weather is grey and murky with a bitter northerly wind.*

He flicked pages:

- *Made stop at Lisbon port today to stock and for QM Joseph to see about the clue he discovered written in the juice of an orange on the back of the scroll . . .*

Pages were skipped:

- *Travelled to Gabon today whereupon . . .*

- *Crew is tested by the heat. I myself am feeling it also. Newly discovered clue Cabin Boy Robert Epping found has a tough riddle but managed to find an answer to it leading . . .*

- *Rounded Cape of Good Hope, Southern Africa today . . .*

- *Wind dropped and caught in becalmed waters. Crew has seen how dangerous it is and are scared and hungry. Food and water gone. Mood aboard deck is tense . . .*

A few entries were missed where Robertson had been away from the Log, starting up again covering the basis of their expedition.

- *Survived great ordeal in Madagascar: Welcomed by local village (tribe) led by Chief Tulyaka (if how spelt). Fed and watered us, friendly connection. Had to collect diamonds to trade for chest. Accused of stealing upon return, convicted and made to face trial by Tangena (if how spelt). QM Joseph claimed chest after facing trial by Tangena, much bravery shown here. Deckhand Hugh Jackson was lost to Tangena and the tribe; may his soul be at rest. Crew are in great spirits upon cracking the new riddle: Australia is new heading, meaning we must cross the Indian Ocean. I hope they are aware of the dangers of the open ocean. I fear they do not understand it.*

- *Making good progress through the Indian Ocean. Wind is strong and persistent, if but temperamental, as expected. Crew are of high spirits after the haul of fish. How long it will last, I am not sure. I worry for them. I have noticed everyone is holding a concealed weapon of sorts. I am on edge, fears of mutiny are a constant thought: have discussed with QM Joseph and he is trying to keep civil with everyone, especially Rigger Dave James after their conflict. I hope QM Joseph has found something in his studies for what to do once we arrive. Boatswain Victoria Penning helping him in studies. I am starting to pray before sleep again.*

- *Progress made. Should arrive in Australia in a week, weather permitting. Rains still falling, crew is quiet. Will this be the day of the mutiny? Keeping check on all Mates and Hands, keeping them busy. Lack of sleep is getting to me. Exhaustion is hard. I must remain strong.*

- *Still no wind. No current. Water is glass. Becalmed waters/ doldrums (too tired to nit-pick on difference, after being here so long I no longer care) holding us tightly. Food running dangerously low. Rations keeping everyone alive yet starved. Store of coconuts is dwindling, and other foods inedible and in need of disposal. Master Rigger Benjamin Smith has sawed bones from pigs and goats for us to suck the marrow from. Rats will need to be caught and eaten soon. Crew are of an anxious state, worse than I have seen of late. I can no longer keep them busy; there are no more jobs to do. I am worried uprising will begin. I fear for my life now. This gang of criminals cannot be trusted. They have evil intent in their eye now we are not making progress. What will happen once we find the chest I do not know. I can only imagine it will not be a friendly halving of the loot. All were convicted for a reason; perhaps I should've been stronger on that first day and stopped them. I now see that I wasn't persuaded, I was shanghaied. I am weak, may God forgive me. As the days pass, I am losing my wits; I hallucinate and wander without a purpose or direction and movement gives a terrible ache. Scurvy is beginning to set in, with me as well as all. Sleep eludes me for three nights in fear of mutiny and of deprivation. Either way, both are present and crushing and I am powerless against them.*

- *No wind. Scant amount of food will be gone in a day. QM Joseph has not revealed any hidden clues and seems to be at a loss. We all are. Hope is as strained as it has ever been. Mutterings common amongst Mates and Hands. It is the only talk between them now. They are joining. I feel their glares; their mutterings are aimed at me: they want command of this ship. Am at a loss of what to do, how to protect myself. Revolt is imminent. God save us all. God save me.*

Joseph read through the last entry and felt a cold sweat running down his face. Robertson had been rather stiff since they began the crossing, but he didn't realise that was through fear of the crew. These were the writings of a man at the end of his tether: a sailor readying for a revolution, a madman's scrawls. *It all looks like something I would write now.* He gulped a dry throat. Nausea washed through him, squeezing his empty stomach tight and sending his head spinning. *He's right. It could be any day now, at any time. The mutterings have grown common. I see the way they look at me . . .* Slowly he looked to the door and the hazy heat outside, thick with anxious tension. Robertson was right; if deprivation wouldn't kill them then a mutiny would.

When and who was involved was a concept he couldn't think about. *Dave: I wager it's his doing. He's behind it all. He always has been. Who else though? How would–*
is Victoria in on it–

will there be . . . He looked back to the Log, to the last entry and felt his gut wrench. *I can't stay in here. Must get out. Must get out!* Quickly, he slammed the book shut and stuffed it back in the drawer and hurried down to the bunks of the berth before his mind tore itself in two.

Benjamin was asleep in his hammock, or was he pretending to be? Was he there trying to listen in on Joseph, to keep check on him? An informant? Was it even Benjamin? Was anyone even there? His head was swimming, disorientation making his legs tremble. Not sure of what else to do, he clambered into his hammock, his breath flitting in short sharp gasps, and he gripped the pocket watch tightly, flicking and twisting the crown as his mind raced before him.

Uncertainty gripped; he wasn't sure who he was, what he'd become. As he lay in his hammock, he wished he'd never went to the Back House that day and heard of Mad Vinny's new job. Wished he'd never heard of the Lost Loot, had never broken into that house and stole the scroll, had never met this untrustworthy band of heathens. Wished he'd never stole a ship and sailed half the world. *Why! Why didn't I listen to Lucy and not go to that house? I could've been at home with her now enjoying the London summer with a stable job as a clerk, drinking the fine cider of the season in warm evenings surrounded by friends. I could've had a full belly, a warm hearth and a soft bed, clean clothes, bank accounts and furniture. I could've married her and had children; two, three, four, been a father, had a family. I could've done it; I could've lived in London the rest of my life. No more stealing, no more reputations, no more Trace. Just Joseph. Just me. Just a future as hopeless as the past. Just a past as hollow as the present.* He stared up at the wood, the possibilities popping and bursting and making him regret. Regret the choices, regret the treatment and the life he'd led. The things he'd stolen, the people he'd neglected, the money he'd made, the streets he'd known, the reputation he'd held; the worries that haunted, the cares that gnawed, the wants that gripped, the dreams that teased, the hopes that things would change and the knowledge they never would unless he escaped.

Yet, at the same time, he knew the dreams of the city life were a sham. Deep down he cared little for the façade society had created; its appearance created a falsehood to keep people happy; to live, to make money, to reproduce, to die. Essential aims to reach. Sounding appealing but feeling hollow. Where was the spontaneity to it?

He had to steal, had to take, had to earn to keep moving forward. To keep living. He loved and despised the street-life simultaneously; the rush of it was addictive but exhausting, the reputation a burden to uphold. He could've left it behind and got a proper job . . . but he didn't. He wanted it all and his greed and selfishness had led him here, to suffer these consequences. The thrill, the kick, the travel; the exploration, the starvation, dehydration and insomnia; rare discoveries and breaking boundaries; meeting tribes and losing friends; guilt-tripping and hallucinating, suffering and wandering, moving, seeking, hoping, finding, reaching the fabled, hated, cursed, poxy chest this had all been about. All in the name of prosperity to better his chances at understanding who he was and what he wanted and what really mattered in this brutal, unforgiving world. *I had to experience everything. I had to learn who I didn't want to be.* His past was gone, his future lay ahead, and his present moment was now; the days to come would be determined from actions made in this time, in this moment and they were his to decide. He was the master of his own fate. The captain of destiny.

As he lay there, feeling his head pound and listening to that constant bombardment thundering in his chest, he considered the first day he'd met them all and realised how wrong he'd been, how quickly he'd judged them. Desperation at getting out was the first big mistake. How was he to know who they really were, who they'd turn out to be. Their motives were a mystery, yet he didn't pry. *Why didn't I? Why didn't I question why they wanted to join?* Motives would've told him everything, their stories could've told their character, *why didn't I ask them? Why didn't I find out more about them before I broke them free and had to live and work with them, before I offered them another future?*

Was it blood they were after? Freedom? Did they want a fresh start, or just to cause violence? Money, was money what they were after? *Of course, it is, it always comes down to money. The only thing that keeps the world turning. The only thing people really care about, believing it'll make them happier only to find out it'll never be enough. It's fucking poison. A con to keep you in the loop. Fucking pennies with royal heads on them, coins and paper; such fickle things to have faith in. Bloody shillings, sovereigns, threepences, sixpences and half bloody crowns. Gold coins. Gold trinkets. Gold and diamonds. Priceless.*

He licked his dry lips, staring up into space with bleary eyes. *If that's what they want, then I'll make sure none of them get it and it's never found! I'll burn the clues and papers for the torture it's put us through, for what it's turned us into. I'll make sure no one will ever claim that blood-soaked hoard. I have the power now. I found the scroll! I founded this mission and sent them on this quest and they're after me for it, for the hardship I've put them through. They want the ship; they want the money and the blood and the violence that'll come with it. I know it is, and that's exactly what they'll get. I am a Winter; this is my life and I've fought too long and too hard to let them get the better of me. I am the master of my own fate!*

Suddenly the crown he'd been unconsciously fidgeting with snapped from its purchase and the pocket watch fell apart in his hands, bursting from its scratched bronze rim. Hands, cogs, sprockets and springs showered onto his stomach and bounced and rolled into his hammock. *Shit!* Joseph gasped, tensing at his own wrongdoing. The sound of clinking metal sounded odd to his ears, unnatural after weeks with only wood and water.

He knew there was no way he could fix it. The instruction from the clue resurfaced: *keep the piece ticking.* Not any more it wouldn't. Squeezing his eyes shut and clenching his jaw he tried to remain calm; there was naught to be angry at but himself, which made him even angrier. *Look what you've gone and done. The clue said to keep it ticking, how am I meant to do that now?* With weak arms he pulled himself up the hammock to get a clearer view of the mess he'd made.

Pieces were everywhere. Who knew there were so many parts that could fit and work together in such a small space; every piece having a function to keep a tick in motion, to keep time moving forward, and now it had been reduced to its bare complex components. A puzzle no one on board knew how to solve. There was something else though, something that didn't fit. His eyes were drawn to it. Poking from the pile of tiny instruments was a corner of cloth.

Gulping, he pulled it out and tried to control the tremble in his fingers. Carefully, he unfolded the cloth and upon it he saw a small writing of hand, a familiar hand he knew all too well. Thoughts were paused, memories were put on hold, functions focused solely on reading the few words he held before him, floating in his watery vision.

> A wasteland is where the chest can be won; rumours
> there are of two moons and two suns,
> Worthy beyond value, pound without pound; to those
> who are lost so you shall be found.
> Turn the holy pages, the key is within this story; a
> witness to the heavens is he that unlock glory.
> We hunt for divinity whereupon and without fail . . .

The cloth was torn.

Only shreds and fibres finished the sentence, the most important sentence Joseph had ever beheld.

There was more. There had to be more, but where? *Where?!* He'd examined every inch of every paper, every cranny of the chests and searched the very nooks of his mind to find an answer to this impossible ending. Now he had a part of it here in his hand; the other had to be here somewhere and by god and the forces of his weakened body he was going to find it.

Quickly sitting up, his head was pounding. *I need to tell them. They need to know!* He swung his legs over the side, the components scattering over his body . . . but his feet did not reach the floor. His leathery, crusted feet, they stopped. The hammock rocked slightly yet his eyes stared dead ahead. *I don't have to tell them. I don't have to tell them anything. I can find the other half to this myself.* And with one thought, the trust betwixt them shattered.

The thought of Victoria surfaced and now his face found a frown. He loved her and soon he would tell her, he knew he'd have to, but this moment was precious, and he was in no mood to share. Naturally, there was a chance she was in on the mutiny too; he'd dared not to consider it, yet there was a chance of it all the same. For now, no one could be trusted, not after the anti-social fog that had descended on deck and the worrisome entries of this creaking tub's Log. Either way, the way he saw it, what good was half a clue anyway? Might as well tell her when he had its entirety.

With his heart thumping rapidly, Joseph tried to hold a logical perception; to start from the very root to get to the fruit in the branches. The other half could be anywhere, which meant one thing: it had to be somewhere. It existed, and it linked with this piece of cloth hidden inside a pocket watch from a chest entrusted to a Madagascan tribe. *Anywhere . . . It could literally be anywhere on the planet . . .*

If the pocket watch came from a chest, then maybe the other half did too? *But I've searched everything we've found; nothing was there.*

If the cloth came from *inside* the pocket watch, maybe the other half is inside another object? *But what, what object?*

If the pocket watch was found, maybe the other object can be too? *Definitely. Keep the piece ticking.*

A notion came to him then; perhaps that was why the clue told them to keep the pocket watch ticking, so that they'd focus on that and realise it wasn't functioning properly because there was a spanner in the works - or in this case, cloth. They'd try and try, then open the egg to fix it only to discover the yolk hidden within. Joseph looked down to the shrapnel on his lap. *An't no chance it'll tick any more.* There was no doubt that neglect and age had ruined its cognitive perfection, but how could they have known it was due to a folded piece of fabric too? It had been no more than a keepsake, a lucky charm. Its purposelessness held a quality to it though, Joseph liked to have it with him, why he could not say. *If it hadn't of been broken, I never would've paid heed to it, its purpose would've been there in front of me, ticking away. Because it was broken, I focused on it better and can now see it had a different role to play.* He sighed and closed his weary eyes, feeling far from the answer. *I just need time to think; time, and a direction to look to.*

Suddenly it clicked.

He tore open his eyes, his gut wrenching.

Jumping to his feet, sending the cogs scattering across the wood, Joseph rushed across the berth to his navy jacket hanging on a hook. He plunged his hand inside and grabbed the item he had deemed worthless from the beginning. A broken thing spinning and struggling to hold true, to stay as the crow flies. A smile broke out on his pallid face as he held the compass in his palm, the compass with the etched J on its back that his grandfather had left him; the thing he didn't want to acknowledge. Now he had to.

From the hold, he retrieved a wooden hammer and opening the metal casing he watched the needle dart and dither, wander, spin and stop. Lost . . .

He placed it on the floor, raised the hammer high and brought it down to the object as hard as his weak hand could muster.

There was a smash, a crash, and Joseph Winter gasped.

Chapter Thirty-Three

The glass shattered and the needle snapped free, the components inside falling apart. Breaking in an odd fashion, Joseph already noticed something was not correct.

He dropped the hammer and gently picked the object up, tilting it and watching the wreckage fall to the floor. Watching as a small, polished rock fell from the casing followed by another piece of cloth: things that should never have been in there, things protected by the distraction of an object void of its use. A deterrent. At that moment, he thought of the regretful old man in his chair and wondered where he found this compass, and doubted he ever knew of its importance. *No, this hasn't been tampered with. Not since the Scott's set this all into play. Grandfather never knew about this.* He couldn't help but to laugh at how foolish Frederick Winter had been; to have had a clue in his possession all along and had not seen anything more than a broken compass. *Maybe that was why he left it to me, in case I ever found anything with it . . . Or maybe he just wanted to rid himself of poisoned memories – that sounds more like old Fred. He would've sold his heart if he could of.*

Picking the small stone from the pile, he examined it, his brows furrowing, not understanding the relevance. He moved on to the cloth and unfolded it, indignant to the fact that he'd been carrying a clue with him from London and had had it with him this entire time, right from the murk of that attic. Shaking his head, he found himself smiling at the slyness of fate. Slowly, he placed it underneath the last piece and began to read.

A wasteland is where the chest can be won; rumours there
are of two moons and two suns,

Worthy beyond value, pound without pound; to those
who are lost so you shall be found.
Turn the holy pages, the key is within this story; a witness to the
heavens is he that unlock glory.
We hunt for divinity whereupon and without fail . . .
. . . we shall bury this lost, rare and precious grail.
Returning it to the earth where it shall linger and wait;
so be it, until people can learn to love and not hate.
When joy outshines greed and days to come are hopeful;
set forth with your shovel and set the earth a'crumble.
The lodestone sampled may guide you to see; for although they live
charged apart their attraction lasts for eternity.
Lest this be the last mystery of our age; many discoveries
lie still unknown, dare to turn the page.
Fortitude and enlightenment are goals to be attained;
explore, discover, and let your life be regained!
Find your feet and seek!
HS ES

Finishing the second half, it dawned on him that this was the final clue. Its language was resolute, and its message gave more than a direction or where to seek the forthcoming part. It gave a sample of what to look for when approaching the loot. A physical idol that sought its equal out there in a land of two moons and two suns. Even though it sounded ridiculous, Joseph now knew better to take it as a literal meaning. *That* was where the treasure was buried: in a wasteland with two moons and two suns, as beautiful and glorified as the gateway to heaven; underneath a rock, a lodestone very much the same as the one he held in his wrinkled, callus palm. *But where on earth can I find a land of two suns?*

He glanced at the shell of the pocket watch and compass and appreciated how appropriate they were for this final part; how one needed the other to reveal the full extent of the clue. How one revealed time and the other direction, just what they needed to finish a trail of this enormity. *Just like the glasses from Lisbon helped me see the clue from Gabon; they all link so tremendously well.* Suddenly he became aware he was the only one, the only man in the world, to know where to look and what to do to find the treasure once they reached Australia, and thus a problem became so painfully clear. Who aboard this ship, if any, was he to tell about his discovery? It was tough. Some would speak, others would squeak.

Suddenly footsteps thudded down the companionway to the berth. He fretted, and quickly stashed the cloths and lodestone away deep in his pocket and swept up the remnants of his fruitful destruction. A shadow folded down the steps, 'Joe, y' down here?' Billy came stepping into the shade; he'd tied a dirty handkerchief around his head, but his curls flopped over the top; his shirt was buttoned halfway revealing a few prominent ribs under a layer of thin sun-bleached chest hair.

'Aye. I'm here.' He replied, 'I was just getting up when the pocket watch dropped on the floor and smashed.'

Billy gasped, 'Blimey, I'm surprised ye still kept that t'ing with you! I didn't think there was much hope with it anyway. As broken as the government, so it was.' He knelt to help clear up the scattered pieces; Joseph hoped he wouldn't notice some parts were of the compass, else there would be questions - questions he did not want to give answers to. 'It's alright, I can do it. My blunder anyway.' He said to distract him.

'Tis fine Joe, I need to do somet'ing to keep me mind a'tickin anyhow. I just came down here to check you're a'right? Haven't seen much o' you over the past few days.'

There's a reason for that. 'I guess everyone's trying to cope with this in their own way.'

'Aye, does seem a bit . . . stressful.' He paused, 'starvation can do funny things to the body,' another pause, 'and mind. Sometimes I don't know whether thoughts are coming from my head or my mouth.' Pause, 'recently I've been dreaming whilst awake and I haven't done that since I was a boy in Ireland when we went through that famine. Dreadful, that was. Felt like I was dreamin' all the time.'

Of course, Joseph knew he was talking about the potato famine of previous years. A hardship faced by many yet overcome by few, causing the Irish population to decline dramatically. 'I'd heard that was a rough one. I read in a newspaper . . . it took about . . . a million lives.' He wasn't aware of pauses any more. Stringing sentences together was a tough feat.

He nodded, 'and a million more emigrated. My family included. Fuckin' blight it was. Tragic. I haven't faced another t'ing like it . . . until now.' From underneath his handkerchief he looked around to Joseph and Joseph met his stare. A thick, uncomfortable silent moment passed between them, and neither said a word.

Just then, a rat scurried along under the gloom of the hammocks, squeaking and shuffling as it hurried to the hold. Billy picked up a cog and threw it, missing the rodent. 'Christ, this ship's crawlin' with 'em!' he turned and looked around to him, 'rats everywhere Joe, I'm tellin' you.' He got to his feet, 'I'm off to catch one. We need something to sup on tonight and I don't fancy sucking another one o' Ben's bone treats, as lovely as they are.'

Joseph looked at him and opened his mouth to say something but found nothing to put his tongue to. Wondering, Billy paused and stared, until the quartermaster forced a vacant smile, 'happy hunting.'

'You too, Joe.' Billy replied with a slow nod, and he descended to the hold.

As he cleared up the last of the sprawl, sweeping it into a pile, his stomach knotted, and his head felt light. Billy Baker knew exactly what he was saying and knew Joseph understood too. *Was that a warning? Does he know? Is he in on it?*

- *Happy hunting.*

- *You too, Joe.*

No, he can't be. If he were, why would he try to tell me?

- *Happy hunting.*

- *You too, Joe . . .*

Maybe he was trying to get me to trust him by hinting at a mutiny, to send a warning?

- *Happy hunting.*

'You too, Joe.' He repeated to himself in the stuffy air below deck. 'You too, Joe. You too, Joe. You too, Joe. You. Too. Joe . . .'

Clambering into his hammock, he took the pieces of cloth out and read them thoroughly, wanting to get to the cabin and make a copy of them but stopping himself from doing so. He wanted to be in possession of the only copy. *They can't know. None can. I can trust no one.* He read through the scrawls again, and again, trying to distinguish a meaning, to pick it apart to find a location until he slipped into a fitful and anxious sleep.

The bell rang long and loud, its chimes the only sound to signify another change of day. Although what day exactly no one could tell, and the month was a mystery no one had the energy to squabble about. It was just another day to them, another sun rising and setting in the exact same fashion as before punctuated only by the sharp, shrill ring of this infernal bell.

This time though, there was shouting with it. A shout that sounded like a scream in the forbidding silence they'd been existing in. '*Up! Now! Up, everyone! Wind has found us!* We have ripples, waves and motion! Get up here now you lazy scallywags and lice-ridden scoundrels, this salty tub needs manning like never before! She's biting at the bit and champing the ground, for the love of God let's let her gallop!'

In a strange flurry that hadn't been seen in days, the crew bounded up to the deck and felt wind on their faces, tugging at their hair and clothes, eager to get them moving. 'Bless my soul, it's here! It's found us!' Benjamin cried as he leapt over to the shrouds. The sails were knocking against the masts, the gooseneck was swivelling, and the lines were rattling, the old sailor knew better than to delay the call.

'Ol' Mother Nature is a cruel wench when she wants to be, but she can show some sympathy.' Dave added with the hint of a smile.

'There's no need to be kind calling her a wench,' said Victoria, 'she's a wicked bitch, make no mistake.'

It was a strong easterly gust, sending waves rolling and rising and cresting in white; returning to the sea its jittering turbulent personality which the doldrums had so viciously snatched. It was a joy to sense wind on their clammy skin, and to feel waves rumble through the wood, oh! What an almighty sensation it was, stimulating and beautiful, letting them forget their hardship for a time. Looking out beyond the bulwark was a multitude of undulating waves reaching to the horizon, movement they had been craving; a sight wonderous and nauseous and productive.

'To work with you all now, my crew! Our time has come! Let us sail this glorious tide and be hindered no more! Man the yards and winch the anchors!' Captain Robertson called to them in a vigorous voice, then laughed in glee. He left the bell and raced to the helm. Dave and Rob scurried up the shrouds on both the mizzen then fore masts to hoist the topsails and mainsails. Billy and Thomas manned the halyards and Victoria and Tess went about hauling the sheets to keep them in the tailwind and setting the correct knots to the belaying pins for the running rigging. Joseph set the spanker and flew from stem to stern winching the anchors and aiding with hands as best as he could with what little strength that remained. For now, cheer was found and shared as the precious winds continued to push them from misery, even if their bodies retained it.

The sails unfurled and were tightened, immediately filling with voluptuous gusts and the ship lurched forward. The motion, although familiar, felt bizarre and the wood felt unstable under their feet, reminding them of their first day aboard *Victoria* when they were but hapless land-lubbers slick with city skin. As the deck lurched and rolled and jolted it was not long before they found their sea-legs once again, moving with the ship as the ship moved with the wave.

Focus was revived from all and all were eager to move lest the wind dropped again and left them condemned in that hole void of life. It was a place they were not to forget, and hoped, in time, the memories would fade, and they could rest easier with light hearts. Even though the movement and thought of land was a shared desire that felt attainable, the crew were too exhausted to smile for long and conversation lagged. Tensions could still be felt; it was enough to dry all personality – each person becoming no more than a blank sheet of paper with their name written on it, enough for Joseph not to open his mouth to anyone in case he revealed what he had secretly discovered.

A blue grey light washed the sky with paleness, and the wind was brisk carrying no warmth with it at all. A cold morning it was, cold enough for them to hurry down to the berth when they had the time and don another layer of clothing until the warmth of the day resided.

As the bitter morning developed, large spreads of dark bulbous cumulus clouds passed overhead; glum and depressing they looked, moody and forlorn as they spread thickly over the sky like margarine ripping up bread instead of spreading over it. The peaks of the dense cumulus were a charcoal grey, darkening to a coal black at their base. Robertson eyed the sky, the horizon and beyond. A darkness lay heavily there, allowing no light through, and to his trained eye a storm looked nigh. It made sense, he thought, *the only thing strong enough to push a gust through becalmed waters would be a storm. Even so, we should be thankful for it.* Silently, he prayed for it to pass them. To be becalmed then hit by a storm was a demoralising concoction, especially when some aboard were feeling particularly vulnerable. *Food and rest are what we need. Maybe that'll stave off the outbreak . . . maybe.* Robertson blinked thrice and tried to focus on the deck. *Just get to land, get back to reality. Your mind . . . is wandering, Jim.* 'Hands and Mates alike to deck!' he called to them abruptly, 'when you're ready and have a moment to spare, go and get something to eat. With what little you can find.' Breakfast was slithers of coconut with a few gulps of its water. Their last two. Far from exciting or nutritious, but just enough to live off. Sadly, the crew hobbled down in dribs and drabs; it was a rare sight indeed to see all together now.

Rob returned to the deck last of all. 'There's nothing left to eat now, Captain.'

He sighed irritably. *As soon as one good thing happens, bad is just around the corner.* Measures had to be made. Realistically, there was food on the ship, live and fresh and furry and plenty to be had and in all honesty, they were not in a place to be fussy. Too many bones were evident. Too much yellowing skin and bleeding gums, not to mention soured attitudes. Soon they'd be beyond recovery. *It must be done.* Captain Robertson made his decision.

When all hands were accounted for, he called out from the helm once more with his words echoing in his head, 'Hands to deck!' Faces turned to him and looked down from the yards; gaunt and pale and skeletal they were with dark rings around every eye. A crew of the dead. Competing with the wind, he shouted, 'catch as many rats as you can today. Catch them big and fat like some of the ones I've seen roaming this bloody ship and let us feast tonight. They've been feasting, why can't we? They may be vermin, but they have flesh and blood and meat, and we need all we can get before we become a ghost ship run by skeletons like the tales of old. Catch them, says I! Round them up so we may fill our bellies tonight and give our withered tongues something else to taste.' *Other than the bitter air this ship now circulates.*

'Have we really reached that point?' Dave complained from the mizzen yard, 'they're nasty little creatures, full o' disease.'

'Yes, we have. Pass on it if you wish, but when you're clutching your belly with cramps of starvation, losing your hair and teeth as well as your mind from scurvy, don't crawl to me for aid. Rats are what we eat tonight.'

No one replied but an agreement was made. Passed was the point to decide what to eat.

Slow hours passed with disdain and time, again, became an irritable burden worthy of complaint, if they had the energy to. A barrel was lashed to the foot of the mainmast to collect the captured rats in a vain hope the sight might restore some satisfaction. One by one each went to give it a try and see what they could manage and gradually the barrel numbered at five. At first the sight was disgusting, but when pushed to the limit of starvation and madness it became a beacon of hope and reward and, as the barrel's numbers increased, so did their want for the day to run its course so they could dine on vermin flesh.

Keeping a wary eye from the maintop platform, the quartermaster observed the deck and who descended below to the ship's hunting grounds for winnings. Thomas Sharp brought forth two to offer to the barrel; a low blow, and Tess Mills also managed two. Benjamin Smith and Billy Baker contributed three each whilst Victoria Penning took the prize with four, holding all by their tails. Robert Epping jumped down from the shrouds and Joseph watched as he slowly thudded his way over to the hatchway and plodded down into the gloom.

Quickly, Joseph shuffled to the shrouds, clambered down the ratlines to the deck and hurried to the companionway, following Rob down to the murk of the hold. The smell hit him first, a vile waft of rot, damp and salt that he had to swallow in order to gain passage; the toll of the hold, and punters needed a strong will not to gag to pass inside. Already he could hear scuffling and squeaking and thudding around the empty barrels and sacks – Rob was hard at work, chasing after his supper tonight.

The wood creaked beneath his feet and the thudding paused, 'oh, you sneaky bastard,' Rob cried to the rat, then, 'who's there? This is my turn down here. My rat just got away.'

'S'alright, boy. There'll be others to catch.' Joseph replied, bemused by the sound of his own voice again.

'Joseph? What're you doing down here? Does Captain call for me?'

'No, no. I just wanted a talk is all.' As his eyes adjusted, he saw the silhouette of the boy at the back, moving with the roll of the ship.

'About what?'

Joseph moved in further, trying to be at ease but the topic was a hard one to bring up, especially since it had been mulling in his head and over-ripening to the point of bitterness. His dagger felt weighted in his belt. He lowered his voice, 'I just wanted to ask, have you heard any funny things recently, suspicious things? Amongst the crew?'

'A few things. Why? Have you?' asked Rob after a time.

'Rumours mostly, how developed though I don't know. That's what worries me.'

There was a pause. *Victoria* creaked. Rob understood what he was conveying. 'Why have you come to me about it? I thought the Captain would know what to do more than I.'

Cautiously, Joseph stepped in further, nearing Rob. 'I . . . I'm not sure who to turn to anymore.' He paused, not sure how best to ask, 'how . . . what do you know of it?'

Rob shrugged in the shadows and seemed to take time in speaking. 'Not much. I wasn't told a lot of it, although the last I heard is that it's been abandoned. That there's nothing to fret over anymore.' Rob tried to find Joseph's eyes but struggled to see them sunk into their sockets as such; he glanced to the ladder.

Joseph refrained from a relieved sigh and tried to keep his voice firm even though he felt like crumbling. 'Is that so? I'm pleased to hear it. Codswallop to it, drivel; that's what it was. Who was behind it all, Rob? You can tell me.' The question had been burning, he had to ask it.

He shrugged again, 'I only heard whispers from whispers. I never knew myself. I didn't want anything to do with it anyway, I washed my hands of gangs as soon as I left London.'

'Aye. Good lad, it's the best route to follow. Better to go at it alone sometimes.' *Like Trace did.* He pried further, 'Why was it all abandoned?'

Another adolescent shrug. 'Not sure. I wasn't told why.'

'Who was sending the whispers? What was the souce?'

'Am I on trial?'

'Not at all. I just need to know.' *Need to know who's been stabbing me in the back so I can keep an eye, and if needs be, a knife on them too.*

'You probably won't be surprised at this, but Dave was the one in my ear. And Benjamin was the one in his, and before that I don't know.'

Joseph exhaled sharply. How many of the crew were involved? Had it spread throughout them all? 'Fuck.' He said, 'well, as long as it's all been abandoned now.'

'That's what I was told.'

Now, he let out his relieved sigh and felt the burden lifting from his shoulders. First the clue, then the wind and now this; it was a rarity, but problems were solving themselves. *Good. I haven't the energy to sort them.* 'That's good news, cheers Rob. I'll let Jim know.' He turned to leave, then turned and found an odd smile on his face, 'happy hunting.'

Upon the deck, the wind was bitter and rigorous and caught his navy jacket in its grasp. It had strengthened considerably and at an estimate the gusts were easily reaching twenty-five knots. *Keep this gale a'blowin and we'll go skidding up the beach when we reach land.* The thought made him smile again and caused his cheeks to ache with exertion. Climbing the ladder, he found Robertson at the wheel and Victoria giving a report. 'I think Thomas could do with a hand down there, Vic, if you've a minute to spare.'

She nodded tiredly and tried to keep her *Boss of the Plains* hat on her head. 'I'll see about it. Thank'ee Joseph.' Down the ladder she went, leaving the captain and quartermaster alone.

Joseph walked to the taffrail, minding the moving spanker and looked out to the waves behind them, trying to make it look like a casual conversation. 'Jim, I have news.' But he received no response. 'Jim. Jim? Captain?'

Startled, he looked behind him, 'Oh! Sorry, I was . . . miles away. I keep drifting like flotsam at the minute. What did you say?'

'The problem has sorted itself, says I. Our infestation has dissolved.'

For the first time in days, the captain's dry lips found a weak smile. 'The rats are all caught? Excellent! How full is the barrel?'

'No, Jim. The *other* rats we spoke of hitherto – they've abandoned their campaign. We no longer have to live in fear.'

His face remained stern. 'Are you sure of this?'

'Yes, I've only just heard it myself from the Young Hare. It's over.'

The captain closed his eyes and exhaled slowly, 'wonderful. This is terrific news, although we must remain vigilant lest they change their mind. The weed is already grown and the roots established, because it has been plucked does not mean it will not grow again. Let us keep talk of the chest and its contents to a minimum; it might be the spark that sets the embers alight once more. We're all vulnerable and prone to sways in this depleted state; the notion of riches and rewards would be enough of a persuasion.' He paused, 'speaking of the chest, any luck with finding anything leading to it?'

Joseph gulped, feeling his defences rise. Looking to Robertson's hazel eyes he felt guilt at hesitating. This man was the captain of this ship after all, if he could trust anyone, it had to be him. *And Victoria. She needs to know what I found. She's been helping me throughout.* Robertson blinked. Joseph Winter made his decision. 'I . . . may have found something of use.'

His eyes lit up. 'This is even better! Well done, my man! If we had any grog left, I'd be raising my toast to you this evening. Unfortunately, all we have are rats and dribbles of coconut water, not exactly things to be thrilled about yet alone raising to celebrate. Does it lead directly to the chest?' he asked in earnest.

'I believe . . .' *you don't have to tell everything, it's your own choice how much to divulge.* 'It might. Only partial things were there, it all needs some thought.'

'Excellent. Oh! How sweet joy feels when misery has taken centre stage. You'd best think up on it then Mister Winter, if this wind prevails, we should reach the coastline in little over a day.'

The news was tremendous as Joseph spied the horizon, awaiting the sight of a coastline. He couldn't remember what land felt like underfoot. Still and sturdy with wheels that rolled and horses that trotted, roads that were winding and buildings that reached to the sky. There were people too, other people with different faces and voices, different stories. The memories seemed surreal, imaginative and altogether frightening. Despite living out in the open for the elements to gnaw upon for months, he felt claustrophobic.

Robertson seemed to sense the apprehension. 'Don't get too worked up now, you old seadog, Australia is waiting. Land and wonders your sailor-salt eyes will revel in. Beauty unbeknown to our washed-up hearts.'

Chapter Thirty-Four

Hesitantly, Joseph Winter brought the flesh to his lips and forced his mouth to open. Despite his mind refusing all appetite for it, he couldn't help salivating; his cheeks yearned for substance, his tongue slick and ready. To make the experience bearable, Benjamin had spent the afternoon skinning so this morsel in his fingers looked less of a rat, alas it appeared even more disgusting – all pink and sinewy with flies buzzing around it. His teeth closed and sunk into the scrawny flesh.

An aching pain rumbled around his gums and made him wince with every chew, pinpointing on particularly weak teeth. They had been yellow and tobacco-stained before, he wondered what colour they'd mellowed into now. *Lemon? Brown? Black?* As he slowly mulled the meat around his palate, it felt like some teeth were about to shatter under the tough consistency. After eating the soft flesh of coconut for so long, this was like chewing on rubber. Yet this was a better day than most. Some days he hadn't eaten anything at all and hadn't wanted to; a clear sign this journey was crushing the life from him.

Once accustomed to the ache, he focused on the flavour. It was stone cold; they'd ran out of fuel for the stove weeks ago, which did not aid in its appeal. It tasted gristly and rusty; *not exactly chicken*, he observed. Far from flavoursome or his choice dish, yet after days upon days of nothing but coconut flesh and bone marrow the taste was refreshing enough for him to take another bite. And another. And soon he found his belly filling and the flesh diminishing. *Go for the tail!* He crunched on the rough hide, ignoring the sparkling pain fizzing through his gums and found satisfaction in crunching on the bones and using his teeth again.

The sensation was familiar and satisfying once he'd passed the painful stage, persuading him take the legs and head and to pick up another rat.

Within a matter of minutes, he finished his second rat and stepped away from the barrel feeling heavy with food, bloated and slightly nauseous. The sky was a strange colour, with a bright yellow-white, fluorescent sunset sinking below a dense dark, multi-layered bank of clouds. Trails of shadowy cumulous fingers clawed out from the cloudbank, grappling the air to haul the darkness closer to their ship - the blinding acidic light of dusk capturing their urgency to reach them.

Dark over Will's Mother's, he observed, *that doesn't look promising.* His gaze falling, Joseph noticed a few of the crew were at work having already eaten their share of vermin, appearing satisfied. Despite dusk being nigh, the sails were still open and full of air, and did not look to be furled any time soon. He frowned and peered up to the main yard where the master rigger was busy with the lines. 'Benjamin! What's happening with these sails? Are they being furled or flying through the night?'

The old sailor looked around, then down to him. 'Oh! Flying the night Quart', Capt'n ordered we sail through it.'

'Well, the bugger never told me,' he muttered, and gave a nod, 'very well!' It made sense; they could cover the distance faster and lord knows they needed it. Their destination was not far now, a final push was appropriate, sensible even; indeed, they'd caught as many rats as they could find and having checked the barrel they would last until morning. However, this was not the only concern. The water situation was of a depressing state; their remaining stores of rainfall had grown stagnant and were greening and browning in their containers. Barrels and scuttlebutts were infected with clouds of floating algae and containers had curdled to a viscous rust-coloured sludge where sea salt had contaminated the freshness. It was a daring risk to drink from them; with such confined quarters it would not take a lot for disease to spread, especially since they were all drinking from the same source. *We've grown our own barrel of cholera; our own special brew of disease;*

the draught of the seas, he thought as he looked out to the waves and felt the rise and fall of the ship. *We're down to eating vermin and drinking bile, here's to your new life Joseph. Cheers to that!* Despite himself, he was already excited for the morning to eat rats again. It felt a rare treat.

Suddenly he heard laughter coming from the forecastle and was taken aback by the sound. It was odd, a pure sound that he hadn't heard in so long. Curious, he walked afore the ship to where Billy was laughing, and Dave and Rob stood smiling. 'What is it?' he asked Billy.

The Irishman turned with a broad smile on his face. 'Why, I was just tellin' Dave something I've realised.'

'What's that?'

'Well, if I'd have known we were going to Australia, I should've persuaded the Judge to give me a penal service, been sent to one o' those Hulks y' see on the Thames and shipped to an Australian colony! Ol' Lord North is t'inking he's getting rid of me when he'd actually be doin' me a favour!' he burst with another fit of laughter.

Joseph's eyes widened at the realisation. 'Well bugger me.' He said and laughed too, 'why couldn't these explorers have told us Australia in the first place! All that hassle stealing a ship and finding clues!' he chuckled, shaking his head his head tiredly before starting on a round of the ship.

Surveying the deck, he noticed loose halyards and sheets from the mainsail which had slackened in the rising winds, loosening around the belaying pins freeing the sail and consequently slowing the vessel, taking her off course. 'Hands to the mainmast! Mainsail, I say! Halyards are loose and the sail's whipping wild! It'll be footloose before long! We're already three sheets to the wind!' Robertson cried before he ominously ordered, 'don your foulies, able seamen! Retrieve the storm sails, pronto! Get them rigged, sailors, the winds are strengthening. We don't want an episode like last time on our hands!' Instinctively, Joseph hurried over, grabbed a loosening sheet and heaved, but the canvas fought and tugged mightily.

Suddenly Thomas appeared beside him, snatching another line and helping to saddle this bucking horse. 'The wind! It keeps taking it!' Thomas yelled out the obvious as if the canvas had ears. They both yanked hard until their hands were sore, and their palms felt shorn, until Robertson cried out, '*Quartermaster!* Where are you? We need storm sails rigged and sea anchors deployed! Reef all sails hard! A hard trim as we did before!'

'Mainsheets! Hang on!' he managed to call back.

'Quart'! You're needed by the Captain.' echoed Benjamin, shouting to be heard above the rising winds.

'I know! Heard him! *Be there in a minute!*'

Victoria then called, 'Joseph? Have you a minute? I need to talk to you.'

'*Main bloody sail! I am busy! Give me a minute!*' he yelled red-faced.

Suddenly Thomas lost his footing and the rope slipped through his grasp, burning his hands in a blaze of fiery friction. He shrieked, and the sail flew looser, with Joseph hanging on by frail fingers and the core strength of a Tibetan mountain goat. The gusts of the wind had grown powerful and the crew knew from experience that gale force winds would follow such a hasty development. A demoralising darkness loomed in the sky above, impatient and foreboding with electricity in the air. A storm was approaching, smothering all light and turning the dusk into midnight. Joseph glanced at the dark clouds and felt the static; a bead of sweat rolled down his brow. He prayed it would skirt around and miss them entirely – the last thing they needed was a free sail amid a storm; the blame would be his.

Before they knew it, the waves rose steeply and dangerously, exacerbated by the gales that now blew. *Victoria* climbed a high wave, her bow sinking into it with powerful force and rising with it before dropping into its trough, sending a barrage of seawater over the deck. She rose again, riding the next wave with a tilt that turned her to port; her bow slicing through the inky waters, cresting with the manes of galloping white horses, then, hogging the wave, she slid and dipped with a slight heel to port, making the crew cling on. Rising, she righted herself at the peak then once again slid into a trough, noticeably deeper.

The gales were now extreme and pummelled the sails, thrashing through the stays and halyards so hard it made them thrum – a foreboding sinister tone, deep and melancholic – the church organ of the seas. The crew hurried about the ship, with those more confident with heights climbing the shrouds to prepare for reefing the mainsails and rigging the trysails. The others scurried from the hold to the weather deck collecting the storm sails and readying them to be hoisted up to the yards. The foremast was quickly rigged appropriately with the mizzen being started on when Robertson exclaimed again, *'the sail! Sort that footloose out, Quartermaster! We've no chance of holding her straight with that canvas running like a whore's skirt in a breeze! Baker, grab a rope and lend a hand you Irish squab, saddle the beast or free it! Just sort it to release us! We must heave-to! We must ride through once again!'*

Just then Joseph felt drops of water on his face, not from the waves but from the ominous sky. *Oh Christ, not yet!* He pulled the sheet mightily, his digits screaming white noise. Billy suddenly appeared next to him snatching the other line and pulling it hard, his muscles already burning. The sail bucked, switching and flipping and snapping back and forth as the winds harshened, bringing with it the rain of the heavens. A biblical oceanic downpour. Within a minute the drops felt like bullets pelting them, a thousand bee stings, a maelstrom of giant proportions, and a stinging face was soon the new pain. Fighting through the sharp pelts, the two men fought with the rogue canvas.

'Get that sail in, men!' cried the captain, *'Make haste! Now, says I! This wind is worsening, and it'll tear the sail or yank it free, taking the mast with it! I need any deckhand free and to spare; get to the mainmast now! If you can't draw it in, then fucking cut it! Cut and run, I say!'*

'Joseph! I really need to talk to you!' he heard Victoria again, shouting to be heard above the gales.

Gritting his teeth, he yanked on the sheet with hands that felt aflame, until suddenly there was a splitting of fibres and a creaking snap. With scouring eyes, he saw the rope untying on itself, spinning, thinning, and the line pulling apart. Rope flung and snapped about the pulley, whizzing through its eyes until the corner of the sail flapped loose, snapping and cracking in the forceful gusts, straining more lines. Joseph flew back into Thomas, and Billy, clutching to the rope, was hauled from his feet and into the air, where he crashed on the ladder and thundered down. The sail loosened altogether and became unbridled, flapping and crashing and whipping its ropes looser, freeing itself. Instantly, they felt the wood stressing as the sail protested the mast, tied so tightly by the standing rigging. *Victoria* crested another high wave, tremors running through the hull as the uneven distribution of weight threatened to snap her in two, before she dropped into another trough, sagging in its bottom.

'*Christ! The sail!*' Benjamin wailed as he shuffled along the mizzenyard to the shrouds and began to descend.

'*Free it! Free it! Cut the bastard loose!*' The captain hollered through the pounding gales, clambering down the ladder to the main deck.

'*My arm! Fuck! For the love of God, my arm!*' exclaimed Billy, his wet hair whipping and dripping. Joseph rolled from Thomas and looked over, seeing Billy staring at his right arm that now had two elbows. His forearm drooped like a wilting plant; the break was blatant.

'*Bosun!*' cried Joseph, quickly hurrying to the injured. '*Boatswain! Surgeon! Where are you, Victoria?!*'

'*Helm! I'm at the wheel!*' she yelled.

'*Loose! Cut it loose now!*' Robertson bawled to them.

The rain began to slash in white torrents, sheeting in a plethora of thick blasts, jetting and surging in a way that would force Noah to consider the construction of an Ark. From afar, thunder could be heard rumbling.

Captain Robertson tried to keep his horror at bay. *Mother of God . . .* he wiped the water from his eyes. Suddenly the sky lit in a dazzling flare; electric cracking through the innards of the clouds, lighting the darkness for a split second. It was enough to see the sail was wild and was loosening and snapping all its lines, ripping as it whipped thither, *there's no way we can catch that now . . .*

Running through the rain and balancing on the bucking ship, Robertson hollered, '*cut it loose now! Cut it! Cut it! We've no hope of catching it! Let it be flotsam and jetsam!*' He ran for the main shrouds, his knife at the ready. Suddenly the ship crashed over a wave, heeling hard to starboard; he lost his footing and fell, grappling onto the railing; he looked up and saw the wheel spinning, unmanned.

Without a second thought, he turned and bolted back up the ladder to the wheel where Victoria was up again, struggling to hold it steady in their direction, especially now a sail was rioting. She hauled and heaved, trying to manage the wheel, groaning in effort. '*I'll take the wheel! You cut the sail!*' he instructed.

She nodded, her hair wet and wild and her clothes flapping. She handed him the rungs. '*I'll order them to furl the topsails!*'

'*No!*' he cried, '*Open! Keep them open!*'

She looked at him incredulously, '*the wind will stress them, damage them! Break the masts! I'll bring them in!*'

'*Leave them! We need them open now; we're not getting the trysails up fast enough! We must ride this storm with the working sail plan! We need this tailwind to push us out of these troughs! We've got Dover Cliffs to climb!*'

'*We'll die in this storm if we're not careful!*'

'*The topsails need to stay open! If we stow them now, we risk losing them and lives of the crew; we'll have no speed or power, we could fucking capsize with the size of these waves! We'll be stranded in this storm with nothing to blow us from it! They remain open, that's an order!*' he shouted with a stern look in his eye, then hollered, '*Go and get the sea anchor and drogue instead! We need drag to control our speed!*' he looked back to the washed-out deck, '*Lifelines! Cabin Boy, secure all lifelines!*'

Victoria turned, biting her tongue, and strode off to see to what Joseph had been calling her about. Instantly, she saw the state of Billy's arm. '*Holy Christ! What're you still doing up here?! Get down to the sick bay now, you fool! I'll splint it later!*' She shouted above the wind. Billy, pale-faced and on the verge of vomiting, got to his feet and stumbled to the hatchway where the hatches banged open and shut with water splashing inside. *'Thomas! Batten these hatches!'* she cried. Then, upon seeing the clutter of barrels and nets strewn about the deck, Victoria forgot about the sea anchors and quickly ambled over and grabbed them before someone got tangled, passing Rob running aft see about saving the mainmast madness.

Rob ran past Joseph and launched himself onto the main shrouds and began to climb. *'Walk-er! Careful, Rob! Keep a steady foot, lad!'* Joseph called out as he got to his feet and looked up to the mainyard to see Benjamin, Tess and Dave aloft, working as quickly as they could cutting the ropes free. The maintopsail was still, shockingly, open, and he was about to climb the shrouds himself to furl it when he lost his footing and clung onto the mast. Suddenly three stupendous white bolts cracked and split as they plunged to the waves, lighting the darkness for a few brief moments. A fourth then dazzled his eyes, before vanishing, leaving in its wake a clap of thunder that boomed like explosive percussion, reverberating through the oil-coloured clouds. Despite the calamity, Joseph felt a shred of relief, of clarity. An almighty sense of balance and initiative, a rush of personal prowess that gave him a confused feeling of enjoyment riding through this chaos. They were within the destruction and riding through the torment, yet he couldn't shake the wonderous feeling of harmony: peace within the peril. Beauty within the horror. A realignment of energy within energy. *It's not over us. It's miles away. Lord bless us, we're on the edge of it.*

Just then, through the rage and gloom, Joseph turned and saw a wave unlike any other; a tremendous, towering vessel easily as tall as one of the buildings in their home city, a real Dover Cliff. Terrifying and sinister it was, rolling toward them – a black impenetrable wall with its crest spouting spray down its back like smoke from a machine, like the flowing manes of a herd of white stallions. A wave larger than the rest, and Joseph knew its name. 'Bless me for a fool . . . *the Ninth Wave!'* he cried, pointing, *'Hold on!'* Their tiny boat struggled to its top, the tailwind gales blasting into the topsails and trysails, heaving them higher as the yards and masts screamed under the intense pressure, whereupon it sluiced through the roaring lofty peak and, after dangerously hogging the wave . . . tipped. Everyone gripped hold and held their breath, squeezing their eyes shut . . . before *Victoria* shot down its back, riding down the giant wave with speed and forces unbeknown to them.

Upon reaching the trough, the bow crashed into the water with such a force that the jibboom and bowsprit snapped, and the storm jibs, headsails and forestays were ripped from the rigging. Water cascaded over the ship in a tremendous tidal force, leaving the unfortunate crew to be no more than flotsam and jetsam. The ship then rose drunkenly and set about ambling up the next wave with the flood still draining from her deck. There was a gurgled shriek, and as Joseph peered, he saw Victoria struggling against the railing as the water surged to starboard.

'*Victoria!*' he yelled and dove into the rushing runoff and haphazardly splashed through to where she struggled, coughing and spluttering and vomiting up water. Barrels and boxes were strewn around, the few that remained, and lengths of rope and netting snaked across the deck, constantly slithering in the movement of water as *Victoria* swooned like a drunkard. He grabbed her and helped her to her feet and took her away from the bulwark with his arm around her shoulder.

'*Bailing buckets! Get the water off the deck!*' Robertson cried as the sky lit again. Joseph's eyes flashed to the mainyard where the silhouettes of the four deckhands were cutting, having managed to ride the ninth wave aloft. The sail whipped and tore with each snapping reef-point and loose lines began to slide, zipping from their eyes and sliding from the spars and mast. The sky flashed a second time and with water running down his face he saw two of them had bumped into each other. Everything went dark. Thunder clapped and banged. With his eye trained on the yard, lightning struck in the distance once more and he saw the silhouettes holding onto the yard, shuffling toward the rigging. The mainsail was freed and was immediately whisked away in a powerful gust. Suddenly the ship felt as if had righted itself somewhat and Robertson, although battling with the wheel, found her easier to steer even though they were speeding. '*Sea anchors now! Drag! We need drag!*'

Joseph took Victoria down to the berth amidst a torrent of rushing water and immediately embraced her soaking body. Her clothes clung to her frame; he could see her comely shape and handsome curves, and her protruding bones. The attraction was lustful, he hadn't seen a woman's body in so long, yet alone Victoria's body, but now was not the time to act upon it. He wondered what she must see when looking at his body through his wet clothes. *A bag o' bones with a heartbeat, no doubt.* 'I must go,' he told her, 'stay here where it's safe. I can't risk losing you.' He paused and made his decision. 'I love you, Victoria.' He said resolutely and kissed her, then turned to descend to the hold to grab the necessities, quickly having to grapple to the wall as the ship listed to port.

As he ran back and mounted the companionway to the main deck, he heard from behind him, 'I love you too, Joseph.' A grand smile spread across his face and a magnificent rush of happiness surged through him as he entered the blast of the elements.

'*Lifelines! Where're those fucking lifelines?!*' cried the captain, '*Joseph! Secure all lifelines! Do it now!*'

'*Aye-aye! Benjamin! Deploy these! Hand over fist!*' He quickly gave the sea anchor and drogue to the master rigger and made haste to the stanchions and flailing coils of rope and set about hitching them to the set of stanchion pins. A frustrating business it proved to be as his cold wet fingers struggled to tie properly, but he managed it. After he'd tied eight, he tied his own about his waist then set about handing them out, bumping into Tess. Her hair was bedraggled, clothes waterlogged, '*I'll take them Joseph! Thomas and Dave need a hand with securing the foresails. Lines are loosening!*'

'*What lines an't loosening?! Where's Rob?*'

She blinked the rainwater from her eyes and yelled, '*he's on the foreyard waiting for–*' another wave cut her short as it blasted over the deck and pushed them both from their feet. Barrels rolled off the ship and ropes flailed around them.

'*For Christ sake! Where are the lifelines?!*' yelled Captain Robertson.

Tess got to her feet, picking up the lines and raced to everyone, handing them their lifelines as the gales buffeted and the lightening smote the tide again and again as if Zeus himself was at war with Poseidon. Suddenly an almighty scream of wood could be heard as the maintopsail lurched forward and snapped the topmast from its peak down to the maintop platform. '*Watch out!*' In a tangle of stays and lines, the sail and mast and rigging crashed to the deck, breaking the spar of the capstan as the broken mess landed upon it in a sodden heap. Joseph just managed to avoid the crash. '*Tophamper down! We've lost half the mainmast, Captain!*' Benjamin exclaimed.

'*Quartermaster! Riggers and hands! Reef the other topsails before we lose any more! Bring in the sea anchor and drogue! Our lack of main tophamper serves as drag enough; we need to pick up speed! We can do this my hearty crew! The worst is now behind us!*' the captain hollered.

'*Aye-aye!*' Joseph cried, praying the captain was right.

Hours passed with the bow rising high and falling sharply, riding angry animated waves that threatened to list them. Hours of harsh winds howling, sails flapping and writhing, masts creaking and lines snapping. One thing was for certain, it did not feel as ferocious as their previous assault from the sky; whether that was due to them sailing through the outskirts, or they were accustomed to such beastly elements, they could not tell. Although, their lack of proper maintenance and wear-and-tear of their tophamper was another matter. Their sails, stays and masts were losing their strength and effectiveness – *Victoria* was falling to pieces. Thankfully, their journey was almost at its end, as was their trusty ship.

Through the night the storm raged on and as morning approached, they limped from its brutal grasp and into its outer perimeter, where only a heavy rain continued to douse from a moody, sullen blanket of grey.

Eventually the winds abandoned their advance, retreating to a calm breeze and the waves grew tired of tossing them, shrinking back to a motion that felt frustrated with its failure, knocking them and splashing hard against the hull. After their restless night, they hardly felt the waves as they walked around the deck, exhausted and soaked to their very hearts. Their clothes clung to them, were thin and torn and, where loose, dangled uncomfortably. Their unkempt hair felt weighted against their heads, plastered by the heavy shower that remained hanging above.

Joseph plodded tiredly to the forecastle, his feet squelching in his boots and his calf aching dully. His wound was still healing and had left a nasty scar, yet he was thankful he still had a leg. He looked at the splinters of the bowsprit pointing to the horizon and saw a lighter sky there. Dawn was approaching; sunrise wouldn't be far off. *And neither will land.* The thought made him smile as he held the railing, feeling the stem split through the waves victoriously. His smile disappeared at the loss of the bowsprit and jibboom; a bitter blow as now all forestays were slack and the major support systems for the masts were missing. Additionally, they couldn't rig any jibs meaning their progress was to be majorly altered. One gale force wind and they'd easily lose more sails and masts. In fact, it was a miracle they'd managed to pull through the remainder of the storm.

'My crew!' Robertson announced. Joseph turned and saw the haggard man upon the helm still holding the wheel white-knuckled, his wet hair hanging over his face. 'Well done on passing through another storm. They never seem to get easier, but we all get harder from it.' He took a tired breath, 'we're all exhausted and hungry, but first whilst this rain persists, we've got to try and catch it. Collect the containers and barrels and scuttlebutts, whatever we have left, and let's catch some fresh water. Then go and find something to eat and, afterwards, we need to rig a spare canvas onto what's left of the mainmast to act as a mainsail; it's a blessing the mainyard wasn't torn down too. Rig a spare spar as a makeshift bowsprit for the headstays. We can't sail with naught support; it would be like taking the crutch from a one-legged cripple. In afterthought, it's shocking we made it out of the storm at all with barely any tension in the stays. Our mighty ship is much stronger than we think, or we're all blessed more than we thought. Either way, we are to sail another day.' His voice resonated through the rain, sounding gruff and depleted. 'Now, off to the mess deck to break your fast on rat.'

Wondering how blessed they really were, they slowly thumped down to the hold and collected the remaining few barrels and scuttlebutts, sitting them on the deck and lashing them to the masts, lidless. Then, one by one they returned to the hold to pick out what was left of their rats to breakfast on. Upon Joseph's turn, he found four left; the last food aboard, and picked a small skinny runt and began to eat it without thought; munching on the scant flesh and crunching down on the bones, caring little for what went in his mouth. Caring little for disgust or emotion; he was too fatigued. Nothing mattered any more, as long as there was food and it could stave off starvation then that was good with him.

Suddenly there was a cry from the deck, a most desired and longed-for cry that sounded so divine the Messiah himself couldn't have said it better. Joseph looked up to the gloomy ceiling of mould, mildew and cobwebs and gulped down the last of his rat, hesitating, wanting to hear it once more to make sure this was not a dream, a hallucination or con, that this was reality. He waited, then:

'Land!' Dave James wailed loudly, 'Land! I see it! It's there! Australia! Land ho!'

Forgetting all his aches and pains, sores and welts and cuts and bruises the quartermaster raced up the companionway as fast as his body could muster and burst out on the deck. A warm rain showered, and the sky looked shades lighter than before. The crew crowded against the railings, all eyes looking in one direction: Ahead, to land.

Joseph threw himself afore the ship to the forecastle and spied the horizon and the jagged silhouette, immovable and rooted. Unmistakable. It was not a mirage or illusion or trick of the eye; it was there, and all saw it. 'We've done it.' Joseph muttered, 'my god. We've crossed an ocean and we're here. The last leg.' He looked over at Billy stretching up to see and noticed his arm had been splinted and bandaged as best as possible. Despite his obvious pain, Billy beamed, his freckled face donning its best smile for the occasion - his companion from the very beginning. *No, there was one before that. Before Billy. A lad who kept hold of my things until I woke up in prison.* He smiled at the memory, at the thought of the friend who had been there with him throughout it all. *Where's Rob?*

Scanning the backs of their heads, he didn't see him there. *Maybe he went for a lie down and doesn't know the sighting yet.* He hurried around the jumble of wood and canvas – what was left of the maintopmast and sail – and down to the berth to Rob's hammock. 'Rob. Mate, we're almost there! Land has been sighted.' There was no reply. 'Rob?' Concerned, he leaned over to look deeper into the gloom and saw the hammock absent of its owner. Frowning, he checked all the hammocks and found every one empty. He then checked the orlop deck and the hold and found them vacant. Hurrying faster, he ran up to the deck, to the rain and merriment and surveyed with worry. The crew wandered back from the railing: all smiles and cheer, without the young lad there. 'Rob?' he called out, 'Where's Rob? Has anyone seen him?'

Faces looked to him in confusion, some shrugged and answered, 'might be eating or kipping. I haven't seen him.'

'What's this? What's happening?' Robertson asked from the wheel with rain dripping from his hat and beard.

'Rob. I can't find him anywhere. Have you seen him?'

He shook his head. 'Nay. Can't say I have. Not this morning. He should be here though; the lifelines were all secured, you did that yourself.'

'I tied them to the pins, but I didn't give them out.' The crew crowded around him, their faces ashen and worried. 'Tess had that job.' He finished, and eyes turned to her searching for answers.

She looked at them all pale-faced, her hair slick. She blinked innocently in the rain, her lip trembling. 'I did. I - I gave it to him. I did . . . I swear it.' Her eyes darted around the deck as she tried to remember. 'There was so much happening, so much going on. I took the lines from you and the wave struck, then I went about giving them out and - and - and – he was on the yard, helping to cut the sail free. Yes! That was where I saw him.' Her clear eyes were hopeful as tears streamed from them.

'Did you give him his lifeline, Tess? Did you climb to the yard and give it to him?' Joseph stepped toward her, his face stern, his voice grave.

She opened her mouth, closed it, and looked to the floor, racking her brains. 'I must've done . . . I'm sure . . . I . . . Oh, what have I done? What have I done?' Tears streamed in full flow now, even in the rain she was clearly crying. Victoria embraced her caringly.

'Did you give Rob his lifeline, Tess?' Joseph asked again, sombrely.

Gently, she shook her head as she began to sob into Victoria's shoulder, her breaths heaving in short gasps. She lifted her head slightly, 'I . . . I must've. I . . . couldn't . . .' she looked to him with her bloodshot eyes and her arms around Victoria. 'Because I'd already pushed him from it . . . I didn't even see him splash.' She said softly, casually, with tears still streaming down her face.

It took a second for the words to compute.

Joseph's eyebrows furrowed in confusion, perplexed. The rain ran down his face, in his eyes; but what he saw before him was oh so clear. He took a step to her, reaching around to his belt for his dagger, his pistol, his fist; anything to cause harm, to stop her. But it was too late. Far too late.

A sudden blast of pain exploded from the back of his head.

Joseph Winter crumpled to the deck in a heap.

Returning to consciousness, he immediately wished he hadn't. A wild, harrowing, debilitating pain burned in the back of his head, as if someone had just branded him. Sparks rushed up and around his head and spread to every limb, making him tingle unpleasantly. The floor beneath felt unstable; he could feel himself rocking. *Am I in a cradle?* Slowly, he opened his eyes. It was more of smell than sight that told him where he was; he sucked in the rancid air of the hold and coughed, feeling the back of his head explode again. Grimacing, he tried to sit up but was smacked hard by a wave of nausea and a pain that felt like someone was taking his skull apart piece by piece. Weakly, he laid back, tasting bile in his throat. Somehow, he couldn't move his hands. Pain swallowed him, a physical and emotional pain; his eyes swelled with tears at the thought of Rob's tragic fate.

'Joe?' he heard an Irish accent say, 'Joseph! Christ, he's awake!'

'Joseph!' a woman exclaimed, and the bleary vision of Victoria hung over him. 'Oh, Joseph I've been so worried! We all have.' She sounded like she'd been crying. 'How do you feel?'

Suddenly the bile rose forcefully, and he gagged, trying to vomit but struggled to get it from his face. He choked. 'Roll him! Roll him for God's sake!' another voice yelled, and he felt someone rolling his body and the vomit spilling from his mouth. With each gag, his head popped like a bullet ricocheting in his skull. He spewed hard once more and sucked in the air, tasting bile and rat meat.

'I feel . . . bad.' He replied, closing his eyes again; they stung in the soft lamplight. 'What happened?'

'Mutiny. That's what's happened mate, and Tess is the head o' it all.' Billy answered, 'it's all been set up, she had everyt'ing planned out: timing, weapons, mutineers - the lot. It's a fuckin' shambles of a situation, that's what it is. And just to add salt to the wound, the bastards even threw my fiddle overboard!'

Victoria then added, 'Just as she told us about Rob, Dave suddenly had a musket in his hands and smacked you in the back of the head with the butt, knowing you'd rise against her as soon as you found out.' Anger rose in her voice, 'then everything went mad; everyone suddenly had weapons in their hands. They had them prepared for that moment. The first sighting of land; that was the trigger to it all. What they had been waiting for. There was shouting and screaming, beating, until they grabbed us and bound our hands and dragged us down here and have closed it off. They'd had this all planned for a long time. I'm fucking furious I didn't stop her; didn't see what she was up to! *How could she do this to us, to me! She was like a sister!* None of us wronged her or treated her badly, why do this?'

'The chest. It's always been about that cursed chest.' He spat remnants of his upheaval from his mouth and shuffled to a sitting position, his head pounding a gong's chime. He still couldn't face opening his eyes. *Oh Rob, poor boy, I'm sorry, so sorry . . .* he inhaled, 'She wants the loot. They all do. It's the only reason they agreed to join this mission. To be honest, I'm surprised it stemmed from *her*. I always thought Dave was behind it.'

Billy shrugged, sounding defeated. 'He was, as well as damn near all the crew. How did they do all this right under our noses? I heard things, poormouthing and the like, but I didn't get involved; I just thought it'd all died down.'

'What?' he ripped opened his eyes, to see only Billy and Victoria with him in the glow of the oil lamp and felt his chest burn with fury and betrayal. Everyone had rebelled. 'The rest are with her?! *Even Jim?*'

'Jim? No. Jim tried to save us. He's with us. As soon as he saw what was going on, he pulled a pistol from his belt and ran down the ladder but t'ey were too organised. They grabbed him, pulled the gun from him and beat him t' the floor. I saw it with my own two eyes, Joe. *My own two eyes*. Despicable.'

'Where is he then?' he started looking around for another face, the face of their captain.

'I'm here.' His voice sounded hard, angry more with himself for letting this all happen on his own ship. So much time spent in denial, distracting himself with the main overlying issues he didn't see the one worsening right under his nose. Hobbling over, Jim Robertson entered the lamplight, his hands tied behind his back and cables tying his upper body tight. His cheek was swollen, lip split and eye blackened. 'It happened, Joseph. It reached us after all this time. We should've been more prepared. We should've *seen* what was happening and sought to stop it in its tracks; I know it would've been difficult, but more should've been done to prevent it. Those *monsters* up there have murdered Rob and taken *my* ship from me! *Traitors!*' he spat, his eyes shadowed dark under his brow, 'Bloody traitors. Disgraceful. We should've thrown them overboard when we had the chance!'

'Then *we'd* have been the monsters, Jim.' Joseph replied, 'there was nothing we could've done to stop it. If we started targeting one, the rest would've risen. If we held one at gunpoint to interrogate, they would've risen. If we'd have thrown Tess overboard; left her behind on an island; threw her on the boat and cut the rope to float away or even keelhauled her, they would've risen in her place and we'd still end up here with our hands tied behind us.' Then suddenly it occurred to him, 'who's at the helm?'

'Benjamin, I should think. He's the experienced sailor, he'd know how to sail a vessel. Although some lines need sorting on the mainmast, every so often she tilts portside and veers. He's got the knowledge of the knots and sheets but sailing her is a different matter.'

'Christ, *Benjamin?!* He's not exactly the sort to go rogue.'

'Neither was Tess, now look at her.' Victoria reminded.

There was a moment of silence, then Robertson broke it. 'Joseph, who told you the mutiny had been called off?'

'Rob did.'

'Did it occur to you he might've been in on it and told you that to cancel any suspicions?'

'No. I believed him, as any good friend would do.'

'You shouldn't have done that. You should've pressed him further, got more information until he squeaked so we wouldn't be here now. You shouldn't have taken his word so lightly.'

Through the gloom Joseph glared, the pain of Rob's departure was still raw. 'He told me he was done with gangs. Anyway, in case you hadn't noticed, Tess threw him overboard and into the stormy sea, so don't try and twist this to make me and Rob look like the enemies when he's now in a watery grave and I'm tied up down here with you all with a head that feels like it's trying to hatch.'

Sensing the rising tension, Victoria intervened, '*stop it now!* Both of you, this instant! This is the last thing we need.'

There was an inhale, then an exhale. 'You're right. I'm sorry. I'm worked up is all.' Robertson lowered his gaze to the floor, deflated.

'We all are.' Billy added, 'we need each other now; we need to work together to get the better of them. Even if we are outnumbered.'

Joseph looked away in agony . . . when a thought occurred. A change in tack, in perspective. There was another side to this they hadn't considered, and now Joseph knew who he could trust he knew it was time to reveal all. Slowly, he turned to them with a small albeit sly smile on his face. 'Even if we are outnumbered, we have a weapon. A secret. They need us. They've kept us alive for a reason. The rest of the clues; they don't have them. They wouldn't know how to reach the treasure or where to look.'

They looked on with hopeful eyes, but Victoria's truth kept them in check. 'We don't either, Joseph. We found nothing in our studies, we've got nothing to offer them.'

A nod and a sentence were all it took to change their outlook; that the four prisoners had the upper hand. 'Perhaps we do.'

Her eyes showed excitement, but her face gave confusion. 'You found something? When?'

'A few days ago.'

'*–And you didn't think to tell us?!* I worked so hard with you on this, helping you to find something else and when you find it you don't tell me about it?' she snapped.

'That's low, boyo, I t'ought we were friends.'

'Now hold on. We were on the verge of a mutiny; it was in the air; I didn't know who I could trust!'

'You couldn't trust *me*? Joseph, *I helped you with it!*'

He retorted, 'So if you found something, you'd tell it to the people you thought you could trust, only to find out *they* were part of the mutiny intent on crushing you? With that stagnant, sour cess pit we were living in, would you feel like sharing your darkest secrets, Victoria?'

'*We weren't part of it though!* I heard things; whispers shared, and mutters passed along but I didn't get involved. I even tried to warn you about it once, but you didn't do anything about it.'

'Aye. So did I.' Nodded the Irishman.

'How was I supposed to know you both weren't involved?' Joseph responded hotly, 'of the entire crew, how was I supposed to know who was in on it when you were all acting the same; or how it was going to spring up and when? Or how to deal with it when it did arise? The best and safest option I took was to keep it to myself; that way it wouldn't spread, and everyone wouldn't know where to look. No doubt it would've been used against us. By keeping it to myself, we can now use it against *them.*'

Victoria wasn't convinced, 'If you didn't trust me when I was helping you with the clues, why did you want my input?' She looked as if he'd just slipped a cold knife into her back.

'Of course, I wanted your input, I always did and still do. I just couldn't take any chances; not with how things developed. I was going to tell you, all of you, once I was certain you weren't involved.'

Billy Baker chipped in, 'well surely you've got to trust us now, eh?'

'As of now, trust, faith and the last piece of this poxy trail are what'll keep us four together.' He said with his head throbbing.

'Aye, yes. Out of a broken arm, a cracked skull and a beaten body, I reckon Victoria here will be the only one keepin' us together; we're all falling to bits.' Billy said with a tired smile.

Victoria pursed her lips and decided to put the matter behind her. She could be angry with him later. She turned to their captain. 'What do we do now then? Our course of action?'

Robertson moved closer into the murky light of the oil lamp, the mellow glow showing his swellings and bruises. His lip was bleeding into his beard. He sighed exasperatedly, wishing things had not come down to this, had not turned the way they had. Alas, nothing could be done now except plan, defend and survive. 'Right . . . Yes. Well then, I suppose the first and main thing we need to settle is the point of our squabble. Joseph, do you have the last piece with you? What does it say, pray tell?'

Just then, the doors to the hold were unbolted and opened and down strode Tess, with Dave and Thomas following. Gone was her calm composure and air of timidity; she walked with confidence and boldness, a manner of swagger of one in power. Every step had a purpose, every movement had been planned and she was proud of the results of her tireless plotting. She'd cut her hair too, it now hung just above her shoulders and daresay made her look evermore striking; it suited her and gave rise to the appearance of change she'd worked so hard to execute. Tess entered the glow of the lamp.

All eyes were on her; viewing her now as a treacherous villain, a vengeful traitor and a cold, witty bitch who had managed to overthrow a ship and turn this journey on its head. A sly smile found her pretty face and the gleam in her eye was venomous. With a tone of superiority and coy pride, she asked, 'yes Joseph, what *does* this last piece say?'

Chapter Thirty-Five

Robertson was the first to burst. '*What have you done to my ship! How dare you, Tess, who the hell do you think you are! Never has a crew of mine mutinied, never!*'

She rolled her eyes. 'Dave, have a care.' Dave walked up to him and delivered a blow to his stomach and around his face that sent him sprawling on the floor, unconscious.

As soon as Joseph laid eyes on her and the two men at her side, he felt the blind fury like that in the Madagascan village; enough to blot out the pain. He knew he couldn't let her get the better of him; he had the upper hand here, but he still couldn't comprehend her motives. Holding back his anger to not scream, he let it fester and released it in a tone that seethed. 'Tess. Why. Why do this? Why murder Rob and mutiny? After everything I did for you, after *everything* I worked so hard to give you, this is how–'

She rolled her eyes again, as if their previous problems were just petty instances. 'Oh, give it a rest Joseph, stop making a mockery of yourself. We all know you're just as selfish as the rest of us. You want the riches of that loot just as we do so stop pretending like you're doing this for us. Some time ago I came to realise the only reason you only broke us out of that place was because you needed people to run a ship. You didn't want to give us new lives, you only wanted to use us for your own wretched gain. Dragged us into it and put us through hell for it.' She leaned forward, and Joseph no longer knew who this person was, what she was capable of. He was scared. 'No more, I say! I'm not being fooled or ruled by men again; I'm choosing my own fate and I'm helping those with me get their second chance, and we can only do that once we find the Lost Loot. So,' she folded her arms, 'I ask again, *what did the last piece say?*'

'Oh, stop giving yourself so much credit – it doesn't suit you. I broke you out of prison to give you all a second chance, to give you all a–'

'*Enough!*' she commanded and sprung over to him and quickly bashed the back of his head against the wall, sending a shower of glittering shards raining over his vision. The pain was agonising. Again, he felt vomit crawling up his throat. 'I've had it with the lies! I've had it with your bold modesty. You've given that same twisted reason so many times you believe it yourself. Convinced yourself the lie is the truth. You used us all, fooled us and manipulated us, becoming the puppet master in this filthy scheme. You can stop with the guilt-tripping, I have nothing to feel guilty for - and it doesn't suit you.' She moved closer and levelled herself with him, her eyes cold and piercing, 'I'll ask this once more: *what. Did. The. Last. Piece. Say?*'

His glare was icy, trying to hide the pain that shuddered through his bones, 'I'll tell you. Once you tell me why you murdered Rob. He was innocent, he'd wronged no one; his conscience was clear. Why did you toss that poor boy to the waves?'

A malicious smile spread over her face, 'you really believed he was on your side, didn't you? You really did think him a friend, no - more of a brother. I knew I'd made the right decision. Since you two were close and you were vulnerable, I knew you'd believe anything he would say. When he told you of the "whisperings" he'd been hearing, and how he "was done with gangs when he left the city", oh, and the cherry to my perfectly layered cake;' she raised her voice to make a mockery of the boy's, '"It's been abandoned. It's not happening anymore, no. I didn't take notice of it anyway." He told you what I wanted him to tell you, he was where I wanted him to be; the perfect pawn – he played his part oh so well.'

'Why murder him then, Tess? If he worked so well, why kill him?' Billy piped up.

She turned her gaze to the Irishman holding his arm, 'he was no longer needed. He played his part, that was his only role; to dissuade anyone that came to him asking about the revolt. To stop him from breaking character and letting something slip,' she shrugged, 'I let my pawn slip. I had to tie the loose end now, didn't I? Plus, I knew Rob and Joseph were close, I knew he could easily turn to his side and become a liability, so I did what I had to do. The mutiny was going to take place with or without him, and to be honest, I missed the thrill of taking a life; what's one less low-life street-rat anyway? There's plenty more in the city, in any city, scraping a living by picking up the waste of others.'

'Monster! *You're a fucking monster!*' Joseph cried, angry and painful tears flaming down his cheeks.

'You callous bitch.' Billy uttered. 'You're crazy.'

Tess rolled her eyes, 'please. You learn a lot as a girl growing up in a world run by wicked old men. Anyway, I thought you thought me pretty? You said so yourself – don't deny it – you thought I was a lovely little thing when we first started out on this godforsaken journey. What's wrong, Billy-boy? No smiles and winks for me now that I've got some power, eh? Still think I'm a lovely little thing now that I've overthrown a ship and rallied the crew to my side, and it's I who makes the decisions? Don't like a woman in power, no?' she moved over to him and squeezed his cheek and played with his curls, '*oh dear!* Grow up. Time to learn women have a say.' She grabbed his broken arm and twisted it, before hitting him hard. Billy dropped to the floor with a sharp thud.

'I'm all for strong women, Tess, but this isn't the right way to go about it. You need to stop this now.' Victoria said resolutely.

Venomously, Tess turned to her. Her eyes were sharp and glassy like a threatened python. 'Not the right way to go about it, so what is the right way, Victoria? Complain incessantly and call it feminism like you? No. I have power now. I've overtaken this ship, mobilised a crew to my side and can say and act however I damn well please without men intervening. I have tipped the scales. If anything, I should be your idol.'

'All I can see is a dictator with a different sex, not an idol.' Victoria met her glare and attempted a different tack. 'I know you. I know who you really are. You don't have to be like this, Tess. We're all here for you, to help you through this–'

'Oh, fuck off with the mother-hen attitude, Victoria. You've been trying to brood me since we got on this blasted ship, but you knew what I was–'

'–I wasn't trying to mother you! Christ, I was trying to be friends! We're the *only* women aboard this ship!'

'Is that so? Friendship was what you wanted. I see. Well, *friend*, you surely spent your fair share of time around Joseph here, as well as a lot of the men. Small wonder why they all like you so much, you're an old bitch making the most of her last heat.'

Victoria looked aghast and tried to wrestle free from her bonds, 'you bitch! We both know why the men flocked to the berth as soon as you went down to your hammock, why Thomas fell for you so quickly! You had him on your side as soon as he stood before the mast, you wagtail slag!'

Tess smiled, 'I know what I like. I know how to win a man's heart. And get a man's heart. Remember our night in Madagascar, Victoria? Do you remember it?'

Victoria hissed, 'I do.'

Tess whistled. 'That was a night.'

Suddenly Victoria turned to Joseph and quickly blurted, 'they didn't rape her. *She killed them!* All three! When I woke from being beaten, she told me she'd been raped and had killed them in defence. I didn't realise it at the time, but now I can see what she'd done: the blood we saw upon her the next morning were the men's, not hers! She'd rubbed blood between her legs to make it look like she'd been raped! She told me not to speak of it, saying she wanted to forget it ever happened, but it was a ruse to cover her tracks that she's a killer–'

There was a loud crack as Tess landed a hard slap around her face that made her fall to the floor. 'Enough now, Victoria. That's enough. That was meant to be our little secret, was it not? Perhaps I should show these men what happened in our pit that night . . .'

'*Leave her! Leave her alone!*' Joseph exclaimed.

'*I didn't tell them!* Please, Tess. *Stop!*' she pleaded with a bright red mark across her cheek.

Tess tutted, 'keep on clucking, mother-hen. This is who I knew you were all along. All for him. You're weak. One slap and you're crumbling.' She shrugged, 'I guess you're used to it after the way your husband treated you, small wonder he did it so often when he was up against such little resistance.'

Victoria looked abhorred and her mouth drooped open. An old wound reopened is a deep wound indeed. Then Robertson's voice emerged from the darkness sounding much calmer, trying to keep the situation under control. 'Tess. Stop this. What would Poppy think of you now?'

Slowly, Tess turned to him cast amongst the clutter. 'How dare you bring her up, Jim, especially to use against me as a tool for guilt. How could you, *after I shared my pain with you!*' She got to her feet and stormed over to him landing kick after kick, '*she would've been proud to see me now! To see how strong I am and have become! To see what I am capable of! I'm doing this for her!*'

Suddenly Joseph realised he'd heard that before, and a cold dawning set in when he saw this mutiny was what Tess had meant. This had to stop, and he knew how to do it. 'Alright! Tess, stop! *I'll tell you!*' he yelled.

At once, she ceased her attack and looked round to him, tucking a lock of hair behind her ear in an innocent motion. 'You will?' she said exasperated, 'I guess I shouldn't be surprised. You'd rather see your only friends face brutality one after the other before eventually telling me what I came down here for in the first place. And don't bother denying it, narcissism is an ugly trait, and it can get tedious very quickly.' She stood in front of him, waiting.

Joseph had to force himself not to roll his eyes at her. He knew who he was, didn't he? This *was* to help them all, wasn't it? He couldn't help but recall his previous thoughts. Was this all for himself? Did he plan to share it out? *Don't let her get inside your head!* With an exhale, he spoke aloud the last piece of the trail. As he shared the final lines, their mouths opened in astonishment – not only at the clue itself, but that he had given away their only leverage.

'. . . Turn the holy pages, the key is within this story; a witness to
the heavens is he that unlocks glory.
'We hunt for divinity whereupon and without fail . . . we shall bury
this lost, rare and precious grail.'

She nodded, thinking. 'See. That wasn't so hard, was it?'

Furious and betrayed, Victoria was peeved. '*Joseph, what have you done?*' she whispered, her cheek was bright red; the slap had been hard to take, yet the sell-out was even harder.

Again, Tess turned to her, 'what he's done is help the cause, Victoria. Perhaps it's time you learned that yourself.' There was a call for her from the deck and she pursed her lips with her gaze fixed, not wanting to leave. 'Yes!' and with the pride of a lioness, she stalked from the hold with Dave and Thomas following.

'Thomas!' Joseph called out, and the man turned back, 'Dave, I can understand; he's always been a prick, but you. We rescued you from that godforsaken island and this is how you repay us. To turn against us, to be with *her*.' He shook his head, 'we should've left you on that island to rot.'

He glared through the shadows to the mellow light they surrounded, 'she's the one that saved me. She's the only one who has shown me love. All of this is for a worthy cause: her cause. I've given her my heart and I'd follow her to the end of the world. We plan to marry after we find the treasure. I've made my decision and am not burdened nor affected by your insults. I know who I am. I've let go of my past; my conscience is clear . . . can you say the same?' With that, he walked back up the ladder and closed the hatches, sliding the bolt shut.

A moment of sullen quiet passed as the clarity of the fracture betwixt them was displayed, but it was short-lived. 'Why did you do that, Joseph? Why give her the clue? For god's sake, that was the only advantage we had against them!' Robertson snapped as he hauled himself within the light of the lamp.

Despite the pain in his head, his arms tied behind him, the crew that had mutinied and the friends that had rallied against him; he smiled. 'I didn't.'

'You bloody well did Joseph! You shouldn't have done that, we all heard you tell her!' flared the boatswain.

'I couldn't watch her beat you anymore. I've already caused you so much pain and I'm sorry, but I didn't. I told her what she wanted to hear. She doesn't know the entirety.'

'There's more to it?'

He nodded, and with a cautious look to the ceiling above, he muttered the last passage he'd found in the compass. 'I haven't had much time to think of an answer yet, or where this land of two moons and two suns is, or *what* it is, but we have something to go on. Something to lead us, guide us, to the trove.'

Their faces were set as their minds began to start, seeing there were two parts to their defence: their advantage still intact. The clue was as much of a riddle as the others, although this one seemed to have a sense of finality to it. Could this be the last one? It was hard to distinguish; the Scott's had been careful planting their clues in obscurity. An object would be needed to lead them on, a key was to be found, another part to find to collaborate with the rest. For all they knew this clue could lead to another chest that led to another clue to another chest, until they arrived back in London where it all began. *Dear lord please let that not be so*, Joseph prayed, *I'm far too tired for any more of this travelling, and there's only so much these traitors will be happy with until they decide to kill us all.* He looked to the floorboards, fearing Rob's fate and thought about their options before their captain spoke up.

He winced as he heaved himself to a sitting position against a barrel. 'Wasteland of two moons and two suns . . . the only thing I can think of to make sense of that are the doldrums. There're two suns, two moons – whatever the sky shows the water reflects. There's two of everything.'

'Tis' is on land though, Jim-o,' reminded Billy, 'unless there's such a thing as an inland doldrum.'

He shook his head, 'not that I know of. There must be something like it in Australia though, surely? They decided to bury it there.'

'T'ey hadn't been there before, remember. They wouldn't have known.' Billy reminded again.

Joseph clarified. 'The clue says "rumours have been heard of two moons and two suns"; they were only following whispers. They didn't know if it was there or not, or if they were going to bury it there altogether – they just made sure their clues led this way.'

'And who in the blue blazers follows a rumour halfway across the world?' the Irishman cried.

The irony of it was almost too much to bear. 'We are.'

Suddenly Victoria spoke up, almost voicing her thoughts, 'it's given us a location and mentions the key to the chest, that much is clear, but what I don't understand is this "lodestone". What is that?'

Joseph plucked it from his pocket and held it between his index finger and thumb for them to see. 'I think it's this; the lodestone it mentions. It was within the compass with the second half of the clue. I reckon this is the reason why the compass didn't work.'

'It had a damn stone in it, that's quite clear to see, Joe.'

'No. From the sounds of it, it's not a stone at all. They called it a lodestone for a reason: it has another quality. The clue says it's charged with another one like it and they'll attract if held close.'

'It's magnetic?'

'I think so, yes. A bigger version is sitting on the ground above the chest.'

'How would we know where to find it though? There's got to be a lot of rocks in Australia.'

He studied the lodestone, the tiny obsidian mineral, and thought logically. 'We'll find it in the land of two moons and two suns, and this will attract to a lodestone larger than itself. A twin sharing the same quality. The only one. That's how we'll know.' What Joseph didn't want to express was his absolute perplexity at how to find the mysterious wasteland in the first place.

A moment's silence passed as everyone tracked their own thoughts, then Robertson added one more query. 'There's one problem: how do we make sure *they* aren't with us at that time? Obviously, we can't let them have it. We need to rid of them before we get too close, and they learn of the second half to the clue. We need a plan. A defence strategy.'

Joseph sighed, *what to do indeed?*

'We stick together and do whatever is instructed until there's a time when we can break away or find a means of losing them. We may be outnumbered but *we* know where the chest is buried. They only have half of the clue, whereas we have it all. Let us see what opportunities arise.' Victoria Penning declared, sounding hopeful in their hopeless situation, which not only gave them strength, but also helped to set their troubled minds aright. Nothing could be done for now but the time to come was where their chances lie hidden, waiting to be discovered and acted upon.

Suddenly *Victoria* jolted and scraped, then turned starboard sharply, enough to make them fall on their sides. Billy cried out in agony as he landed on his arm. Barrels and loose objects rolled as she swayed and swerved, wobbling to right herself. Jim Robertson instantly looked up to the ceiling, wishing he could see the surroundings. 'Something's happened. The wind must've changed, or . . . if we're nearing the coast . . . oh good Lord.'

'What? What's going on?'

'Benjamin won't know how to manoeuvre properly, and with a sail lost, a makeshift bowsprit and snapped lines, it'll be a struggle to maintain a straight course. I need to be up there. Now. He'll wreck this ship!'

'What're you talking about? How?'

'Rocks! Crags, snags, corals and reefs!' Robertson exclaimed, 'under the surface of the water, they're hidden, he won't see them! It's a challenge enough for any experienced captain, yet alone a rigger at the wheel!' He got to his feet and hobbled to the ladder.

'Jim-o, it's wrecked anyway! The crew is against us, how will they listen?' Billy called.

'They don't need to listen to us. They felt that judder as much as we did, and they were rocks I tell you. They know it as well as we do. Benjamin will be struggling to hold her up, at any point we'll list and then we're all done for! Tess!' he cried banging against the door, 'Tess! Dave! Bloody anyone! Release us now!'

There was no answer for a time, only the constant tilting of *Victoria* as she leaned from one side to the other. Another great judder and scrape then sent her tilting hard to port. Water began rising through the seams in the bilge as the wood stressed. Grappling in the gloom, the four struggled to stay in one position. Then suddenly the bolt slid open, and Thomas burst in, sweating, 'get up there now, man! Tess has called for you, for all of you. I think we've hit something!'

Robertson shoved him out of the way, 'of course we have, you witless fool! Untie me now!' Thomas quickly untied his bonds and he rushed up the companionway. The others followed as quickly as they could with the Irishman last of all, holding onto his arm like it was a delicate glass piece.

Joseph stumbled onto the main deck where the light of day was blinding, and the wind was fresh and cool, but the stability was frighteningly unsteady. Everything moved and rolled and fell hither and thither, and suddenly there was another bump and a judder, wood scraped, and Robertson yelled to take over. *'If we hit her once more, we'll split the damn keel!'* The spare canvas had been rigged for the mainsail, Joseph spotted, and the makeshift bowsprit was just getting by. The tension of the forestays and flying jib was stressing it though, as well as the strong headwind. Joseph also noticed the spanker was torn; no wonder why Benjamin was struggling to keep her from the rocks.

His head was pounding. As *Victoria* swerved, he rambled to the bulwark where he leaned against it, wishing for his hands to be freed in order to hold on. Looking portside, he saw a distinguished coastline with raw colours and rugged shapes. *We've reached the coast. I thought it was miles away! How long was I unconscious for?* There were cliffs, rocks and plants, plants that grew over the edge of gullies, growing in between rock and crag. There were high verges with steep drops and rocky crops of tarnished sun-bleached stone. Waves crashed against the barricade, splashing and bucking with heads of white foam to bring down this impenetrable fortress. There were birds too; white-bellied sea eagles soared against the overcast sky; silver gulls perched atop their lofty crags in nests barely habitable.

With pointed eyebrows and a mouth agape, indignancy grew. Surely this couldn't be the coast; it had to be another hallucination, a wild dream of land he'd been fanaticising about. It looked too good to be true. Although only rocks could be seen, it was a sight craved for; serene yet rugged, beautiful beyond recognition. However, it was not a port. They had to keep sailing. Before he could observe any further, she swayed again and turned starboard, away from the fantastical images of solidity. Joseph pushed against the bulwark and peered at the water, seeing the reason for Robertson's urgency.

Poking from the waves were fingers of stubborn rock, although these were the easy obstacles; underneath was where the traps lay. Hiding just under the surface or breaching in the wash were crops of haggard stone threatening to tear the keel and shred it to splinters. His eyes widened as he understood the danger. If they were to wreck here, they were still far from any landing point, that's if the longboat wasn't already claimed by the mutineers, who were evidently concerned more about personal gain than aid of others. Tess then called out, 'grab those prisoners, men, and lash them to the mainmast! We don't want anyone trying their luck when we're this close!'

Arms grabbed him and hauled him before he could realise what was happening. He was shoved against the wood, hitting the back of his head and saw stars rain down his vision. A white torturous pain burned through his body as if his veins were pumping the strongest of Russian vodkas instead of blood. A thick hawser was wound around the three, concluding any spontaneous ideas they might've had.

The vessel turned sharply again and heeled hard before righting herself and scraping again, hobbling frantically from this death trap. Lines were loose, sails were fighting, and pulleys squeaked. The mainyard knocked one way to the other, loose after its battering, testing the new sail's limited strength.

Joseph battled with the agony, forcing himself to stay sharp, knowing he had to stay alert. The breeze on his face helped him root to the present. He viewed the frantic deck, a chaotic riot of people running hither and thither; tightening lines and retying knots, securing sails and trying to stay upright. Benjamin was hobbling as fast as his little legs could carry, Thomas was billowing through the deck making a hash of his jobs under the intense pressure and Dave was as stern as ever, ruthless and mechanical. *You've got a crew of three trying to work a ship meant for nine, Tess. Poor timing of your mutiny, deary. If you'd just untie us, you'd have more hands . . . to throttle you with.*

Despite Tess's accusations, he still found it odd to not see Rob aboard and hurrying stem to stern and yard to deck. A part of him still believed Tess was lying, only telling him of Rob's misconduct to emphasise the frailty of trust in the crew. Surely there had to be another side to it, maybe the lad *was* telling the truth; he had partaken in the preparations but decided against the campaign and in doing so earned himself an immediate ejection from the ship. Joseph closed his eyes; not wanting to think about the boy thrashing in the writhing inky waters of an ocean storm.

He opened his eyes as Dave hurtled by. 'Dave! Release us! Untie these ropes and we can help you!'

The man slowed and turned, sweat dripping from him, 'Not a hope in hell, Winter. You stay tied. Even Robertson's got his hands tied to the rungs of the wheel.' Then he ran afore to the mast where the lines were slack. Joseph gritted his teeth as the mast juddered behind him.

'You'd have better luck askin' a plank of wood for a hand, Joe.' Billy noted from the other side of the mast.

'Joseph?' Victoria muttered. 'I'm sorry for shouting earlier. I understand why you kept it to yourself.'

'Don't worry, Victoria. Let's focus on how to get out of this.'

Twenty minutes passing felt like two hours, but eventually they escaped from the rocks and pulled away from the treacherous waters where they sailed roughly through the westerly wind and unpleasant tide. With the mainmast half gone, the mainsail haphazardly rigged and the halyards straining; the makeshift bowsprit loosening with a jib barely hanging on; a ripped spanker and crew running ragged, *Victoria* looked a sorry sight hobbling from the ocean waters.

Rare sights were then seen bypassing them; schooners, merchants, trawlers and fishermen were upon the water with full sails and flying flags. For a moment, the crew stopped to watch, mesmerised – it seemed almost bizarre to witness neighbours on the water. There were other people, other faces and stories as they manned their vessels to earn money to keep their families afloat. Pelicans bobbed on the waves whilst brown booby's flew in from the day's fishing out at sea. It was a sign they were nearing land, nearing a port, edging ever closer to civilisation; a thought which served as a final push to reach it.

The quartermaster felt an urgency surge within him, a thrashing combination of excitement, apprehension and finality. *This is it. Our final stop. The end of the road.* What they were to find was a mystery, and where they were to find it was a bigger one still. These concerns had to be replaced for now, as docking and finding food and water was the centre priority. He wondered if Tess had thought about how this situation would look to the dockers and officials surveying the port when they sailed to the jetty or rowed to shore from the shallows. When that happened, he wondered what to do. *Run for it, Joseph. Run away. Grab the clues and bolt. Disappear. You've done it before; you can do it again.* The memory of Lisbon popped up; a harsh reminder that his body was barely able to move without aches sparkling in his every joint and sinew. *You wouldn't be able to make it from the boat. You're not the man you were, you're just a salty old seadog too weak to bark.*

With his long hair flying in the breeze, he turned to look at the coast again and saw an altogether contrast. Gone were the cliffs and crags and in their place was a placid bay of white sand and a belt of greenery sprouting from the top of the beach. Trees were there, plants and flowers and vegetation; colours his bleary eyes hadn't observed in a long time. Above, in the distance, the clouds were thickening and falling, shedding weight in refreshing showers. It was so different from the cliffs it looked to be on another continent, as if this were not land at all but another wave changing shape and form every time a back was turned. In fear of another illusion, he blinked hard and confirmed it was rooted in reality; deliciously solid and unchanging. Now more than ever he wanted to walk upon it and feel the earth beneath his feet.

Victoria turned abruptly, before another bump and scrape shuddered through the wood as the hull grumbled over another patch of hidden rock. Robertson began barking, 'Dave, half reef that sail in! The wind's slowing us, and Thomas lend your hands to that–' suddenly he was cut off, and as Joseph looked up, he saw Tess had delt a hefty blow to his stomach.

'No more!' she instructed, '*I* command my men, they take orders from me now.' Flying down the ladder, she was already yelling to the high heavens orders she'd picked up and taken on, trying to manage the ship through these rough waters. 'Tom, heave that halyard harder and call yourself a man! Benjamin! Climb to the yard and see about that foremast canvas! Work with it to give us a few more knots; this westerly wind is fighting us! Dave! Get to the hold and see we an't taking on water! That hit was hard, I do not want to breach now when we're so close!'

'Would it matter, Tess? Land's only over t'ere.' Billy nodded.

She turned to him, 'Oh, a terrific idea. Let's abandon ship and row to shore where then we have to walk miles upon miles to reach a town or the nearest port, assuming we head in the right direction, and then beg for food and water, hoping someone would listen and feel charitable. Feel free to jump over and begin your hike, Billy.' She retorted, 'Thomas! Pull harder! That rope is still slack! Come on men, bring her closer!' Joseph examined her with an open mouth, surprised at how commanding and disciplined this woman, once so quiet and polite, had become. She looked a natural leader, *no wonder the men joined her cause. Look at her!* She stood poised on the main deck, eyes darting and fingers pointing, seeing the problems and seeking a hand for the solutions. *Who in god's name is this woman?!*

Dave rushed to the deck. 'We're taking on water, Captain. There are a few feet of water in the hold from the last few hits. She won't last much longer.'

Her face stern, she nodded. 'She doesn't need to; we're closing in. There must be a port ahead.' Veering closer to the shore, detail became increasingly distinguished, and the land became greener with less sand and more rocks. Sheltered coves and bays became frequent and rugged crops of sharp exposed coral rose from the water in places up the beach forcing the waves to breach. Joseph spied the water, breaking over the rocks in white plumes, rushing back to the tide in wild glittering showers of a million dancing drops.

'Ships!' Benjamin hollered as he pointed from the rigging, 'more ships heading away! We must be nearing port now.' Checking the distance, Tess ran to the forecastle and surveyed their heading in the spyglass. There, in the grey light of the cloudy afternoon was a sight divine and miraculous; a harbour, equipped with a long jettison stretching out into the water to aid in trading, leading into a busy port.

'Port spotted! Prepare to reef all sails and lower the anchors a fathom, not to bed but let them swim – await my call!' she commanded, the westerly breeze running through her hair. With beady eyes, Joseph looked ahead and saw it; a busy port situated at the very tip of a narrowing stretch of land that had a steady curve to it, creating a large bay they were sailing through. Attached to the port was a long, floating platform that accommodated two vessels already docked with sails nipped up tight, and two more were anchored in the shallows, unloading their goods via longboat to the port to trade. Other ships were berthed in the harbour on the other side.

She's not docking us; she's lowering anchor in the shallows and rowing us all into the port. Docking would create too many questions and a fee we can't pay for. Joseph could see her logic – it was a smart move; another reminder of how well she'd planned everything. He sighed and lowered his head, worried that if any opportunity arose for them to rid of them, she would be quick to the draw and end it before they'd even noticed. *And I thought Dave was the mastermind - he's nothing more than a misery. She's the real fiend. No wonder she wanted so many of the dogwatches, so she could continue plotting!*

At last *Victoria* entered smooth water where she could wander freely amongst the waves without fear of tripping, even though she was sinking. The bay was tough to get into from their route but once entered, it was calm and sheltered; a perfect location for trading and working. What port this was, though, was a mystery they'd have to discover – not that it would make much of a difference. It was land. It was civilisation and by god they needed it. Nonetheless, to not arise suspicion or attention, the correct procedure had to be administered, and Tess saw this from the other anchored ships: 'Jim! What flags do we need?'

Robertson glared at her from the stern, visibly sweating after that horrific sail. Secretly, he'd been hoping she wouldn't have realised; it would've aroused suspicion and resulted in questions upon arrival, which would give those tied a good stead. Now, those hopes were squandered by her superb tactics and observation. *She'd make a great pirate* . . . There was no use in lying to her now. *No, Jim, she is a pirate.* 'The Red Ensign needs hoisting to show we're a merchant ship of the United Kingdom, then fly the Courtesy Flag beneath; there should be an Australian one in the hold somewhere; to let them know we aren't a threat.' *But you are.* He called back, 'Any hand; go and grab those flags and hoist them, fly the colours.'

Tess began to march up to the deck again, her fists clenched, 'I *told* you my men do *not* take orders from *you*!'

Robertson gritted his teeth. 'Fine. Go order *your* men to hoist the Red Ensign and Courtesy Flag then. Or don't order them, and we'll see what happens when we reach land.'

She levelled, frosting the glare with ice. 'Thomas! Grab the Red Ensign and hoist it, then the Courtesy Flag.' She instructed without looking away. Eagerly as Thomas's frail body could move, he fetched the flags and hoisted them, seeking her approval with a longing eye.

Tess stepped to him and pecked him on the cheek, appearing as if she did it just to keep him satisfied, then headed for the forecastle to keep her eye wary. The ship was slowing as she lowered into the water. 'Start swimming the anchor and drop it half to bed, then unfurl all sails and let them catch this rogue wind to slow us. Ready the longboat!' She declared without taking her eyes off the port they now closed in on.

The jobs were completed very gradually as fatigue crept in on them; their burst of energy was over, they were spent. *She's run them ragged without even a thought,* Joseph noticed, *it's a wonder we even managed to keep sailing.* Eventually, they slowed to a stop in the bay where the anchor was put to bed, a mile from the port was what was left to row. A mile left until they stepped on the final shore. *And then how many miles?*

Tess then ordered them all to wait for dusk, where they could row to the shore unnoticed under the cover of darkness. Another cunning ploy. Everyone was thankful for the rest and after an hour the sun began to set, shrouding the port and harbour in an ashen misty gloom. In a bitter, restless wind, they began to climb down into the boat, exhausted and desperate. The three prisoners were then untied from the mast and from their bonds and clambered down into the longboat one by one. Joseph was last of all, and, with Tess's permission, he collected the papers, scrolls and objects and slipped them all into a canvas bag that he shouldered. He walked the last walk, seeing the memories of the deck play out past him.

It was here that Poppy danced with Rob to the merry songs Billy strung with his fiddle; Harold sat on a barrel in a warm African sunset smiling at the crew's banter as he carved chunks of softwood. Hugh smoked and laughed as he placed his winning cards down and raised his cup of grog. Victoria's face softly smiling as he asked her to dance on the night the ocean glowed. He remembered their evenings on the deck, eating supper in a glowing sunset, smoking pipes and cigarettes listening to Benjamin tell stories of the sea.

He thought of how much had changed; the recent horrid mutterings, the mutinous glares and eventually this violent rift between them now, and felt it was time to let the past lie. Keeping only the memories that really mattered; holding onto the memories rich in warmth and feeling that he could look back on with joy. Then he stepped onto Jacob's ladder and climbed down to his seat on the centre thwart next to Thomas, ready to row.

Again, it was sadly strange to not see Rob aboard, looking out to the shore with wonderous eyes. He sighed, *time to let it go . . .* They pushed off, listening to the lap of the waves licking the bow as they rowed toward the last stop.

After a few minutes, Robertson and a few others glanced back to the exhausted ship and he took his hat off, putting it to his chest. 'Goodbye, old girl.' He said sadly, and the ship settled into a sullen silence, lowering deeper into the water as she sank.

As Joseph pulled the oar, his tired mind plucked the memory of his grandfather once again and instead of the clunking rowlocks, he heard the gravelly voice of the beaten man: *Travels. Is that what you want to hear, boy? About my explorin' days? There an't no point to it I tell you! No point says I . . .*

Chapter Thirty-Six

29th April 1770.

. . . Waves lapped against the bow of the longboat as the two oarsmen pulled the six men toward the beach. The air was thick, heavy to breathe but they were used to the heat now; their pacific voyage thus far had a hot climate. Nevertheless, rowing this boat was enough to make Frederick Winter sweat, as well as the thought of their destination.

A smile spread across his face as he remembered the number of ailments he used to suffer from when they first departed Britain. Sores and welts, bleeding blisters and seasickness, *blimey, I can't remember what that feels like anymore.* Two years at sea had changed him. He'd left home a boy, a humble apprentice shipwright, and the world had changed him into a man; had nurtured him into a hardy sailor of twenty-two with a body of a weathered rock, hands as tough as bull's hide and a spirit invigorated by the brilliance of exploration. As he lay in his bunk at the end of each day, he wondered: What else was out there hidden in the blank spaces no one knew of? New lands? Islands? Continents? More importantly, colonies to plant the flag into . . . The blossoming empire always needed fresh soil if she wanted to expand, to grow into a superpower of the world, and he was proud to be a part of it.

Out of the one hundred men that set sail from Plymouth two years ago, he felt privileged to pull the oars toward another undiscovered land. The thought reminded him of George Carter, his best friend who had persuaded him to travel with him to Plymouth and try their hand at manning ships instead of building them. *Come on Fred, let's do it,* he heard Georgie-boy say, *I've saved up 'nough to get down there now. Five pounds an' a few shillings. We can do it, together. We've learned 'nough from these 'wrights now, let's go and learn for ourselves. Yer never know, we could find a brand-new land!* Frederick smiled warmly, already excited to inform George how the landing went upon their return to the *Endeavour.*

He glanced behind to the beach and saw another adventure, and this voyage had certainly had its fair share. They had faced storms, bloodshed, disease and deceit all whilst exploring the southern regions of the Pacific Ocean, all thanks to their royal commission from good old King George III two years previously. It was thanks to him a ship was available when the two boys arrived at Plymouth dock. God save the King!

After crossing the Atlantic, they rounded Cape Horn and reached Tahiti, where they observed the crossing of Venus before stopping at unknown islands claiming them as Great British soil, planting the Union Jack and adding more countries to the ever-growing empire. It had been a matter of weeks since they had charted New Zealand's coastline and waters and, after spotting a butterfly at sea, they realised more land must be close by. Intense searching began until they spotted glimpses of another coastline squatting on the horizon. Excitement grew again and, anchoring in the shallows, six of the crew manned the longboat and set sail for the coast, unsure of what this new land had to offer and, crucially, if it had already been claimed.

This was the first time Frederick had been an oarsman to the first boat to shore and his exhilaration was second to none. Only his imagination had given him these feelings before watching from the bulwark as the captain and scientists made the initial discoveries, but now he had earned his keep. These were feelings of experience. Nerves tingled and his stomach knotted but they did nothing to dampen the wondrous spirit he held dear. He was an explorer now; nerves were a part of the job.

Facing the sea, Frederick could not see the beach or how far they had yet to go but it couldn't be long, the *Endeavour* was getting smaller in the distance. He pulled the oar to his chest and pushed it away in a circular motion, feeling his muscles pump and burn and hearing the clunk and splash as the oar rolled in its rowlock. It was in perfect unison with his fellow oarsman, allowing them to propel the boat quicker to shore. From his view, he could only watch the eyes of the scientist, (or *botanist* as they kept reminding the crew) Daniel Solander, to register his reaction of how close they were to the shallows. . . and what this new land looked like.

Now, Solander's eyes were wide and intrigued. If no other hints or signs of western civilisations were sighted, then their suspicions would be correct: no one else their side of the globe would have seen these views before. Frederick's anticipation to jump off and explore was hard to hold onto. *I'm here, I'm making history!* Solander's eyes were growing wide and excited, reminding him of how he must have looked two years ago as a twenty-year old lad taking those first few steps onto the great *HMS Endeavour,* captained by the true legend James Cook himself. The clarity of that memory still resonated to this day; the buzz he had felt had not worn off. Cook was already known for his feats in the Royal Navy and his skills at surveillance and mapping – to work for him aboard his own ship was an honour to the name of Winter. *I want to do it, I want to explore as he does so people will remember me for my travels, so Winter can be a renowned name in history. A name people will know and smile upon.*

Adventure welcomed him with an adrenalin-fuelled embrace and had not let him go – it gave him the confidence he had needed, as well as an enthusiastic spirit of those who lived their lives off the pages of the map. He was an explorer, a pioneer. No doubt death had prickled his spine once or twice, or thrice, but it was worth the risks for the adventure. Again, he thought about that close episode with scurvy and the brush with destiny when he lost his footing during that storm. He regretted nothing and took on those challenges knowing that whatever happened, he would become stronger because of it, and he hoped that, in a way, when he returned home, he would be a better man than the one that left the dock.

They rowed for a further fifteen minutes, making a beeline for the beach and slowly the scene materialised into shapes and forms with earthly roots. The clear shallow waters transported them to the warm white untouched sands of the mystery wonderland. What they would find, what they would see, *every* experience made was a new discovery. No other man had ventured this far. No other man from their side of the world had set foot upon this soil. Every step they took would literally be charting the very bottom of the map; they were colouring in the blank space unknown to the northern hemisphere. To them, they had journeyed to the very edge of the earth; and were about to jump off. About to make history.

The tide lapped gently along the side of the varnished wood - the water crystal clear. An unpolluted clarity. It was definite now no other ship had been here before.

The longboat brushed up onto the sand.

A warm breeze folded around them.

A tantalising moment, an apprehensive and exciting moment as all six of them looked to the land ahead. Frederick Winter could not believe his eyes.

The white beach stretched up to a segmented broken line of brush, including small, rounded bushes that were a mottled green but did not look like they supported much life; if anything, it looked like algae had coated the branches instead of thickets of leaves. Sooty oystercatchers scuttled from the tideline and into the wiry collections of twigs and buds, joining the undergrowth, skittering over the dry dusty ground that looked like it rarely received much rain. Beyond that, a small area of trees grew, offering some shade from the harsh sunlight that burned brightly. Beyond that, however, was another mystery entirely. Where were they? What land was this? That was up to them to decide. The only question that was out of their control was the unnerving concept of company. Was this land inhabited? If so, by whom? *Hopefully not by people practising human sacrifice like that island of Tahiti . . .*

It didn't look like much; undiscovered lands never did, but Frederick could see potential; every island, bay and piece of soil had it. Once the Union Jack was planted, the possibilities were endless: a new colony. Another piece for the growing British empire. Claimed. Theirs by right, by law: another piece of Britain, expanded and developed. It was the future. As Frederick looked at the sand, he could see it; a hundred years from now this land was to be bustling with people. People working jobs, earning money to support their families. Colonies. Towns. Cities. Guided by a government who answered to the King or Queen of England on the other side of the world. Civilisation. All made possible by his and his Captain's discovery today.

'Jump out, Isaac.' Cook addressed the man behind him and turned with a giving look on his face. It was one of the most generous of gestures, letting one take the first step – it was always something every explorer wanted to say; it was what they were to be remembered for, if not for anything else.

The midshipman Isaac Smith nodded and smiled back to his cousin, a film of sweat on his forehead. He said nothing. There was nothing to say. If Cook had ordered Frederick to take the first steps onto an unknown land, he wouldn't be able to find the words either; he would have just nodded, smiled, stood up and looked down to the sand, just as Smith did.

Frederick watched in awe at the historic moment as Royal Navy Officer Isaac Smith stepped out from the boat and onto the shore, officially sealing this land's fate. He walked up the beach and placed his hands on his hips, scouring the ground before him.

'Let's explore.' Cook said to them all with a smile, and hopped out of the boat . . .

. . . He walked up the beach feeling uneasy, the sand slipping beneath him. It felt bizarre walking on such terrain. The ground felt solid, immovable and rooted. Joseph Winter fell to his knees, losing his balance after expecting the land to rise and fall with his step.

A great fatigue crept over him as the gravity of making landfall sunk in – a momentous occasion, physically and mentally, after suffering the strain of the journey for so long. He felt the ground under his hands, the sand in his palms and the enormity emphasised;

the clues, the objects, decisions, suffering, everything, had led to this place, to this land. Somewhere out there, buried in the ground, was their objective. Their grail and holy covenant of deliverance. Scott's Trove itself. *'We're so close.'* He whispered to himself, the weight of the world on his shoulders. The moment was short-lived, however, as priorities gripped. There were more important things to think of.

Food, water and rest.

Robertson stood over him and held out a tied hand, looking gaunt and weary. 'Come on, Joseph. Let's go see where we are.'

Faithfully, he took it and got to his feet where the crew were already stumbling to the nearby buildings. To where exactly none knew, the scene of civilisation was overwhelming; there was no longer a berth to sleep in and a deck to work on, there was much more, and everything seemed to move so quickly on land! Time, it seemed, picked up pace on this alien solid landscape.

Led by Tess, the group slowly ambled over to the closest buildings; pubs, brothels, fisheries and warehouses looked to be the main running businesses, and a few houses lined down the straight road heading away from the port. Old and weather-beaten they were, with crumbling bricks, blasted joints and slanting windows, but to the crew they were lavish mansions with rooms, hearths and a roof.

They spotted candles in the windows and firelight brightening, shadows were stretching on the ground; the hubbub of the port and harbour were slowly winding down as the evening began to take its weary form. The last few people were working the docks, hauling in the day's catch and negotiating any other trades that were visiting. The day was ending. The perfect time for them to arrive, and the worst.

As they walked, Benjamin approached Joseph and Robertson, his eyes crumpling in wrinkles as they squinted in the gloom. 'I've been ordered to take the ties from yer now. Won't be no good to turn up with people arrested. Too many questions, aye, there would be.' He began to untie them, 'there an't no point in tryin' to run or get to us now. We've got it all figured out; we have.' He grumbled.

'Why Benjamin? Why are you in on this? What could she possibly have given you to persuade you to her side?' Joseph scrutinised, seeing the old man in a new way. An old man he was, but a man against them. An enemy.

'Worth, master Joseph. She's made an old seadog feel worthy of somethin' again and to me, that makes all the difference.' He replied.

'You *were* worthy! You manned the ship; you joined this mission. That's got to be worth something.'

A stern look passed his craggy features. 'I was just another hand to move. That's all we were. Just cogs to keep the clock tickin', to keep yer journey on its feet. No more, says I. This one's ours now.' Benjamin hobbled away to untie the others, his ripped trousers flapping, his shirt crunching with the movement of the dried salt.

Joseph pursed his lips, nursing his own self belief that he *was* a good man, yet doubt was forming, maybe he was just another monster that had found its way to sea after all. *No! Stop it now. This an't who you are. Don't listen. Just focus. On the chest . . . Find it and end this . . .*

Suddenly he noticed Tess and Thomas had stopped outside a house. A small house with fishing hooks and harpoons leaning against the front wall and brickwork that had been blasted of its joints from the awesome coastal gales. In its window, firelight glowed warmly against the dusk outside. A fisherman's house perhaps? A whaler's cottage? Was anyone in?

Gradually, they trickled in her wake, stopping outside the front gate. Tess checked behind her and, seeing all in order, she knocked on the door and waited.

The door opened with a squeak and a short woman looked out. Joseph could only see features from the gate: greying hair, high blushed cheeks, crow's feet and a small mouth. An expression of concern and confusion flickered on her friendly face, but before she made a move to slam the door shut or to call for help, Tess dived into her plea, her throat heaving and clutching as she attempted an exhausted cry. 'Please, miss. Have you any food; room to spare? We've just arrived from a long journey, we have nothing. Please. Help us. All we ask is for food and water and a roof over our heads.'

Surprisingly, the woman's face conveyed recognition and she nodded, before turning to call back into the house. 'Kinny! They're here, love! The ones you were watching from the windah. You were right.' She turned back to them, 'we thought you moight come to us. We're the closest house to the port. Plenty of sailahs visit us when they stop by, so we're quite used to strangers. Come! Come in. We've some fish cookin'; the fire's hot and my pot's empty so I can russle up a hearty stew for you all, too. You look loike you could do with a decent meal.' She opened the door and ushered them all inside her house. The feel of the heat was soothing, the smell of the fish was tantalising. Their host introduced herself, 'I'm Charlotte Dodger, but eiveryone knows me as Charlie.' The courtesy and honesty of these people were self-evident; hospitality was clearly a most important rule.

'Thank you.' Tess whimpered, 'God bless you.'

To fit everyone in, Charlie spread them out to different areas of the house. It had small rooms but had a second floor with two vacant rooms which, to the Londoners, was something only the rich and able could afford. Clearly out here the population was not half as expansive. Charlie showed them to places where each could stay, mostly sleeping together on spare bundles of sheets or spare sacks of fishing material. In one of the rooms was a straw bed with a flat pillow; the most beautiful piece of furniture they'd ever seen. Charlie couldn't be thanked enough.

Joseph, Robertson and Billy were led into a room outside; a storage shed that smelled of fish and was full of bundles of nets and sacks with hooks hanging from the ceiling and a rack of harpoons lining the wall. Boxes gave the desk some form of organisation, but the space was messily strewn with objects and homemade knick-knacks half finished. By now, it was hard to distinguish much detail, only fading silhouettes. She placed her hands on her hips, 'sorry for the mess, loves. My husband, Kinny, is a fisherman; the port's lovely and full 'o tuna and kingfish, and he's quite the oyster-catcher too.' Charlie then sighed at the mess on the desk and smiled, 'he's always makin' new little doodads to sell along the port, bless 'im. I help with some of it; it earns us a few more coppers and that's always noice to have. It keeps us floating. Anyway, you can bundle some 'o those nets up or unravel them sacks to sleep on and I'll be back in a whoile with the stew.'

'Thank you, Charlie, we really appreciate it.' Robertson said as she left. She smiled and nodded, her long greying curls bobbing. The three men stumbled across to the nets and sacks and arranged them as best as they could with Billy struggling with his one functional arm. Too tired to talk, they moved in silence in the darkening evening; too tired to think, they cared little for their plans for the morrow. For the time being, none of it mattered.

Soon, Charlie returned with a jug of water and bowls of stew; chunks of vegetables, meat and herbs cooked into a rich fatty broth, and bade them goodnight. A simple dish to cook, yet its treatment and taste was exquisite beyond compare, as if jets and sparkles were exploding on their tongues and melting down their throats like warm butter. The flavours, oh! the flavours were fantastical as well as the meal being cooked, not to mention the nutrients, vitamins and minerals; all of which were drugs to these poor punter's veins. Joseph couldn't remember tasting anything better, and after a drink of fresh water, they settled down on the netting and pulled their caps and hats low. *What to do about Tess? How can we . . . get through this? How can we . . . find . . . it . . .* he yawned, and slipped into a peaceful sleep without thought, regret or emotion clouding the craved slumber.

Chapter Thirty-Seven

In a fit of anxiety, Joseph awoke breathing rapidly, sweating in his bed of netting. His tongue felt thick, his throat a strip of sandpaper. Racing thoughts blurred cognitive motion and he found himself disorientated in the fisherman's shed. The back of his head ached bitterly, as if a chunk of smouldering char was melting through his skull, slowly burning a fleshy hole to nestle into. Suddenly his guts wrenched painfully, and he hobbled outside to find the latrine. The stew had gone right through as his insides, once again, had to adjust to an influx of sudden consumption. Aching after the bout of diarrhoea, he stepped back in the shed and laid on his makeshift bed, wide-eyed.

Knowing there was no chance of getting back to sleep, he pushed himself up to sit and held his belly. Nausea flowed through him in ebbing swells as his mind and body tried to realign itself after being roused in such an abrupt manner. The cause of it was unclear, but after the development and climax of such a strenuous sequence of events he could guess at a few things that kept him on edge. *No doubt Hugh was in there somewhere, screaming his way through every fucking memory I have.* He groaned and rubbed his eyes in the mellow light of a fast-approaching dawn.

Robertson and Billy were sleeping soundly, so Joseph decided to walk out and watch the break of day to ease his baffled brain. The air had chilled overnight; the overcast sky had been blown free leaving a sky as clear as glass. He wandered around the shed and found a well, where he pulled the rope and retrieved the bucket, drinking the freshwater deeply. With water dripping from his beard, he looked out to the shore beyond the house, to the horizon blending its pale lemony grey watercolours into the dark oily tones of night.

As Joseph viewed the pale rising sun and remaining stars, he felt at peace, with half of him wishing to go back to that night in the doldrums to witness the phenomena all over again. The vision burned bright, the memory a glowing strobe of hope. A whisp of cold air brought him back, and he looked out to the calming lap of the waves rolling along the sand, to a dark silhouette of a ship anchored in the settled morning mist of the sheltered Australian bay. Shadows of pelicans flew seaward for the early morning catch, diving into the dawn. This, it seemed, was just as nurturing.

With a calmed mind and a slight shiver, he turned back to the shed and found an old man sitting on a roughly made bench against the wall, smoking a pipe and watching him watch the sunrise. 'Ye alroight mate?' he asked, and puffed, his thumb flicking up and down over the bowl and moved the pipe from one corner of his lips to the other. 'I didn't wake you, did I?'

A moment of confusion, then, *Ah, you must be Kinny.* 'No. I had a . . . a bit of a start when I woke up and wanted to clear my head a bit.' He noticed him smoking and surprisingly felt nothing. *When was my last smoke? Do I even want one anymore?*

The aged Australian slowly nodded and smiled in the early light. He had a friendly face, just as his wife did. 'Aye, and a thirst that could make a fish jealous, I see.' He nodded, 'you've caught a good toime though; dawn is one of my favourite toimes o' the day. I come out here nearly eivery morning to watch it. Anyway, I'm Kinny Dodger, as it happens. I watched you all row in and got some bits together, thinking you moight come a' knockin' on our door. You've all been asleep for the past day, and you're lucky it's a Sunday else I'd be up n' out already.' He shivered and rose, 'you must be famished! Let's go in and get some fish cookin' for brekky. The mornings are gittin' chillier and I'm gittin' older.' He motioned for him to follow and they hurried inside, slipping quietly into the main room where the embers in the hearth still had a flicker of red. The pot with which Charlie had cooked the stew remained above the ashes, and Joseph hoped there was still some leftover. He was starving. Kinny quickly rustled the red ash with the poker and added some tinder and kindling and readied a pan, lowering gutted fish onto it. Then he pulled chairs from the table in the corner of the room and sat down next to the hearth with a sigh. 'Ye smoke?'

Joseph's eyes, however, were not on his breakfast. Lying on the floor with a rolled blanket under her head and a big throw covering her and Victoria, Tess watched him with open, glassy eyes. She made not a move, but her clear greys said it all. *Make a move, Joseph, go on. Try and get me.* He gritted his teeth as he knew he was powerless. She needed him to help with the search and could not make him look the enemy, just as he couldn't throttle her with a vicelike grip without being made to look like a vicious killer. For now, whilst in Kinny and Charlie's home, it was neutral ground, and both knew it.

'Ye smoke?' Kinny asked again.

Blinking, Joseph focused, unsure of what to say. 'Y-yes. I do. Can't remember the last one; it's been a while. I don't have my papers or pipe on me though.'

Kinny waved it off and brought out some of their newspapers stacked next to the fire. He took out a sheet and expertly tore it into strips and handed his pouch of tobacco. 'Ee-yar. It's all a load o' shit in them papers anyways.' He smiled.

Joseph took the offering and tried to remember how to roll, but it didn't take long for his fingers to pick up the habit. He took the match Kinny offered and lit the cigarette, inhaling the tobacco smoke deeply as he used to, then got caught in a coughing fit. His eyes began to sting and weep as Kinny laughed. 'Loike most o' the country, the baccy's got some bite with her.'

'Christ!' He coughed, then tried again, now tasting the richness and slight spicy flavour. It was different from the London pickings, and it left a warming aftertaste. Still, he'd had nothing but clean sea air in his lungs for months, to breathe in smoke again was tough and it didn't give him the same satisfaction. After a few disappointing puffs, he nodded, 'Thank'ee.' Lowering the cigarette, he couldn't bring himself to finish it.

Kinny nodded and smiled, then prodded the small fire that now flickered and added some more wood before sitting the pan on a small railing above the flames next to the pot. 'There. That's got it right. By a' toime eiveryone's up they'll be lovely and smoked as a fox in a hole. There's some leftover stew too if you want it.'

'Thank you, Mister Dodger. For everything. We all appreciate it. I don't know how we can repay you.'

He waved it off. 'Ahh never you mind. It's an old tradition to always help out those in trouble from the sea and Charlie n' I keep to it as much as we can. We loike a bit o' company, since our kids have got their own sticks now. An' please, call me Kinny. Eiveryone else does.' He drew in a breath and puffed the pipe. As tall as his wife and as honest, Kinny also had tanned skin, a head of receding yet combed back grey-white hair and white stubble, retaining some of his looks of youth. Alas, age and the weather had taken their toll leaving him with crow's feet etched around his eyes, wrinkled skin like that of a crinkled cloth and crooked fingers from a life pulling ropes and hauling tuna. He thumbed his braces against a dirty shirt, and puffed again, motioning Joseph to move nearer to the warmth of the hearth. His eyes gleamed darkly like coal, looking small roofed under such low bushy brows and narrowed by such an inquisitive squint. Another puff, then, 'Where's it you all come from then? If I didn't know any bettah, I'd say that's an English accent.'

He nodded, 'aye, we're all from London, born and bred; know all the streets as if we're kith and kin.'

'Well, crikey! My grandfather was from there. He was one a' the first few colonists that arrived for penal service all o' them years ago. From Camden, I think. Oh, I can't remembah, but definitely a man o' the streets he was, but old Jimmy had a falling out with the law.' He winked, 'that's why I call myself an Australian now, else we'd be calling ourselves kith 'n kin!'

Joseph smiled, 'I know quite a few that managed to get themselves a one-way ticket on the Hulks o' the Thames.'

Kinny returned the expression, 'Y' moight see 'em round mate. We've had no end o' boat loads of Pommy's turn up over the last few decades.' At Joseph's confused expression, he explained, 'Prisoners of Mother England is what they're officially called. That got shortened to P-O-M-E's, and we shortened them to Pommy's

- ye get it. I've seen quiet dusty roads turn into colonies, to little villages and towns, branching out loike roots of a plant – from the amount of aboriginal land the colonies have taken up, it's no wonder why they don't like us.' He looked a little unnerved, then continued, 'The Pommy's I've met sound loike you, others have different English accents I struggle to grasp. Strange though mate, anyone would think that country o' yours is using this noice bit of soil as a dumpin' ground for your criminals.' He winked again, knowing fully well that was what Britain was doing and had been doing since 1788. 'Although from what I hear, those politicians might be ditching the "outta' sight outta' mind" idea soon and dealing with the criminals properly in Britain, rather than carting them out to here.'

Just then there was a shuffle of footsteps from the doorway and Charlie Dodger walked in, wearing a flowery blouse with her hair in plaits that joined around the back of her head. 'G' morning to you, mister . . . bless me! I'm sorry, I never caught y' names.'

'Oh, Mister Winter. Joseph Winter.'

She almost took a step back in surprise. 'Winter, y' say? As in relation to Frederick Winter?'

Joseph nodded, *nearly the same reaction anywhere I go, what was so great and admirable about this man?!* 'He was my grandfather. How is it you ken him?'

Kinny took his pipe out, 'Know o' him! Well bless me! The second Winter stepping on our soil! In our house too, Charl'!' he laughed and coughed, putting his pipe back between his lips and nodded, 'he's a part a' folklore around here, mate. Cook founded our nation and Winter was a big helper in setting up the first few colonies; the ol' fella couldn't seem to get enough of our southern air. And with the money saved from it, he managed to fund his own expeditions. Didn't he tell you of it? Did y' meet him?' he sat forward listening.

Charlie turned the fish, adding seasoning, before stirring the stew. The smell that wafted through the rooms was a delicious wake up call. Slowly, one by one, the crew slipped into the room and sat on an available chair or stool, looking refreshed, and hungry. Joseph found it difficult to focus on what he was saying when such beautiful delicacies were nearly ready to eat. 'We weren't close, and from what I remember of him, he was a different man. I think his travels must've changed him; he barely told me anything about what he did. I never knew he helped to build the colonies.'

A look of disappointment spread over his face, but it was Charlie who answered, 'ah, lives can take different routes along the way and spirits can get lost - or found. Y' remember ol' Nick, Kin? He was a different man when he came home.'

Kinny puffed the pipe, 'aye he was. Ol' Nick was a blacksmith but never took pride in his work – to me, I'd say he just looked loike he didn't know where to put his foot next; always tentative and nervous an' one day he upped sticks and left for - what was it Charl? A year?'

'Yes, about a year I'd say.' She replied, lifting the fish to check them.

'About a year he was gone; eiveryone thought him dead - a snake or spider we said, but he came back, and he was, well, he was loike a new man! He crafted the finest metals and became quoite popular. Good for him, I say. Went out and done it with only the clothes on his back an' it done him good!' He suddenly caught sight of Benjamin as he walked into the room. 'Now there's a sailah if ever I saw one! Come in, we're just about to have some brekky. An' what's your name, mate?' Kinny asked with a grin.

'Benjamin Smith, sir, and might I just thank'ee for letting us stay in your home.'

Another wave, 'ahh, never you mind mate! Come on in. An' who moight you be?'

'David James, but I prefer Dave.'

'I trust ye slept well?'

A flicker of a smile looked odd on his face, 'the best I've slept for a while.'

Then Billy walked through. 'Bless me! Your arm!' Charlie cried, 'let me splint that properly and bandage it. I was a nurse once, a long toime ago. I should hope I know what to do. Come with me mister–?'

'Billy Baker.'

'An Irishman! Kinny, he sounds just like that other one that stayed once, y' know, that one who said he kissed a mermaid an' she swam next to his ship for a week waiting for another. Oh, what was his name?'

'Ol' Micky?'

Charlie smiled and clapped her hands, 'that's the one! We never could agree on our versions of *The Wild Colonial Boy.* He always said it was Jack Duggan in the song and we kept reminding 'im it was Jack Dolan instead, especially when he was here on 'Stralian ground!' she laughed.

Soon, the room was full of chatter and smoke as those who enjoyed a puff were eased into the local Australian blend. As easy as that, the aging couple liquefied the friction and drew the crew from their shells, asking them questions about their journey and lives in London. Conversations flowed and laughter was shared, reminding Joseph of the buzz of the Back House; he'd forgotten the feeling of it, and realised how much he'd missed it.

As her new character bloomed, Tess mellowed and chatted to them as if they were part of her family. She was fresh and charming, layering her persona with a sweetness that was sickening for the four prisoners to see. She almost reminded Joseph of himself when he changed character depending on the situation or job, except she was far more convincing, clearly having more practise. *Christ she's good. She's even fooling me, and I know the real her!* Even Victoria looked around to him with wide eyes. *Can you believe this?!* Was her expression, but now was not the time, or the designated opportunity, to mention anything. For now, they had to keep quiet and let her charm their hosts.

As they talked, they found out Kinny and Charlie had four children who were all grown and had five grandchildren who rarely visited, leaving them missing the company of a full house. To salvage the problem, they began to offer their shelter for sailors in dire need of the necessities and help them as much as they could. 'You're lucky you chose our door to knock on mates.' Smiled Kinny, and as daylight grew brighter in the room, Joseph noticed photographs framed and hanging from the cracked walls and handmade ornaments sitting on the mantlepiece. A rug carpeted the floor and blue-painted waves gave feature around the base of the walls.

The fish and stew were then dished up. The crew tried to eat as civilised as they could, although all they wanted to do was tear the fish to shreds. A jug of water was passed around, as well as second helpings of the stew, silencing them all as they were reminded of the beautiful flavours that came with cooked food. 'Eat up loves,' Charlie ordered, serving the last fish in a cloth, 'we've seen enough sailah's to know what the brink 'a scurvy looks loike.'

As they ate, Kinny asked, 'where's it you sailah's are off to then? Don't mind an ol' fella loike me saying, but you all don't look the usual sailah sort we get knockin' upon the door.'

Joseph pursed his lips as he thought how best to put it. *You've got to mention something; he might know of the wasteland we're looking for.* With the stash of papers and objects feeling heavy in the canvas bag on his lap, he gulped the last of his stew and sighed, *just tell them. What harm can they do?* 'We're looking for something. Something we've travelled a long way for. Something we've sacrificed a lot to get.'

The Australian sat back in his chair and gave him a quizzical look. 'Well, I take it yer not merchants then.' A smile spread, and they noticed he had two gaps where teeth should've been. 'What is it yer looking for?'

Joseph leaned forward with a strange feeling of having a full stomach and glanced at Tess who watched his every move. *How can I word it, so she doesn't know but he does?* He hesitated, and Jim Robertson quickly responded, thinking the same thing. 'We an't sure yet, but we have a vague idea of what to look for; pointers to lead us, if you will.'

'What are they? We know the area quoite well I should hope!' Kinny took his pipe out to laugh. 'That's if you don't mind taking directions from crazy ol' bats loike us.' Charlie shot him some daggers as a wife would do to a husband who had said something he thought to be funny but gave a wrong impression.

Robertson looked to Joseph and Joseph pursed his lips and nodded, not knowing how else to reveal the clue with Tess and her gang in the same room. The captain looked to the couple in earnest, 'we're looking for something hidden somewhere in this land. A lost chest. Our only hint of where to look is a wasteland with two moons and suns. I don't suppose either of you know anything about it, or where that is, do you?'

With a careful eye, Kinny scrutinised them and, seeing their intent and drawn faces, knew this was not a joke. All were serious. All waited for them to answer. He picked a match from his pocket and lit his pipe again, taking a drag and puffing out the smoke, 'wasteland o' two moons and suns, ye say? Well, I'm sorry to disappoint you but I've never heard of it. You, Charl?'

She looked confused, 'Land o' two suns . . . can't say I have.'

'It makes sense now though,' Kinny added with a scrutinising squint, '*I* know what you all are. You're Rushers!'

'What?'

He smiled, 'You're treasure hunters! Gold diggers! *Prospectors!* An' don't you worry y' selves, you're not the first ones to come our way. We've lived here for, crikey! must be twenty-five years now, eh Charl'? And in the past twenty years or so we've had hunters from all over since someone found a golden nugget out there, and ever since then there's been a rush for it. Seems loike our soil is littered with the stuff! Around the port, n' I wouldn't be surprised if it were round the others as well, us locals just call those gold diggers Rushers, as they're involved in this gold rush – and they're always in a bladdy rush too.'

'It's more loike *him* that calls them that.' Charlie sighed tiredly. 'There's no need to worry y' selves, loves. There's some diggin' sites about we can point y' to. A few of our friends around the port and from the city have visited a few sites and troied their luck.' Charlie added.

Joseph shook his head. With a trail as complex as the one they'd unravelled; this was not just a matter of shards and nuggets of gold in the ground. They'd not come all this way to join a site that everyone else was digging, but there was a chance someone had dug up something other than gold. Maybe in a wasteland of two suns as well. *Cor, we should be so lucky.* 'Did they find anything? Apart from gold?' he asked, leaning forward.

Charlie thought about it and shook her head, 'not that I know of, Joseph. I–'

'No, wait, you're forgitting William, Charl'. Remembah what he told us that night? He knew of someone who found somethin' else.'

'William? William who?' she quizzed.

Kinny gestured for her to remember, 'You know, you remembah, William Webber? Ol' Willy who troied to tame that wild wallaby once?'

She smiled and laughed, 'Oh! Willy Webber!'

He laughed, 'Ye know it!'

'How could I forget him?'

'And Willy Webber knew someone who found what?' Billy chipped in, unable to take the suspense any longer. All were nearly on the edge of their seats.

Taking his pipe from his lips, he told them that William knew of someone who'd found a book buried deep in the ground; 'wrapped in a cloth he said it was, to stop the pages from rottin' out. Whoever buried it there wanted it to be found intact. Why, I can't say. Must a' been a special one I guess.' He said with a shrug.

Victoria crossed her legs and looked inquisitive, 'what book was it?'

His bushy white eyebrows crunched up, 'you know, I can't remembah–'

'A Bible.' Charlie Dodger answered, 'it was a Bible he dug up. A lovely discovery I'd say.' It was then that they noticed she wore a cross around her neck.

'Oh, how blessed are we to have stumbled across your wonderful home, Charlie, it was almost predetermined by the good Lord himself. I'm a Christian too.' Chimed Tess, ringing her saint-like bell. 'I used to volunteer at church and help out those in need back home. Nothing made me happier.'

'I'm sure you helped out plenty, Tess. Helped lots of poor young lads on the street.' Joseph countered bitterly.

She looked to him with a saintly eye, but her tongue gave sinner's words. 'I guide them to find the Lord, Joseph. Sometimes all it takes is a slight push and they're there.' she smiled maliciously.

Charlie beamed, 'Oh Tess, that's truly lovely to hear. The world needs a helping hand sometimes. We do our bit, Kinny, don't we? Any weary travellers are welcome under our roof, just as Jesus wanted.'

With his bandaged arm spreading flames up his shoulder, Billy's patience was wearing thin. Even Benjamin looked tired. 'Aye, aye, aye. Yes, tis' a lovely thing. God bless us all. Now can y' tell us where we can find this William?'

Kinny lit his pipe again and itched his head whilst puffing, his skin brightening in the morning glow spilling through the front window. 'Hm. Ol' Willy lived just outside the port once . . . then he moved because of a spider infestation, and now he lives a few moile out.'

'No, he moved again, Kinny. He's not there anymore. From what I heard there was a nest of tiger snakes out in the bushes near his front door and his house was starting to sink. Bad foundations or something loike that.'

'He did?' Kinny gave a look of surprise, 'well he never told me n' I see him down the bar nearly eivery week!'

'Well, I heard about it. Maybe you just weren't listening; wouldn't be the first toime, love.' She said pursing her lips, 'but yes, he's now livin' with a friend of his just near the shop, off the road a bit. Down a track. Y' know the one.'

'Oh, I think I know where. And I reckon I can guess at his "friend" too, the cheeky devil. Him an' that Mary have always had something there, I doubt even her dearly departed husband knew about it.'

'He'd have been the only one that didn't, nearly all o' the community knew what they were up to. Nice fella, ol' Willy, but he never did shy away from pretty women.'

Robertson intervened before their conversation could develop further. 'And where is this track near the shop? We need to talk to William.'

Kinny took his pipe out and blew the last of the smoke. 'Not far mate. Just down the road. Keep followin' the road, pass the houses and you'll get to a few shops, fishmongers, smithies and what have you. Pass an ol' gnarled tree then a bit further on there's a dusty ol' track leading away from the road, and there you'll find him. An hour's walk maybe. You've just got to be careful of the critters out there; bare them in mind. Stay outta' their way and they'll stay outta' yours.' He advised with his wife nodding.

'You won't make it far though, loves.' Charlie added, 'not with how you are. We've seen what scurvy's like; Kinny has seen it claim innocent lives that thought they were well again. I can't let you go out there into this winter until you've got some meat back on your bones and your teeth and joints have stopped hurtin'. Your skin looks lemony; I can't let you leave until I at least see it a little pinkish.'

Robertson nodded, 'aye, I agree. I've seen it too.'

'We need to go now, Charlie; this is important.' Tess quickly answered, sounding less angelic and more of her true devilish self.

Victoria turned to her, trying to keep her voice pleasant but sounding evermore sharp, 'by all means, *you* can go. I, for one, don't want to keel over on the side of the road, but feel free to leave, Tess.'

After a moment's hesitation, Tess revaluated. 'Actually, it would do us good to rest up and gather our strength. It's just a matter of patience, something of which I've got experience in.' Before she could let Victoria retort, she turned to Charlie. 'We'll take you up on your generous offer, Missus Dodger. Thank you for your kind hospitality, I don't know how we can repay you.'

'Ah don't worry y' selves about that! We aren't anything fancy, crikey we've only one bed to spare, the rest are just bundles of sheets and blankets.'

'And netting.' Billy smiled; 'an' might I add it's some o' the comfiest I've slept on.'

Charlie beamed, 'I'm glad y' slept well. Now that I think of it, there are some things you can do whilst you're recovering . . .'

Over the next two days they ate delicious meals; Charlie making sure to give them all the proper nutrients a body needed to get them out of their pasty skin-tone. They ate and ate, never seeming to fill, until they all crashed and slept for hours upon end. Whilst recovering, all offered to help in any way they could and were told the mess in the shed and around the house outside could be tidied and cleared as a repayment for their stay. When they were not tidying or eating, they rested as much as they could and gradually regained some of their strength. Each had a warm bath too, a divine luxury after months without one. Charlie also offered them a cutthroat razor and a pair of scissors and shears for them to cut their hair and shave their beards whilst she washed and mended their clothes.

After a time, movement no longer ached; their joints lubricated by vital minerals and their crawling teeth were eased as vitamins were reintroduced to cement them back into place. Sleep nurtured their exhaustion and water rebalanced their weak frames, physically as well as mentally, clearing their cluttered minds and reorganising thoughts back into order. Charlie was right, they had been far worse than they thought.

Upon the fifth morning of their stay, a warm and windy day with sunny outbreaks pouring light through passing clouds, they all agreed they were strong enough to leave. They thanked their generous hosts profusely and walked out the gate to begin searching for William Webber, when Kinny approached Joseph. "Ang on there, mate. I want to give you something.' He gave him one of his handmade ornaments wrapped in a cloth. It was a polished wooden pipe that had been ornately carved into the shape of a fish; its mouth was open to form the bowl and its curving hollow body formed the shaft where the raised and smoothed tail then hooked for a set of lips, parted and ready to smoke the rich Australian tobacco. It was painted beautifully in shimmering shades of blue with hints of purple around each scale; the fins were yellow with tints of red and the head was a light periwinkle, glinting in the early morning. He was stunned; the craftmanship was very impressive, but a guilt gripped him. 'Kinny, I can't . . . it's beautiful; it's too much. You could make a decent sum of it. I've nothing to offer.'

The old Australian waved a hand and smiled warmly. 'Ah never you mind, cobber. It's just a small way of saying thanks for yer grandfather's efforts, and a little somethin' to remembah us by.'

Joseph could feel himself welling up; the generosity of this couple was astounding but he couldn't crumble now. He gulped the emotion down and wrapped it before slipping it in his pocket. 'Thank you, both of you. For everything.' He said and shook both their hands before departing, swinging his canvas bag over a shoulder and joining the rest of the crew already walking down the road.

The day would've felt hot if it wasn't for the breeze that whipped through the port, sending dust clouds sweeping across the road. Nearby trees, naked and empty, rattled and the sprouts of grass breaking through the rough road were flung back and forth as the wind tried to tug them from the ground. People strode past, holding onto their bonnets and hats. As gusty as it was, the crew felt invigorated with their new strength, stepping with force and feeling human again after their ghostly arrival to land. It reminded Joseph of his moments emerging from a successful job, reattaching his flesh and blood to the ghostly figure that never left a trace. As he walked, he shrugged the memory away, leaving it to billow free in the coastal breeze to allow space for fresh growth.

After half an hour's walking, Victoria matched his pace. She walked close beside him. Her hair was neat and fresh having been washed and trimmed with no knots or mats and was styled into a relaxed chignon. Her skin had regained its smoothness and radiancy; she looked healthy and attractive. He himself had bathed too and had cut his hair and trimmed and neatened his beard to look a little more sociable. After some thought, he'd decided to keep his beard, a trademark of a new chapter in his life, plus he liked the look of it. By the look of Victoria's warm smile, she did too. 'You're looking a bit fresher.'

Joseph nodded, squinting in the bright sun that moved and folded with the passing of the cotton clouds. 'You know, I never knew how much I'd appreciate a warm bath. Amazing what a bit o' fresh water can do.' He side-glanced at her casually and smiled, 'you look lovely, Miss Penning.'

She smiled as her loose strands of hair and blouse played in the breeze. 'As do you, Mister Winter.' Then Victoria faced ahead and checked that no one was lending their ear. 'I've thought of something we can do.'

A nod said *continue* . . .

'When we find this man that found the Bible and we get him to take us to the discovery site, we bind and gag each of them in the night and leave them behind, so they'll never know where to look.'

'She'll know, Victoria. She's anticipating something. We've got to be unpredictable.'

'Alright. We grab whatever weapons we can when they least expect it; we threaten them and take them to the nearest police station.'

'They'll talk.'

'We gag them.'

'They'll fight.'

'We bind them.'

'The police will wonder.'

'We tell them what happened.'

Joseph sighed, 'We underestimated her before and we're underestimating her now. She's planned everything Victoria, right down to who she'd kill, what to do if anything arises and how to handle a tough situation, and she's told her henchmen as much too.'

'Indeed, I have.' Tess said in front of them, making them stop, not giving them a chance to wonder how she'd heard. Her hand looked primed for the dagger she had tucked away. Thomas, Dave and Benjamin stood watching, waiting for any spontaneous movement. 'And you're right, Joseph, I have thought of everything, including the second half of the last clue. Oh, close your gaping mouth you stupid fool; you can't be that shocked. Did you really think I wouldn't notice? I knew it didn't sound right. Give me the second half. Now.'

Rage caught flame within him. No matter what they did she was always a step ahead. This time he had nothing to offer her, what was left was all they had. The last half was their last hope. Their only protection. *If I don't tell her, she'll beat us until I do. If I tell her, she'll kill us all. Either way she'll get it, and she knows this.* There was no use in lying. Sooner or later, it would have to be revealed.

He looked to Victoria, to Billy, to Robertson, then sighed and closed his eyes. To the horror and shock of the others, he uttered the last half to her eager ears. Just as that same malicious smile was about to hook her lips, he continued. 'Spare us now, Tess, and give mercy. You owe us that at least.'

A momentary look of confusion glimpsed across her face, and she shook her head almost amused. 'I owe you nothing.'

'On that day behind those prison walls, I offered you all a proposal to help me on this journey to its end. To the chest. To a new life. You agreed to that. It was my idea, and all played their part; we're here, but we're not at the chest yet. A new life is not so far away, buried under this very earth. I've held up my end and got you here alive and now you have what you want – *spare us*. Let *this* be our new life, even if it is from here to the burial ground of the Lost Loot itself.'

Her complexion softened slightly, then hardened to stone. 'Did my sister get her new life? Do you see her here? Or Harold? Is Hugh standing alongside us? You got us here alive – *what a crock of shit!* You can't even support your own words.'

'Their deaths were accidental! I did nothing to–'

She went to grab the dagger, ready to strike.

Just then Dave James suddenly spoke a word that stunned them. Joseph most of all. 'Wait.' He said commandingly, 'Tess. He has a point. Their deaths were results of the journey; you can't blame him for that.'

Tess turned and glared with bitter animosity, fangs out and venom dripping. '*Dave* . . . you disappoint me. After all the contempt, you want to let the monster live. After everything he's put us through! *After everything he's done!*' she hissed.

He shook his head. 'I'm saying we give them this one. Then, when we reach the site, he's mine. He'll get to the very end but never see the chest or the treasure inside; I'd say that's a fair comeuppance for everything he's done. That is the worst torture for him. His "new life" is to be a short one and I want to be the man to take it from him, to feel his blood run through my fingers as I watch his strength fade. Nothing could bring me more joy.'

Slowly, Tess nodded, considering, and looked back to Joseph. 'Your death warrant is set, as is your executioner. Enjoy your last miserable days.' She made her way back to the front of the group, leading them onward under her iron fist.

Chapter Thirty-Eight

With a clammy palm, Joseph knocked on the door of the small wooden shack and waited. Stress weighed heavy on his shoulders and riddled his back with enough knots to make a sailor jealous. Freedom of speech was now chained, every move had to be tactical to stay alert, to stay ahead. To keep moving forward. If any step appeared to be lagging or a purposeful dawdle to stall for time was spotted, there would not be a second chance. As of now, every moment was observed by Tess and her ever-watchful henchmen. As of now, every moment counted.

Sweat trickled down his brow. *Come on, answer the bloody door!* His fists clenched in anticipation; an involuntary tremble had begun. Anxiety was back with a vengeance; strangely, he'd almost begun to miss it – the uncontrollable thunder in his chest reminded him he was alive. Adrenalin in all its glory.

Suddenly the door opened, and a tall man wearing a cotton vest and a pair of trousers looked out with eyes as blue as the waters of the Indian Ocean. Those eyes searched for recognition, then reason. 'Ello?' he said in a deep voice, 'y' alright there, mate? What can I do for you?' He appeared to be in his forties but had aged well with his body retaining some of its youthful look; only slight wrinkles, pronounced veins and numerous scars gave the impression of his experience in the world. With a chiselled jaw dusted with dark stubble, he could have passed as handsome.

'Hello. Are you William Webber?' asked Joseph, trying hard not to stumble on his words.

The man's eyes narrowed in a suspicious squint. 'I am. An' who are you?'

He nodded, 'I'm Joseph Winter. We've all just come from Kinny and Charlie Dodger's house and we were told to pay you a visit; you know of someone who we need.'

'What's this about? Who do you need? I don't know anyone round here. I've recently moved.' He held onto the door apprehensively, ready to swing it shut.

Keep your wits. Give him a wrong answer and that door is slamming shut and you're dead meat. 'We're looking for a man who's dug up a Bible somewhere out there, and we've been told you know him.' He paused in thought of what to reveal, then decided. 'We're looking for something, something that means a great deal to us and this man could help us find it. If you would help us find this man, we'd be indebted to you.' He licked his dry lips, his throat dry.

Relief spread over William's face and he sighed with a smile that revealed two missing molars in amongst his yellows. 'Well, that's alright then! Crikey, you gave me a jump mate, I thought you's were coming for me n' Mary. O' course I'll tell you. Come on in, cobbers.' He led them all inside the shack that, to their surprise, was bigger on the inside than what it looked from the front door.

Oil lamps hung from the ceiling, giving a murky light to the shadows of the shack, but giving enough to see the rare assortments studded to the walls and hanging from hooks. Jawbones of sharks were arranged from large to small on the wall next to an old photograph of a group of arranged uniformed soldiers. There, propped in the corner, was a hand-painted aboriginal shield. The crew felt a sense of wonder at what else this couple had collected. Then they saw, in the other corner, a large authentic, colourfully painted and patterned digeridoo. 'That was a gift from an aboriginal tribe, as a thanks for helping protect their land from being invaded. Most 'Stralians don't like them, but I just think they're misunderstood.' He noted their wide eyes at his variety. 'I'm a bit of a collector. We both are. I love somethin' just as wacky as I am. Y' know, I even troied to tame a wild wallaby once? Nasty little bugger it was.' He smiled and motioned for them to sit on the woven colourful rug they had on the floor. It was clear the couple were living in poverty, but their humility and hospitality were inspirational.

'You were a soldier?' Thomas asked, inspecting the photograph.

He nodded, 'I was. Service o' fifteen good years too. Then on a tour I got bit on the leg by a viper. Buggered if I knew that was there, but it was either a choice of the poison or the chop,' he lifted his trouser leg, 'and would y' look at that - a wooden leg. Gone are my days in the field, as well as my days dancing. Maybe a ship is the best bet for me now; I just got to get myself an eye-patch an' I'll be off roaming the seven seas. Adapt to survive an' all that.' He smiled playfully.

'Believe me, it's harder than it looks.' Billy remarked, looking around at their wild collection.

A voice then came from a separate room. 'Willy, at the rate you're at, you'd then get bitten by a shark instead.'

He chuckled, 'Don't y' worry darl', I've got the wooden leg now. It'd get a jaw full of splintahs!'

'Splintahs? More like toothpicks when it's finished munchin' on your old bones.'

Willy laughed with a slight shake of the head, 'She's a rascal that one. Sorry mates, we've only got two chairs n' Mary needs one; she's delicate at the minute. Mary? Sweetheart, it's alright love. It's not who we thought.'

They sat down, wary of any "rattlers" or "crawlers", as Kinny had called them, and looked on as Mary struggled through with a ballooned belly. She gave a lovely smile and had her hair, a beautiful light sandy colour, tucked and tied behind her. She had pretty green eyes with a narrow face and crooked teeth and wore a maternity dress. 'Crikey, there's more o' you's than I thought. G' day.' She smiled warmly, 'can I get you some wautah?'

'Don't worry y' self, I'll do it.' He helped her to a chair and poured some water into cups for them to share. Unsurprisingly, she was much younger than him, in her twenties they soon found out. They looked to be a lovely couple, but from the simple shack and remote location, their relationship was not approved of.

'How much longer do you have, Mary?' Victoria asked after taking some gulps of water.

She stroked her belly, 'three more weeks to go. I'm getting a little nervous now, but I'm excited too. It'll be nice for Benji to have a brother or sister.'

Benji, they were told, was William's son by another woman; a divorced man with a bastard child who was cradle-snatching with a woman half his age – they could understand their trepidation at letting anyone in. 'Who were you expecting at the door?' Joseph asked as they were chatting.

William shook his head in exasperation, 'frustrating in-laws, shall we say? Not wanting their daughter to be with someone loike me. 'Specially after the last hubby who was heir to the railroad fortune an' heir to the gold rush fortune an heir to the bladdy moon for all I know. Money an' titles didn't save him from that venomous boite though, those snakes don't give a shit who you are.'

Joseph glanced at Tess. *You've got a point there, Willy.*

He made his way to the chair next to his wife, his wooden leg clunking on the floor. 'Now,' he exhaled, 'what's it you wanted to know?'

Robertson answered for them, 'we were told you know of a man who found a book, a Bible, buried somewhere out there. Who is he and where can we find him?' He got straight to the point.

William nodded slowly and he replied, 'well that would be a Mister Jack Potts. A well-known prospector, although I'd call him an opportunist. I've visited prospecting soites a few toimes with him before, although nowadays he goes digging by himself lookin' for new soites. New gold. Eiveryone knows the first pick is the pick most golden so he troies to get there first, although ol' Jackie rarely foinds much. One toime though, not too long ago, he digs up something other than a nugget or a shard.' He licked his lips, 'the next toime I saw him over a beer, he tells me about the Bible and says to me, "and that's not even the strangest part Willy, this book, roight, well it was wrapped in a cloth." A cloth? I say. "To preserve it, why, I don't know. There's plenty of Bibles out there, just walk in any home or church and there'll be one."

'An' I say to him, "this one must be special mate. Y' can't sell it or toss it. That's a bladdy sin." And he laughed, "it's just a book, Willy. Pages stitched together with writing on 'em, just like every other book. I served god before as a kid, y' know what my old mother was loike, but he never turned up when I had that accident."

'I told him to keep it anyways, it could come o' some use one day, and well, here you are askin' about it.' He leaned back in his chair and swatted some flies that had found interest around his head.

Joseph looked to Robertson, his heart racing, and Robertson looked back. It sounded hopeful; against all odds they had found a ray of light leading them on through the darkness. 'Did he tell you anything else? Does he still have it?' Robertson asked.

William thought about it, then shook his head. 'Nah, this was up the bar and conversations were flowing as easily as the beer. I can't remembah him saying much else about it; there wasn't much more to say I guess.' He answered with a shrug.

'Where can we find him? Where can we find Jack Potts?' Subtleties were overlooked now; they didn't care how eager they looked. Especially now the stakes were high; they couldn't afford to lose any time.

'Crikey you're a fast lot!' he exclaimed with a laugh, 'city-folk, are you?'

Joseph nodded, 'originally, yes. But time an't a thing we can lose at the minute.'

Holding up her hand passively, Mary waved it off. 'Ah, never you mind. Our pace can be slow out in these lovely sticks.' She smiled, 'Ol' Jackie lives in the next town along. Most know him, so he can be found easily enough.'

'That's if he's not out diggin'.'

She nodded, 'ay, he's a busy body, y' could say.'

'Where's the next town along?' asked Tess attentively.

Lifting a crooked finger, William pointed, 'off that way, along the road; about half a day's roide by horse. A day to walk it, but under our 'Stralian sun it'll feel loike a week.' He winked.

'You can't all leave now though; you'll be walking through the night and it can get dangerous. All sort o' critters out there. You'll be best to wait till morning. Stay. Eat with us.' Offered Mary with a welcoming smile.

The crew looked to each other, knowing it would make sense and agreed, thanking them for the kind offer. Tess, now knowing she was sleeping under another roof, reverted to her former angelic state helping Mary out as best as she could, acting as a devoted sister. The rest were not impressed and tried to constantly undercut her to get her to slip but she was sharp, aware and always managed to stand tall.

Whilst Mary cooked a simple meal of chicken and vegetables, William showed them around the rest of his collection and readied bundles of sheets and blankets and what little else they could offer for their beds. That evening, as the sun set and darkness loomed, their host made a fire outside and placed logs around it for everyone to sit on. After a time when talk subsided, William brought out a flute and began to play to the mystical contortions of the flames. Billy then showed him his Madagascan flute, which impressed William so much that he then continued to play from it. The crew watched the fire dance to the playful tune as they finished eating with tired smiles on their faces. They quietened, enjoying the warmth and music as the night sky came alive, sparkling in a million white pinpricks above, reminding them of the peaceful nights spent anchored off the coast of southern Africa. It was the same sky and the same stars, but the feeling that came with it was far from tranquil.

Joseph sat next to Victoria, wanting nothing more than to put his arm around her and comfort her but the triggers that could set Tess off were widespread and he didn't dare push his luck. He didn't even take out his new pipe for a trial-run smoke. Her glassy eyes watched his every move.

The next morning, after thanking the kind couple copiously and taking a container of water and some food, the crew left the shack and entered the heat. The wind of the previous day had died, leaving in its wake large fluffy rolling clouds building in the distance and a shimmering haze from the powerful yellow idol they all knew too well, making the road seem unstable as it waved and undulated on the horizon. Now the shifting air had left them, they quickly grasped William's meaning only half an hour into their trek to the neighbouring town.

The heat was as relentless as they had known, reflecting from the brightly coloured landscape as much as it did out on the open water. A force of might that was bent on crushing them to the ground and cooking them like the corpses of the creatures unable to seek out sweet serendipity in the shade of a tree. The air became stuffy and stagnant, an effort to breathe, and their sweat became sticky with the rampant humidity. Flies soon clouded around them, swarms desperate to cool off in the sweat emerging from their bodies and forcing themselves in any open orifice, be it a nostril, earhole or eyeball to claim their due moisture. Ridding of them was a pointless act that used far too much energy and they needed every scrap to reach this town. Soon, they became desperate and using jackets and spare clothing, they covered their heads leaving slits for eyes to stop the pests from burrowing too deep. Depressingly, the only thing they could do to speed things along was to keep walking along this hot road. To endure the sore welts, cracks and corns pressing into their soles like a torturous form of acupuncture, made worse by them swelling in their boots, baking like potatoes in a cast iron stove.

As before when the heat intensified, none talked. If there was to be a conversation, it had to be cut fine. Inhaling this horrid air was awful enough, yet alone talking with it, resulting in everyone focusing on the dusty road underneath and their passing surroundings, which quickly became interesting. Despite the conditions, the Australian countryside was stunning, offering a range of things to look at as they passed along this rough track, far more interesting than their oceanic passing.

Patches of wattle and gum trees, white from the bleached bark, spilled bright orange sap and stretched from the dry ground on stilt-like trunks, before expanding in a multitude of branches bristling with thick hardy leaves. Large termite mounds as tall as a man rose like fingers from the red dusty earth. Witchetty bushes stretched along the track, joining the trees and filling the air of the day with creaks, chirps and whines of insects taking refuge in the shade. Small birds like the galah flitted from the branches, darting overhead with a beautiful pinkish plumage. The common bronzewing chased the butterflies with feathers of brown and splayed-white and spinifex pigeons plucked at the crickets, proud of their wonderous pointed crests. Strange calls of a cuckoo began to repeat, named appropriately after their distinctive song.

The further they walked, the more greenery bloomed and thus more creatures. Meadows soon spread; sporadic fields of long, lush moss-green grasses sprouted from the bright orange earth, and within these meadows large ponds sat stagnant; giving life to the creatures who dwelt there.

Large, peculiar mammals browsed, hopping from one place to the next with large muscular legs, small arms and a long rodent-like face. Ten were in this group with some, they saw, bearing pouches. Billy stopped for a moment, and they all halted with him, taking a moment to observe the native wildlife. They were so *odd*, so bizarre, they looked like enormous rats. He wiped the sweat from his forehead, 'Bless me. I never t'ought I'd see 'em with my own two eyes. Not in t'is lifetime anyway.' He huffed, 'I heard of 'em and t'ought t'ey were strange, but now I'm seeing - what're they called again?'

'Kangaroos.' Robertson answered.

'Aye, now that I'm seeing 'em with my own two eyes they don't look strange at all. Beautiful creatures they are, I mean, would ye just look at them legs!' He smiled briefly and nodded, before turning away to continue down the road.

As the day wore on, it turned out kangaroos were not the only fauna to pass by. A strange, brown spiky animal called an echidna crawled across the dirt to a bush where a snake lay curled, its tail rattling as it glared through glassy slit eyes. A koala was spotted by Thomas sleeping in a nearby tree; round and grey and fluffy, it drowsily looked around to their passing, unfazed. A peculiar-looking striped dog then wandered along the road in the distance; a

Tasmanian tiger was something they'd never seen before and hoped they wouldn't see on the prowl – they kept their distance. A mob of wallabies was seen bouncing in the hazy distance, kicking up dust clouds on the dry, red, stony earth that now only grew wiry sprouts of green weeds; melting into a mirage that cruelly reminded them of their crippling thirst.

Late in the afternoon, they spotted a man and his mule towing a dray back in the direction of the port and upon seeing their dilapidated state, offered to fill their container that had been long empty. He was a young man, making his business transporting goods from the port to the next town along. 'How far to the town?' Tess asked, shielding her eyes.

The man nodded down the road. 'Not far. Three moiles. Although you lot better get cracking if you want to reach it before dark. That's when the dingoes come out to play.'

'Great. Thanks for the advice. And image.' Victoria added dryly.

The man tipped his hat and rode away, disappearing into the hazy reddish afternoon like an apparition.

By the time the sun lowered, and the heat lessened, they were completely out of water and were ravenous. Fatigue suckled on their energy, draining them quickly after a day of battling with the merciless flaming dictator above who had been intent on squashing them into the dirt.

The fluffy rollers of the distance they had seen this morning had enlarged as they pushed inland, capturing the warm evening colours on their turreted cotton peaks. A beautiful soft blend of pinks, limes and creams mellowed together upon the large splaying roof, where, underneath this gentle beauty, an ominous shadow lurked, darkening with the oncoming night. Streaks shed from the dark underside as if a painter had slipped on his paintbrush, and a slight change in air brought with it the smell of rain.

They walked on with a newfound vigour, intent on missing the oncoming washout; trekking in the blistering sun and *then* torrential rain was an ugly concept none wanted to partake in. Then, as the warm red dusk was enveloped by the looming shadow, they spotted civilisation ahead and began to run. The pain was acute, shooting up their legs as if they were stepping on pins but they cared little for it, for rain had already begun to fall and had a pace that beat their weary legs. It began as fat splodges, but these intensified dramatically and within a matter of minutes a lethal storm was upon them, unleashing the full force of nature's flare. Soaking them to the bone, the lashing rain made the town look like a grey-streaked oil painting with flecks of amber hearth-light glowing in the windows of each humble home.

They ran into the town heaving deep breaths, their hearing muffled by the slash of rainfall, and slowed as they passed the buildings. The streets were wide, and the boxlike structures were spaced apart. Compared to the sprawling city they'd known; this was positively tiny. Suddenly lightening flashed, and a rumble of thunder made the clouds moan overhead. Yet to them this felt underwhelming. After experiencing vicious tropical storms aboard a bucking ship, to be on flat land whilst in one seemed extraordinarily dull; tame beyond belief, yet it was still unpleasant after a long day walking. Joseph stopped and looked about the deserted streets drenched in runoff. *Where do we go now? Where is Jack Potts?* As he walked by windows, he peered in to see people huddled around their fire, some looking out to the storm; ignoring the strangers caught in it.

Walking on and beginning to shiver, they grew despondent; where then a woman's voice called out to them from across the street, 'Y' not murderers or thieves, are you?'

There was a pause as lightning jumped from the clouds and thunder rolled by, and because they didn't know how to answer. *Actually, yes. Yes, we are.* 'No.' Joseph shouted above the rain to the woman at the window.

A door opened and she motioned to them, 'come here then and get inside outta' this storm!' she cried and they dutifully obliged, hurrying over to the open door where they filed inside a tight hallway with a staircase and many closed doors. They followed her into a room on the left where candles were flickering, and a fire was roaring. It was a small room and barely furnished. A bed was in the corner under the window that had a long spreading crack through one of the panes and a table with two chairs stood against a drab and cracked wall where a lone photograph hung. Atop the mantlepiece were two profile portraits of a man and woman looking to each other. Over the floor, straw was strewn. Coming in from the storm however, this was a perfect apartment; bathed in the comforting glow of candles and a fire that gave warmth and a cosiness. A home. To whom?

The woman of the window came to them and it was now they saw she was barely a woman; sixteen, perhaps seventeen, wearing a simple cotton night gown, but she ushered them in all the same and emptied a jug to fill the kettle and hung it above the flames. She was not alone, they noticed; a young girl was huddled on the bed, more terrified of the storm than the strangers in her home. 'Stand by the fire; all 'o you are shivering to the high heavens!' She sat on the bed beside her sister and tried to comfort her, 'your clothes will dry soon. You can all stay here the night if you'd loike. I doubt the landlord would approve, but if you all keep quiet, I'm sure you'll be fine. We haven't got much room and it'll be a tight fit, but you're welcome to it.' She gave them a smile.

Robertson turned from the dripping huddle around the fire and tipped his hat. 'Thank you, miss. You're truly kind.'

Benjamin nodded, shivering hard, 'aye. Thank'ee, miss.' Dave thanked them too, his clothes clinging to him.

She shrugged, 'I'd help anyone stuck out in this storm. Being lost is one thing, being lost in the rain is another. I just had to check you weren't any criminals I'd be harbourin'.'

Billy smiled with his hair dripping, 'aye, tis a good t'ing we're not.' His arm throbbed heavily after the awkward run; his bandages were soaked.

Noticing there were just the two, Victoria asked caringly, 'are you here alone?'

She nodded, her light freckles seemingly emboldened by the firelight and framed by her short dark brown hair; a small scar was on her young but worn face. Mature and brave; a young woman who had known hardship, she earned their respect. 'I'm Amelia, and this is my sister Chloe.'

They all introduced themselves as the shivers subsided. 'Lovely to meet you girls. Are your parents nearby?' Victoria asked, giving a smile as she wrung her hair out, 'in another room?'

Amelia shook her head, 'Mother passed in childbirth and Father works in the port for the week, docking, coming back eivery other Sunday. He sends money when he can. I doubt he'll come this Sunday though,' she looked at the window to the storm outside, 'not with this.'

'He might. Have faith and hold it tight, little ones.' Tess said gently with a sickly smile that frankly Joseph was getting tired of.

Amelia didn't seem to take it and in an adolescent manner she shunned the false pleasantry with a confused and suspicious nod and a frown. 'Right . . . Anyway, where is it you folks are off to? Y' don't sound loike you're from round here, or look loike it either. If anything, you look loike sailah's.'

Joseph answered for them, 'we've travelled a long way and we're looking for a man called Jack Potts. We were told he lives in the town. Do you know of him?' he then realised his shivers were gone.

She smiled, showing off her gapped front teeth and shook her head, almost seeming to laugh. 'Ay, I know of him. He's a funny guy, a man o' sorts.'

'What do you mean?'

'Ah don't worry, you'll know what I mean when you meet 'im.'

Suddenly lightning flashed and thunder grumbled angrily, making Chloe jump. Amelia put her arm around her, wrapping her in a blanket. 'Shh, there now. It's alright, love. It'll pass.' Then the kettle began to steam and squeal; she got up, retrieved it and poured the water into two mugs, both with chips in the rim. 'Tea. Pass these around, it'll warm you quicker.'

'Thank you, Amelia.' Robertson took a sip and passed it to the next pair of hands. 'You wouldn't happen to know where Jack lives, would you?'

She paused for a moment in thought, 'well he does git about a bit, but last I knew he was just along the street. Got a room in the house with the green door. Moight be in; if y' lucky. Usually, he's off out with his horse or diggin' up some other patch of earth.' Climbing back on the bed, she cosied up to Chloe who was trembling. Pushing a lock of wet hair out of her face, Tess went over to console her, trying to look the part, whilst Amelia ignored Tess's façade and continued to draw her sister closer.

Joseph struggled to not roll his eyes at Tess's efforts and he could see Amelia was apprehensive of her too. He pursed his lips and mentioned to them all, 'we'll go and find him as soon as this storm lets up.'

Their faces drooped at the thought of searching in the darkness, but the only vocal protestor was their young host. 'Y' can't go anywhere tonight; it'll be damp and dark and miserable. Stay, and in the morning, you can head off to find 'im.'

With her hair still dripping, Victoria worried, 'are you sure? Will there be enough room for us? We don't want to be a burden.'

Amelia waved a hand, 'plenty! No drama. I can't turf y' back out there in this.' She motioned to storm beyond the cracked window. 'An' if any o' you's are hungry, there's some biscuits and oatcakes in that tin on the table; share 'em out if you want 'em. I can always bake more.'

Struggling to not look completely desperate, Thomas took the tin, opened it and passed around the goods. It wasn't the grand meal they needed after a long day's walk, but it was better than eating raw rat-flesh and sucking marrow from pig's bones. They tasted wonderful, especially with the sips of tea, reminding them of fond memories back in London drinking a rare cup of tea with some biscuits, talking of each other's day beside the fire.

As he mused on this, Joseph found a glimmer of affection in the otherwise oppressive and guilt-ridden memories. *Keep those ones to look back on; it's only the harmful memories that'll hook you in and pull you under to drown in the past.* There was only one true direction in which to move now. Ahead. If there was one thing the gruelling days and endless travelling had taught him; it was that a positive outlook was fundamental for hope to exist through a dark time. Hope was, indeed, an integral part to life.

After some shuffling, they found room and slept on the straw beside the fire, resting their aching legs. Then, in the morning, after plenty of thanks, they donned their damp boots and left Amelia and Chloe to the new day which had calmed after the stormy night, looking overcast with air that was fresh and breezy.

As Joseph walked along the puddle-stricken street, he realised that out of everyone they'd met and stayed with; none had wanted anything in return. Only to help weary travellers along the way. It was humbling and refreshing, the hospitality endless and inspirational. He couldn't believe the difference from their origin. *Nothing was free in that smoky city. Something had got to be gained. Someone had to prosper. There had to be a price for everything, how petty . . .* he walked and wondered, *there's so much more to life than profit. So much more worth in kindness and spreading it. There are better ways to live and find joy than seeking it in pounds and prices . . . what have I paid for to get here?* In terms of physical amounts: Nothing. Not a farthing. Yet the toll this odyssey wanted was more of a personal exchange. He looked down to his holey boots and the lesion-riddled feet within them, saw how his clothes hung on his skeletal frame. The welts, the sores, cuts and blood, the loss of his identity. If there was a price, he'd paid for it. He hoped.

A breeze gently pushed the overcast sky as the sun speared holes through the intricate tapestry of clouds that moved south toward the coast. It was a fresh morning, and Joseph could almost hear the knocking of the sails against the masts eager to catch these streaming gusts. His eyes fell to the ground, indignantly missing the old creaking tub, barnacles and all. After all the contempt and anguish upon those decks, he found himself yearning to feel the waves rumble through her weather-worn wood and feel the sea breeze run through his hair. *Nice day for a sail,* he thought, suddenly wishing to be afloat again. He slipped his hands in his pockets and followed the group quietly.

In the corner of his eye, Robertson stopped suddenly, and the rest stopped around him. A green door stood in front of the captain; the paint was cracked and flaking, yet it was green all the same.

There was a pause and he glanced around to them with a look that said *we're here,* then he knocked.

Nothing.

He knocked again.

The door remained unmoved.

Then, with a groan, the door opened a crack and an eye peeped through, checking them over. It then opened further, and a tall, muscularly toned man looked out at them with bleary cobwebbed eyes. His shirt was half unbuttoned and untucked and he wore no shoes. His brown hair and sideburns were tousled and unkempt. One of his braces fell from his shoulder and half his trousers slackened. Upon his narrow but handsome face, a frown showed his utter confusion and he was just about to open his mouth when Jim Robertson smiled and held out a hand. 'Mister Jack Potts.' He said sounding relieved; the dirt on his shirt giving a clear sign of identity.

Reluctantly, the man took it and slowly shook it, then shrugged, 'g' day mate. How are we doing?' he smiled easily, showing off two golden teeth in amongst his yellows. His relaxed attitude made them feel comfortable already.

'Tired, but alright. I'm Jim Robertson. Can we come inside? We need to talk.'

'Let me just ask one question. What's an Englishman, and other English muckers I presume, wanting to talk to *me* about at the crack o' dawn on a day loike today?' His hand was on the door, ready to shut it if they answered wrong.

By the look of her face, Tess was about to jump into another one of her personalities when Joseph took the pleasure of cutting her off. 'A Bible you found.'

Jack looked taken aback, 'that old book? Is that all? Well, crikey, course you can! I thought you's were here asking after the gold I found,' Then he paused, and his eyes widened, 'of which . . . I haven't found and do not have in my possession in this very accommodation at this point in toime.'

Joseph couldn't help but laugh; he'd make a terrible criminal. 'Just the book is all, and where you found it. A man told us to find you if we wanted to know more.'

'Who's that?'

'William Webber?'

'*Oh!* Old Willy Webber! Great guy. He's seen some soights, I tell ya'. Even tried to tame a wild wallaby once the old cobber did, what a laugh.' With a wave, Jack motioned them inside, 'come on in you's lot before y' let the cold air in.' They followed him and filed through the door into his one-roomed apartment. It was a large space, with a fireplace in the wall to the right and the hearth gently smouldering. A window faced onto the street with a curtain half drawn and another curtain separated another room to the back. Boxes and knick-knacks filled the corners and covered the table under the window, stacked on each other, and numerous black and white framed photographs lined the oaken lintel above the fireplace. It was clear Jack was not a poor man, yet from his home he was not wealthy either, or that was just what he showed. To them, it looked as if he was too excited and curious about everything than to be brash or boastful about money. He had it; he just couldn't be bothered to show it. Against the far wall next to the curtain, a bed was seemingly occupied. To their surprise, Jack hurried over to a bottle of alcohol and took a swig, then picked his fallen brace up and thumbed it on his shoulder, before leaning over to a woman under his sheets and roused her gently. 'S' alright love, we've got some company here to see ol' Jackie. Toime y' get going, sweetheart. Your money's on the table.'

The woman looked tiredly around to them, then pulled the sheets up to her neck and blushed with her long black hair in a messy tumble. She was pretty, and naked, and the men of the group stared with Benjamin and Robertson turning out of courtesy. Jack had a fine taste; she looked to be expensive. Joseph glanced to Victoria, who looked at him plainly with pursed lips, knowing his thoughts. He pretended to look around at the collection. 'Sheila, y' moight need to slip something on, y' stark nuddy.' Jack whispered in her ear.

'*You let them in here when you knew I was still in here?!*' she hissed.

He looked at her guiltily, 'they needed questions answering, love, and they've come at the crack o' dawn so it must be important.' Handing her some of her clothes, she slipped some on under the sheet and grabbed the rest, storming out of his room in a fluster.

'You're a mongrel, Jack Potts! Rack off!' she cried.

He went to the door after her, 'aw now don't be like that Sheila, Sheila! *Sheila!* Ah she's gone.' A pause, 'come back soon, love! Miss you already sweetheart, safe journey home!' he waved, then shut the door.

Just then a young girl walked through the curtain, rubbing her eyes sleepily. 'Daddy, what's going on? Who are they?'

He ushered her back through the curtain. 'Just some friends my chickadee, no drama. Don't you worry. Go back to bed now, there's a good girl.' With a swish, he closed the curtain and looked back to the group of people waiting in his room.

Billy looked through the window and grinned, 'a foine woman indeed, sir.'

Benjamin looked sheepish, Joseph had a sly smile and Dave had reddened, as the woman looked like his former wife. Tess stood with her arms folded, 'the philanderer father. Is that setting a good example to your daughter? How often does she see things like that?' With a glare, the quartermaster looked at her, *a mother figure now, are we? First the murdering pirate then the God-loving Christian, the endearing friend and now the judging mother. Why Tess deary, it's like you can't make up your mind.*

Jack just shrugged, 'I do my best to care for my children. It's why I dig so much and foind new soites, to get the gold to earn the money to feed the five hundred.' He gave them a golden smile. 'Life's given me only a few pleasures, and I'm afraid women is one o' them. I never mistreat a single one, I'll have you know. Now, what is it y' wanted to know?' He took another swig from the bottle and began to add tobacco to a sheet of old newspaper and lit it with a match. Then lit Billy's cigarette and Benjamin's pipe too.

Robertson got straight to the point. 'The Bible you found. Do you still have it?'

He nodded, 'yep. I kept it wrapped up; I didn't want to disturb anything or ruin it.' The man wandered over to his bed where he knelt and pulled a trunk out from under it. Holding his cigarette in the corner of his mouth, he opened the trunk and picked through his collection of rare and valuable finds and handed the wrapped book to Robertson's waiting hands.

They huddled for a closer inspection. The cloth still had dirt on it and was worn, fraying but otherwise well preserved. Carefully, Robertson began unwrapping it, then he stopped. 'Joseph, you should be the one to open it. You found the clues, you got us here. You have this honour now.' He offered, and a brief smile passed over his tired face. Joseph paused, then with a nod, he took it and carefully unwrapped the cloth revealing the thick, aged book inside.

Despite having the same psalms and testaments as every other Holy Book, this one had an age to it that made it worth more than any gold. Invaluable. An artefact of a bygone age, a missing piece of history they now had possession of.

'What do we need it for?' Thomas finally spoke.

A thought then occurred to Joseph, a passage of the last clue that suddenly had a slight alteration in perspective. Making him think of it in a more literal sense, rather than metaphorical or allegorical. Now seeing the Bible here in front of him, a sudden rush of comprehension made his head spin. He reeled as pieces suddenly and abruptly fit crucially together, a key sliding into the lock and turning the tumblers of his mind. *Turn the holy pages, the key is within this story . . . a witness to the heavens is he that unlock glory* . . . 'We're looking for a passage.' He uttered, the book feeling heavy in his palms. 'A psalm.'

'How do you know which one? There's got to be hundreds in that one book.' Victoria queried.

'You know it. We all do. We've come across it before, a long time ago in another clue; at another place: we just thought it was for something else.' He smiled, 'Psalm 16:11.'

With careful fingers, he peeled open the cover and flicked through the pages to reach the New Testament where he stopped and felt himself welling with emotion. There was a reason the Bible was so heavy. A gasp spread, and Joseph Winter read aloud for all to hear, "'You make known to me the path of life; you will fill me with joy in your presence, with eternal pleasures at your right hand – Psalm 16:11.'"

There, cut into the pages of the New Testament of this Holy Bible, kept safe six feet under, was a key.

The key.

Suddenly, drastically, it made sense.

When in such dire conditions, when hope is strained and choices are narrow with limited possibilities as Eve and Henry's were at their end, faith in a solution prevailed. In these times, people put their faith into the hands of God, or in this case, put their key into his holy pages. Proof that faith, indeed, was a timeless force.

Chapter Thirty-Nine

With trembling fingers, he picked the key from its nest within the testament, prying it from the pious pages of the psalms. It was slightly larger than the rest and looked older, its metal glimmering in the light spilling through the window. No rust had touched it, no elements had invaded or corrupted. *It wasn't a Bible that was buried,* he mused, *it was more of a safety deposit box. A biblical bank.*

The hushed silence was then broken by a very perplexed Australian. 'Well would you look at that! A key was in there all along! Why, if I'd have known that I'd have opened it a long toime ago. It would've made a monk o' me.' He smiled, his two gold teeth glinting and wandered around to get a better look. Placing the cigarette back in his mouth, he asked, 'What's it for?'

There was a pause from them all as they hesitated. How much was he to know? They could've lied, said it was for a house, a safe, a lock for the secrets of their souls . . . but there was a fact to consider. He *had* found the Bible, he *knew* where it had been buried and, if they guessed correctly, the book and chest had to be in the same vicinity. The two objects were linked, they had to be buried close by. Surely . . .

Then again, this was an obscure trail they'd followed. Who knew where the chest could be, though perhaps a good starting point was the burial site of this holy book? Joseph felt eyes on him; they were looking to him to decide what to say, apart from Tess whose eyes were locked firmly on Jack with mounting hostility. 'It's for a lost treasure. Scott's Trove.' He quickly jumped in, making his decision. When it came down to it, essentially, they needed him. 'We've been hunting it since London, picking up clues along the way and it's led us here. To this book, to this key, and to you. All we need now is a location, something only *you* know, Jack. Where did you find this Bible?'

A look of surprise and excitement overcame his features, and his hands began to noticeably tremble. 'You lot are treasure hunters? Well, ladies and gentlemen, that makes me your new best friend! You've found the roight guy – I love me some diggin', and I love findin' something even more. Crikey, I mustah found thirty-odd nuggets o' gold with that trusty shovel over there, two of which I even had moulded to replace my missing teeth.'

Tess took a solid step toward him, 'that's great. Now tell us where you found that book.' Her tone had changed, as had her demeanour.

Jack took a step back and closed his mouth, suddenly realising the gravity of their case, and, upon seeing how exhausted and desperate they looked, understanding how much they'd endured to get here. With their dark-rimmed eyes staring at him, he slowly nodded. 'I - I found it north. In aborigine territory. Two days roide to get there, maybe three. I'll take you there if you want me to. If you'll let ol' Jackie in on the hunt.'

Robertson nodded and donned his weathered hat, 'if you can take us there, you're in.'

Jack Potts nodded easily and threw the end of the cigarette into the hearth. 'Course, course. I can get y' there, no drama. I've just got to sort a few bits first then we'll set off. Help y' selves to food if you're hungry, there's some in the larder.'

Two hours passed where Jack organised provisions for the journey and care for his young daughter and saw to his horse, making her ready for the journey. As the crew ate breakfast from his larder and drank some water, Jack attached a small cart to the horse with enough room for their supplies and a few passengers and readied a barrel of drinking water, lashing it to the frame.

Locking the front door behind him, he hurried over to his horse and climbed into the saddle before any of the passing pedestrians asked any questions about the cart and strange people in the back of it. Jack adorned a dusty brown fedora hat and whipped the reins and clicked at his dark brown draft horse. 'S' alright Daisy, on y' go, girl.' The cart clunked and began to roll along the wet street, the wheels splashing through the puddles from last night's storm as they passed the townsfolk tipping their hats to the friendly prospector.

Exiting the town, the company progressed north following the muddy track leading them away from civilisation when Jack suddenly exclaimed. 'Aw shit!' He pulled on the reins and leapt from his horse, hurrying back to the town, back to his house. Upon his return, they saw he was carrying something long. 'Crikey that would've been a mess,' he tossed the shovel into the cart, 'imagine that, going all that way only to find out we forgot my lucky shovel!'

Even though the town itself was relatively new, only built within the last thirty years, the rising traffic's cartwheels had worn deep tracks in the road. The tell-tale ruts were an indication of businesses inclining at a steady rate, flowing deftly as the developing country (almost new in the scheme of other global powers) rapidly caught up with its neighbours. Colonies were now towns; untouched lands had become agricultural, and ships of people continued to boost the white population to fill this new soil. Like a supreme plant, once the seeds had been sown, they grew in fertile land as did the communities of this continent. Jack pondered on this subject as he mused, thinking of his company's back grounds after hearing their thick English accents. Listening to the thud of hooves and the creaking wheels in the rutted tracks, he turned back and asked them a burning question. 'So, where are you lot from then? Where have you been to get to this point?'

Victoria gazed at Jack from her perch, jostling with the movement of the cart. 'We're from London originally. All of us. We sailed to Portugal to Lisbon port and picked up a clue there. Then that led us to the beaches of Gabon in western Africa where we found another, which then led us to an ancient tribe on the east coast of Madagascar where we claimed the next clue. We crossed the Indian Ocean and arrived in Australia, tracking the mystery of a Bible and a prospector who'd found it.'

'Crikey! Y' don't half get about a bit, do ya'? That's a fair ol' trek! What's been your favourite place?'

There was a pause before she replied, 'Madagascar. We trekked for hours through the rainforest to get to this underground cavern filled with diamonds – it was astounding. We saw fruit bats and birds with great long colourful beaks and monkeys were everywhere. I've never seen anything so green and full of life before. It was beautiful.' She smiled at the memory.

'How about you?' he turned to Dave walking beside the horse.

He, too, thought on it for a moment. 'Lisbon. The first place we stopped at; first place I've been to outside London. It was similar in some ways but was warmer, and felt, I don't know, exotic? I've never been to a foreign country before. The different smells and foods. I could've stayed for longer.' They all looked in Dave's direction, surprised at how open an answer he'd given. He barely said a word to anyone on good day.

Jack nodded and gazed into the distance with his eyes shaded in the rim of his fedora. 'I've never been out of Australia, but I'd *love* to go to London. What a place.'

Joseph walked beside the cart and added, 'you wouldn't be saying that if you've lived there.'

'Aw well, no, but it's loike that for any place where you live; the novelty wears off. I could say my town is absolute dung, but to you passing through you'd think it a lovely spot. You'd say London is a dirty dunny, I'd say it's the centre of an empire, a place y' can glimpse at the future, 'specially with all them wacky new inventions you English lot keep coming up with. Eivery other month I hear o' new things being invented and patented: a machine or a small whirring doodad. And they're not the only inventions; you've got Dickens reinventing Christmas with his books and Darwin reinventing theology with his theory of - what was it he came up with? Natural selection? . . . I don't know, but I fuck'n love this new speed of change.'

'You think change is good?' Joseph asked.

'I do, for sure. Change is normal, a part of nature and of life. I don't think the tree resists change when it's time for its leaves to fall, just as it doesn't hold onto what the winter forced it to do – the tree just changes with the season and knows it can bloom again, letting it happen. Why, if we didn't change, we'd be stuck thinking the same thoughts our ancestors conjured and be living out prejudices and judgements from a time long gone. Once a widespread opinion is forced upon children, you're then in the generational game and in it for the long run – trying to eradicate an outdated mindset engrained into the system. Crikey, that could take hundreds of years. I mean, do you really want your grandchildren to fight the same war you fought? Hate the same people you hate? Think your thoughts? Nah. Let them live their own lives in their own time, discover their world for themselves; it'll be different from the one you grew up in. As for me, I'd rather have my own mindset and pick my own thoughts rather than live out ideals someone has forced upon me to uphold. I'm all for change, mate. That's what the future always gives you the option to do.'

They were all stunned into silence, and once again Joseph found himself awestruck. He'd never heard anyone speak like this before; he wondered what else rattled around Jack's head. As if wondering herself, Tess chirped up. 'What do you think of it then?'

'Think o' what?'

'The future? Are you a gypsy?'

He smiled, squinting in the bright morning, then picked out another shred of newspaper and added the tobacco, lighting it and drawing breath. 'Nah. I'm just interested in where us lot, as human beings, are headed.' He blew out the smoke with the cigarette in the corner of his lips. 'From the direction we're heading in with these machines – *they're* the future I say. Technology. I reckon – and don't take this's gospel, these are just the words of an old Australian who moight drink too much – but I reckon we won't be needing horses in the future. We'll be riding around in machines on wheels and sailing boats powered by steam-less engines. Wars will be fought and won with guns and bombs and technologies we can't even comprehend, and, soon after that, humans will take flight into the air like birds and soar.'

That made them all laugh. 'Christ, Jack I've never heard such tripe!'

'Lad, I've seen some things in my time, and I can honestly say I don't think that's gonna' happen.' Benjamin answered from the cart, 'men can't fly. We don't have wings and we an't going to get 'em.'

Jack nodded, 'Ay, I know that, but at some point along the line, in the turn o' the century or after when us lot are either old and wrinkled and knockin' on death's door, or we're already six-feet below, we'll hear a strange tale about how man will fly.'

'And how do you think that'll happen then, Jack?' Robertson tried.

'Artificial wings, Jim. Fake wings. That, and a fuck'n heap of ingenuity and bravery. I tell you's lot, you will hear that story and you'll say to y'self, "crikey, old cranky Jack Potts was roight! We *can* fly!" All it takes is a slight change of thinking, a side-lining thought and with a bit of funding and work, history will be made.

'The great thing about us as humans is, we can learn from the mistakes of our past to make things bettah for the future. I mean, look how far my country's come in the past hundred years – ovah hundred years ago there's only aborigines here with huts and spears, and now we're here with economies and societies. Then, soon, we'll have our own machines and after another hundred years development, our great-grandchildren or descendants will be driving them on these very dirt-track roads.' He patted Daisy's side, 'whatever will y' do Daisy, you'll have so much toime to spare!' He laughed to himself. 'That's why I'd love to go to London cobber, I'd love to see the changes with my own two eyes. The future's coming at us whether we loike it or not, moight as well embrace her instead of trying to scare her off.'

'What a fascinating thought,' Thomas uttered, bewildered, finally meeting his eccentric match.

'Well bugger me Jack, what on eart' have you been drinking?' Billy exclaimed and laughed, unable to hold his thoughts, or tongue, any longer.

Jack laughed heartily and took off his hat, 'life, my dear friends! The future is ahead of us and the present is now, I just try and make light o' both. I enjoy the present cos it's strong but ever so fragile, merely a whisper; the next moment it's gone and become the past and I don't live there – it's not as important. There're only two uses for the past; so I can learn from it and so I can revisit happy memories again. And I speculate on the days to come 'cause that's where my track leads. Where it goes, I don't know, but it's only in the present will I find out which direction will take me to it. Ay. That's what I say.' He stroked Daisy's neck, 'I've only got this one chance at living, and I don't want to look back on the day o' my death and wonder where it all went, so I choose to live as much as I can.'

Joseph looked up to the man on the horse with his golden smile. A deeper layer to his character was then seen, a fresh coat was added to his perspective: as it turned out Jack was not just a womaniser, alcoholic and father, he was an advanced philosophical futurist with an eye on the world that Joseph hadn't seen before, not even from Thomas. His views were something he had never heard of, and yet they didn't seem completely deranged – if anything, they seemed plausible, possible, if but slightly far-fetched. It was an intriguing listen indeed, a one he wasn't sure he could totally believe. His gaze fell to the ground and he felt compassion for the peculiar Australian they'd just met – more than that – he felt inspired, which was an odd feeling he wasn't sure what to do with. Undeniably though, Jack Potts was enlightening.

They travelled in a ponderous silence for a time, feeling the heat of the day rise as the carpet of clouds was heaved away, leaving scudding remains scattered across a blue expanse. What Jack had been talking of had sent their minds reeling, yet some refused this gypsy talk outright. There was a good story, and then there was ridiculous slur. Eye-rolling ideas, they couldn't be taken seriously.

As they reached noon, they stopped, ate lunch and took some water, before swapping places on the dray. The silence thickened. The horse's breaths amplified, hissing and puffing as her strides became heavy clopping plods. The clunking of the turning wheels sounded like a great whirring factory machine. The flies buzzed and whined. Jack struggled to hold it together. 'So, any o' you's lot got any kids?'

A few shook their heads, but Billy nodded, as well as Robertson and Benjamin. 'Aye. Grandchildren too,' the old sailor said, 'I used to see a few every so often but then they slowly faded away. I do miss 'em.'

Robertson added, 'my son doesn't want to know me. We've become alienated over the years.'

Jack nodded, 'can be hard to keep track of 'em that's for sure. I got seven o' the ankle boiters.' He grinned, 'eldest is middle twenties and youngest you all saw. Two from me first woife, three from me second and the last two were, well, let's say not planned. But I do what I can for 'em, I care for 'em all. I love 'em to bits.'

'Your youngest daughter caught you kicking out a prostitute whilst holding a bottle of whiskey. Hardly a fitting example of prime fatherhood.' Tess commented harshly.

Jack shrugged in the saddle. 'As I say, I do what I can for 'em. Anyway, little Marie knows Shelia, she loikes her and Shelia loikes Marie. And I loike Sheila as well.' He smiled slyly, without shame.

Within a matter of minutes, all talk slumped and once again tension between them ripened as before. As Joseph looked to Victoria walking beside the horse, he desperately wanted to talk to her, to check she was alright, to ask her if she had any ideas of how best to rid themselves of these parasites. To ask her if she would stay with him once this was all over. Now was not the time, though. Tess and her men had the ears of a fox; there was no use in trying to send a message, which resulted in a thicker silence.

Hours passed in this torpid state, where not even Jack opened his mouth. However, what the journey lacked in conversation the scenery picked up on. Again, they saw lush meadows of greenery with pools of water, tall wattle and gum trees with wiry branches and tough leaves and shrubbery that reached the horizon. Wallabies lazily gazed up at their passing, kangaroos hopped away from them as Jack waved his arm, 'G'won, get going y' mongrels.' He quietly muttered, fearful of this encroaching shadow that loomed over their space. It was uncomfortable and unpleasant; he sensed something was ripening, thickening, rising.

As the large red sun lowered, its evening light cast beautiful crimsons and coppers over the dry landscape, and they noticed the road no longer seemed a used route. It was more of a dirt track, only distinguishable by the imprints of hooves pressed into the worn earth. 'Careful where y' walk down here; rattlers and snakes and spiders will be out at this sort of toime. If y' see one, or hear it, just back away slowly.' Their guide offered, 'not a lot of people come down this way, this is aboriginal land. I'm good friends with them though, they know me and let me through.' Bumpy and cracked, the old road tested the wheels of the rickety dray and as they followed it further into the brush, Joseph felt his chest being tested too as it tightened and squeezed the air from his lungs. Knowing this journey was almost at its climax, he knew his chances were dwindling. He'd seen Thomas glancing at him, checking he wasn't making any moves; Dave walked closely behind. Tess constantly had him under supervision; every breath was observed, every step recorded.

Worries gnawed at him by the time they stopped for the night and Jack prepared a fire amongst the witchetty bushes. Anxiety began to warp his thoughts, giving them lesions of paranoia like deep-rooted corns on a hardened heel. Leading him to believe a knife would, at any second, be slid across his neck or pushed into his back as smooth and as silent as the approaching darkness. His heart was loud in his head and he struggled to gulp.

Over the fire they roasted the corpse of an armadillo they'd found along the way, its hardened shell offering a free pot that cooked the flesh wonderfully. They drank water sparingly and stayed close to the fire, especially after Jack's warning of the wild dingoes that roamed these areas.

Once more, no one spoke and silently, tense and rigid, they watched the embers flitter up into the darkness like dancing fireflies against a starry night. Tonight though, clouds had spread, covering their chances of a hopeful glance. Insects buzzed and clicked in the brush surrounding them; peaceful, if it were not for the terrifying anxiety that infected them all; each too afraid to move. Jack made another cigarette and lit it, taking a drag, then took his hat off. 'Right. That's it. I've spent all day with you lot and this silence is fuck'n awful, like waiting for a croc to leap at ya'. *What is it?* What is going on? What is it I don't know?' he cried, looking around at their weary faces in the firelight.

Some looked down and away, others looked at him with eyes that desperately wanted to inform, to implore him to not ask, but couldn't in fear of getting him involved. Eventually it was Tess Mills who answered. 'Jack. You don't know what's going on here and I wouldn't ask questions like that again.' Her gaze was sharp and tireless.

Jack did not reply, and instead he stared at her cautiously, then turned his gaze to the flames with concern deflating his lips flat of their usual and often smiles. Without another word, the group dropped one by one to snatch what sleep they could with such vicious predators prowling, and not just the local fauna. As Joseph lay with his back to the fire pretending to sleep, his eyes were wide and unblinking as he fretted about what tomorrow would bring.

Under a wiry bush he spotted a sandy-coloured snake, coiled and silent, glaring back at him with fiery eyes reflecting the light. There was no rattle, but he was silently perturbed; unnerved to see such a sinister predator so close. *There's a snake there and a snake behind you . . .*

'Well, I guess I'll take the first watch then.' The Australian muttered to himself, and Joseph felt a surge of relief. *That's one snake wrangled.*

Tess replied with a sickly sweetness in her voice. 'No need Jack. You rest. You've been riding all day.'

'Oh. Don't you worry, love. I'll take the first watch. From the sounds of it, *you* need your sleep more than I do.' He said, puffing smoke away.

A faint smile found its way to Joseph's lips and he closed his eyes with the key feeling heavy in his pocket and his canvas bag held tight to his chest.

As the faintest light was seen on the horizon, turning the black into a translucent grey, the company rose to smouldering ashes coughing up the last of its smoke. It had been a slow night indeed with almost all unable to find rest, reminding Joseph of their night around the tribal fire before their trek to the underground cavern. *A lifetime ago, that feels like.*

They sipped water and quickly nibbled food before setting off, heading north. Glimmers of a sunrise began to glow and soon, a bright orange head peeked above the eastern horizon into a sky of soft pinks and delicate creams, highlighting strips of thick cloud that looked as if they were homemade cigarettes that had been rolled between God's fingers. The higher the sun rose however, this spread of hopeful cumulus was smudged out, fading into the heavenly colours like lost spirits ending their purgatory. The rays lanced strikingly, emboldening the silhouettes of the bottlebrushes, ferns and kangaroo paws they passed.

As they walked, they noticed colour returning to the extensive flora; reds and pinks popped and burst into the exploding waratah flowers and the sharp spikes of the banksia were now a bold yellow, as were the opening buds of the desert cassia. The vegetation was contrasting in all manners of shapes and sizes; they couldn't help but think of the Madagascan rainforest at dawn, with life bursting into the darkness – it was a glorious morning worthy of impression.

Although, the wonderful dawn of this southerly continent did nothing to grease the friction between the company as all trudged in a strained silence. All were ashen faced and fatigued, even the mutineers were looking agitated and irked. Tess, however, was mechanical and ruthless, walking behind them all, keeping a watchful eye over everyone. Supervising Joseph especially, who walked beside Victoria, trying to keep his thoughts aligned and his stomach below his throat.

Kookaburras chirped, insects droned, leaves rustled, and the cart continued to creak and moan. Then an Irish voice abruptly added, 'Where's t'is discovery site t'en?'

Jack almost jumped at the sound of a human voice and pointed, 'not much further. We should reach it by late afternoon, by then all this will have gone, and it'll be desert and salt.'

'Salt?'

He nodded, 'Yep. I found the Bible out in the salt-lake. Or salt-plain, whatever y' want to call it. I came out here diggin' every day for about two weeks, so I know the route well. A long dig you could say but I dunno, I also loiked it. The salt crunching under your feet is comforting, and there's nothing to see for moiles and moiles; everythin' is so clear and still and oh! When it rains mate, it's great. It fills up, but not to lake-standard, you understand, just a layer o' wautah ovah the top, but the salt in it makes it briny and shine like a bladdy mirror! Looks loike there's two suns sometimes and it's hard to tell where the sky stops and the wautah starts. Beautiful mate, absolutely beautiful.'

Suddenly Joseph's ears pricked up and he looked dead ahead at the man on the horse. 'What did you say?'

Jack turned and looked at him, 'What?'

'Say what you said again. About the mirror.'

Confused, he repeated his simile and Joseph felt his breath catch. He blinked, not sure whether to smile or cheer or run, instead he found himself whispering, *'that's it.'* The riddle's answer became instantly clear, like a gust of wind blowing fog away. *A wasteland is where the chest can be won; rumours have been heard of two moons and two suns* . . . it was a salt-lake that acted as a mirror when water was within it, briny and sharp. An inland doldrum. This was it, it had to be.

At a faster pace now, they pushed down the track, ignoring the protests of the dray and its unhappy wheels. They pushed on until the plants gradually disappeared and the brown, orange earth became sandy with a cracking crust breaking in the heat of the day. Now the answer to the last clue had been accidentally discovered, a newfound motivation overcame them – a final push.

Joseph sat in the back of the cart with his eyes trained ahead. All signs of the track had vanished, leaving them with mounds of sand to plough through and a horse that seemed to know the way. A salt-lake was ahead, they could smell it in the air. They were not far away, and he could hardly control his racing heart. Thoughts now swayed in the direction of the chest and its contents, and a phase of fragile excitement replaced the hostility.

All of it has been leading to this, he pondered, *right from the very beginning. Right from Eve and Henry nearly a hundred and fifty years ago . . . to Frederick on the Endeavor . . . to my birth and life and career, to Mad Vinny giving that tip off . . . it's all led to here. To some spot out there, to a–*

Arms suddenly grabbed him from behind and yanked him from the side of the cart and into the hot sand. He heaved as the breath was snatched from his lungs. Sand was thrown into his eyes; he wailed and clamped his lids shut. A cacophony of shouts and cries and yells, unintelligible and incomprehensible, shrieked around him.

Hands pulled and tugged, heaving him and turning him. He punched and kicked and writhed and wriggled with eyes weeping, a throat burning and lungs heaving for breath. A powerful kick sent spasms of pain from his stomach, then to his chest, his head, breaking his nose, sending jets of blood showering over the sand.

Stars rained down in front of his eyes, stars of pain, stars that brought comfort. He stumbled on consciousness, his mind tripping, hearing a woman scream his name . . . and Joseph Winter sunk deep into the sand into a dark, unfeeling void.

Chapter Forty

A breeze played over the sand, whipping the grains over the undulating landscape in great sweeping masses, like sea spray billowing down the backs of rising swells. Desolation it proved to be with no signs of life anywhere – a wasteland. Even the few reptiles that managed to call this place home found what little shelter they could, hiding from the intense afternoon heat under rare rocks and tinder-dry plants. All was quiet, apart from the occasional brave gust and a trickling sound as grains rolled over each other. Then suddenly there was a scream, a harrowing cry full of anguish, that echoed loudly throughout the wilderness.

Joseph sat up sharply and coughed the sand from his mouth. Heaving in desert air, he felt it grate down his throat as if he were sanding down his oesophagus. A formidable thirst gripped, and he coughed dryly and struggled to swallow, suddenly fearing that he was going to choke. Flies buzzed around him in swarms, their tiny high-pitched whines surrounding him as they pined for his body's moisture. Slowly, he opened his dry eyes and surveyed this barren landscape; the foul memories of how he got here clicking back into place. *They've left me out here to die. They dragged me from the cart, beat me and left me in the sand for the dingoes and vultures . . .* Suddenly an insurmountable rage boiled from the very pits of his soul. It was Tess and her mutineers. *Tess fucking Mills.* Muscles locked, his fists clenched, and he screwed his eyes shut. '*NO!*' he howled helplessly, but despite the multiplying echo it reached no ears.

One thing became rapidly clear; the animosity *had* to wait. Too much energy could be wasted when it had to be conserved; he had to calm down and push through his hatred of that brilliantly awful woman. *Focus. Senses. Breathe. What is around you?* He scanned and saw nothing. Only then, as his bloodshot eyes scraped around in their beds of grain to look at his surroundings, did the depth of Tess's despicability become truly transparent.

He was alone. Desperately and intensely alone. Left for dead in a desert, a warzone where the elements were at an eternal quarrel; where the sun beat relentlessly, and the sand never surrendered. Both sides were merciless; there was no safe ground nor sanctuary. In the thick of it, he had nowhere to shelter from the barrage, from the onslaught that sought to eradicate him through a test of gruelling attrition. If he didn't die from dehydration, starvation would finish him off and if it were not that, heat exhaustion would kill him. If it were not that, there was the threat of lurking predators as desperate as he was.

Suddenly he realised he'd dreamed this before; one of his night terrors aboard the ship. Only now he saw it had become a premonition, and it didn't end well. 'Fuck!' he cried, realising the towering odds stacked so loftily against him.

Spotting his reddened, cracked feet poking from the sand, he saw they were bootless and burnt. *Why would they take my boots?* Then suddenly it became clear. This baked sand was to be his bed of hot coals; his penance, and he was to walk through it or die. He grimaced and could already feel the pain. The sand, bright and hot, was everywhere, as far as his sore eyes could see. Rolls upon rolls of rippling reddish dunes gave no sense nor sign of direction. How was water to be found, yet alone the way back to the town? It was already hard to think straight with the heat, yet alone the thirst which, he knew, was a debilitating force once it gripped hold.

Dehydration would soon come, damming his sense and sanity like a beaver would to a running stream and then . . . he shook his head, not wanting to consider the repercussions. Not now. Not yet. Not when he was still trying to pick himself up off the ground. Once again, Joseph found himself as an inexperienced sailor, bobbing on the tide with no sense of direction and no knowledge of this strange alien world. *As soon as I manage to handle one bloody ocean, I'm thrown into a similar one,* he reflected, *except this time I am the captain and I have no idea what I'm doing.*

The sun continued to blaze a fiery trail through a cloudless blue sky he was all too familiar with. Already his throat cried for liquid, even more so since he knew he had none to provide. As he tried to move, his skin felt scorched and ablaze, begging the question of how long he'd been lying unconscious for. *A long time. An awfully long time, but now it's time to get up.* He placed his cracked dry hands beside him and felt an object on either side.

Pulling them from their mounds of collected sand, he found the metal bottle William Webber had given them and a weather-beaten sailor's hat. Robertson's hat. His eyes widening, he quickly pulled the cork from the bottle and tipped it, feeling a rush of water extinguish his flaming pipes. The need to keep drinking was easy to give into, but his mind yanked the reins. *Stop! Conserve!* Taking a careful measured second gulp, he forcefully corked the bottle and put on the hat, feeling the shade of the rim and the powerful rays being deflected. 'Thank you, Jim, thank you.' He sighed tiredly and closed his eyes, imagining the captain imploring Tess to have mercy and at least let him leave his hat behind.

With a clearer mind, he got to his feet sending showers of sand from his clothes and wobbled, dizzy with the heat. Pain smouldered his soles, heating his legs and body even more. Wincing, he tried to block it. *Tracks. They would've left something, movement of some kind.* Alas, the wind had taken care of that; smothering Tess's tracks for her like ripples fading on water, leaving not a trace to follow. Joseph remembered the smell of brine as they approached the salt-lake, but upon attempt he realised she'd also taken care of that; a broken nose clogged with sand and blood made sure he was not to use it. He couldn't help but to feel impressed. Her ingenuity was boundless.

With no sense of direction, disorientation took a firm hold making the world spin faster. At a loss, panic began to swell. Worries and thoughts jumbled together making it impossible to gauge anything, a rising pulse and short breaths took away any hope of staying calm. Not only did his own problems mount, but the thought of his friends was agonising – if she was able to do this to him, whatever had she done to *them.* '*Victoria!*' he cried, 'Jim!

Billy! Jack! *Anyone!*' but the only person to answer was his own voice. The thought of Victoria tied up and strewn in the sand for the sun and dingoes was hard to bear. 'Oh Victoria, my sweet, my love. I'm so sorry.' He closed his eyes and fell to his knees as the stress crippled him, taking his strength whilst making him notice his absent prized possession.

'*My bag!*' He cried. She'd taken it, as well as his pipe gifted to him from Kinny and Charlie dodger. He tried to remain calm, then thought to check his pockets. Digging his hands inside he found nothing but a scrap of paper. A ripped-out page of what looked to be a diary entry. *No, I recognise this . . .* it was the last entry he'd read from the Ship's Log aboard *Victoria*, describing the worsening situation and threat of mutiny. A cruel jape to play upon a broken man. Trying harder to stay calm and not shred the paper into a million tiny pieces, he carefully folded it and in doing so, found writing on its back.

Find us, Joseph. End this.

The note was written in Robertson's hand. He must've slipped it in his pocket whilst Tess's back was turned. Joseph pursed his lips feeling guilt rip through his chest. 'It's alright, Jim. I will find you; I will end this.' He vowed and slid the note back into his pocket, then realised what the missing bag meant. He gulped and felt the air being torn from his lungs. *She has the key . . . and the lodestone . . . the guide . . . and a shovel. Not to mention my fucking boots. Can she take anything else from me?!* She had everything she needed to find the treasure. To find it and take it. Rage swelled in a formidable wave; he ground his teeth to contain it. The thought of her digging and taking the loot was enough to send him to the brink; enough to get him to his feet, to grab his nose and crack it back into place, to blow hard on it before sucking in the desert air as if it were his last.

The pain was agonising as it spread around his sunburnt face, but the air he inhaled was the saltiest he'd tasted - a wonderful briny scent. Turning around, he faced its direction and sniffed again, confirming his throbbing nostrils functionality. With the thought of Victoria and his friends, he took the first hot step toward the smell. The first step of many on this long road of redemption through this field of hot coals.

Over the first mound he trod, wincing and grimacing at the heat of the sand; each step feeling like a mile. His soles were leathery, yet even leather could burn. Daring not to look down at them, he knew of the sheer state they were in. The cracks between his toes would be filling with sand; his corns were forever a nuisance, kneading the balls of his feet as if they were a tough dough making them ache, sending his already limited balance off. His plantar was already twanging like a taught bow. Grunting and groaning, he moved as vigorously as he could with the little energy he had left, trying to keep to a straight line. This was a challenge in itself as the sand rippled like a beach and the horizon flickered like candlelight and melted like wax, dripping in the hazy heat of the Australian outback.

Soon, he found the hat did nothing to shelter him. The heat was unbearable, making him wish for a roof, a wall, a rock to hide behind. He envied the lizards that were small enough to burrow into the sand and the snakes that could swim across the dunes with ease. The circling birds above watched in anticipation, awaiting his demise as they hovered on warm desert drafts. It was not long before the heat enveloped his thoughts making it the focal point of awareness. *I'm hot. So hot. I can't breathe properly. My lungs are burning, melting; my skin is slipping from my bones.* Sand was everywhere, one colour and unbearably bright. He squinted harshly to see through the torturous reflection, gouging deep troughs of crow's feet wrinkles from the corners of his eyes like cracks in mud during a prolonged drought. It reminded him of the doldrums - a dry doldrum - with more sand and less water but equally as hellish.

After an hour, his feet were beyond raw; numbing, and the only reason he looked down to them was to check they were still there. After two hours, his straight walk veered and strayed; he stumbled often, dropping to the hot sand where his hands then felt the horror, teaching him that balance was as important as the few gulps of water he had left in his bottle. *It'll . . . probably be . . . boiled now.* He forced a laugh at his own dry joke, *even my humour's drying out.*

Slowly, as the afternoon turned into evening Joseph noticed his wits beginning to wander. This was his land, and he was king of it, the lord of the outback, master of the sand with no rivals but the faltering wind daring to usurp him. Struggling to hold onto a string of thought, a sentence became drunkenly slurred; words slipped and crashed into each other in his head, and he found the further he walked, the less time he spent in the external world. Since there was nothing to look upon, no stimuli to engage with, and his landscape was so brutally forsaken, Joseph gently slipped inward in an effort to escape. To save his mind from wrecking itself. This time though, he wasn't crushed under an atmosphere of anxiety, and his wits openly wandered, drifting throughout time and space. He wondered as he wandered, wondering and wandering in a free-flowing state. His mind a river with currents neither moving forwards nor backwards; meandering with no true direction.

Despite his feet plodding unconsciously, his mind travelled far. To eccentric thoughts and fading memories, to conversations spoken and wished for. Back to his previous life as a city rat, squeaking out a living in a populous nest of snakes.

He thought back to the memories of his childhood, seeing them as visions displayed upon the glowing sky. He watched the days running barefoot with clothes tatty and mud-streaked, scaring horses pulling hansoms and pick-pocketing any punter who wandered into his vicinity. To a growing interest in economics and the law and how best to cheat them both. To a dead father and a mother who drank too much but worked tirelessly to keep them both fed.

He watched his teenage years, back when he started finding small but honest jobs as an errand-boy but finding more success in joining gangs and honing his skills in theft. To pulling off bigger jobs for the bigger fish to set up contacts and build a career; to initiating a string of jail sentences, and a string of escapes. To the first time he visited a brothel and made inexperienced love to an older woman, and visited again, and again.

Back to his twenties when he enjoyed independence with a developed career; thieving on a large scale, sifting through stocks and shares to manipulate the weakest for extortion, getting hired to set up jigs and hits to make deaths look like accidents for the extra profit. To the addictive gambling and bare-knuckle boxing – the banging of fists against the ring from the screaming crowds and the dishonest money that flowed in steady streams. To the backstreet whores and violence on the streets; to relationships and mistresses and neglecting them all, using them for his own gain.

Back to a reputation that was hard to maintain with everyone knowing him, everyone admiring him, even though he despised them all. To meeting Lucy and renting a room in a through-house, earning more but spending more yet never on the right things. Never being able to quit, never being able to walk away because of the insatiable greed and overpowering ego; the love of the rush, the hit and the score in the life of the infamous Trace.

Risking everything to uphold his name, caring for little apart from those that gave him what he needed; creating a façade that led him to believe he was a good and loyal man. Stopping at nothing to attain the dream of limitless money, only to eventually give up Trace and buy the generic life like all the other fuckers, so when he grew old, he could look back and say his days had been meaningful and honourable despite living a false factory-made existence society had generated to make it all look worthwhile. It was this he had run from, fearful of the same fate as everyone else, knowing he could never be happy with normality and so his alter ego - the almighty, unbreakable Trace - lived on and thrived through him in the constant thieving. The violence and the deaths. The whoring, neglecting, cynicism and greed. The egos and contempt for everyone and everything. The pride, envy and lies. They were Trace. They were Joseph. They had become all he lived for.

These memories and traits, however distasteful, he pinned onto a mental wall to better understand their ways and strung them together, searching for meaning. Eventually the mass web categorised into successes and failures, money gained, money lost and hopes for the days to come. Taking a step back, he examined them in detail and grimaced at who he thought he was proud to be. Those old things were from a past life, from a different man than the one whom he was now. He scanned the last section avidly; it was dark, obscured – he wasn't sure what his future was to be. A question mark was all he had. *Those old traits aren't me. Who even is "me" anymore? Who am I?*

He'd never wanted a normal life, but others and their judgements would've forced it upon him, and he knew, in time, he would've crumbled and succumbed to it. Hating the system and himself even more until he returned to it and ended those that tried to stop him living life without a Trace. *I never wanted to make a trace . . . I wanted to be a ghost, to observe the hardship and toil without it affecting me . . . and I knew if I had the normal things the hardship would eventually clamp its manacles around me and chain me down until I became just like . . . everyone else.*

Truths had to be faced, regrets had to be acknowledged. Wounds had to heal; and as he trudged through the sand following the salty scent with the red sun sinking below the horizon, he spoke aloud to himself. Not because he wanted anyone to hear, but because he needed to front a major problem and address it without restraint. 'I'm a self-righteous bastard. I am a vile beast; a cynical, villainous, egotistical, disgusting man with beliefs that I am above everyone. I am a wholesome, heartless cunt. I believed if I did not partake in the norm, I wouldn't have to be chained to responsibility the rest of my life and I could be free. A free agent, but I wasn't free at all. I was chained to my reputation, the judgements and opinions of others. I'd made myself a prisoner, rotting behind bars of my own creation, behind bars of greed. I earned money, treated people badly and rejected everything I wasn't a part of in fear of eventually understanding it and wanting it. Tess was right about everything she said. But that's going to change. I am going to change. That man is a part of me, I can't deny it, and without him I wouldn't have known what I know now, and wouldn't be the person I am today, but that man is not who I am any longer.' He looked up to the glowing horizon, to the rays of gold and pink and amber as the great hazy sun lowered and knew he could be a better man.

A man to let go of the past in order to have a brighter and happier future. A man to forgive, forget and move on. A man to make decisions based on joy and wisdom instead of judgements and greed. A man to understand the importance of money and not be consumed and controlled by it. A man to enjoy laughter and warm company with close friends as a member of society; to appreciate raw human interaction and to care for people and the world surrounding. To reignite the wonder of the soul by observing, involving and remembering precious moments of beauty where the world emitted peace in gentle soothing waves. To be the light in the times of darkness and give all he could to ease the toils and burdens those dark times brought. To wander freely with the light step of simple living and a light heart, to love and be loved. To wish for nothing more than to hold a loved one by the side of a warm fire and feel fulfilled under a beautiful starlit sky.

To be happy in whatever this tremendous life had to offer along the way.

As night enveloped the desolate landscape, he did something he never thought possible. He forgave himself. Absolving the guilt, the sins and the shadowy ego he realised he'd been carrying his entire life, becoming heavier as this mystery began and this journey progressed. In a grand and unexpected rush, he felt his shoulders slip their weights, freeing their burdens, and a great ease overcame him; a sensation of complete freedom to make his own destiny, to manage it without judgement or loathing from the self. Everything he was had become gangrenous, his ego a festering limb, and he cut it loose now, so he could reclaim his own identity in a way that brought forth the very best of who he knew he could be. He realised he needed to love himself in order to give love away to others. An incredible wealth of happiness then surged up from unknown depths and made him fall to his knees and knuckle the ground, breathing the night air deeply.

Awash with emotion, he felt the thrum of the earth in the sand and a pulsing throb of awareness, of focus and centrality realign his vision to an absolute clarity. He lifted himself, opened his arms and gazed at the wonderful, twinkling stars and laughed gently and with ease. Not because of how bad the situation was, but because he needed to; laughter for the sake of laughter, so he could hear its joyous tone again.

Out here, in a barren desolation with no boots to walk in, a battered body and tattered clothes, with no certain direction to follow or help to guide him along the way, he felt an overwhelming sense of perfect serenity, of acceptance. Deliverance. He realised this journey had not just been about the chest and the treasure within, it had become an acknowledgement of his past to allow him to move on, to give him the freedom he'd always wanted – a liberation of his own soul. This odyssey had become a road to redemption, and he'd found it. It was ecstasy. He laughed with tears streaming down his face. It was as if he had had to endure this long godforsaken journey from the drab streets of London to conquer his chequered past and attain absolution here, in this desert, with no one but the stars and a great white moon to bear witness.

Through his tears of joy, he marvelled at the sky and knew it was time to make amends. 'God. I am at your mercy. Do with me what you will, I am tired of fighting. I surrender . . .' He saw how beautiful the stars were, seeing everything with divine eyes. He made his peace with God and was finally able to listen to the whispered truth from within telling him he need not search nor be burdened further, that he was and would always be welcome in the Kingdom of Heaven.

Joseph dropped to his side and pulled the necklace of the carved wooden elephant from his neck. He dug a small pit and buried it under the stars, knowing it was time to let everything go. He smiled freely as he covered the guilt-ridden memories and tormenting burdens, realising it had become an emblem for his writhing ego. Laying his head down, Joseph slipped into a peaceful sleep without thought, regret or memory. There was silence. A beautiful, glorious tranquil of freedom.

When he awoke, the stars were still in the sky, but the edge of the horizon had mellowed into a light grey and navy blue. Dawn was not far off. There was not a moment to lose. He took out the cork from the bottle, took another gulp and squeezed in the stopper. Looking ahead, he noticed a slight shift in the landscape; no longer were there divots and ripples of undulating sand, but a flat expanse of a different shade, a lighter shade. White. Like salt. A smile hooked his dry lips, splitting them and causing a slow bleed into his sandy beard.

Wasting no time, he walked at a brisk pace with feet that felt renewed on this cooler surface and headed for the salt-lake. By the time the sun broke over the mountainous eastern horizon, he was at the edge of the final stage. Somewhere out there, within this plain of crusty salt, were his friends and the love of his life, searching tirelessly for Scott's Trove. He licked his lips and stepped out onto the crust, feeling it crunch under his feet. Walking a few steps out, he noticed he left footprints where the salt had broken. *Perfect. Just as I thought.*

Jogging along the outer rim he scoured the ground ahead, searching the crust for disturbance. Joseph didn't stop to think if he was heading the right way along the edge; he followed his initiative and knew that as long as he kept his feet moving, he had hope. Then suddenly he spotted it, distinct in the amber rays of dawn hitting this dried lake at an angle. Footfall, hooves and two deep gouges heading inwards. Once he reached the marks, he stopped to breathe and looked in their direction, to their trail leading into the salt-plain. Of course, there was only one way to go.

Onward.

Starting off at a walking pace he kept to the tracks, making sure to keep them in his vision. They were his lifeline, his driftwood to cling to so he didn't float away. Keeping his eye on the glowing horizon above the layer of settled mist, he saw a large mound set against the sky, a hill of sorts, dark in the morning light. A heading, and if he kept it in his sights, he would find them eventually, wherever they ended up.

As he strode, he imagined what this lake would look like when rains had come. He pictured a layer of water stretching out as far as the eye could see, flat and without ripples, dense with brine allowing a perfect mirror image of the sky above. A wasteland of two moons and two suns, rising and setting at the very same time. A spectacle. *I want to see it; I want to walk the line between heaven and earth.* A smile then spread over his face as he realised; he was already there.

Time ticked by. The sun climbed higher, rising the temperature by a few degrees, making him sweat already. The mist clouded over the flat landscape, staying as low as possible to evade the coming of the day but out in this desolate land there was nowhere for it to hide. With the light of day brightening, he watched the mist dissipate and saw movement in the distance. It was small - so small he had to strain his eyes to make sure it was not a ploy set by a tired mind. Alas, the flickers of movement continued. Confirming that the end of the road was nigh, and, comfortingly, that he had not toppled from sanity.

He walked with a faster pace along the track, his eyes trained unwaveringly on the movement. Jogging, he ignored the pain shooting from his feet and hurried as the flicker of movement materialised into a form that he deflatingly saw was not what he had hoped.

As he approached, he spotted two four-legged creatures scrapping ahead. His heart pounded in his chest, fearing the worst. Two large sandy-coloured dogs stopped and looked up at his approach, their large ears raised and twitching. *Not dogs - dingoes.* They were not scrapping for the sake of it either, they were fighting *over* something. *Oh god no . . .* Joseph waved his arms, 'Go!' he cried, 'leave! Off with you! Hook it!' His legs feeling weak, he ran closer until the two young predators scarpered, leaving their prize in the ground.

The dingoes had been digging a mound of disturbed earth where a leg had been pulled out and mauled on the surface, mangled with the boot pulled off. The stench of death became overwhelming. With tears welling in his eyes, Joseph quickly dove to his knees and started pulling away the earth until there, resting with dirt in his beard and upon his weathered face, lay Benjamin Smith.

Joseph gasped and tried to remain collected. Even though he'd joined the mutiny, seeing his dead face in the ground with his leg almost torn away was a hard sight to come by. From what he could see, Benjamin's pale face was at peace; a sign he did not die in a brawl. The poor old man wouldn't have stood a chance. Joseph looked at Benjamin's face and rested his hand on his forehead. 'I'm sorry.' He said with tears streaming down his cheeks, 'I'm sorry I wasn't there for you when you needed me; I should've helped you instead of pushing you away. May you find rest now and forgive me for the man I was. You were a good friend, an honourable man and the finest sailor I have ever met. May you rest now and find peace.'

Gently, he pushed the dirt back, covering Benjamin's face and pushed his mauled leg back into the ground, burying it as best as he could. *It's a sign they were here, but where did they go . . .*

He found the track again having strayed from it and, without looking back, jogged across the salt until he began to see old rectangular pits dotted around the area. They did not look fresh; he guessed they were from Jack's numerous attempts to find anything out here. *I'm close.* With bloodshot eyes scanning the distance, he watched for further movement.

Soon the track began to wander freely, with footprints branching out from the cart to small rocks that had been overturned and shallow holes had been dug. *They've been testing the lodestone to find its partner . . .* Wanting to curse himself for his actions, he wished he'd never told Tess the second half of the clue. *But if I hadn't, we'd be dead by now. All of that has passed anyway; it doesn't matter. It's gone; there's nothing I can do except act on the present.*

Jogging along the main track, he suddenly spotted bigger movement now; bodies and a dark blob in the hazy morning heat that looked to be the dray and horse. From the movement, a figure was digging. He felt the air being sucked from him and a formidable anger swell again. The serendipity of the previous night had passed; this was raw and had to be released. 'Found you.' He growled and began to run.

Immediately, pain jarred up his legs, grinding the joints of his knees and hips as if his crackling cartilage were being milled to make flour from his broken gristle. His feet felt like they were being hit by hammers, as if each bone were being shattered, pummelled by the lesions and welts rooted into his soles. *Keep running.*

His legs cracked and fired off exploding tingles into his thighs as they were reminded of how to generate power for him to manoeuvre at a faster pace. His stomach tensed and roiled. His chest heaved as his lungs sucked in powerful breaths. His heart thundered as it charged his body to keep it moving. To keep it running.

Muscles awakened, joints eased but his mind screamed at him to slow down as the pain was insurmountable, begging the question of how on earth he managed to do this every day around tight streets and bustling markets. *No. I will not stop now. I refuse to be brought down by this body. I will keep running.*

Stop! You can't do this!

I can. I will.

Shutting down his thoughts as he spied the digging figures, Joseph focused on his motivation to keep his legs moving:

Run for Billy Baker, Jim Robertson and Jack Potts to save them from a disastrous fate, for friends to respect and give loyalty to.

Run for Victoria Penning, for love and a house with her, for shared incomes and shared happiness, for children, for fatherhood and teaching the lessons life had given. For a boat to sail in a gentle bay, for a fire to share with those close by, for laughter, love and humility. Run for the eternal smiles.

Run from your past and let it be, let it go, taking only the lessons it gave and moments of cheer to look back on.

Run for your future as a better person, to be positive and noble and superior to your former self; for a place in society, for a place to belong. Run for existence and a happiness that could never end.

I know what I want now. I know who I want to be, who I can be. I know I can have a future as open and as free as a wandering wave in an ocean of possibilities.

I know the secrets to life.

I know.

Heaving in the warm morning air, Joseph Winter ran through the salt-plain clutching a weather-beaten sailor's hat and a bottle of stagnant water. He ran fast, his pace constant. Endurance was key in desperate times like these.

Spotting Robertson digging with Tess standing watch over him, he knew they'd found it. Robertson was already knee-deep in the earth with a pile mounting beside him. Dirt flung from the hole, almost touching Billy, Victoria and Jack gagged and bound beside the cart under the watchful eyes of Thomas Sharp and Dave James.

So engrossed by the digging they were, that they hardly noticed Joseph running toward them, hurtling behind the cart, around the horse and diving into Tess Mills, tackling her to the ground with the snarl of a pouncing jaguar.

She fell flat with a squeal and immediately began wriggling and writhing, grabbing his arms, his face; anything she could get her hands on. He raised a fist and punched her hard whilst she grappled with his face, scratching deep gashes down his cheek. As he punched her again, feeling her cheek shatter, her hand scrabbled to get beneath her, to her belt, to the knife tucked away. Joseph grabbed her arm, *'don't you fucking think about it!'*

She slapped him and kneed his groin where he wheezed, and she rolled him to the ground and straddled him. *'Tess!'* cried Thomas, running to her aid.

'Leave me! I have him!' she commanded, hissing, 'and you, keep digging!' She pointed to Robertson, holding her other hand tight to Joseph's throat.

Joseph peered around and spotted the three prisoners wriggling and trying to call out to him. Spotting Victoria with bruises on her face, gagged and bound was one of the worst sights he'd ever had to witness. A great surge of fury swelled, forcing him to throw his arms wildly, hitting any part of her he could.

Tess's grip was firm, closing on his windpipe like a lioness at her kill. He could feel his throat closing, his Adam's apple crushing, his lungs struggling for air; his eyes beginning to bulge. His arms frantic, they punched her stomach and breasts and sides weakly, reaching for her head but her control over him was immense and hellfire was in her eyes. She'd killed before, she knew how to do it. As his arms dropped, he quickly remembered a vital tool. Snatching the handle of the knife she had behind her, he brought the blade out and swung it to her throat.

Her surprise was genuine, and she instinctively pulled back, releasing her grip, allowing him to rise from the ground, push her to the dust and straddle her, holding the knife to her throat.

'*Release them, now!*' he cried, 'I don't want to kill you, I don't want to be like you. *I'm not a monster anymore!* I've had it with you and your tyranny, your plots and slimy characters - *this mutiny ends now!*' Tess struggled and wriggled against the knife. 'Don't make me do it.' He hissed. With her lip bleeding and cheeks red and swollen, a strange smile spread upon her face, revealing her teeth coated in blood - a red segmented sheen. He could feel the rise and fall of her chest and a shudder ran through it, as if she were holding back a laugh.

'You still don't know, do you?'

'I know perfectly well how *fucking* awful you are, you wretched bitch! Now release them, stop playing these fucking games!'

She shook her head, her red teeth glistening. 'I was only a piece. A player of this game. I wasn't the one who set it up in the first place. I'd have thought you of all could've seen that.'

'Seen what? What are you talking about?'

There was a slight click from a pistol and a hard barrel gently touched the back of his head. 'Don't worry, Tess. He's been blind from the very beginning.' Jim Robertson's voice declared, 'which was why he was perfect for this role.'

Chapter Forty-One

Holding the knife, his hand began to tremble. *What . . . no . . .* Joseph felt his breath catch, '*Jim?*'

'Get off her and get to your feet, you vile cunt.'

He hesitated as he tried to find a grip, a handhold on the situation. *What . . .* Suddenly his hair was yanked. Joseph shrieked as he was lifted and thrown to the crusty salt, dropping the knife. As he turned to the rising sun, the silhouette of Jim Robertson stood tall with a flintlock pistol pointed at him, the smell of gunpowder was on his fingers. 'Oh Joseph, how I've longed for this moment. How I've longed to see you beaten and bloodied, dazed and confused in the dirt with nothing. Not even boots on your feet.'

'Jim. What . . .'

'All along you've been acting as the hero of this tale, but you're not. You've been the tool. The fool. You're nothing. You're pathetic."

Suddenly anger replaced the confusion and impatience seized his tongue. '*Explain yourself!*' He cried, wanting to yell, to cry, to beat the ground and implore it was not so.

A stern face gave him a dark expression, made darker by his overhanging brow. 'Must you make me? Come now Joseph, we've been through a lot together and I know how smart you are. This has been one long trail picking up pieces, try picking some up now.'

In shock, he didn't know what to think, where to start looking. What pieces? What was there he didn't see? He got to his feet and gently shook his head, 'I don't . . . I don't know what you're talking about. What pieces?'

Captain Robertson was disappointed. 'I expected more, especially from how well you did getting us here. From the beginning. Start there. Where did things go wrong for the mighty *Trace?*' he said sneeringly.

He was about to reply when he stopped. It was the way he'd pronounced the last word. His alter ego from the backstreets. How did Robertson know, Joseph had never mentioned it . . . Searching through his London life, the whole of it had been shambolic and corrupted but there was a beginning to its demise. 'Mad Vinny.' He started.

There was a coy and slimy smile. 'Ah yes. How could anyone forget old mad Vinny Jenkins?'

'You *knew* him?'

'Of course, I did. That stupid drunk small-time pawn dealer with a great ugly scarred V on his forehead acting as the head of an intricate criminal network from his booth in the Back House. What a jape that was to the bigger fish; what a disgrace. Did you *really* think he sorted that map-job by himself?'

Joseph's mouth hung open, unable to believe what he was hearing. Robertson didn't give him a chance to reply.

'Of course he fucking well didn't. *I* was the one who gave him the tip-off about the house, telling him it was from a maid, suggesting *you* to be the perfect man for the job because I *knew* you would take it on. Your excessive ego, boisterous pride and famed reputation were ugly things and they preceded you – landing you in a trap. You'd never say no to something Vinny offered. Even though you thought yourself self-employed. I bet you even thought of saying no, of walking away, then considered - *this is Mad Vinny, why not, for old time's sake. He's never let me down before.*' He smiled, 'as a pawn dealer, he was the first pawn moved along the board. Along *my* board. I thought it was fitting.'

He knew me before I even stepped on the ship. He knew exactly who I was. 'The map in the attic . . . the compass. How did you . . . how could you have known?' Slowly, shakily, he got to his feet.

Robertson took a step forward, the gun raised. 'Known? Come now Joseph, you're sharper than that. I had the map in my possession and had found your grandfather's compass. I placed them in the attic, and I did my research on your back grounds; not that I needed much, since everyone seemed to know your family's history. I knew that compass was what your grandfather had left you, so I added it in to make you feel like this was your destiny. As if fate had truly intervened for you. I wanted to get you off the ground and get you on the water.' A sickly smile hooked his lips – he was enjoying this.

Joseph could feel the earth spinning faster, yet his feet stood stock still. 'But the house. That house. Why that house? How could you have placed them there; how did you get in? Vinny told me about the tunnel, how could you have known about it?'

He looked away in disdain. 'My parent's house has always been a burden to them, only buying it for a fucking impression to keep up with their wealthy neighbours. To show off their fortune. Their own wealth made them wretched creatures: selfish and paranoid; loathsome brutes. Growing up, I was their prissy son, always pampered and having to stand straight with correct clothing and combed hair. What a chore; I fucking detested it. I didn't care for their money, just as they didn't care for me. I was raised by nannies and shown no love – I was just a liability to them, another excuse for them to fret over expenditure. I couldn't wait to get away. I used to use that tunnel all the time, sneaking out as often as I could. They told the maids to keep an eye on me, but I found my way around them.

'I got sick of all the petty scandals and the sly corruption they partook in, so I escaped, joined a gang, made some new friends and some new enemies, discovering how best to break the law and how best to evade it. Surely you of all would know what that's like. I preferred a life where the corruption was out in the open and in *my* control, rather than on paper hidden from view. Ruining lives with a signature and a slimy back-handing of notes, why not just stab their petty colleagues in the back themselves–'

'Like what you're doing? You sound just as bad as them.' He quipped sharply.

He leapt forward and smacked the butt of the gun in his face, dropping him to the ground with a thud. '*Don't. You. Fucking. Dare compare me to them or interrupt me!*' Robertson hissed. 'That was a particular lesson I learned often; except I received a cane when I interrupted. After they found out what I'd been doing, I wasn't allowed back, and I didn't want to go back. They tossed me to the streets thinking I'd be lost without them, thinking I'd find life so hard, but I'd found my own way. I enjoyed my years pilfering and pawning, then grew tired of it. I slowly put down the life of crime and settled with a wife and new-born son, working on the docks and ships, learning about sailing, working my way up through the decks. Things were settled for a time, until a mugging killed my wife and my son moved out.

'To heal from the pain of losing everything, I focused on this lost chest and how best to get it. It became an obsession. I knew it was out there, gold and riches, the lost loot of history. The mystery of the Scott's treasure had always fascinated me; I believed in it, and after a lot of searching I found and stole the scroll, but I couldn't understand it. I needed someone to crack riddles. Someone to solve problems and have the confidence to act rashly but cleverly. I needed someone with such self-belief they could follow the trail blindly, recklessly; I needed someone who wouldn't leave a trace.

'When I discovered my mother, that petty sow, was ailing, I knew my time had come. Time to get you in that house to crack the hunt I'd set up for you, as a test to see if you were good enough for the bigger game.' He smiled, 'you didn't disappoint, I'll give you that. Credit where its due.' Nodded Robertson.

Joseph seethed with his cheek aflame in a web of blotchy burst vessels. 'And the peelers waiting outside the tunnel? You as well or was that Vinny?' He spat blood to the salt.

He shook his head, 'you give that docile doorstop too much credit, Joseph. What a waste of a man. The peelers were of my own doing; I told them I'd seen you breaking into a wealthy property, and as soon as I told them I thought it was the infamous Joseph Winter, they were champing at the bit to get you. They'd have believed anything I said they were so desperate for a collar such as yours. And I must say, watching the performance of, what was his name? Constable Nicholas Locke? Impeccable, and before you ask another stupid question, yes, I was in the courtroom too as a witness, and was responsible for the note you received. That fat lump of lard would've written anything to get my pistol away from his V-scarred head. You know, for a man who got us all this far, you're slow on this trail.' He sighed, exasperated.

'In prison, I'm guessing you were there too?' He slowly got to his feet, trying to think of a way around him, a way to defend himself and attack. Alas, focus was hard to come by when a barrel was pointed at him and the trigger was about to be pulled.

'Don't be absurd! I sent others in there, paying them well, to cause as much trouble as they could. You did your part too, I'm sure, but the others were violent beasts; just to make sure the guards were kept busy enough to give you a better chance at getting out, with whomever you decided to bring along. Then I readied myself,' another step closer, 'I prepped my ship, paid some dockers to load it and readied my crew. We'd served together twice before on small duties, so I'd gained their trust. As soon as a scout of mine reported a prison break, I hoisted the Blue Peter. Why, I'd had that Blue Peter flag flying for nigh on two hours, making excuses to the officials to stall for time to make you believe I was about to leave, so you'd pick my ship and jump on as quickly as you could. I had to contain my laughter when I saw your efforts to get aboard. But again, credit where it's due. You managed.'

Joseph couldn't believe what he was hearing. This entire venture, it seemed, had been set up from the very beginning and, as he thought on the journey itself, points of confusion became suspicious. 'If you made such an effort to get me on board, why did you nearly leave Billy, Rob and I behind in Lisbon port?'

Robertson seemed taken aback by his question, yet he almost relished the fact that he'd picked up on a part of the game. His face said it all: *Fair play.* 'Ah. There was a mix up.' He answered, 'we were loaded up and ready, we had no choice but to leave to prevent further attention. Believe me, I was panicking at leaving you behind. I needed you. I would've sent a rowboat back to fetch you though so there was no need to fret.'

He remembered another point he found disturbing. 'Not for Harold though? Remember him? That was you, wasn't it? You were the only one with the musket. You shot him whilst we were separated and alone in Gabon. It was you that killed him.'

A smile spread, 'now you're showing your colours. That's the Joseph Winter I know.'

'You killed Harold and tossed your musket in the water so none of us would suspect anything, to make it look like you truly were escaping from the tribespeople.'

'You're almost there, but details are missing. How could you have known though.' He lifted the gun higher, aiming for his head, 'no. I didn't shoot him. I stabbed him. Twice. In the stomach, so he would slowly bleed out, then I shot the air to get the local tribes alerted to the coast. And Harold, well I must say his fate fit to my plan perfectly. He managed to get to the beach as we were heading back to the ship, so you could all see he *almost* made it and he *was* alive and it had nothing to do with me, then the savages came and took him; that was a nice touch I must admit. Then I filled you all in with some half-arse bollock story for you to believe me.' He shrugged, as if it were all too easy.

'You bastard.' Joseph shook his head as he tried to manoeuvre himself around to a better position. 'And you call me the beast. No. Jim, that's you. I bet you told Dave to steal those diamonds from that cave too, to get us all imprisoned by the village.'

Surprisingly, he shook his head, 'that one wasn't me. No, it was *Hugh* I hinted at to fill his pockets, and being a ragtag rapist and common scum, I knew he'd do it. People like him only need slight temptation, a minor slip-of-the-tongue - I only gave a playful suggestion to get it in his head: he did the rest. And Dave stole them because he saw what I saw.' He dug his hand in his pocket and brought out a handful of the precious rubies from across the ocean. 'Rare and invaluable, priceless items. I liked the look of a few as well; I thought they wouldn't mind.'

My god you're worse than the lot of them combined. 'You caused the death of Hugh Jackson, Jim, and very nearly the death of Dave, Rob and I.' He said sombrely.

'Joseph, he was a multiple rapist, a common thief and a bad man. Rotten to the core. He deserved his fate after all he'd done. The city is full of men like him, what's one less to anyone?'

The words were an echo to Joseph, reminding him of the pain in the back of his head as he dropped to the deck. Another part emerged and he narrowed his eyes. 'The mutiny. Tess. *You* staged the mutiny, didn't you? You made Tess the face of it to cover your own tracks, but it was–'

'–my idea? Yes. Of course. I'd been spreading, branching out; things were developing under the surface and when you came to me saying you'd heard some whispers, I knew the first stage was complete. All that talk of an infestation of rats, and there you were telling the source of its own squeaks. You were right to not trust anyone. Shame about our cabin boy though. Pushing Rob during that storm was all on Tess, I had nothing to do with that, but I must say it did add some fibre to it. My god, even I believed her when she said she was the head of it all. And when she kicked me down in the hold and gave me abuse, blimey, I felt young again. I was always administered harsh discipline, I administered it to my own child, and Tess just seemed to know. Honestly, what an astounding woman, and right to the very end she never let anything slip.' He turned and glanced at her as he said, 'I knew you had it in you, I saw your potential from the very beginning.'

Tess looked round to him, with Thomas dabbing the blood from her face with a damp cloth, and smiled, giving a curtsey.

'Why?' Joseph asked plainly, feeling sick. He stepped further. 'Why do all this?'

His face gave nothing away. 'This chest, this fable: Scott's Trove. The mystery has always been an interest of mine. No one has come close to finding the Lost Loot, so everyone deemed it to be false, but I knew it was true. It had to be. The last relic of the Golden Age of piracy and exploration and *I* wanted to be the one to dig it up. *I* wanted to be in the history books, the famed explorer who'd cracked the mystery and reaped the reward. The Lost Loot's Livingstone. I just needed someone to do the leg work. Which is where you came in. Since you're the grandson of that crotchety insect Frederick, I knew you'd dive into it - seeing it as "unfinished family business". Plus, I wanted you to learn a lesson in humility, to live a torturous and punished life totally apart from everything you had known in London, and it worked. I could see your demons hanging over you night and day.'

In part, he was right. Joseph had believed it to be family business, but still, something needed clearing up. And he needed more time to get into position. Without taking his eye off the gun or the cunning man behind it, he replied as calmly as he could, knowing Robertson's patience was thinning. 'I found the clues, solved the riddles and got you here, why not just kill me as soon as we reached land, or on the road to the town? Why did you keep me alive when you knew my part to play was done?'

Robertson shrugged, 'I thought I owed you another day. You're a filthy self-inflated gutter-rat but I think you're trying to be a good man. I liked giving you that glimmer of hope, making you think you had a chance, dangling a future in front of you like a gormless donkey with a carrot.' He almost had to retain a laugh as he shook his head. 'But by god I would've never let you near it. Not my treasure.'

Joseph slowly shook his head, 'It was never your treasure.' He stood over the large black mineral, the corresponding partner of the smaller lodestone. 'It will never *be* your treasure–'

'–Jim! Look out!' Tess cried, and Robertson looked around to her.

In that fleeting moment, Joseph seized his opportunity and grabbed the lodestone, smacked the gun from Robertson's hand and dived, tackling him to the ground in a cloud of dust. He raised his elbow and jammed it into his chest as hard as he could muster, wishing he had more strength left in his weak arms to finish this. With his other arm, he swung his fist hard and smacked him in the cheek with the mineral and blood sprayed from his mouth. He raised it again and brought the lodestone down hard into Robertson's face, smashing his nose. It was clear now who had pulled him from the side of the cart, who had emptied his pockets for the key. What was perhaps more despicable was the note and hat left to him to reinforce the feigned loyalty a final time. To make him still believe he was on his side whilst he took his true position in the revolt. There was no need to ask the question. '*You left me in the desert to die, you bastard!'* He clenched his fists hard and delivered blow after blow until his knuckles reddened and split, then clenched his hands tight around his throat.

Robertson fought hard to stop it, landing a blow to Joseph's jaw, knocking a tooth from its purchase in a bloody splatter, clawing at his face and eyes until he subdued and instead clawed at the hands around his throat.

Joseph clenched his fists tightly with blood dribbling from his mouth, wringing out the man's windpipe like a wet cloth. Suddenly he saw Tess in his periphery, moving for the knife he'd dropped in the salt and, knowing her intention with it, he foolishly jumped off to grab it.

Tess snatched it up before his eyes, making him realise it was a ploy to get him off and give Robertson a chance. Suddenly Robertson was up and delivered a powerful blow to his spine, making him scream in agony. Then, in a blur of motion, Robertson grabbed his head and was about to sharply turn it when Joseph grabbed his wrists and pulled them away with a grunt.

Seeing another opportunity from behind, Robertson wrapped his arms around Joseph's shoulders and held the back of his head, locking him in a chest-opening position where Tess then brandished her knife and made to strike. *'Finish him, Tess! Finish this!'* Jim Robertson cried with his face bloodied and broken.

Joseph writhed and kicked, grunting and groaning, his legs swinging but Robertson's grip was formidable. Years of pulling lines and manning ships had turned his hands into five-fingered vices. There was no way he could escape – the kicking had delayed Tess's blade but as soon as he missed one kick, she would be ready and –

Crack!

The sound of a gunshot was like a bomb exploding in the salt-plain; ear-splitting and loud, it made all of them startle. All except the three stunned prisoners watching the fight, seeing who had pulled the trigger.

The horse whinnied and bucked in surprise, trying to pull away.

Robertson winced and gave a surprised gasp. He released his hold and dropped to his knees. Joseph ducked and held his head to his chest. He squeezed his eyes shut, waiting to feel the excruciating agony of a bullet blasting its way through his back and a knife shredding through his front.

Then there was a click as the flintlock loaded, and another gunshot echoed through the salty waste.

Joseph jumped, tensing, his heartbeat loud and dramatic. Listening to its pulse the last few times.

There was no pain though. All of what he imagined to be involved in a gunshot wound and knife attack hadn't affected him. *Is it numb? Have I been shot? Am I already dead?* Slowly, wincing and trembling, he opened his eyes . . . and saw Tess lying dead on the ground at his feet with a gaping bloody hole in her pretty face with bold, red, blood spreading into the white crust of the baked salt. The knife glinted in her lifeless hand; it hadn't touched him. *What . . .*

'*Tess!* Oh my god! *Tess!*' Thomas wailed, rushing to her side, his eyes already streaming. Turning back, he cried to the perpetrator, '*why did you do that?!*'

Joseph made a gradual turn and saw Robertson clutching at a blooming red mark spreading through his clothes from the bullet lodged in his back. A look of perplexity gripped his face as he stared at his red palms, slick with his own lifeblood. 'What?' uttered the indignant man.

Joseph looked up and was astonished to see a smoking barrel held by a man who'd barely said a word the entire trek from port to salt plain. The bastard from the beginning.

Dave James released the trigger and dropped the pistol, his hands visibly trembling.

The muffled screams of the prisoners, the shouting, cursing, grunts and groans of pain – it all stopped. The silence was deafening as they tried to comprehend the unexpected sequence of events.

Gradually, Dave's eyes met Joseph's and he blinked, uncertain of this untrodden ground between them. The man's gaze then fell away, and Dave methodically stepped around to fill Robertson's vision, his feet crunching on the salt whilst Joseph hurried over to the three prisoners, releasing them from bonds with white shaking hands.

Jim Robertson looked up at Dave, perplexed and paling in the warm morning sun. Ghosting on the salt. '*You?*' He questioned weakly. 'You - you did this?'

'What does it feel like?' He asked, lowering to look him in the eye.

'What?'

'What does it feel like, being shot in the back? Having a bullet tear through your skin? Is it hot? A burning pain, like being branded by a hot poker. Does your flesh want to crawl?' He looked down to the ground sombrely and said with an unusual calm. 'Mine does. Every day.'

'David, how could you do this to your own–'

He shook his head and forced a laugh, 'to my own *father*? Oh Jim, you stopped being my father a long time ago. Ever since you abused me and abandoned me to fend for myself. You said so yourself, we've become alienated.'

The five observers watched on in shock.

'You were a man.' He croaked, 'you didn't need me to look after you.'

'I was seven-years-old. A boy. A child. After Mother died, you were never the same, you were obsessed by this obscenity. I was young, but I could see it. You valued this treasure over your own treasure: Your son. I'm still recovering from the trauma you caused me; and these scars on my body will never leave. I am cursed and I blame you for it all. You, who never showed me any love, who taught me to see the world through eyes of hatred, were the very source of the suffering in my life.' He smiled, almost in relief, 'but not anymore. No. I'm becoming freer the more you slip from this world. I've waited a long time for this, to find the strength and the perfect moment to pull that trigger. To see you waste away to nothing in a pit of agony. What victim wouldn't want to kill the abuser that ruined their life? This *is* revenge, Jim. Cold-blooded, primeval revenge, for all the woe and sorrow in my life that stemmed from your wrongdoing. You must've known this was coming.' When he didn't reply, Dave continued, 'you knew me from the very minute I stepped aboard that ship, yet you said nothing to me. You didn't acknowledge me as your son. *Why?*'

Robertson frowned and groaned, as white as the salt around him, as the ground he knelt in reddened.

Dave reached over and pressed hard into the rupture and listened to Robertson howl. He screamed harrowingly, torturously, as Dave repeated, 'Why?'

'Because–' he gulped, 'because I couldn't face you. I couldn't–' he whimpered, 'I couldn't bring myself to acknowledge you. It was too painful.'

'Why?'

Robertson began to fall. Dave reached over and held him up. 'No. No. You will not die yet. I already know the answer, I just need to hear you say it.' He pressed his fingers into the bullet wound until the man hollered.

'*Stop! Please. No!* No more. Wait . . .' He gasped, his eyes on the ground, then he took a deep breath and suddenly reached out to grab him, to grab his neck. Dave fell back with his father on top of him, grappling for his throat, his long greying hair in a tangle. There was a scuffle; Dave grabbed his weak wrists and pushed him off, letting him collapse to the ground with a cry.

Quickly, Dave reached in Robertson's pockets and pulled out the diamonds and rubies he'd stolen from Tulyaka's tribe. They glimmered richly, beautifully, as he jammed them in his father's mouth, lacerating his tongue and palate, stuffing them inside until small red glittering stones fell from his face and tangled in his wiry beard.

Robertson struggled, writhing on the floor with red spreading further out from his back. Dave's hands worked rapidly, picking out a long diamond and jamming it hard into the man's mouth. He closed his jaw and held it shut. Despite the sinister act, he forced himself to watch the life fade from his father's eyes, becoming freer as time ticked by.

A moment later, Robertson's body dropped heavily and slumped. His limbs folding out with a slight twitch in his fingers. Never to move again.

Dave James moved from him and got to his feet, his clothes and hands were smeared in blood, but his face had never looked calmer. He looked to the sky. Clouds were beginning to sweep over in wild forms; some fluffy, some thin and stretched as if they'd been scraped over the stratosphere. He breathed heavily, and Joseph saw a new light to this venture; for Dave, this journey was more than just reaching the chest. It was stewed revenge, retribution to a father that had abused and abandoned him when he was young. Now, as the man turned, Joseph saw small attributes to his face that looked like Jim Robertson and wondered how he never saw it before. *The power of perspective,* he thought, noticing a tremendous weight lifting from Dave's shoulders. Instead of retribution, there was absolution. Peace in his tired eyes.

Then, shockingly, he held out a hand, without saying a word.

No one moved, but Joseph understood. He stepped over to him, and with pride, took his hand and shook it.

Dave smiled and nodded. Then he strode over to Thomas's side, weeping at Tess's warm corpse and tried to console him.

Walking up to the half-dug hole, then looking up to the scene before him, Jack Potts's eyebrows furrowed in vexation. 'Right. Well. Firstly, *what* in the fuck'n name of the sweet Virgin Mary was all that about! And secondly, *who* the fuck are you people?!' he crossed his arms, one eye was swollen and black and his lip was busted.

Billy squinted in the bright daylight. 'Never y' mind who we were, see us as what we are; ordinary people with hard pasts hoping for a better future.' He paused in thought, then turned, 'Dave? I don't get it. How can you and Jim be father n' son?'

Dave looked down, as if finding the strength to admit it. 'My full name is David James Robertson. I can never face calling myself a Robertson though, not after what he did to me, so I tell people what I want to tell them. I want no relation with that man.'

Joseph listened on, still partly in shock, then stepped to the cart and rinsed the blood from his mouth before drinking deeply from the water barrel. The gap in his gum felt raw and mushy, but the pain from all his injuries could wait; he had to check on someone more important. Stepping over to Victoria, he could see how exhausted she was. With eyes reddened and puffy, it was clear she had been crying as well as beaten. Her hair was knotted, and her bruises were bright. Joseph felt like crying, then embraced her lovingly. 'I'm sorry.' He whispered, 'I'll never let that happen again.'

She hugged him back tightly. 'I thought I'd lost you. The way they'd beat you; I saw it all. I tried to yell, to tell you that Jim was behind it all, but you were already gone. It was awful. We all thought you were dead.'

'Not quite yet.' He replied, 'I think I've got some years left in me, and it would be wonderful to share them with you.'

Her eyes filled with tears, and she nodded.

'Sorry to interrupt a lovely moment, but Joseph, would you like to do t' honours?' smiled Billy, holding out the shovel.

Joseph released her and smiled tiredly. Taking the tool, he stepped over to the half-dug hole and jumped inside with the sun beaming down on them from the heavens. Everyone watched in anticipation, waiting to hear a thump. Even Thomas managed to stand with them after a time.

He dug the shovel in deep, heaving out clumps of mud and earth. It was hard and sticky; the earth was wet as soon as he dug below the dry line where the sun had baked the ground. Despite the sweat and the effort, this was nothing – a small chore after their journey's toil. Cutting against the sides, he made sure the hole was accessible and big enough. Deeper, he continued working the earth until the surface of the salt-plain came to his chest yet there was still no sign of any chest.

Keep going. Keep digging. It all leads to this. He formed a large pile outside and noticed how everything was considerably cooler at this depth. *No wonder all the lizards and snakes dig holes. This is bliss.*

As he shovelled, he thought of his old life and the man who he'd been and with each shovelful he pictured it gone. Lifting one heap out, he dug away his cynicism, his judgements and bad attitudes, tossing out his issues with commitment in a dirt-filled spray. Lifting another was shedding himself of the regrets and the guilt, the lives that had been damaged or taken because of him. As he dug, he made room for optimism, care, wonder and prosperity; love, happiness, satisfaction and fulfilment - everything he needed to become a nobler person and a better man. Digging away his past, he sought the future deep within this cool, dark hole. He sought the truth. He sought life.

After a time, concern began to spread. Thoughts were being shared unspoken. *What if nothing is down there? What if it was all a hoax? What will we do?* And for a moment, Joseph became concerned too, as more and more earth was flung from the pit. Just as he was about to stop for a breath, a resounding thump was heard from the shovel. It did not scrape as if it connected with a rock. It did not clink as if it connected with metal. It was a solid thump, as if it had connected with a chest.

All eyes suddenly looked down and hairs stood on end. With wide eyes, Joseph looked up at them all as he shared this momentous occasion and a pure, wonderous silence settled, until the Irishman couldn't take anymore. 'Don't just stand t'ere starin'! Get the bastard thing up here!' exclaimed Billy Baker with his usual impatience, leaning down to the edge of the pit to get a closer look.

Using Jack's prospecting tools, he carefully removed the thin layer atop it and scraped around its edges to get a clear idea of its size. It was large, larger than any other chests they'd found, about the area of a trunk. But how deep? How much could it carry? He carefully nipped away at its edges and chipped around its perimeter to loosen its hold; his hands trembling and his mouth dry, until they could fit their hands either side. Jack jumped down to help and they slowly excavated the chest from its purchase in the earth: its home of over a century. Cautiously, they all lifted it, easing it up to the surface, and placed it onto the salt beside the hole where the sun welcomed it into this new age of an old world. To this new age of empires, industries, ideas and populations; dug up by these brave old seadogs and wonderful, wizened criminals. Dug up by these worthy people seeking redemption and reward.

Looking at it was like looking at a dream, a figment of imagination. It almost didn't seem real, but with the sun highlighting its edges and curved lid, shining on detailed metal strips that encased beautifully ornate oak and spotlighting a lock at the very front; it became a part of them.

Joseph licked his dry lips and gulped a dry throat, still indignant to this trunk at his feet. The Lost Loot. Found. Turning away, almost dreaming, he walked to Robertson's corpse, reached into his pocket and took out the key. With his feet seeming to float, he returned to find everyone parting to make way for him, looking upon him with earnest, thankful eyes. They parted for the man that managed to get them here. For the man who had taught them a most important necessity of life and showed them how to use it: to believe. To believe in a better and prosperous life, to believe in themselves again and to hope when all else is lost.

Joseph dropped to his knees and brushed away the collected mud, before slowly inserting the key.

And turning it.

There was a clunk as the chest unlocked.

In his own chest, his heart drummed but his mind was transparent.

In a gradual movement, Joseph Winter lifted the lid and they all gasped as their eyes marvelled at the fabled hoard. The Lost Loot itself. Scott's Trove in all its glory.

'Crikey.' Jack Potts inhaled.

The contents glittered and shined, glowing in the warm sunlight, finally able to sparkle after a century shut away. Gold and silver filled majority of the chest, countless coins and trinkets and jewellery dazzled in the wooden box making their faces glow as they inspected. Scattered throughout the loot were beautiful diamonds and minerals twinkling all colours of the spectrum like beating hearts pumping value into the veins of this fantastical old chest.

Extraordinary jewels and gemstones of all colours poked from the trove, collected from across the world over a lifetime: glowing navy Tanzanite stones from Africa, vibrant Fire Opals from Mexico and colour shifting Alexandrites from Russia. There were other special gems and minerals too, like amethysts and quartz that seemed to fluctuate colour as they settled into a sunlit ray. Rubies and jewels sparkled with a newfound wonder, the likes of which they had never seen. The diamonds and jewellery they'd stolen from shops were not like this. Never like this. These were far more intricate and gleamed brilliantly, giving life back to relics from ages past, from a different world than the one they knew. Sparkling and glittering, the contents of the chest revived their surroundings making the salt-plain appear to be a glorified patch of heaven that had fallen from above and had dried in the Australian sun. These were not crusting salts at all; these were baked clouds they walked upon, a land where two suns could share the same sky.

Joseph reached out and slowly dug his hands inside, feeling the gold coins rub against his fingers, feeling the riches melt in his palms. A treasure-hunter's dream. Yet as he groped, he felt a peculiar shape and brought it forth to the light of day. Within his palms sat a magnificent rock, an oblong stone of the smoothest touch with curved ends as deep and as black as the darkest night, as smooth as ink, yet within its centre lay secrets he never knew existed in this mortal world. Within its solid length, a transparency gave a window to its core, revealing a sublime beauty he could not take his eyes from. A charm that reigned supreme. This belonged to Olympus, to rest on podiums carved of the finest marble stone, in a pantheon of divinity for only the omnipotent to marvel upon.

In his hands, he observed the rock seeming to glow from within, and move. He examined further and saw rich translucent ambers of the rarest trees trickling into flaming reds of spewing molten lava; moving and folding, mixing and merging as they were caressed by fingers of glorious light dropped from the sun itself. A perfect flame burning in eternity, forever flickering upon a wick of obsidian stone. Just as it looked to be guttering out, a brilliant spark ignited, and the formation enveloped into an entirely new masterpiece. As he marvelled, he felt things he'd never felt before. Awe-struck; it was abject amazement to any onlooker, and he pitied those who could never see such a beautiful thing.

Unable to take his eyes from it, it was with great difficulty he passed it to Victoria with one thought, *are there more?* Looking back to the chest, the gold and diamonds appeared drab in comparison to what he'd witnessed and, moving the coins aside, he searched for another.

There, buried within the gold, was a sibling and he carefully plucked it from its golden nest. This one was different and felt cold to touch, but fresh, as if he'd plucked it from a fast-flowing stream. Within its window, shards of ice had frozen, forming a watery glass that a cobalt blue wave swelled against; ebbing up the smooth glacial walls. Immovable and unconquerable, the glaciers encased such a fine clarity of which he'd never known; trapping a section of the bluest sky and giving it freedom amongst flakes of intricate snow it had never bore witness to. Just when the ice began to melt, it moved and flowed and formed into different shapes, giving different motions before freezing once more – allowing transparency into this complexity, allowing a simplistic glimpse into a finely-tuned system incomprehensible to the mortal eye.

As he held this shining rock, this beacon of immeasurable intricacy, he felt connected to it as if he were a part of it. As if it belonged to his being, his consciousness and mind. Amazed, he passed it to Victoria and hoped she would feel the same.

He found another amongst the jewels. Another that felt cool to touch with marvels encased by a shell of the darkest obsidian yet had hints of violet within the stone, as if they had been forged together as one. Joseph investigated it, was absorbed by it, seeing a scene before him he recognised, and again desired to kneel before its wonders. Layers upon layers of twinkling stars and swirling galaxy masses, fiery and white, burned together in harmony. All were joined by lengths of purple twine, always moving them, always rearranging; clustering and spacing, forming and joining, before expanding them far apart. Expanding to the furthest reaches until he could see them no more. Then, just when it looked as if they were so far away, they'd disappeared, they were back. Swirling, circling around a centre that was as bright and marvellous, as remarkable as they're own solar supremacy that brought light to the horizon at the end of each dark night. He witnessed a galaxy in the universe forever expanding, developing to unknown reaches, creating once more: Genesis encased in this polished rock, held by his weathered, mortal hands. Such was the astonishment of this stone, he wondered how this came to be, how such magnificence could fit into such a small yet miraculously large opal stone. He felt as if he was holding galaxies within his palms, a universe cocooned in this formidable egg, ready to hatch and expand, to join, to form, to create, to be at one with the divine the pious worshipped.

Then, as he passed it along, the image was no more, and it became a simple stone plucked from a wooden box, begging him to question his perspective.

'Joseph . . . what are these?' Victoria gasped, marvelling at her eye's desire.

Whilst holding them, he'd thought of an answer to what they were. He'd concluded that they, indeed, did not belong to this lump of rock they called home. He looked to her, to them all. 'I think I have an idea.' He smiled as he remembered the first scroll Eve and Henry had left to the world. Getting to his feet, he walked to the cart where he sifted through his precious canvas bag and found the scroll Robertson had taken from him. He unravelled it and read aloud, '. . . *The end of days is what she seeks, the edge of horizon is where Polaris weeps, bleeding in the black, crying in the night, wishing for the idol that lost its light.*' He looked to the chest, 'it was here, all along. Telling us what the chest contained. Idols. Fallen stars – meteors. Blinded by our own views of value, all we imagined was gold – the height of wealth from a human's view, whereas what they were collecting, the real treasure, was nothing so simple. They explored the world searching for these meteors, these fallen idols. These fallen stars. The rarest items on the planet, and the most valuable. These stones don't just give worth, they give emotion to the heartless. A beat to a flat line. They're incredible. No wonder they wanted only the worthy to find the chest; for only the worthy could understand them, could see what they truly are.' He smiled as he remembered a line from the last clue and understood its meaning better – knowing all of them had experienced its instruction; 'to those who are lost, so you shall be found.'

'What's the gold in there for then? And the diamonds and jewels?' Dave asked, looking stupefied.

Joseph mused, 'you know, I reckon the gold wasn't theirs in the first place. The gold and treasure are from the loot of Black Bart. I've been thinking of the tale too, and how it all connects. I believe Eve was the daughter of Black Bart that no one knew of, and since he died, they found wherever he'd hidden his loot after a successful pirating career, and in this chest is what's left of their funds after they travelled the world exploring. They probably visited countries before they were even known, before their waters were charted, but since they weren't commissioned by a king or funded by a crown, they left everything untainted. They had nothing to prove, nothing to gain, nothing to claim for an empire or country's sake.' He beamed, 'they didn't become failures, since they were never striving for success; their goal was a personal one. Exploring because they could, because they wanted to. It was their passion. They were lapidaries, looking for the perfect diamond, the perfect gemstone, searching for another fallen idol, and they travelled the world whilst doing so. They were free. Just as we are.

'This gold, these trinkets, these brilliant opal stones; they're ours now and as I promised, we share this gold equally to build a new life, or to get drunk and throw wild parties.' He smiled with a face that hurt and bled. 'It's yours to do with as you please.'

After discussing their options, they decided to take the trove back to Jack's home and settle the shares there, where they didn't have to stand in the rising heat. Closing the chest, they hauled it on the cart and Joseph collected his items from Robertson's pockets. They removed the rare red rubies from Jim Robertson's gaping maw and lowered the bodies into the pit, filling it and drawing the drama to a close.

The journey back to the town was to be long and tiresome with swarms of buzzing flies, but the air was now clear, and they breathed happily with light hearts. They were victorious, not only over the journey and the mystery of the Lost Loot, but more importantly over their own fates. As they passed through the desert and back into the fields of flowers and forests of eucalyptus where koalas watched them sleepily, they shared tales of their origins and journey with Jack, laughing freely and smoking the rich Australian tobacco. That night, Victoria cleaned up Joseph's wounds and face as best as she could but the missing tooth, she could do nothing to aid. When it stopped bleeding, Jack informed him of his own smelter that could fashion a tooth from gold to fill the dark gap and that he should look him up when he had the chance, and Joseph agreed, now having enough gold to spare.

With pure elation, they realised the night was to be clear and they happily camped under the stars, observing them with a newfound interest. In a way none could explain, they felt connected to them having held them in their palms, feeling a sense of belonging under their shining gaze.

The following day they quietened, giving in to reflection and exhaustion. Thomas walked apart from the group, his face pale, his eyes puffy and bloodshot. In a way, Joseph could understand his pain – to fall in love for the first time only to have it torn away in a glimpse. Before, he would've avoided him and let him endure the pain, but now he slowed his pace and walked beside the glum fellow, and after a moment, tried his best to console him. 'I'm sorry for your loss Tom, I know it's hard to lose someone.'

He didn't look up, 'do you? Have you seen your only love being murdered in cold blood right in front of you?' he sniffled and whimpered, 'she was my first love, my only love. We were to be married.'

Joseph paused before he replied, 'I don't know much about love, I'm only beginning to understand it, but I know that it can be renewed. Rediscovered. If not in someone else than in yourself – the rest will follow from there.'

Forcing a smile, Thomas nodded and returned to his downward gaze.

Giving him the needed space to mourn, the company travelled in light spirits through the dirt track then into the road's ruts, realising their journey was almost at its end. Surprisingly, an overwhelming sense of melancholy enveloped, causing silences none knew how to break.

The sad silence stretched along the road to the flaking green door of Jack Potts's abode. Upon their return, they unloaded the cart and brought the chest into his main room as Jack took Daisy back to her field, and when he returned, he picked out separate wooden boxes for them all.

Billy lifted the lid of their legendary loot and smiled in the radiance of the hoard. 'Christ, y' can see why pirates used to like this stuff so much. Would y' look at that glow!' Daunted by the amount, they began the long process: sifting through amounts and shares, finding new gems and opals hidden within the piles of golden coins and pieces of silver. Keeping it as fair as they could, Jack made sure his efforts within this venture were also recognised. 'Now don't go forgettin' old Jackie here, I may not've come all the way from London, but I played a part.'

Joseph nodded, 'you'll get some mate, don't you worry.' Soon, the chest began to empty as the separate boxes filled, each partaking in their wants from the chest with some favouring rubies and diamonds and others golden trinkets. The chest emptied gradually, whereupon more stones were found. Two more, with two contrasting windows; one displayed lush greens and browns, earthly mixes of precious life, whilst the other showed roiling greys with flashes of white, as if a raging storm were trapped within. There were enough for them all to have one, and they chose whichever they favoured the most.

The lid closed, and then the lids to their boxes, and a deepening silence spread between them. Looking at each other, they knew it was coming. Slowly, they all stood.

"Ang on there a tick. Got to finish it all off properly.' Jack suddenly blurted, hurrying over to a cabinet where he retrieved a bottle of cherry brandy. He smiled at them all, 'my favourite,' and, collecting six glasses, he poured a tot in each and passed them around.

They looked down to their brandy, and Victoria raised hers. 'To new friends, a strong ship, a bloody long journey and a chest of gold. Scott's Trove is ours.'

'To the happier days to come.' Added Joseph, and they all toasted and drank the glasses dry.

Joseph Winter sighed, not knowing how to begin. 'There's a lot I could say to you all, yet now I find myself lost for words. So, let me start simply.

'Thank you, to you all. Thank you for the part you had to play in this. It was not an easy road; it's the paths not commonly trodden that make the hardest journey, but onto success our road was led.' He looked at their faces, their worn and emotional faces, and smiled. 'You wonderful people.' He gulped, 'I hope this is not the end, but a beginning to new friendships, and, once you're settled with a house or cottage or shack under the sun, send me your address and I'll have a map at the ready and my boots on ready to find you. I wish you all luck and happiness in whatever future you choose.'

All stood in silence, before Dave James bowed his head and held out his hand. 'Thank you, Joseph. For the opportunities I was never given and the peace of mind I've never had. God bless you, and thank you, my friend.' Taking his hand, he shook it, trying to swallow the tears. Picking up his box, he then turned and walked through the door.

Thomas was next, forcing a smile through the tears. 'Thanks to you all, for saving me. For giving me a life again. It's a fresh start for me. I'll stay in touch.' He nodded and took his box through the door, trying not to break into sobs.

Billy wiped away a tear. 'Men aren't supposed to cry, but when it comes down to it, I don't care anymore. Ah Joe, from the beginning to the end, eh? From our damp little bunk in that dark cell, to riches I've never known in my life, and opportunities I now can choose from. It's all thanks to you. You saved us all and gave us everything. Thank you.'

Joseph held out his hand, 'just don't go gambling it all at once, alright?' he smiled.

He chuckled as he wiped away another tear, 'ah. Nah. I'll give it at least a week. The luck o' the–'

'Don't say it. Don't you fucking say it.' Joseph laughed, embracing his dear friend, knowing this wasn't to be an end. 'I'll see you soon mate. Take care of yourself.'

'Aye, I will.' He wiped another tear, 'take care Victoria, and God bless you both.' He embraced her, then took his box and walked from the room.

Turning to Jack, Joseph couldn't help but smile at him. The man had a soft look and arms that were folded. 'I never thought I'd see the day when people would value honour and gratitude over gold. Not one of you squabbled about amounts, none fought. You all seem more emotional about goin' separate ways than what you've got tucked under your arm.' Jack said, shaking his head.

'Ah, they've probably slagged us off as soon as they walked through that door.' Victoria smiled. 'Thanks Jack. For helping us finish this. We couldn't have done it without you.'

Jack nodded, giving his famous golden grin. 'I can't really say it was my pleasure since I had a shit toime of it, but what a tale my friends! What a grand tale to tell.' He reached out and shook Joseph's hand, 'I'll be sharing your story Joseph. Both o' your stories. Why, I've never known a story that gave a bunch o' poor people from the big city so much hope, so much determination that led them all to freedom. I take my hat off to you's folks. Now go. Go and enjoy it, an' know that if y' ever need a friend to talk to, you seek out ol' Jack Potts. I'll be here.' He let go of his hand and shook Victoria's too, 'best o' luck for the coming days. Bless you both.'

They bade goodbye to their Australian friend and picked up their boxes, walking out of the door and into the fresh air outside, breathing it in as new people with new hopes, sharing the same ideas. 'Wait a minute,' Joseph stopped, and fished around in his pocket. When his hand came back out, he held a beautiful diamond ring he'd picked to be in his share; the most remarkable ring she'd ever seen. Victoria gasped.

He put down his box and took to one knee, and holding the ring out for her, gave a proposal with astonishing clarity in his eyes and a sureness he'd never felt before. 'Victoria Penning, will you make me the happiest of men and be my wife?'

Tears streamed down her tired face as she took a step back. 'Joseph, you do this now when I'm looking my worst after a long journey, in front of all these people?'

He nodded, 'where else and when else.'

She beamed, tears flowing down her cheeks. 'Of course.'

He beamed and slid the ring on her finger as the surrounding townspeople clapped. Amelia and Chloe applauded too, with Jack Potts cheering from the doorway and Billy, Dave and Thomas hollering from the end of the street. 'The future is ours, Victoria, and I can't wait to share it with you.' He whispered as he embraced her, holding on.

Chapter Forty-Two

Two years later.

Taking off his boots at the front door under the climbing wisteria, Joseph stepped inside their house and hurried into the bedroom where he slid off his dirty work clothes and found a clean vest and some trousers to slip on. His muscles ached from the manual labour, but his soul felt soothed, helping the local bricklayers build the orphanage they were funding. After their impoverished upbringing in London, Joseph and Victoria endeavoured to help the next generation by giving them a solid and healthy start and give them, at least, a small chance in life. Yet their orphanage had not been the start to their generosity.

Once they'd bought their own place to call a home and rested, they paid a surprise visit to their kindly hosts, giving small fortunes to Kinny and Charlie Dodger, William and Mary Webber and their new little girl Eliza, and Amelia, Chloe and their shocked father. They'd all declined the wealth, as the couple thought they would, yet only took it when Joseph and Victoria insisted.

They then married, a small but joyous event on the beach of their small bay behind their house, celebrating with all their friends present, including Billy's, Dave's and Thomas's fiancés and wives. They stayed for a time, before itchy feet made them take to the road, exploring this new country they called home. Upon the road, however, they realised their future held more than just a home and a family, and their fortune had a purpose worth pursuing.

Whenever they came across a poor beggar or a struggling family, they donated small fortunes to them, doing all they could to help; to be the light in their times of darkness. They had learned that the light of a candle could be shared amongst other wicks without the candle losing any brightness; just as joy could be shared without losing any potency. If anything, the potency increased. Taking on this mantra, they tried to emphasise the teaching in whatever they put their minds to. The orphanage was now their new project and they worked hard to share the light further.

Even though their fortune was very prosperous, and they were wealthy beyond comprehension for the rest of their days, Joseph enjoyed the feeling of a solid, honest day's work, keeping him busy. It was enough of a reward. Money was not the source to joy, he'd told the bricklayers, helping others was. Giving was just as good as receiving. He called out from the bedroom. 'Victoria?'

'Just outside!' she called. *Blimey I swear she loves those chickens more than she loves me.* He walked into the kitchen and looked at the view of the bay from the window. Just past the decking and roofed veranda sheltering two padded chairs, a path of wooden slats paved a route through luscious green grass, leading down to a quiet bay where a strip of curving white sand hugged a lagoon of clear calm water. The sky was a gorgeous tint of red and amber as the sun, a great, hazy, red disc, slid lower to the horizon. The summer evening was warm, and a soothing breeze swept through the bay causing a few ripples on the water and the grass to play and dance. *Lovely evening for it . . .* he pondered scratching his cropped beard, hoping Victoria would be well enough for him to enjoy it.

Whilst she was outside, and whilst he remembered, he wrote a letter and wrapped a pair of handmade glasses caringly and slid them inside a small box and wrapped the package, addressing it to be delivered to a Mrs E Lake, in Lisbon, Portugal, as he'd promised. He smiled, then prepped for dinner and began to cook so when she came hobbling back inside, she sighed with relief, 'Ah lovely. Thank you. I was just about to start. I've been studying all day and the chickens offered a wonderful respite.' She put her hands over her pregnant belly, walked to a chair and sat down beside her notes – her experience as a ship's surgeon had inspired her to follow a passion, and hopefully career, in nursing. Her hair was trimmed and clean, tied up, and her face was radiant, its glow quick to return. Her beauty and charm were unmistakable and made Joseph gleam every day.

'You should leave me to clean them chooks, especially in your condition.'

'This "condition" is a one *you've* put me in Mister Winter,' she toyed playfully, 'so I'll keep doing what I'm doing until I can't get up. Oh, by the way, you had some men knocking for you today. Well, knocking for both of us. I told them you were at work, so they said they'll pop in later; could be any time this evening.'

Joseph turned, confused. 'Really? Who were they?'

She shrugged, 'they didn't say, they just asked about our journey.'

'Our journey?' He said, surprised. 'God, I hope they don't come when we're eating, that happens every time.'

'You know, I'm sure they wait at the door until they hear cutlery scraping and *then* decide to knock.'

'I wouldn't be surprised if they were out there now listening to us and smelling my glorious cooking.'

'Joseph, if they could smell your cooking they'd be running *from* the door, not to it.' She jested.

'Oh, ouch. Although, I forget, who *is* it that's cooking tonight?' he turned and faked a stern look, with hints of a smile.

Victoria pursed her lips, and smiled back, 'sorry, sorry. Continue.'

Once the dinner was cooked, they sat down at the table and began eating, when there was a knock at the door. 'Oh. My god. I should've checked that damned door earlier, I swear.' He slammed down his knife and fork as Victoria laughed and went to the door where two men were waiting.

With sideburns and bowler hats, wearing waistcoats and jackets, they gave him a flashback of men's fashion in London. *No, it was high tops, not bowlers.* He smiled as pleasantly as he could knowing his food was waiting, and they addressed themselves politely. 'G'd evening sir, moight you be a Mister Joseph Winter? My name is Charlie Munson and he's Alex Drayson, and we'd loike to ask a few questions about some things to do with a remarkable journey you've been on; we were told it had the power to give hope where none seemed possible.'

He gave a look of confusion. 'I am Joseph Winter, but might I ask who told you all this?' *Well Jack, you've got a big mouth as well as golden teeth.*

'A Mister Jack Potts.'

Joseph couldn't help but smile, showing off his own golden tooth. He liked it, and Billy, Dave and Thomas did as well when he showed them. Each, too, now had their own children with more on the way; each enjoying fulfilment in their paths and budding careers. 'I might know of the man. Come in. We're just eating, so if you wouldn't mind waiting, we can talk about this after.'

'Of course.' The two men entered and were shown into the drawing room near the hearth that Joseph quickly set up and lit, then went back to finish his meal.

Once finished, he entered the room and sat down. 'Is your wife available for a chat too? We were told Missus Winter had a part to play as well.'

'Of course. Victoria darl', you there? They want to talk with you too.'

There was a clink of plates and she awkwardly walked in and took a seat. 'Hello again, sirs. Sorry for the mess, I'd have tidied up beforehand.'

'Don't worry yourself, there's nothing to tidy.' The two men smiled in the glow of the flames, where Charlie then began. 'Now you're both here, we were wondering if we could talk to you about an adventure, a journey you both, and others, endured, all to find a fabled chest, a Lost Loot, I think it was called, that turned out to be very much real. Is this correct?'

They nodded, 'why do you ask?'

'We're extremely interested in your tale. Mister Potts tells us it's a tale of fates, and a passage to freedom. We are writers and we were hoping to take notes and eventually write a novel about it, with both of your permissions, of course? It would be a work of fiction, written in third person perspective, yet authentic and visceral, as if the reader were there.' Alex Drayson asked politely.

Joseph shrugged and looked to Victoria, who also shrugged and nodded. 'I can't see a problem with that.' He replied, 'it's a . . .' he paused, wondering whether he wanted to revisit the memories and relive the trauma, there was so much to share, but he knew in the long run it would help to let everything out and let everything go: acting as a confession, in a way. 'It's a long tale to tell. Have you the time?'

They both nodded with their fountain pens hovering and ready above pages of blank paper. 'All the time in the world . . .'

Epilogue

For the following week they talked; agreeing on points and disagreeing on others, collaborating their views on an extraordinary tale unknown to the world apart from a few. All whilst Charlie's and Alex's pens scribbled away on paper that filled quickly. When they'd finished, drawing the points to a close, the two writers looked at them with tears in their eyes. Speechless, they struggled to find words to put into sentences. Eventually, Charlie Munson managed to utter, 'I must say, I've never heard a story loike it. You've certainly had some adventures, yet how you all managed to pull through and find success, happiness and peace, is astounding. Your charitable work and the orphanage you're building is incredible. I am inspired and I'm sure others will be inspired too. And to see a little one on the way is a beautiful thing. Jack was right in what he told us. A tale of fates and freedom, indeed.' He told them with a smile. 'The details you can keep to yourself, but the story we will transfer to manuscript to the best of our abilities. Moight I ask, do you still have the clues? May we see them?'

Joseph nodded and collected them from a drawer in their bedroom and gave the stack to them to take notes from.

After a time, as Charlie scribbled, Alex slid a piece of paper their way. He explained, 'this is just a rough idea. A first draft, if you will, but this is what I've got in mind for a start. It'd look something loike this.'

Joseph and Victoria leaned over and read his handwritten paragraph:

Heaving in cold morning breaths, Joseph Winter bolted through the dirty, cobbled streets; one hand clutching his bulging jacket pocket, the other gripping a felt black bowler hat. He ran fast, his pace constant- endurance was key in desperate times like these; the body had to be ready for a quick dash, a swift escape, if he wanted to stay out of that godawful place again. By now, Joseph didn't mind the running; after years of it he quite enjoyed the exercise. One thing he enjoyed more though was the thrill of the pursuit, and even better, the art of the steal.

'Blimey, look at that.' He marvelled, surprised at seeing his experiences written down. 'I like it.'

'I do too.' Victoria added with a smile.

'As I say, it's only a first draft. It needs working on, but we'll make it work, eh, Charlie?'

He packed up his notes and papers, squaring them and putting them into a leather case. 'Aye, definitely. Thank you both so much for your toime, and congratulations for the new arrival – I've got two myself. Good luck.' Charlie winked and held out his hand for both to shake and Alex did the same. 'G'day to you's both. Crikey! It's evening?' he shook his head, 'honestly, where do the days go? Well, instead I'll wish you both a good evening and the best of luck for the future. We'll be in touch.' He tipped his hat and they both walked out the door, heading for the town to search for a hotel room.

'Thank you for your time, and for listening. We can't wait to meet whoever this little one will be. Goodnight.' Joseph waved, closing the door and locking it.

After a moment, Victoria turned to him, 'Joseph, what happened to you that night in the desert?'

'I'm not sure. Something profound, inexplainable. It was . . . incredible. It changed my life, just as you have.' He replied, remembering the night well.

She smiled and hugged him, then asked, 'did you really think I was beautiful when you first met me that day?'

He nodded, holding her. 'Of course. And I have ever since.' She beamed and kissed him. 'Right. I'm hopping in the bay for a while.'

'Alright. Do you fancy a fire tonight too?' she asked.

He nodded and looked tired. 'Blimey, it's all I've wanted to do since they walked through the door the other day.'

She laughed as he slipped on his boots and exited the house, passing photographs on the walls and a gorgeous rare red ruby taking pride of place on the kitchen windowsill; the evening light refracting in remarkable rays as it shone through. He breathed in the warm evening air, and running down the wooden slats to the sand, he scared off the gulls and oystercatchers and walked into the water where his small sailboat was anchored.

Jumping inside, he hoisted the mainsail and jib, tightened the halyards, lifted anchor and settled himself beside the tiller. The breeze pushed into the sails and the boat moved effortlessly, sliding across the calm water, riding the slow current that pulled him further out.

He breathed deeply, listening to the gentle waves lap against the hull, to the creak of the lines in their eyes, to the slight breeze that made the boom squeak gently as it pushed the sail and played around him, ruffling his hair and clothes. Looking out, he watched the deep orange sun slide lower through the clear sky, heading for the wavy horizon to end this long summer's day.

Joseph sighed relaxingly as he belayed the sheet to the pin and held the tiller gently. Priming the hand-carved pipe, he lit it and puffed, not because of need any longer, but because of want; it was all his choice. Independence from addictions, he'd found, was a wonderful virtue, but he kept a small pouch of tobacco handy for occasions such as this. Closing his eyes, he understood what Thomas and Jack had been talking about all those years ago. Breathing deeply, he felt an emotion that was hard to come by but easy to reach once he knew how; a beautiful presence that sharpened colours and brought forth a sense of ease, making him feel light, as if the breeze was to carry him away. Freedom, in all its glory.

As the sun sank lower, dusk grew and darkness spread, forcing him to turn back, heading for the glowing light coming from the beach. The glowing light of a fire. Beside it, a pregnant woman sat in a padded chair under a blanket, her content face illuminated by the flames; the most beautiful woman he'd ever known.

Dropping anchor in the shallows and stowing the sails, he jumped from the side into the water and walked up to the warm glow of the fire where an empty chair waited beside his wife. Victoria smiled and lifted the blanket open for him. 'Felt like you were gone a long time.'

Joseph smiled back, 'don't worry, my love. I'm home.' He said, sitting beside her, wrapping his arm around her shoulders and feeling the warmth of the fire under a sky filled with stars, twinkling like the ceiling of that Madagascan cave. Stars that twinkled and expanded; moving and forming, burning with the graceful fire of eternity, like the opal stone that glittered wonders upon their mantlepiece.

Glossary

Victorian slang, phrases and insults:

Apple lady – a hard cider.

Back slang it – to go out the back of a dwelling.

Beer and skittles – to have a good time.

Benjo – a busy day in the streets.

Betty fang – to thrash or beat.

Bitch the pot – another term for pour the tea.

Bit o' jam – another term for a pretty woman.

Bonneted – to have your hat pulled down over your eyes: a popular joke in Victorian times.

Bricky – to be brave or fearless.

Cabbaging – another term for stealing.

Chignon – a type of woman's hairstyle where the hair is pinned to the back of the neck or the back of the head. There were many variations of the style, but a basic chignon was popular in Victorian times.

Chin music – a conversation.

Chuckaboo – another term for a close friend.

Cop a mouse – another term for a black eye.

Comforter – an old-fashioned term for a scarf.

Collie-shangles – another term for arguments.

Cupid's kettle drums – another term for breasts.

Damfino – unsure of what it is about e.g "damned if I know".

Dark over Will's Mother's – a term to describe approaching dark clouds, a precursor to rain or a storm. The origins of this term are unknown.

Dash my wig! – a term of exclamation.

Dance upon nothing – to be hanged at the gallows.

Dip – a type of candle.

Don't sell me a dog – another way of saying "don't lie to me".

Dog days – the hottest days of the year.

Done to a turn – something has been completed satisfactorily.

Evening wheezes – false news, another term for newspapers.

Fancy girl – another term for prostitute.

Flapdoodle – a sexually incompetent man or woman.

Foozler – a clumsy person.

Fresh fish – a new recruit.

Frousy – another word for tatty or unkempt.

Gibface – an ugly person.

Gigglemug – a smiling face.

Got the morbs – temporary melancholy; sadness or depressed.

Going down the line – going to a brothel.

Grinning at the daisy roots – a term for death, six feet under.

Hard case – someone who is rough and tough.

Hedge-cropper – another term for a prostitute.

Horizontal refreshments – another term for sex.

Hornswoggler – a fraud or cheat.

Hook it – to tell someone to leave or move, another way of saying "be off with you!"

Hornets – another term for bullets.

Hunky Dorey – another term for terrific.

Jonah – a person believed to be jinxed or hexed.

Jollocks – a fat person.

Kenned – 'ken', to know something.

Kith and kin – one's relatives.

Killing the canary – shirking or avoiding work.

Links – coarsely made torches that lined the streets in Victorian times before the installation of electric streetlamps.

London Mud – the streets of London during Victorian times were clogged with waste from horse and human alike that has now become known as the London Mud.

Make a stuffed bird laugh – another term for preposterous.

Meater – a coward.

Mumbling-cove – a shabby person.

Mutton-shunter – a policeman.

Nanty-narking – another term for great fun.

Neck oil – beer or alcohol.

Oil of gladness – an alcoholic beverage.

Old Scratch – a nickname for the Devil.

Open the hall – to begin a battle or fight.

Orf chump – to have no appetite.

Pigeon-livered – another term for cowardly.

Podsnappery – a person ignoring problems in belief they're too good to sort them out.

Poked up – another term for embarrassed.

Possum – a best friend or buddy.

Poxy – cursed.

Ratbag – a general term of abuse.

Riding a Dutch gal – to consort with a prostitute.

Robin – a young child beggar.

Shin plasters – paper money, pound notes.

Shoot into the brown – to fail.

Skedaddle – to run away fast.

Skilmalink – shady and doubtful, secretive behaviour.

That's the ticket – the proper thing to do.

Tickle one's innards – to have a drink.

Tight as a boiled owl – another term for drunk.

Uppity – a person who believes they're above their station in life.

Up the pole – another term for drunk.

Vazey – another term for stupid.

Wagtail – a promiscuous woman.

Walk-er! – a cockney expression of astonishment or surprise.

Welch wig – a cap knitted from smooth yarn.

Wooden spoon – an idiot.

Billy's Irish slang and phrases:

Acting the maggot – to be a fool.

Batter ya – to beat someone up.

Chancer – a dodgy character, manipulative for their own gain.

Clean on – another term for good looking.

Craic – to have a good time.

Cut to the onions/to the bone – to be fed up.

Doin' a number – to cause discomfort, upset or stress.

Drobes – another term for bits and pieces.

Eejits – another way of saying idiots.

Gas – a laugh, someone or something funny.

Hatchet – another term for brilliant.

Head like a bag of spuds – stupid or ugly.

I could eat the twelve apostles – I'm very hungry.

In tatters – to destroy or be destroyed.

Kicked and booted – to assault or be assaulted.

Knackered – I'm exhausted.

Layin' boots – to kick someone whilst they are already down.

Like a blind cobbler's thumb – something ugly or messed up.

Mad as a box of frogs – crazy.

Muppet – a fool.

Noodle – describing a head.

On the lash – to go out drinking.

Plugged – another term for pregnant.

Poormouthing – to talk bad about someone or something.

Racked – I'm exhausted.

Rawny – describing a delicate man.

Rumbly – dodgy job or person.

Sell the eye outta' your head – a persuasive salesman.

Shebang – the whole thing.

Sticking out – another term for doing well.

Stook – an idiot or fool.

Ship - nautical terms and phrases:

A.B.S – Able Bodied Sailor. The backbone of the ship, they were expected to have knowledge and experience in all areas. When this was called, this meant anyone on deck.

Aback – when there is a strong headwind, to rig the sails aback means to brace them the opposite side in order to catch the wind to reduce speed. This is done to assist in tacking and heaving-to when there is extreme weather during a storm.

Abaft – toward the stern, the rear of the ship.

Afore – the front end of the ship.

Aft – the rear end of the ship.

Ahoy – a cry to draw attention aboard a vessel.

Aloft – to be in the rigging or above, to not be on deck.

Anchor – a heavy object used to slow or stop a vessel's movement, usually in the shape of a hooked plough.

Anchors aweigh – this term is meant to be said when the anchor has cleared the seabed and is no longer anchored.

Anchor ball – a small black floating object that indicates the ship is still anchored.

Anchor home – when the anchor has been winched above the water allowing the vessel free movement.

Anchor winch – a small capstan that is used to winch the anchor up from the seabed.

Argosy – a type of merchant ship.

Aye-aye – a reply to an order to confirm the order has firstly been heard and secondly will be carried out.

Avast – to stop or cease what is being done.

Backstaff – a navigational instrument used to measure the altitude of a celestial body, such as the sun or moon.

Backstay – a stay or cable reaching to all the mastheads from the foremast to the mainmast and the mizzenmast, which then runs down into the lower rigging. This stay supports all masts of the ship beyond the forestay.

Belay – to fasten a line around a fixed fitting such as a cleat or pin.

Belaying pins – a removeable wooden pin in a rail which running rigging and standing rigging are fastened to.

Bend – a knot used to join two ropes together, or to attach a line to a fixed object.

Berth – the deck where hammocks and bunks are stowed and hung, where the crew sleep.

Bilge – the bottom flooring of the ship.

Blow the Man Down – a classic sea shanty sung to give motivation.

Blue Peter flag – a flag that indicates a ship is about to sail.

Bulwark – the railing of the ship; the sides above the level of the deck.

Boatswain – the role on the ship charged with supervision of duties, maintenance and inspection of sails and rigging as well as supply stores. The Boatswain also is charged with deck activities such as hoisting sails and where to drop anchors. Also colloquially known as "Bosun".

Bonnet – a length of canvas attached to a sail to increase surface area in order to catch more wind.

Boom – a spar extension that can be added to a yard on a square-rigged ship in order to give more length for the sail. On a sailboat, the boom is a spar that greatly improves the angle and shape of a sail.

Bosun's chairs – a short board or strip of canvas secured by winches and ropes that is used to hoist a man aloft or over the side of the ship for maintenance.

Bow – the front curve of the ship, also known as the "stem".

Bowsprit – a spar running out from the bow of the ship. With the extension of the jibboom, the forestay, forestaysail and jibs can be fastened to this.

Cabin Boy – an attendant to the crew, who is charged with menial jobs such as tidying or swabbing and maintenance. Usually a young man with little or no sailing experience.

Cables – a band of tightly woven ropes used for heavy lifting.

Capstan – a wide revolving cylinder powered by spars used for hoisting objects from the deck or winding rope or cables.

Captain – the master of the ship, in control of navigation, discipline, setting duties and general seamanship.

Careen/Careening – maintenance such as ridding of barnacles, caulking or painting, usually performed when the ship is beached but can also performed when the ship is afloat.

Carpenter – responsible for the repair and maintenance of all woodwork aboard a vessel.

Cut and run – cutting the anchor in order to make a quick getaway or cutting loose a hinderance such as a rogue sail.

Companionway – a set of stairs leading to a lower deck.

Courtesy flag – a flag that is hoisted when entering foreign waters as a sign of respect and to show there is no threat.

Crosstrees – a cross of struts at the top of the topmast used to rig the topgallant mast for the topgallant sail and royal sail.

Crow's Nest – a small platform, usually a barrel upon a nineteenth century square-rigged ship, attached to the main mast near the masthead for use of a lookout for other ships or nearby rocks.

Deck – the top of the ship which is worked on to keep the ship sailing. There are at least four decks on a ship.

Deckhand – the role of the deckhand is anything from supervision and maintenance to swabbing to helping another role; anything that needs an extra pair of hands.

Devil to pay – an expression on deck for unpleasant and impossible tasks, usually known as a punishment for sailors with bad behaviour. Usually associated with caulking the longest seam of the ship known as the garboard seam or devil's seam.

Devil's seam – also known as the garboard seam, a long and difficult to reach seam.

Dock/Docking – to moor a ship in order to transport goods to the port or for maintenance purposes.

Dogwatch – a watch period, usually the nightshift.

Doldrums – a patch of becalmed water where the wind and tide are absent and only drifting on the passing current can move a ship.

Dover Cliffs – a slang term for rough seas: high waves with whitecap peaks.

Dressing down – to treat thin and worn sails with oil or wax to renew their effectiveness.

Drogue – a type of sea anchor to slow a vessel, usually comprised of a small parachute, or an earlier version consists of largening slats of wood around a pole.

Dutch courage – false courage induced by alcohol.

Even keel – a vessel floating upright without listing or heeling.

Equatorial counter – the belt of the equator where, due to the earth's polarity, currents are forever shifting leading to harsh weather or becalmed waters.

Fathom – a nautical measure of depth of water equal to six feet.

Fife rail – a horizontal fitting rail located below each mast with which belaying pins are used to belay the mast's stays and standing rigging securely.

Figure-of-eight knot – a type of stopper knot that prevents the rope from running through or out of certain devices.

First Mate – usually the first officer below the captain, with the same responsibility as the captain and quartermaster.

Flotsam – floating debris after a shipwreck.

Footloose – the foot of a sail that is not attached or secured properly.

Footropes – ropes connected to a yard on a square-rigged sailing ship for sailors to stand on or put their legs through whilst furling or unfurling a sail.

Fore-and-aft – a sailing rig that sets its sails along the line of the keel, such as yachts or sailboats.

Forecastle – a raised deck at the front of the ship.

Fore tophamper–

- **Mast** – the mast closest to the stem of a ship.
- **Masthead** – the top of the mast.
- **Sail** – the larger sail of the mast.
- **Sheet** – the line that adjusts angles and positioning of the foresails.

- **Shrouds** – the standing rigging connected to the side of the deck to the foretop platform that gives access to the yards and higher foremast tophamper.

- **Stay** – a long taught line or cable connecting the bow of the ship to the masthead to support the foremast. This then connects with the standing rigging and fife rail at the base of the mast.

- **Top platform** – the platform giving access to the foreyard as well as shrouds leading up to the foretop yard.

- **Topmast** – the upper mast set above the foresail and foretop platform where the foretopsail and foretopsail yard are rigged.

- **Topsail** – the smaller sail rigged above the foresail.

- **Topsail yard** – the shorter yard or spar that the foretopsail is rigged upon.

- **Yard** – the longer yard or spar that the foresail is rigged upon.

Forestaysail – a triangular sail that is strung with the other jibs upon the forestay.

Fouled up – when the motion of a ship or a line aboard is obstructed, entangled or collided with that hinders further movement and effectiveness. For example, a rope gets tangled, or an anchor gets snagged on hidden obstruction.

Foulies – clothing to be worn in rough weather, such as coats or waterproofs.

Furl/Furled – to roll up or stow a sail against its mast or yard.

Garboard seam – the longest seam of the ship that is the hardest to reach when caulking, also known as the "devil's seam".

Gangway – an opening in the side of a ship's bulwark to allow passengers/crew to enter and exit when docked.

Gooseneck – a swivelling connection for the boom to attach to the mast, allowing better movement for the sail.

Grog – rum diluted with water.

Guineaman – a type of ship slavers sail.

Halyards – Ropes used to unfurl a sail, or to hoist any other object to the mast's yards.

Hatches – an opening in the deck of a ship where cargo can be loaded and accessed.

Hawser – thick cables or ropes, usually used to moor or tow a ship.

Headstays – stays rigged between the bowsprit and foremast.

Heel/Heeling – a lean on a ship caused by strong winds on the sails.

Helm – the steering apparatus of a ship; either a wheel or tiller.

Heave to – to rig the sails so they will catch the headwind to slow the vessel, as well as lashing the wheel of the ship and deploying a sea anchor and drogue (depending on the speed of the ship.) This tactic is a usual manoeuvre when sailing through a storm or harsh weather in the open sea and shelter cannot be reached.

Hitch – a type of knot used to tie a rope to a fixed object.

Hog/Hogging – when the peak of a wave is in the middle of the keel, causing the hull to bend as the weight of the stem and stern are unevenly distributed, sometimes resulting in the keel to be warped.

Hold – The bottom deck where majority of the cargo is stored.

Holystone – a block of sandstone used to swab/scrub the decks with. Named after the kneeling position sailors adopt that looks like praying and the stone itself is rectangular in the shape of a Bible.

Hull – the body of a ship.

Inner jib – the next jib after the forestaysail.

Jacob's ladder – a rope and board ladder used to climb the side of a ship.

Jetty – a wooden platform extending into shallow waters allowing easier access for ships to moor/dock and for the crew to enter or vacate a vessel.

Jetsam – floating debris from a shipwreck.

Jib – a triangular sail set ahead of the foresail, attached to the forestay between the foremast and jibboom, used for extra velocity and to give additional accuracy to steering.

Jibboom – an extension spar connected to the bowsprit to give extra length for additional jibs to be attached and rigged.

Keel – the base of the ship around which the hull is built.

Keelhauling – a punishment for any sailor by which one is dragged under the keel of a ship whilst still attached by a rope to the bow.

Knots – one knot equates to one nautical mile, used to measure the speed of a ship.

Ladder – all stairs on a ship are called "ladders".

Laudanum – an alcoholic solution containing morphine and opium, formerly used as a painkiller.

Line – all ropes upon a ship are called "lines".

List/Listing – a large tilt on a ship when there is an uneven keel.

Lodestone – a mineral with natural magnetic qualities.

Longboat – a rowboat a ship carries to act as a tender, to either transport goods or people from ship to ship or ship to shore.

Lubber's hole – a hole built into the top platform of all masts to allow access to the platform as well as onto the yards or shrouds.

Mess deck – the deck where crew eat, or if there is no mess deck aboard, the berth becomes the mess deck.

Main deck – the open deck of a ship, also known as a weather deck.

Main tophamper –

- **Mast** – the middle and main mast of a ship.
- **Masthead** – the top of the mast.
- **Sail** – the larger sail of the mast.
- **Sheet** – the line that adjusts angles and positioning of the mainsails.

- **Shrouds** – the standing rigging connected to the side of the deck to the maintop platform that gives access to the yards and higher mainmast tophamper.

- **Stay** – a long taught line or cable connecting the foremasthead to the mainmasthead to support the mainmast. This then connects with the standing rigging and fife rail at the base of the mast.

- **Top platform** – the platform giving access to the mainyard as well as shrouds leading up to the maintop yard.

- **Topmast** – the upper mast set above the mainsail and maintop platform where the maintopsail and maintopsail yard are rigged.

- **Topsail** – the smaller sail rigged above the mainsail.

- **Topsail yard** – the shorter yard or spar that the maintopsail is rigged upon.

- **Yard** – the longer yard or spar that the mainsail is rigged upon.

Man the yards – a term to have all the crew of the vessel off the deck and aloft to spread along the yards.

Mast – a tall vertical pole with an arrangement of horizontal spars in which sails and rigging are attached.

Mate – All deckhands or A.B.S are called mates aboard a vessel. Mates are charged with maintenance and routine daily inspection, reporting any errors to the Quartermaster, First Mate or Boatswain. Also, they take care of hoisting and dropping anchors and all duties when arriving at a port.

Middle Passage – the section of the triangular trade in which slaves were transported from Africa to the Americas.

Mizzen tophamper –

- **Mast** – the mast closest to the stern of a ship.

- **Masthead** – the top of the mast.

- **Sail** – the larger sail of the mast.

- **Sheet** – the line that adjusts angles and positioning of the mizzensails.

- **Shrouds** – the rigging connected to the side of the deck to the mizzentop platform that gives access to the yards and higher mizzenmast tophamper.

- **Stay** – a long taught line or cable connecting the mainmasthead to the mizzenmasthead to support the mizzenmast. This then connects with the standing rigging and fife rail at the base of the mast.

- **Top platform** – the platform giving access to the mizzenyard as well as shrouds leading up to the mizzentop yard.

- **Topmast** – the upper mast set above the mizzensail and mizzentop platform where the mizzentopsail and mizzentopsail yard are rigged.

- **Topsail** – the smaller sail rigged above the mizzensail.

- **Topsail yard** – the shorter yard or spar that the mizzentopsail is rigged upon.

- **Yard** – the longer yard or spar that the mizzensail is rigged upon.

Moor/Mooring – to dock a ship upon a jetty.

Ninth Wave – after a build-up of high waves, it is said to be the largest wave in a storm.

Orlop deck – the level below the berth deck, also known as the "tween deck".

Old Pulteney – a type of malt whiskey.

Old salt – a slang term describing an experienced sailor.

Opium – a widespread drug in the nineteenth century for its use in treating pain, dysentery, diahorrea and other illnesses. Contains high levels of morphine and originates from poppy seeds.

Outer jib – the next jib after the inner jib.

Poop deck – the highest deck aft on a ship, also forming the roof of the cabin below.

Port – nautical orientation to turn left.

Quarter deck – a ship's upper deck, usually where the helm is located.

Quartermaster – the role on the ship charged with maintenance, discipline and navigation. During the Age of Sail, this role was voted on by the crew and was one rank below the captain.

Ratlines – the rungs fastened between the shrouds to act as a ladder so the shrouds can be climbed. Also known as "rattlins".

Red Ensign – a British flag insignia flown by merchant ships to show they are part of the United Kingdom's civil ensign. Also known as the "Red Duster".

Reef/Reefing – to reduce the area of a sail exposed to the wind, either to slow the vessel or to protect the sail against strong winds.

Reef-points – lengths of rope attached to the sails, used to furl and stow sails when they are not in use or to secure a reefed sail.

Rigger – charged with maintenance and control of all rigging and sails from keeping tension in the stays, adjusting angles and positioning of sails and hoisting and trimming sails. Perhaps the most dangerous job on a ship since they were always aloft on high slippery yards without any safety harness.

Rigging – a system of ropes and cables which support the masts and adjusts the angles and shapes of the sails.

Royal sail – the highest sail of the topgallant mast. This would only be rigged when there is fair wind and would speed up the ship considerably.

Rudder – an attachment at the very base of the keel connected to the wheel by tiller ropes, used to steer a ship through the water.

Running rigging – rigging that is used to control the spars and sails including the shape, size and angle as well as the raising and lowering of the sails in order to give the best conditions for a ship's movement.

Sag/Sagging – when the ship is in the bottom of a wave's trough, forcing the shape of the hull to warp as the stem and stern of the keel are higher than the middle.

Sail-plan – a set of traditional sails that can be changed to adapt to the changing weather. For example, a working sail plan is changed to a storm sail plan in rough weather.

Scally cap – a cap worn by sailors. Otherwise known as a flat cap or newsboy cap.

Scuttlebutt – a large barrel with a hole in it containing the ship's drinking water.

Sea anchor – a stabilising object, usually in the shape of a small parachute, deployed in the water to provide drag to slow the speed of a ship whilst heaving-to in harsh weather.

Sextant – a navigational tool used to measure stars to calculate latitude and longitude whilst at sea.

Shanghaied – the involuntary service of a crewman working upon a ship; to be forced into service.

Sheet – a line, used to control and adjust the angle and positioning of a sail in relation to the wind direction.

Ship's bell – a bell fixed to the main deck, rung when there is a change in shift, to draw attention or to make an announcement.

Shrouds – standing rigging attached to the side of the deck to the mast in order to climb to the yards or upper tophamper.

Sick bay – a sectioned off part of the berth where crew or passengers with injuries or ailments would be taken to be treated.

Skipper – another term for the captain of a ship.

Spanker – a fore-and-aft sail that is rigged upon an extended spar from the mizzenmast at the stern of a ship, used to keep a vessel stable and balanced when moving.

Spar/s – horizontal wooden poles set upon masts used in the rigging of a ship to carry and support the sails.

Spar deck – a temporary deck constructed of spare spars and canvas to provide shelter for watchmen during rough weather.

Spyglass – a small extendable telescope used to see over a distance.

Square-rigged – a sailing rig that sets its rigging and sails across, or "square", from the line of the keel and line of the masts.

St. Elmo's Fire – a weather phenomenon in which luminous plasma is created upon the tips or ends of sharp and pointed objects within the vicinity of a strong electric field in the atmosphere, usually generated by a storm, causing them to glow a bright white or blue colour.

Stanchion/s – a sturdy row of vertical posts used to support lifelines and other lines.

Standing rigging – rigging that supports the masts and spars, including shrouds and stays. These are not usually manipulated or adjusted apart from their tension.

Starboard – nautical orientation to turn right.

Stay – a strong rope running from the bowsprit to each of the masts to support their weight. Jibs can also be rigged from the stay between the bowsprit/jibboom to the foremast; these are called headstays or forestays.

Staysail/s – sails that are rigged upon a stay line. For example, jibs and headsails.

Stem – the front of the ship.

Stern – the rear of the ship.

Storm sails – a set of sails that are smaller and more robust than the usual sails and can withstand harsh weather. Also known as "trysails".

Stowaway – a person/s trespassing on a ship.

Sun's over the yardarm – a phrase aboard a ship to describe the appropriate time of day for lunch or to begin drinking.

Surgeon – a medically experienced sailor charged with treating ailments and injuries.

Swabbie – although not technically a job, this was a role that every deckhand took part in which consisted of swabbing decks and keeping everything as tidy and clean as possible.

Tack/Tacking – zigzagging through the water when there is a strong headwind. This manoeuvre is usually performed whilst heaving-to or whilst sailing through harsh weather or strong winds.

Taffrail – the rail of the poop deck at the very rear of the ship.

Tender – a smaller vessel, usually powered by an oar, to transport goods or people from ship to ship or ship to shore.

Topgallant mast – a mast extension that can be rigged from the crosstrees to make the topgallant sail and royal sail available for use.

Topgallant sail – a smaller sail rigged above the topsail, rigged when there are light to moderate wind speeds in order to gain more knots.

Tophamper – a collective term for the masts, spars, sails and rigging that stands above deck.

Three sheets to the wind – when the bottom three sails are loose resulting in a drop in speed and for the ship to meander. Also, a phrase for a sailor who has drunk too much and is stumbling.

Tiller ropes – ropes connecting the ship's wheel to the rudder, enabling the ship to turn in any direction.

Trim/trimming – adjusting the area of a sail to boost its efficiency.

Trysail – sails that are part of the storm sail plan. These sails are smaller and more robust, able to endure harsh weather conditions.

Turnbuckle – a small device used to adjust tension in stays, lines or shrouds in the standing rigging.

Unfurl/Unfurling – to open a sail from its purchase upon a yard ready for use.

Weather deck – the highest deck exposed to the weather, also known as the main deck.

Wheel – a device at the helm used to steer a vessel by use of tiller ropes and rudder at the stern of the ship.

Working sail plan – the normal sail plan that is in use regularly when there are variable weather conditions.

Yard – a horizontal spar from which all sails are hung from and attached to. All spars upon a ship are called "yards".

Longboat terms –

Bottom boards – the bottom flooring of the boat.

Centre-thwart – the middle plank of the boat where the rowers (usually two) would sit on to row.

Gunwale – the lip of the boat.

Quarter-knee – the stern corners of the boat.

Rowlock/oarlock – a curving device that allows free movement of the oars as they move but will not allow them to slip out

Stem post – the post that joins the inner frame (rib) at the front forming the bow.

Stern sheets (stern thwart) – the board that curves around the quarter-knee giving the stern passengers a place to sit.

About the Author

I have a full-time job as a qualified bricklayer and have a passion for creative writing, with years of experience. When I'm not building houses or on the trowel, I'll be writing books. I like to write gripping stories with a range of interesting characters with their own tale to tell. It's something I find therapeutic; almost like slipping into someone else's perspective to see the world through their eyes. It gives me courage and freedom in day-to-day life, enabling me to find the power to shape my own future and fate.

I live in Cambridgeshire with my family (not to mention the dogs, cats and chickens) and love to get home in front of a warm, crackling fire after a cold winter's day working on site. I also like daily yoga and to paint when I can, and I love to travel, seeking new adventures and discovering different cultures and ways of life.

Seadogs and Criminals is a series of two books (so far) and is the first work I have had published.

9 781839 756689